Hearts at Play

The Bradens, Book Six

Love in Bloom Series

Melissa Foster

“A sinfully sexy and heartwarming series.”
—*Bestselling author Amy Manemann*

ISBN-13: 978-0-9910468-3-6
ISBN-10: 0991046838

This is a work of fiction. The events and characters described herein are imaginary and are not intended to refer to specific places or living persons. The opinions expressed in this manuscript are solely the opinions of the author and do not represent the opinions or thoughts of the publisher. The author has represented and warranted full ownership and/or legal right to publish all the materials in this book.

Print Edition
V1.0

Cover Design: Natasha Brown

WORLD LITERARY PRESS
PRINTED IN THE UNITED STATES OF AMERICA

A Note from Melissa

Hugh Braden is a fast-talking daredevil, and I knew it would take a special woman to capture his big, loving heart. Single mother Brianna and her daughter, Layla, were as unexpected as they were perfect for our loyal, loving hero, but Brianna is a careful woman who has no room for a man in her life. Or so she thinks…

If this is your first Braden novel, get ready for a sexy, romantic ride. If you've already read each of Hugh's siblings' love stories, prepare yourself for a side of Hugh you never imagined. I hope you love Hugh, Brianna, and Layla, as much as I do.

The best way to keep up to date with new releases, sales, and exclusive content is to sign up for my newsletter.
www.MelissaFoster.com/news

About the Love in Bloom Big-Family Romance Collection

The Bradens are just one of the families in the Love in Bloom big-family romance collection. Characters from each series make appearances in future books, so you never miss an engagement, wedding, or birth. A complete list of series titles is included at the end of this book, along with a preview of the next book in this series.

You can download **free** first-in-series ebooks and see my current sales here:
www.MelissaFoster.com/LIBFree

Visit the Love in Bloom Reader Goodies page for downloadable checklists, family trees, and more!
www.MelissaFoster.com/RG

For those who dream of fairy tales

Chapter One

KAT BURST THROUGH the stockroom doors of Old Town Tavern, nearly plowing into Brianna.

"Jeez, Kat. What the hell?" Brianna Heart had been working since noon, and she had another two hours to go before her ten-hour shift was over. She didn't have the energy for Kat's drama. Not tonight, when she still had to muster the energy to pick up Layla, her five-year-old daughter, from her mother's house, get her to bed, and then make invitations for Layla's birthday party.

"Patrick Dempsey is here. I saw him. He's sitting at a table in the bar. Oh my God—he is even hotter in person." Kat flipped her long blond hair over her shoulder and tapped her finger on her lip. "I wonder if he's looking for a date."

"Kat." Brianna shook her head. "You're crazy. You always think you see famous people. Not a lot of famous people are clamoring to get into Richmond, Virginia."

"Bree, I'm telling you. I think I need to change my underwear." She looked at Brianna and furrowed her perfectly manicured brows. "Oh, honey. Here. Let me help you with your hair. You could be the prettiest bartender slash waitress out there and you know it. Well, besides me, of course." She began fluffing Bree's straight, shoulder-length brown hair.

Brianna shook her head. "Please. If it is Patrick Dempsey, I'll be the last person he's looking at." She wiped her hands on the little towel she kept looped over her belt at all times—because she didn't have time to breathe, much less go searching for something to dry her hands on.

"Oh, come on, Bree. Don't you want to get out of this place? What better way than with a famous sugar daddy?" Kat looked at her reflection in the glass and flipped her long blond hair over her shoulder again.

"*Ugh.* No, thank you. The last thing Layla needs is that kind of lifestyle, and the last thing I need is to stand in the stockroom talking about fictitious people. I love you, Kat, but I gotta get out there." She patted her back pocket. "I need the tips. Layla's birthday is coming up."

"I can't believe she's going to be six. Gosh, that went quick. What does she want?"

"A puppy, a kitten, a bigger bedroom." Brianna sighed. "But I think I'm gonna get her a winter jacket. Kill two birds with one stone." She winked as she headed out of the stockroom and up to the bar. A quick scan told her that Patrick Dempsey was definitely not there. She snagged the empty glasses from the bar and wiped it down.

Mack Greenley, the manager of the bar, sidled up to Brianna. She'd worked for Mack for the past five and a half years, and though she was twenty-eight and he was only thirty-eight, he'd taken her under his wing as if she were his daughter.

"Booth." Mack was a big man with a mass of brown hair and a thick, powerful neck.

"Got it." Bree wiped her hands on the towel, grabbed an order pad, and went to the only occupied booth in the small bar. It was Thursday night at seven o'clock. Another half hour and the bar would be packed for Major League Baseball playoffs. Brianna focused on her order pad, thinking about Layla's birthday and wishing she could afford the time or money to get her a pet, like she wanted. But as a single mother, she couldn't balance working fifty hours each week with taking care of Layla *and* a pet. It was just too much. She pushed the thought away and feigned a smile.

"Hi, I'm Brianna…Bree. What can I get you?"

The guy in the booth lifted his head in her direction, and Brianna's breath caught in her throat. She felt her jaw go slack. The man's thick, windblown dark hair looked as if someone had just run their hands through it. *While kissing his glorious lips and feeling that sexy five-o'clock shadow on their cheek. Jesus, he does look like Patrick Dempsey…on steroids.*

"A sidecar and a glass of water, please," he said.

Brianna couldn't move. She couldn't breathe. She couldn't even close her damn mouth. *Shit. Shit. Shit. Shit.*

He cocked his head. "Are you okay?"

Are you kidding me? Does your voice have to be so damn smooth and rich? That's so unfair. She cleared her throat. "Yeah, sorry. Long day. One sidecar coming up." She cursed at herself all the way back to the bar.

Kat grabbed her arm and pulled her toward the sink, their backs to way-sexier-than-Patrick-Dempsey steroid guy. "I told you," she whispered. "Jesus, you're lucky. What are you gonna do?"

Brianna looked over her shoulder at the handsome man. *Trouble.* That's what she saw. She'd known men like him before. Hell, that's how she ended up with Layla.

"Nothing. He wants a sidecar. You take it to him." Brianna handed her the pad and went to help the woman she and Kat called Red—a slutty redhead who spent every Thursday night trolling the bar for men.

Brianna focused on making Red her cosmo. The din of the customers fell away. Her mind circled back to the Patrick Dempsey look-alike's voice. It was so…so…different from any other man's voice. He didn't speak as if he were rushed, and he looked at her eyes instead of her breasts, which was also different from most of the male customers at the tavern. She started when Kat touched her shoulder.

"Bree, come on. You do it. I can't take him from you. He's probably a big tipper. Look at that jacket."

Brianna glanced at the brown leather jacket hanging on the end of the booth. "It's okay. You go. I'm good." She handed Red a cosmo.

"Do you know who that is?" Red lifted her glass toward the handsome man.

Bree shrugged. "No idea." *But I'm sure he'll take you home.*

"I think that's my date," Red said.

Isn't every man? Brianna watched Kat bring him his drink. Her crimson lips spread with a flash of her sexiest smile. Brianna knew Kat's next move. The hair flip. Then she'd touch his shoulder and…She watched Kat throw her head back in an exaggerated laugh. Brianna sighed and turned away. *He's probably an ass.* She'd made it this long without a man dragging her through emotional hell; she wasn't going to cave now. She pulled her shoulders back and rotated just in time to see Red sliding into the seat across from him.

ALL HUGH BRADEN wanted to do was disappear in the fog

of a few drinks, then go back to his house and chill. Instead he was stuck waiting for a blind date, and with a race around the corner, there'd be no drinking for him. A beautiful woman with the most contemplative eyes and the sweetest face he'd ever seen had taken his drink order. At least he could look forward to seeing her when she brought it to him. He had planned on ordering seltzer water, but one look at her and he was unable to remember what he wanted. *Sidecar* came off his lips like he ordered it all the time, and he'd had a sidecar only once—and that was several years ago. Now he'd have to stare at the damn drink all night.

It had been a grueling day. Hugh didn't know why he'd let his agent talk him into the stupid photo shoot, and just as he'd anticipated, it had been a painful few hours. They'd taken the photos at the track and had scheduled another shoot for Saturday morning. The photographer was cool enough, but fake smiling and posing in positions he'd never stand or sit in made his already sore body ache. Ever since he won the last three Capital Series Grand Prix races, he'd been hounded by the media. *Damn sponsor obligations.* As much as he was thankful for the sponsors, he rued the attention, and he needed another racing magazine cover like he needed another expensive car or another house.

A blond waitress set his drink on the table. "Hi. I'm Kat. Enjoy your sidecar."

Really? This is definitely not my night. "Thank you." He peered around Kat, looking for the dark-haired beauty who had taken his order. *Bree.* He spotted her taking a drink order from a stocky blond man in a flannel shirt. The first thing Hugh had noticed when she'd taken his order was that she looked as if she was thinking about a hundred things and taking his order was white noise to her internal thoughts. In the space of a breath, she'd struck him as interesting, beautiful, and intense in a way that had nothing to do with sexuality—which in and of itself struck him as strange that he'd notice something like that. But he had. And now he was unable to look away as she moved from one customer to the next, focused and efficient and completely oblivious to him.

Hugh had picked the Old Town Tavern to meet the blind date because it was out of the way. A little bar with a smaller restaurant. The last thing he wanted to deal with was another group of sex-craved or money-hungry women eyeing him like they hadn't eaten in a month and he was a big juicy steak. He'd hoped he could go unnoticed. When Brianna had finally lifted her eyes to his and her jaw dropped open, he'd worried that she'd recognized him. But she'd ditched him and sent Kat as a replacement. Hell, she hadn't even taken a second look. He might not want to be recognized for who he was, but being noticed as a man rather than a race car driver and then rejected by Brianna was a whole different story. This was definitely not his night.

He'd accepted the damn blind date only because his buddy and crew chief, Art Cullen, had claimed he had the perfect woman for him—smart and beautiful, and best of all, she had no clue who he was. Now, as an overdeveloped redhead slid into the booth across from him, he questioned that decision.

"Hey, sugar. Are you Art's friend?" The redhead put her glass on the table between them and ran her red fingernail around the rim of the glass. "I'm Tracie. That's with an *I E,* not a *Y.*"

I'm going to kill Art. Tracie looked like a dime-store hooker with overprocessed hair and a tight red dress that was three sizes too small across her rounded hips and breasts. Hugh pressed his lips together and forced himself to lift his cheeks into a smile. "Hugh. Nice to meet you."

"Art said you were handsome, but I never expected you to look like that guy on television. McDreamy? McSteamy?"

She laughed, and Hugh sighed. At least Art had promised not to tell her what he did for a living. *No more fan girls.* Based on the other patrons' eyes locked on the pre-playoff show on the large-screen televisions, and the lack of attention from any of the guys in the now-packed bar, Hugh assumed he was safe from being identified. *Might as well make the best of it.*

"Yeah, I've heard that. Patrick Dempsey," he answered. He was already bored. He glanced at the group of guys coming into the bar, each one louder than the next as they approached the bar. The blond waitress, Kat, picked up a tip from a table, then headed back in his direction, seating two more people on her way across the floor.

Kat appeared by his side and scowled at Tracie, then flashed a smile at Hugh. "What can I get you, darlin'? Another sidecar?"

If looks could kill. One more drink. Then I'm out of here.

"Get us both another one. On me," Tracie said, fluttering her false eyelashes.

On you? Right. Women like Tracie were made of hollow offers and a boatload of needs. Not that Hugh needed anyone to buy his drinks. He eyed his untouched beverage. *Not very observant, are you?* "No. I'm good." He nodded at his full drink, wishing he could escape the booth and sit by himself—or maybe at a table where the cute brunette would take another order he wouldn't drink.

"My pleasure," Tracie said.

There's that sex-hungry stare again. *No way in hell.*

"Thank you," Hugh said, showing the manners his father, Hal Braden, an affluent thoroughbred horse breeder from Weston, Colorado, had instilled in him. With a bigger trust fund than he could ever spend, Hugh didn't need women buying him drinks, but dealing with the wrath of a woman who felt put off would be worse. He could spare another half hour, have a drink, then politely excuse himself.

He watched Kat return to the bar and whisper to Bree. Even her name was appealing. She wiped the counter with a serious look in her eyes, served up drink after drink, and dodged a guy putting his hand on hers—"Behave, Chip," she said with a shake of her head—all in a matter of seconds. She didn't look at any of the men at the bar. In fact, she seemed to be purposely shifting her eyes to the counter every time a guy spoke to her. She was the only person in the bar not smiling—besides him—and Hugh wondered why.

He turned his attention back to Tracie, who was rattling on about *Grey's Anatomy*. Hugh didn't watch television, and after Tracie finished her next drink, he looked at his watch with a loud and purposeful groan.

"Well, Tracie, this has been nice, but I'm afraid I have to run. I've got an early meeting tomorrow." He stood and extended his hand. "Thanks for coming out to meet me. I appreciate it."

She climbed from the booth. "I don't have my car here. A friend dropped me off. Can you drive me home?"

Are you freaking kidding me?

Kat appeared by his side again. "Leaving already?" She glanced at the fifty-dollar bill he'd left on the table.

"I'm afraid so. It's getting late," he said. "Thanks for everything."

Red wrapped her arm around his, and Hugh noticed Kat's eyes narrow.

"Right," Kat said. She snagged the money from the table and stalked back to the bar.

As Hugh pushed the door open for Tracie to pass through, he noticed Kat and Bree watching them leave. He smiled—and this time it wasn't forced. Kat waved. Bree turned away.

Chapter Two

"THERE IS NO way that beautiful man just left with that whore," Kat snapped. "I swear, there is something cosmically wrong with this world when that happens."

"Oh, please. He's a guy. She's easy." Brianna shrugged. "What's not to get?"

"You're so cynical. That could have been you walking out with him, Bree."

"In case you haven't noticed, I've been off the dating train for quite some time." When it came to men, Brianna was a master at turning off her emotions. She'd been doing it for six years, and she planned on doing it for another twelve.

"All I'm saying is that you don't have to be a bitch about it. You could have smiled, waved. I don't even get why you're on an eighteen-year celibacy plan anyway. That makes no sense to me."

"Excuse me. Can I get a drink?" a tall guy hollered from the bar.

"Sure, darlin'. Just a sec." Kat brushed Brianna's hair from her shoulder. "You take him. Patrick Dempsey left a great tip. I'll share it with you."

"You don't need to do that." She smiled at Kat. When Brianna came back home after graduating from the Rhode Island School of Design, where she'd focused on photography, she hadn't known she was pregnant. She'd put the pieces together two months later, after failing to find a job and writing off her nausea and missed periods to stress. Her mother was not exactly thrilled that she'd gotten knocked up at a graduation party by Todd, a guy she'd dated only a few times, and Brianna had to admit that she wasn't thrilled either. But the minute her doctor had told her she was pregnant, her hand instinctively went to her belly, and there was no question in her mind about what she was going to do. Layla had become a part of her at that moment, and even though she and her mother had a falling out shortly thereafter and she'd stopped looking for a job in the arts and took the bartending job so she could make the rent payments on her new apartment, she'd never regretted her decision. Not when Layla was a colicky infant and stayed up for hours on end and not when she was two years old and colored with crayon all over the walls.

She looked at Kat and sighed. During those early months of Brianna's pregnancy, when Brianna's mother had been less than supportive, Kat had always been there. She'd supported Brianna's desire to keep her baby, held her hair back while Brianna had bouts of nausea, and she'd never once judged her for getting pregnant. Kat had been the sister Brianna always wished she'd had.

"I'm not dating because Layla needs a stable mother, not a mom who's caught up in the drama of worrying about a man. I brought her into this life, and she's the best kid in the world. I don't want to mess her up. It's the least I can do."

Kat hugged her. "I wish you'd have been my mom. Now go help the hunky dunk over there. Yummy."

Brianna didn't mind Thursday nights. With the noise of the game and the cheering of the drunken fans, the hours moved fast. *Another twenty minutes and I'm out of here.* Brianna bent over a barstool as she wiped it down.

"This seems to be the only free seat. Do you mind if I take it?"

She froze at the sound of that rich, delicious voice. *Get a grip.* She lifted her gaze to see that the handsome man who had left with Red was back and she was staring at his broad, muscular chest. She swallowed hard. At five foot five, Brianna was not a short woman, but next to this guy, who was almost a foot taller than her, she felt petite and feminine…and like her heart was on speed.

"Sure. Sorry," she managed.

"Thank you." He took off his jacket and folded it over his arm, his gaze never wavering from hers.

His eyes weren't just brown; they were a warm shade of cocoa. She also noticed that his five-o'clock shadow wasn't all black after all; it had a little lighter shade of brown sprinkled in. Oh, how she'd love to photograph him in black-and-white. Profile shot, maybe. He smiled, revealing the cutest dimples she'd ever seen. *Patrick Dempsey. Definitely Patrick Dempsey. Only hotter. Sexier. Stronger. Oh God, shut up!* Brianna realized she was staring, and a flush heated her cheeks. She spun on her heel and returned to the safety of the opposite side of the bar, racing heart and all.

She eyed Kat fixing drinks and flirting with a group of guys at the other end of the bar, wishing she were beside her. Kat could tease her out of her momentary lustfulness—or she'd give her crap for not acting on it. Brianna took a deep breath and focused on wiping down the counter.

"What'll it be?" *Don't look at him.* She felt like she was standing in front of the real Patrick Dempsey and if she looked again she'd be awestruck, she'd go mute, and embarrassed beyond recovery. That was the stupidest thing in the world, and she knew it. She forced herself to lift her eyes and clenched her jaw to keep from making an idiot of herself.

He smiled again and—*Oh God*—when it reached his eyes, he didn't look like an asshole at all. Maybe she was misjudging him. *But he just left with Red and he's back for more already!* She clenched her jaw tighter.

"Seltzer water, please," he said.

Seltzer water? She took a few steps away and focused on pouring his drink at the back counter. Kat was by her side half a second later.

"He's back? Already? That doesn't say much about his bedroom skills," Kat whispered.

Brianna glanced back at Hugh. Thankfully, between the noise of the customers and the distance between them, there was no way he'd heard her. "Shut up."

Kat touched her arm. "You're shaking." She drew in a loud breath. "You're shaking. Bree. Oh my God. Because of him?" she whispered.

"No. I'm tired, and I need to go home."

Kat gave the guy at the bar a quick once-over and then waved as three large groups left the bar. "Twenty minutes. Can you handle it? Want me to take him?"

"Nah. I've got this." Brianna wasn't about to let some guy get the better of her. She'd learned her lesson six years earlier. She headed back toward the far end of the bar, where Hugh appeared to be people watching. "Here you go. Enjoy." She handed him his drink and picked up a tip from the bar.

"Is it always like this in here?" he asked.

It took a second for Brianna to realize he was speaking to her. "Ah, I guess. On Thursdays, anyway." *Where's Red?*

He nodded. "Happy crowd."

"Playoffs tend to bring out the smiles. And sometimes the fists, but luckily not tonight." She watched him sip his water; then she began putting the bottles away.

"Is your kitchen still serving dinner?" he asked.

Dinner? She glanced at her watch and then back at him. "It's almost ten." She shrugged. "Sorry. They close the kitchen at ten. Maybe you can grab something at Bob's, down the street." *Why am I still talking?* She watched Kat crossing the bar to wipe down the booths.

"Nah. It's okay. I'll grab something at home."

"I haven't seen you in here before." She glared at Kat's back, wishing she'd come save her from her own inability to stop speaking. *What is wrong with me? He's just another customer. Then why does my stomach do a little flip every time he speaks?*

He looked around the bar. "I've never been in here before tonight." He finished his water as Kat came up to the bar.

"Done with Red…err…Tracie…already?" She crossed her arms and tapped her foot.

He shook his head in question. "Done with? I just gave her a ride home."

"No one *just* gives Red a ride home." Brianna removed the towel from her belt and folded it, then set it on the counter behind her.

"Whoa. If you think I…" His eyes ran between the two women. "Sorry, ladies. That was a blind date, and she was definitely not my type."

Kat leaned over the bar and smiled. "What is your type?"

Brianna shot her a look that said, *The seductive voice? Really?*

Kat ignored her.

"That's a bold question." He held out his hand. "I'm Hugh, by the way."

"Kat." Kat shook his hand.

He held his hand out toward Brianna. She narrowed her eyes. He was definitely a player. *A really smooth one.* There was no way she was touching his hand. If his voice made her stomach flutter, then who knew what kind of deluded thoughts his touch would give her.

She crossed her arms. "Brianna. Bree."

He held her gaze and her pulse sped up.

"Yes. I remember."

You remembered.

"Well, Kat and Bree, I guess I never thought about what my type is. I just know she's not it."

He looked away, and the way the light caught his dark eyes made Brianna wish for her camera again. *One day I'll be able to afford to get it fixed.* His features were unlike those of anyone she'd seen before. His almond-shaped eyes were on the small side, and on any other man they might look too small, but they were in perfect proportion to his luscious mouth, and the way his thick neck gave way to his strikingly broad shoulders was more masculine than any model she'd ever seen. She realized only too late that she'd missed half of what he'd said.

"Smart and honest, I guess. Family oriented, that's a must for me. I guess if I had a type, that would be it." He ran his hand through his hair.

Family oriented? Smart and honest? Holy hell. No way. She scrutinized him again. There was no tension in his forehead. He leaned his forearms on the bar and appeared comfortable and relaxed. Between school, photography, and bartending, Brianna had studied people's faces for enough years to know a bullshitter when she saw one. Hugh was either a very adept liar, or he was not at all the type of person she assumed he was.

Kat pushed herself from the counter where she'd been leaning and looked at him with a soft, dreamy gaze.

"Bree, it's ten, hon."

Mack's voice pulled her from her thoughts. "Thanks, Mack."

"I'll walk you out back when you're ready," Mack said.

"Is that your husband?" Hugh asked.

Kat laughed too loud, and it made Brianna laugh, too.

"He's my boss. I park out back, and he doesn't like me to go out there in the dark by myself. He walks Kat out, too, when she parks there." She was still smiling about his *husband* comment.

"After I pay, I'll be leaving. Want me to walk you out?" Hugh asked.

Kat wiggled her eyebrows at her.

Yes! No! Bad idea. Truly bad idea. Brianna thought of Layla and came back to her senses. She looked down and straightened her T-shirt. "No, that's okay. Mack will take me. It was nice meeting you, Hugh. Kat, I'll see you tomorrow."

"When are you on?" Kat asked.

"I'm at Claude's in the morning. Back here at four, after I get Layla." For the first time in longer than she could remember, as Brianna said her daughter's name, an uncomfortable feeling prickled her nerves. When she'd first had Layla and she was learning to shut out the male population, she'd had a few uncomfortable conversations with men about having a daughter. Now she felt that twinge of discomfort, and she hated herself for it. Why should she care if he knew she had a daughter? She was proud of Layla, and everything he'd just said was probably not true anyway. What man says he wants a smart, honest, and family-oriented woman? His good looks must have stolen her ability to think straight. *That has to be it.*

"Have a nice night, Bree," Hugh said with a nod.

As Brianna and Mack headed out the door, she wondered what her name would sound like coming off his lips after a long, sensuous kiss.

Chapter Three

"ART, WHAT THE hell?" Hugh spoke into the speakerphone as he drove his liquid-silver Mercedes-Benz SLR McLaren Roadster through the gates of his ten-acre estate. He couldn't stop thinking about Bree, but the thought that he'd been sitting with Tracie when he could have been trying to get to know Bree better pissed him off—and Art was about to pay for that.

"Was she that bad?" Art asked.

"Was she…? Art, you're my buddy, man. What are you trying to do to me?" He pressed a button on his visor and the garage door lifted. Automatic lights illuminated the interior of his four-car garage.

"I'm sorry. It was a favor. She's a friend of my sister's best friend."

"Dude, really? You're supposed to protect my image. She was like…I don't even know what. I'm off the market. Officially, as of right this second." Hugh ended the call and headed inside the brick Tudor home he'd added to his real estate collection a few years earlier, when he'd found two naked women in his hotel bedroom and had to call security to have them removed. Hugh loved naked women as much as the next guy, but he liked his privacy. Even though he wasn't in any state for very long, he returned year after year, and purchasing homes alleviated the need for hotels altogether. And after watching his four older brothers and his older sister fall in love over the past few months, he'd begun to feel a pull toward settling down, and he'd begun to want more. With a degree from Cornell in finance, he knew he could never settle down with a woman who wasn't his intellectual equal, which meant most leggy models and fan girls were out of the equation. For months he'd been actively separating himself from his previous lifestyle.

He grabbed a copy of *The Art of Negotiating* and kicked back on a leather couch in the large great room. He clicked a remote, and the enormous propane fireplace bloomed in flames of orange and red; then he dimmed the overhead lights, and with another flick of the remote, the reading lamp that arced artfully over his left shoulder brightened. The house had many bells and whistles, which Hugh enjoyed, but he would have preferred something a little smaller. Since he'd purchased during the recession, it had been too good of a deal to pass up, and with the market recovery, he'd already doubled his original purchase price in equity.

He'd just slipped off his loafers and kicked his feet up on the glass coffee table when his cell phone rang.

Savannah. "How's my newly engaged sister?"

"Happy. How are you?" Savannah had always been a positive light in Hugh's life, but since getting engaged to Jack Remington, she'd been ridiculously cheery.

"Eh, you know. Life is good, my cars are fast, and my women are, too." His usual statement fell off his lips like a bad habit, which is just what it had become. It even tasted wrong.

"Are you ever going to settle down?" she asked.

He thought about Tracie and cringed. Then he pictured

Brianna's beautiful face. "Maybe one day, but she'd have to be a hell of a woman for me to even consider it." Hugh didn't know why he was still playing the off-the-cuff answer to Savannah, but as he said the words, his mind traveled down a different path, realizing that what he'd been looking for just might come true after all.

"Yeah, well, when you're not looking, you'll find her. That's when I found Jack. Treat will tell you fate steps in. Dad will tell you that Mom has her hand in it. But I think it's just luck." Savannah was an entertainment attorney, and her fiancé, Jack Remington, was an ex–Special Forces officer, a bush plane pilot, and a survival-training guide. Hugh pictured her in her Manhattan loft, probably packing to go to the cabin Jack owned in the Colorado Mountains, where they'd been spending their weekends.

"Yeah, yeah. I'll believe it when I experience it. What's up, Vanny?"

"We're having an engagement party at Dad's, and I wanted to know if you could fit it into your schedule. It's kind of short notice."

"Of course. When is it?" Everything in the Braden family was short notice. They were used to dropping everything and coming together for one of their father's backyard barbeques even though they lived so far apart.

"Two weeks from Saturday."

Hugh mentally ran through his schedule. "Yeah, that's perfect. The final race of the season is next weekend, so I should be clear for that. Did you talk to everyone else? Were you able to reach Dane and Lacy?"

"Yeah. It turns out that there's some sort of function for Lacy's work in Massachusetts the next week, so it worked out perfect for them, too. Josh and Riley, Treat and Max, and Rex and Jade will all be there. I'm so excited that you can make it."

It struck Hugh that his siblings were no longer referred to as Treat, Dane, Rex, Josh, and Savannah. Each one was now paired with their forever love. That was a comforting feeling, and something in him longed for the same connection. He sat up as the emotion—which had become even more familiar as of late—gripped him and refused to let go.

"Me too, Vanny. Tell Jack I said hi. I'm gonna go chill. It's been a long night."

"Love you," she said.

"Love you, too." After he ended the call, he stood and paced. He looked out the French doors at the starry sky. Hugh had always been a confident, borderline cocky guy who lived life in the fast lane. He wasn't a guy who felt uncomfortable in his own skin, and tonight, as he looked around the enormous house, he realized why he wasn't enamored by the size of it. It made him feel very alone. Maybe even lonely.

He returned to the couch and read a few pages, but his mind kept drifting back to Bree. He wondered who Layla and Claude were. He imagined Layla was her sister. It was Claude that he stumbled over. That name he couldn't write off as a sister or a pet, and the way her eyes lit up when she'd said it, he didn't think it was her brother. She wasn't wearing a wedding ring, and when he'd thrown out the comment about her boss being her husband, he saw the reaction he'd hoped for from both Brianna and Kat. Brianna definitely wasn't married. *But who is Claude?*

He closed the book, draped his arm over his eyes, and thought about going back to the bar the next evening. It didn't dawn on him until a few minutes later that he'd never looked past Brianna's face. Yes, he'd definitely have to go back. That gorgeous of a face had to be attached to a hell of a body.

Chapter Four

"ALMOST READY SWEET girl?" Brianna zipped her knee-high black boots that Kat had given her for her birthday over her skinny jeans and gave her outfit a once-over in the hall mirror. The gray boatneck sweater hung loosely over her slim figure, stopping just short of her hips. Her wrist bangles clinked as she brushed her hair from her face.

"You look really pretty, Mom," Layla said.

Brianna kissed her cheek. "Not as pretty as you do, princess, but thank you. I'm helping Claude with a photo shoot this morning. Do you have your invitations?"

Layla shook her head, tossing her two long brown ponytails from side to side. "I'll get them. Can we get a pony for the party?" She ran into the kitchen in her black leggings and blue long-sleeved shirt and grabbed the bag of birthday invitations Brianna had written up the night before.

"A pony? That's like a million dollars. I think we have to skip the pony. But we can have ice cream and cake," Brianna said.

Layla looked at the invitations. "These are so cool! You taped lollipops onto them! Now everyone will come for sure."

"Everyone will come anyway, because they all love you. Put

them in your backpack so we're not late for school." Layla had many friends, though not many playdates because of Brianna's schedule.

Brianna remembered what it was like when she was gathering a bundled baby in her arms and rushing out to the sitter's before work only to come back ten hours and two jobs later to pick her up each afternoon. After her mother's initial freak-out about Brianna's pregnancy, she'd eventually realized that having a baby wasn't the worst thing that could happen to a girl—despite her own experience with a husband who'd left her when Brianna was only eight—and she'd come around. And although Brianna's life wasn't what she'd envisioned for herself when she was eighteen, she was happy. And so was Layla. That was all that mattered.

Her mother had helped when she was able, but she had also worked full-time when Layla was born. Her mother had recently rearranged her hours to work earlier in the mornings, freeing her up to watch Layla after school while Brianna worked. Now, as Brianna pulled up to the school and Layla unhooked her seat belt and climbed from her booster seat, Brianna leaned over the backseat to kiss her goodbye, and she felt like those exhausted days had taken place a lifetime ago. Somehow, between Layla becoming more self-sufficient and Brianna throwing herself into motherhood and accepting that this was her future, things had become easier.

"Have a good day, princess. I'll pick you up after school and take you to Grandma's. And I forgot to tell you, Grandma wants you to spend the night tomorrow night."

Layla drew in a loud breath. "Really?"

"Yup. She said there's a play at the theater that she wants to take you to see. Is that okay? I'll come get you Saturday after the play."

Layla climbed over the seat again and hugged her. "Yes, yes, yes! Oh, I love plays so much, and Grandma always takes me to lunch. This is gonna be so fun!" Her smile faded. "What about you? Don't you want to come?"

Brianna made a mental note of another mommy moment that she wanted to remember forever. She had so many of them now, she needed to learn mental shorthand. "I might have to buy a certain little girl a birthday present."

"A kitty?" she asked hopefully.

Brianna pretended to zip her mouth closed and toss the key out the window.

Layla groaned.

"Love you, princess. You better get going so you're not late."

"Okay. Two Musketeers?" Layla said with a smile, exposing the dark hole where her front tooth would hopefully soon grow in.

"Always," Brianna said, and blew her a kiss. Layla had started calling them the Two Musketeers two years earlier. She'd asked about her father—again—and Brianna told her that sometimes God gave children just one parent because the child was too special to share. Layla had looked at her with a serious stare and said, "Then we're like Grandma says. We're the Two Musketeers."

She watched Layla run up the walkway and join two of her friends before disappearing through the front doors of the school. Her mind drifted to the Patrick Dempsey look-alike. Despite herself, she let herself recall his name with a silent sigh. *Hugh.* Just thinking about his sexy voice sent a flutter through her stomach. Layla was doing great, and Brianna knew that entertaining the thought of anything else in their lives would only add confusion to their already chaotic schedules. *Who am I kidding? I'll never see the guy again anyway.* The thought was strangely comforting and upsetting all at once.

"BREE, CAN YOU please tweak the lights one more time? I'm getting a shadow again." Claude Delaney moved with the grace of a swan as he glided around the young, scantily clad couple on the bed. They'd been shooting the Regency Linen commercial for five and a half hours, and Brianna wished it would go on forever. Gorgeous didn't begin to describe the couple on the bed with their perfectly sculpted and tanned bodies. Just watching them was more action than she'd had in years. If she didn't count her bouts of self-gratification. A woman had to survive somehow. In reality, it was Claude's photographic techniques that held her interest.

She'd been filling in for Claude's assistant, Stella, on an as-needed basis for the past two years, picking up hours while Stella was on vacation or too sick to work, and she hoped to one day secure a full-time position with Claude. Brianna was a realist, though, and she knew that was a pipe dream. No one left Claude's employ. Stella had been working with Claude for fifteen years, and he was sought after by all the major commercial players on the East Coast.

"Two-twenty, Claude," Brianna reminded him.

He pursed his lips and lowered his eyeglasses to the bridge of his nose. "It's a good thing I love you." He pushed his glasses back up his nose with his index finger. "Five more minutes. Then we'll wrap, so Bree Bree can go get little Layla."

She saw his cheeks rise behind the camera and knew he was teasing.

"Had a fab shoot yesterday. Wish you were here. The guy was hunkier than hunky," Claude said as he climbed a stepladder.

Brianna listened to the *click, click, click* of the shutter, longing to be the one behind the camera. She found the sound as soothing as Layla found rubbing the ear of her stuffed Piglet doll and as inspiring as a writer's muse.

"Did you hear me, Bree Bree?" Claude asked.

"Yes, sorry." *I was busy fantasizing.* "Not interested. Thanks."

Claude sighed and waved his hand at the models. The contrast between his cream-colored linen shirt and his coffee-bean-brown skin made Brianna wish once again that she had her camera in hand. It would be a long while before she would be able to replace her broken camera, but she held on to the dream of one day seeing the world through the safety of the filtered lens once again.

"Great job. Thank you for a hard day's work," Claude said to the couple before turning his back to them and whispering, "Beauty makes for a tough life. What I wouldn't give to roll around on the sheets with that one." He nodded to the lithe male model crossing the floor wearing nothing but black bikini briefs.

"You're terrible. You say that about all the male models."

Claude pulled his glasses down again and peered over them. The lights reflected off of his pointy bald head. "Good. Maybe some of my lusty leering will wear off on you."

"Okay. On that note, I'm going to take off and get my lovely daughter from school. Is Reba coming by to help put things away?" Reba Wilkes was the sweet fiftysomething woman who ran his cleanup crew.

"Always," Claude said. "I meant what I said. I really do wish you were here for that shoot. This guy had soulful eyes, and you could just tell he was a good one, despite his fame."

Brianna waved as she walked toward the door. "Daughter, daughter, Claude. Talk to me in twelve years." She hesitated at the doorway. "Love you for thinking of me, though."

"Fine. Twelve years it is, but I need you on Saturday. Can you make it? Ten o'clock."

Brianna bit her lower lip and closed her eyes. Saturday was going to be her first full day off in two weeks, and she'd planned on shopping for Layla's birthday gift and taking Layla to the park later in the afternoon. They hadn't been in ages, and Brianna had wanted some one-on-one time while the weather was still warm enough to enjoy it. She'd made enough in tips last week to splurge on lunch out, too, but the extra money from Claude would help toward her birthday party. She hadn't told Layla about the park yet, so…

Claude must have seen her hesitation. "Stella won't be back in time. I'll throw in a little extra bonus."

"Sure. Yes." *Sorry, Layla.*

Chapter Five

HUGH ROUNDED THE racetrack at one hundred and eighty miles per hour. He'd been at the track since eight in the morning, after spending an hour at his home gym and going for a three-mile run. This was his last practice run. The world outside his windows went by in one thick blur, but Hugh didn't see the bleachers melding into one another or the blob of fans standing outside the fence with their noses pressed against the gate. His vision was focused on the hood of the car, the road just beyond, and the curve of the track. His body, completely in tune to the vehicle, felt a slight drift to the right around the bend, and beyond the pristine roar of the engine that vibrated through his body, the only thing Hugh heard was his own mind noting the drift and calculating the strategy for the next race. There was no bigger thrill than race day, but practice came pretty damn close.

He downshifted on the straightaway and pulled into the pit. The pit crew flew around the car at lightning speed.

"Fix that drift," Hugh said as he stepped from the car and felt the familiar sensation that everything around him was still moving. It took a few minutes for the hum of the engine to leave his body, and when it did, it stole a flash of the exhilaration from the ride.

"We've got it, Hugh. No problem," Art assured him.

Hugh stood to the side as his heart calmed and the earth stopped moving under his feet. "Art." He waved him over. Art was thirty-five with short, sandy hair and honest green eyes.

"Boss? Listen, we've got thi—"

Hugh put his arm around Art's shoulder and walked him away from the crew. "Art, no more of that shit like last night, okay?"

Art smiled and held up his hands in surrender. "I heard you last night. No more setups. Got it." He looked out over the track and then back at Hugh. "Was she really that bad?"

"Worse." Hugh smiled. "The only good thing that came of it is that I found a place I can hang out without being recognized."

"No shit?"

"Yup. Hell, if I'm here for a week or two, I might as well have a place to grab dinner."

Art pointed at him. "See, now, that's why you need a wife."

"Oh hell no. That's why they make restaurants. I'm off the market, remember?" There was a time when Hugh would have fought to the death to protect his bachelor status, but now, as the words left his lips, his vehemence deflated. He didn't want a wife to cook for him, but every day he was growing more certain that he wanted to have a real relationship with a woman. Something more than *wham, bam, thank you, ma'am* with women he barely remembered ten minutes after they were done in the sack.

"Hey, you told me to tell you when it was three. It's three fifteen. Sorry." Art held up his arm for Hugh to see his watch.

Hugh patted him on the back. "Thanks, man. Let's go over

the notes for tomorrow; then I'll take off."

HUGH SHOWERED AND dressed in a pair of distressed jeans and a white T-shirt beneath a black cashmere sweater. He splashed on Eros by Versace cologne and slid his feet into his favorite pair of black boots before heading out to his garage.

He drove his Roadster to Old Town Tavern, contemplated parking behind the building, where Brianna had said she parked the night before, then thought better of it. He didn't want to take a chance that she'd think he was a stalker, even if he was there for a second day in a row specifically to see her as she arrived at work. He mulled over not going in and taking a chance in a day or two. As with everything else in Hugh's life, he was less than patient. *The hell with it.* He drove down the street and around the corner and parked in the public parking garage.

As a thirty-one-year-old race car driver, it took a lot to make Hugh nervous, but as he pulled open the heavy wooden door to Old Town Tavern, his nerves were on fire. One quick scan told him Brianna wasn't there. He let out the breath he didn't realize he'd been holding, and disappointment settled heavily on his shoulders.

The blond waitress he recognized waved from behind the bar. "Hey there." She pointed at herself. "Kat, remember?"

"Of course. How's it going?" he asked as he climbed atop a barstool. He hadn't given much thought to Kat's looks the evening before, and now, without the distraction of beautiful Brianna or fluorescent Tracie, he noticed that she was quite attractive with big blue eyes and a tall, slender frame, though she wore a splash too much makeup and too tight of a push-up bra. Hugh had never been into blondes for more than a roll in the sheets, and tonight was no different as his mind drifted back to Brianna.

"Can't complain," she said with a smile. "Nice to see you again, Hugh. Sidecar?"

"No, thanks. Water would be great, thanks."

She opened a bottle of Perrier and set it on the bar beside a glass of ice. "Who comes into a bar and orders water?"

"You're right. Give me a sidecar, too." He checked his watch. It was four forty-five. *Where is she?*

"Now you're talkin'." Kat made his drink.

"It's pretty dead in here, huh?" he said, hoping she'd say something about Brianna. "Will it get busier when the game comes on?"

"Oh, yeah. It's still early." She leaned against the counter behind the bar. "So, Hugh, did you just move to town?"

He laughed. "Not really. I've owned my house for a few years, but I travel a lot."

"Oh, what do you do?"

Hugh took a sip of water, trying to form an answer other than the truth. He really didn't want to out himself in the one place he could let his guard down.

The door flew open, and Brianna hurried across the floor, looking down as she stuffed her keys in her purse. "I'm sorry. I swear I hate my stupid car. It wouldn't st—" She stopped cold. Their eyes locked.

Hugh's pulse kicked up a notch as he drank in the rest of Brianna—all the lovely curves he had missed the night before. Brianna didn't just have a nice body. She was smoking hot. He couldn't help but drag his eyes down to her perfect round breasts, slim waist, curvaceous hips, and long, luscious legs in tighter-than-tight jeans that disappeared into knee-high black boots. Hugh felt a smile stretch across his face. He drew his eyes back up to her face and knew that it didn't matter what kind of killer body she had. It was those thoughtful, intense eyes that drew him in. *Shit.* She wasn't smiling.

"Hi, Bree," he said.

Brianna looked at Kat with her lips set in a tight line. Kat, on the other hand, sported a playful grin and raised her eyebrows.

"Um. Hi…Hugh," Bree said before training her eyes on the floor and hurrying toward the back of the bar.

Despite his better judgment, Hugh felt himself turning on his stool, and watched her disappear through a door marked *Employees Only*. In thirty-one years, he'd never been drawn to a woman's face the way he was drawn to Brianna's, and for the first time ever, Hugh had no idea what to do next.

Chapter Six

"SHIT SHIT SHIT." Brianna paced the stockroom floor, her hands fisted, her face a tight mask of nerves. "What am I going to do? He's just a customer. Ignore him. Yes, I'll ignore him." She covered her face with her hands. "Damn it. Why is this happening? Shit shit shit."

"Should I be worried about you?" Mack leaned against the doorframe of his office.

Brianna whipped her head around. "Oh my God. I had no idea you were in there. I'm sorry. I'm fine." *Great. Now Mack thinks I'm nuts, talking to myself in the stockroom.*

"A person who's fine doesn't talk to herself with a look on her face like she'd rather be locked in the cooler than behind the bar. Is someone out there bothering you?" He pushed from the doorframe and headed toward the bar.

She ran to his side and grabbed his arm. "No, Mack. No one is bothering me. I'd tell you if they were."

Mack drew his eyebrows together and crossed his arms. "Wanna clue me in about who is *just a customer*?"

Brianna's voice softened. "Not really."

"Fine, Brianna. But I think I'll hang around the bar tonight just the same."

"You don't have to do that." She snagged a clean towel, tucked it into her belt, and followed Mack into the bar. She watched him eyeing the customers, then glance at her, scrutinizing who held her attention. Brianna made a conscious effort not to look at gorgeous, heart-stopping, breath-stealing Hugh.

Thankfully, more customers had arrived, and there were at least a dozen men between the tables and the bar.

Mack looked around again. "I'll be back. If you need me, come get me." He headed into the restaurant, and the constriction in Brianna's chest eased a little. She took a deep breath and grabbed an order pad to wait on the booths. Kat grabbed the pad from her hand and pushed past her.

"I'm on booths tonight." She was halfway to the corner booth by the time Brianna called out her name.

Damn it, Kat. Brianna busied herself behind the counter, serving drinks and purposely not making eye contact with Hugh, who was talking to the guy next to him about baseball. *God, I love his voice. What is wrong with me? He's a man. That can only mean trouble.* When he held his hand up in a little wave meant for her, a chill ran through her. She smiled despite herself, then dropped her eyes to the bar and began wiping it down. She noticed his water was empty, but his sidecar hadn't been touched—again. He hadn't touched his drinks the night before, either. She opened another bottle of Perrier and set it alongside a glass of ice in front of him.

His hand grazed hers when he reached for the glass. She drew her eyes to his.

"Thank you, Bree," he said.

"Sure," she managed.

"You look nice tonight."

She felt her cheeks flush again. *Damn it.* She felt like a

schoolgirl blushing all the time.

"Thank you." She eyed the alcohol in his glass. "Was your drink made poorly?"

He didn't even look down at the glass. "No. It's fine."

Then why aren't you drinking it? Brianna saw Tracie enter the bar, silencing her before the question left her mouth. Tracie's eyes ran from table to table, lingering over a group of two handsome men, then traveled to the bar and locked on Hugh.

"Your girlfriend's here," Brianna said before walking away.

"What?" Hugh turned just as Tracie sat beside him.

"Why did you leave him alone with her?" Kat whispered with her side pressed against Brianna's back at the counter behind the bar.

"What am I gonna do, stand there and gawk? I can't even speak when I'm near him." She looked at Kat and bit her lower lip. "Kat, you can't let this happen. Don't let my stupid hormones ruin my ability to think straight. Please. Layla is counting on me."

Kat rolled her eyes. "Layla wouldn't care if you dated a cute guy. You just use her as an excuse and you know it."

"Not true. Look at my mother. My father left when I was eight. Todd was a weekend fling who clearly wanted nothing more, and look at your own father. He left when you were twelve. Men suck. They're great for alleviating our needs, so to speak, but that doesn't mean we have to mess up our lives for them. I'd rather go without, thank you very much." She looked over her shoulder at Hugh and Tracie. Tracie leaned in close and Hugh leaned back, stiff, with a pained look in his eyes. Brianna groaned at Tracie's brazenness and turned back to Kat.

"Not all men are like that. Look at Brad Pitt."

"Great example." Brianna rolled her eyes.

"Oh yeah. I totally forgot he was married when he met Angelina. Shoot." Kat laughed. She peeked at Hugh. "Go save the poor guy before she eats him alive."

Brianna took a deep breath. *Why is it my job to save him?* Hugh awakened all her girly parts and prodded emotions she hadn't felt in a long time, and besides, he seemed like too nice of a guy to be preyed upon by Tracie. She handed another customer his drink and headed for Hugh.

"What are you having?" she asked Tracie.

"Cosmo," she said, inching her long red fingernails toward Hugh's hand on the bar.

Hugh slid his hand off the bar and lifted his eyes to Brianna's. She read, *Help me*, in his gaze, but heard, *Kiss me*, in her head.

Brianna's stomach tightened. "Coming right up." *I can't believe I'm going to do this.* She carried the cosmo in her shaking hand. Tracie leaned toward Hugh and her dress fell open, exposing a deep valley between her enormous breasts. Brianna narrowed her eyes, took a final step and then stumbled. The drink flew from her hand into Tracie's lap.

"Hey!" Tracie jumped up with her hands held out to the sides, her dress dripping with the pink cocktail. "What the heck?" She grabbed a handful of napkins from the bar.

"Oh my gosh. I'm so sorry." Brianna reached across the bar and *accidentally* knocked Hugh's sidecar over, splashing a second drink onto Tracie's already wet dress. "Oh goodness!"

Hugh stifled a laugh, which spurred Brianna's smile into motion.

"It's not funny. Now I have to go home and change. Ugh!" Tracie stomped out of the bar.

"I'm so sorry," Brianna said to Hugh as she mopped up the counter. She noticed Mack standing at the entrance to the restaurant, shaking his head. She cringed and mouthed, *Sorry*.

"That was brilliant," Hugh said with a laugh.

His smile lit up his face and lightened Brianna's anxiety. "You looked like you needed saving."

"That, I did." Hugh lifted his water to her and took a sip.

"I'll get you another sidecar." She took a step away, and he touched her hand as it trailed the edge of the bar.

"Don't."

She glanced back.

"I'd rather talk than drink."

Brianna scanned the other customers. No one was asking for a drink. Kat had the booths and tables covered. She had no excuse not to talk to him—and she'd been looking for one only halfheartedly. Another quick glance at Hugh's dark eyes sent the search for an excuse away for good. "Okay."

For a moment he just looked at her. She was hyperaware of every breath. Every second passed as if it were in slow motion, every movement magnified—the slight lift of his lips, the sparkle in his eye, the way he licked his lower lip, leaving his lips parted just enough that she could see the glistening stripe where his tongue had just passed.

"Hello?"

Brianna blinked out of her trance and realized that the older man standing next to Hugh with an angry look in his eyes had already tried to get her attention several times. "Sorry. What can I get you?" She felt Hugh's stare like heat from a laser.

"Bud Light."

"Coming right up." She focused on filling his drink. Her mind ran in seventeen different directions. Her life was work and Layla. What could she possibly talk to any man about? She handed the angry man his drink and then served a couple and a single woman. One of her favorite customers, Bill Carson, a gray-haired man with thin, gangly shoulders sat beside Hugh. Brianna felt Hugh's eyes following her, and the emotions she'd been stifling for so many years came tumbling forward. Her stomach fluttered. Each breath felt too loud. She tried not to look at him, afraid she'd be mesmerized into stupidity again.

She handed Bill his usual Jim Beam on the rocks. "Haven't seen you in here this week. Are you okay?" Her heart hammered against her chest as she forced herself not to look at Hugh.

Bill nodded. He was a retired postal worker, and Bree swore the flattening of his fingertips was caused by years of dealing envelopes across the postal counter. Bill had aged ten years in the last three, since his wife, Millie, had died. A road map of wrinkles covered his cheeks and forehead.

"You sure? Missing Millie?" she asked.

"Oh, you know. I miss Millie every day. My son was in town. I spent a few days with my grandson, but they went back to California." He sighed. "How are you, Brianna?" Bill looked around the bar. "Busy tonight. They treating you okay? Because if they're not, why, I'll—"

Brianna loved how Bill pretended he'd stand up for her, when in reality he was so old and thin that a strong wind could blow him over. She was used to dealing with drunken men, and she didn't feel she needed protecting, but she found it cute that he offered—and she wondered if Hugh was the kind of guy who would fiercely protect his girlfriend. *Stop, stop, stop.*

"They're fine, Bill. But I know you've got my back." She touched his hand. "Excuse me." She went to serve another customer. The three that followed amped up her anxiety.

A table of guys in the middle of the bar began playing quarters, and between the *whoops*, cheers for the game, the searing heat from Hugh's gaze, and Kat rushing in and out of the bar area, Brianna could barely hold on to a coherent thought. By the time the game ended and the crowd thinned, she felt as if she'd walked a hundred miles and, still feeling drawn to Hugh, felt as if she could walk a hundred more.

"What a night," Kat said with a loud sigh. "That was insane. How are you holding up?" She rinsed a rag and squeezed it out in the sink.

"Okay." Brianna glanced at Hugh. "He's still here."

"Of course he is. The man came to see you. Jesus, he's watched you like a hawk all night. You might as well talk to him. I'm going to mop up the booths." She leaned in close. "Stop being afraid. It's a conversation, not sex. Give the hot man a thrill."

It's the thrill I'm worried about.

HUGH LEARNED A lot about Brianna by just watching her, and he hadn't enjoyed an evening as much in a very long time. She handled the customers with kindness and strength, pulling away when her professional attentiveness was met with flirtatious advances. She was nothing like the women he was used to. The models and fans he used to date would never have given the likes of these guys the time of day, and there she was, asking the old man beside him if he was missing his wife. She came around the bar to pick up money a customer had dropped and gave it back to him.

When a young guy grabbed her wrist and pulled her close,

leading with his lips, Hugh stood from his stool. His chest expanded with a deep breath. *I'll kill you.* Before he reached the guy, Brianna smiled like she was going to allow the kiss. Then she snapped her wrist over, breaking his hold, and grabbed his thumb and twisted it back and down—hard, causing him to writhe in agony and beg to be released. Hugh watched Mack escort the numskull out of the bar and then brought his attention back to Brianna, who was wiping down the bar once again as if nothing had happened. Hugh noticed the slight tremble in her arm, and the light that had found her eyes was gone again, replaced with a serious darkness.

"You okay?" he asked.

She nodded. "Happens all the time."

"It does? That's not a good thing, Bree." He didn't even know her well, but at that moment, Hugh wanted nothing more than to take her into his arms and hug away the fear she was trying so hard to hide.

She wiped her hands on her towel. "It's really not a big deal. He just got carried away."

"Bree." Mack appeared beside Hugh. "You okay?"

"Fine, Mack. Thanks." Her eyes darted to Hugh, then back to Mack.

"You sure? I can take care of…" Mack glared at Hugh. "Anything you need me to."

Hugh smiled at the burly man and extended his hand. "Hugh Braden. Nice to meet you."

"Braden? I know that name." Mack shook Hugh's hand.

Shit. How could he slip up like that? "You've probably heard of my brother, Josh. He's a big-time fashion designer. His name is in all the fashion magazines." Hugh had to push the conversation in another direction before Mack exposed him.

"I'm not here to harass Brianna. I was just making sure the guy didn't hurt her."

Mack nodded, still scrutinizing him like he was unraveling a mystery. "Bree?"

"He's fine, Mack." She went back to work cleaning up the bar.

"Braden, huh? I'll figure it out." Mack headed toward the back of the bar.

Brianna stopped wiping the counter and folded her arms over her chest. "Thank you for asking if I was okay. But why are you here? You didn't finish your drink and you didn't watch the game. Should I be creeped out?"

Hugh leaned on the bar and answered honestly. "I'm not sure. Maybe." He shrugged. "I was drawn to you yesterday, and I thought I'd come in and talk with you tonight. So you tell me. Creepy?"

She looked down and blushed. "Sort of."

He laughed. "Yeah, I guess it sort of is, but how else does a guy get to know a woman around here? Do you want to have coffee with me after you're off work?" He saw her flinch. "Listen, no pressure. I was just offering."

Her eyebrows drew together, and she glanced at Kat as she approached.

"What's going on?" Kat asked. "Way to nail that creep. What an ass, grabbing you like that." Kat looked between Brianna and Hugh. "Am I interrupting something here?"

Brianna lifted her eyes at Hugh. Damn, those eyes killed him.

"Okay," Brianna said softly.

"Okay?" *Yes!*

"Okay what?" Kat asked.

"Coffee. I'm having coffee with Hugh after work."

"You are?" Kat lifted her thin brows. "That's great. Where are you going?"

Hugh shrugged. "Wherever Bree wants."

"What about Layla?" Kat asked.

Worry sailed through her eyes. "She's with my mom for the night."

"Perfect," Kat said; then she looked at Hugh.

With your mom? She's got a kid. Shit. She has a kid. Hugh loved children, but he hadn't ever considered dating a woman with a child. He must have looked as concerned as he felt because Kat elbowed Brianna and nodded in his direction.

Brianna crossed her arms again. She looked at Hugh with those beautiful eyes that seemed to be filled with serious thoughts every second of the evening. "I have a daughter. Layla Michelle. She's going to be six in a week. If you'd rather skip having coffee, that's fine. I'd understand."

One look in her eyes and he knew he wanted to get to know her better, but he also knew he'd have to be careful. Dating a single mother introduced all sorts of tangled webs into the equation.

"Brianna, I'd love to have coffee with you whether or not you have a daughter."

"Really?" She arched a thin brow.

"Really." Risking his emotions was new, considering the women he'd dated in the past never struck anything other than lust in him, but risking a single mother's emotions—or her daughter's—was dangerous. He thought of his own father and how he had never been with another woman after his wife died, and he wondered how he would have felt, as a child, if his father had.

His father's voice sailed through his mind—though it was Hugh's own thoughts that he heard. *Tread lightly, son.* Hugh didn't know the meaning of treading lightly. He was an all-or-nothing guy who moved fast and trusted his gut. The thought of treading lightly scared the shit out of him, but not enough to forgo coffee with lovely Brianna.

Chapter Seven

"I HAVEN'T BEEN on a date in almost seven years, much less had coffee with a handsome guy. I can't even believe I'm doing this." Brianna and Kat stood before the mirror in the cramped ladies' room. She brushed her hair, and Kat handed her a tube of lipstick. "No, thanks."

"Come on. You'll look great with a little color," Kat urged.

"He's seen me working for the last seven hours. He knows what I look like." She pulled away from the mirror. "Jesus, Kat. He sat there all night. *All night.* Who does that?"

"The hottie who's out there waiting for you now," Kat pointed out.

"No, really. I mean, it's one thing to hang around for an hour or even two, but all night? And did you see him? He didn't watch the game."

"Calm down. You're having coffee, not going home with him. Although…"

Brianna narrowed her eyes. "No. No, no, no. Don't even go there. Coffee. That's it. And I'll call you if he turns out to be a freak, so leave your cell phone on."

THEY WALKED DOWN the quiet city street to the only place open so late, Dunkin' Donuts. Brianna shivered in her sweater. Hugh shrugged out of his jacket and placed it around her shoulders.

"I'm okay," she lied.

"I'm sure you are, but I was hot and you looked like a great coatrack." He smiled as he opened the door to Dunkin' Donuts. "After you, madam."

A gentleman and funny? No way. "Thank you." Brianna thought she'd be struck mute from nerves, but being alone with Hugh was easy. He didn't make innuendos like the guys at the bar did and he didn't look at her like she was a piece of meat, which she was thankful for. She still didn't know what had possessed her to accept his offer for coffee, but now, sitting across from him in the corner booth, she was glad she had.

"So, let's get past the awkward first-date stuff." Hugh's dimples deepened when his smile reached his eyes.

Did the walls just start closing in? She'd been so relaxed. She hated that the minute she realized there would be questions about her personal life her chest constricted.

"I was kidding, Bree," he said. "You look like I asked you for your deepest secrets."

"I'm sorry. I haven't been on a date in a very long time. It's all a little scary to me." She wrapped her hands around the warm cup. "I'm afraid I'm not very good at small talk, either."

He put his arm across the back of the booth. "Then I'll make it easy for you. I'm the youngest of six. I've always had to be a little loud just to be heard. Tell me what you'd like to know and I'll answer as best I can."

"Gosh, I don't know. You have five siblings? That must be fun. I'm an only child."

"It is fun. I've got four brothers and a sister, and I love 'em all." He took a sip of his coffee. "How long have you worked at the Old Town Tavern?"

She looked down, biting back the nagging embarrassment about what her life had become. Then she thought of Layla and her confidence returned. She looked him in the eye so she could read his response before she heard it.

"I've worked there since I graduated from college. I got pregnant the week I graduated. It wasn't planned, and the guy was just a guy I hung out with for the weekend. I know that sounds awful…" *I sound like a slut. I might as well leave now.*

"Why? Anyone can get pregnant by accident. It's a miracle there aren't more graduation-weekend babies around."

He smiled again, and she had an urge to thank him for not judging her. "I've never looked at it that way, but you're right. I mean, tons of college kids have sex, but condoms don't always break." She covered her face with her hands. "I can't believe I just said that. I'm sorry." She looked up at him and cringed. "I told you I'm not good at this."

"Honesty is a good thing. Tell me about your daughter."

She sat up a little taller. *This*, she could handle. "Layla is going to be six next week. She's smart and funny, and she's the most thoughtful child. She loves art and going to plays. I imagine she'll want to be in the drama club when she gets old enough, and she is totally hung up on all things princess at the moment."

"She sounds wonderful. Does she see her father?"

Brianna shook her head. "No. I never heard from him again after graduation. We'd met at a party, hung out for the weekend, and then he was gone. When I found out I was pregnant, I tracked him down, but…he was less than welcoming about the idea. He made it clear that he wanted nothing to do with me or with Layla." She couldn't believe she was telling him her darkest secret, but the confession came easily. "Sometimes I feel guilty that Layla doesn't have her father in her life, but I can't imagine forcing him to see her out of obligation."

He nodded. "Brave."

"What?"

"You must be very brave to take on raising a child alone right out of college. Weren't you scared?"

His thoughtful gaze held her still. No one had ever called her brave before. "Um. I never really took the time to think about if I was scared or not. I loved her from the moment I found out I was pregnant, so I just..." She shrugged. "You know, you make a decision and then you do the best you can."

"Trust me. Brave is a good word for you," he said. "She's with your mother tonight, so your mom lives nearby? Was she there to help when she was born?"

His voice was sincere, as were his eyes. Brianna was struck by his interest. "She doesn't live far. She was pretty upset at first. I mean my dad left when I was eight, so she raised me and saved her money to send me to college, and then I come home pregnant and unable to find a job in my field. It was really hard for her, but she eventually came around, and she adores Layla. My mom's taking her to a play tomorrow and now I'm working in the morning, so it worked out perfectly."

Hugh leaned forward. "Tell me about you."

Her stomach lurched. *I'm exhausted and I spend every minute trying to make ends meet and make sure Layla's okay.* "There's not much to tell."

"Come on. I watched you in the bar. You're really good at your job, but I can see the gears of your mind clicking away.

What do you think about? What do you like to do?"

"I'm afraid I'm pretty boring. I work two jobs and take care of Layla. Until tonight, I haven't been on a single date since I got pregnant, and I'm not sure why I agreed tonight, to be honest." *What happened to me? I can't stop talking.*

"It's because you felt sorry for me for rescuing yourself from the dirtbag who grabbed you instead of letting me be your knight in shining armor."

"Oh, is that it?" She laughed. "I wondered why I'd cave from my twelve-year-plan for some guy who sits in a bar all night but never drinks."

"Wait. I'll answer you, but what's your twelve-year-plan?"

Shit. How could I let that slip? She wrinkled her nose. "Did I really say that aloud?"

"Yeah, I'm afraid so. Now you have to explain. I mean, twelve years is a lifetime. How do you plan twelve years ahead of time?"

She drank her coffee, debating her answer. She'd come this far and he hadn't run away. She might as well expose it all. "Twelve years is how long it is until Layla turns eighteen." She shrugged. "If I don't date for twelve years, her life is easier."

He drew his eyebrows together. "So you weren't planning on dating until she was eighteen? That's admirable."

"I've made it six years already, so I'm a third of the way there." *God, has it really been that long?* "I figure the less confusion the better. Besides, when it's just me and her, I know where our emotions are."

"So you haven't dated since you got pregnant, and you're doing this to avoid emotional contact?" Hugh's serious tone caught her off guard.

"No, not to avoid emotional contact, just to protect Layla.

You know how relationships are. They're like roller coasters. They're good; they're bad; there's jealousy and feelings taken for granted. And then when you finally relax, the other person takes off. So it's just easier to avoid all of that when she's growing up. I'll have plenty of time after she's eighteen. I'll only be…thirty-nine." *Thirty-nine. Holy shit.* That was the first time she'd calculated out her age in accordance with her plan.

He leaned forward again, and Brianna's heartbeat sped up.

"Do you have any idea how commendable that is?" Then he took her hand and whispered, "Or how sexy?"

His touch sent a zing of excitement through her. His big, warm hand felt like heaven. *It's been way too long. I'm losing my mind.* "Kat just calls me crazy."

"My mother died when I was a baby, and my father has never been with another woman. He still talks to her." He leaned back in the booth. "You know, I don't think I've shared that with anyone. Anyway, you're doing what you think is best for your daughter, and there's nothing sexier than that."

She covered her face. "You're making me blush again."

He reached over and pulled her hand away from her face. "Your face is too pretty to cover up."

"You're either a really smooth player or just about the nicest guy I've ever met. God, what have you done to me? I don't ever talk about me and Layla, well, except to Kat or Mack." She looked into her empty coffee cup. "Did you put truth serum in here?"

ON THE WAY back to her car, Brianna wore Hugh's leather jacket, and she looked so damn cute that he couldn't wipe the stupid grin from his lips. It was refreshing being out with a woman who wasn't clamoring to be taken to fancy restaurants or to be photographed with the paparazzi. Hugh wondered if he could hide his identity a little longer.

"I had fun tonight. Thank you for inviting me for coffee."

One look in her trusting eyes and he knew he wouldn't lie to her. "Bree…" He didn't know what he wanted to say, but when she stopped walking and looked at him, he had the desire to kiss her. He closed the gap between them, wrestling with the urge. He didn't want to hurt her or her daughter. She was trying so hard to do the right thing, and Hugh knew that if he pushed, she'd give in, and then what?

"Yeah?" she said just above a whisper. She licked her lower lip.

Don't kiss her. Don't kiss her. "I'm glad you agreed to have coffee with me," he answered.

Her lips curled into a half smile, and disappointment shadowed her eyes. *Did you want to kiss me?* He was so confused. They walked back to her car behind the bar, and a fist tightened in Hugh's gut. He thought he understood women pretty well, but Brianna had knocked him off kilter.

"Well, thank you for a really fun night." She took her keys from her purse.

Brianna looked beautiful under the stars. Knowing she had such a big heart that she'd put her life on hold for her daughter, Hugh found her all the more alluring. He wanted nothing more than to take her in his arms and feel her lips against his, to taste the sweetness of the honest, selfless woman before him. He put his hand on the small of her back and felt her body stiffen beneath his touch. He put his cheek against hers and whispered, "I'm honored to be your first date in almost seven years." He kissed her cheek, inhaling the scent of her perfume. "You smell sun-kissed, like a warm summer breeze." He stepped back before he ended up kissing her in a way that he knew he'd never be able to stop.

Chapter Eight

BRIANNA TOUCHED HER cheek where his whiskers had just grazed and his breath had warmed her skin. She could barely breathe. *Sun-kissed, like a warm summer breeze.* He was handsome and romantic? How does a girl respond to being told she smells sun-kissed? *Thank you? You should see how good I taste? Oh my God, what is happening to me?*

Hugh opened her car door.

"Thank you," she managed as she climbed in. She was so conflicted. She didn't want the night to end, but she knew if she kissed him it would be hard to stop, and she didn't need that kind of complication. She'd come too far to lose herself in one night of passion. *Been there, done that.* But as she slid the key into the ignition, she felt a loss, knowing their evening was ending and he hadn't asked for her phone number. Oh God, maybe she'd blown the whole night and hadn't realized. It had been a very long time since she'd had to worry about dating etiquette.

He stood beside her open door, his hip close enough for her to touch. She twisted to put on her seat belt and realized she still had his jacket on. She climbed from the car, brushing against his firm, muscular thigh.

"I forgot about your jacket." She pulled one arm out.

He gently touched her arm. "Keep it. It's chilly."

"But it's leather." She tried to pull it off.

Hugh moved in front of her. "Keep it," he whispered. "I'll get it another time."

Another time? Another time!

Without any thought, she put her palm on his chest. Even with her heels, the height difference was too great for an easy kiss. She felt his heart beating beneath her palm.

"Are you sure?" she whispered. *Kiss me. Just kiss me already.*

He nodded, then leaned down and kissed her forehead. He took a step back again. Could he send her any more confusing signals? She wanted to really kiss him—full-on, tongues tangled, chests mashed against each other, their heartbeats connecting, sharing a rhythm, and exchanging oxygen—so badly she could practically taste the coffee on his tongue.

She climbed back into the car and pulled his jacket tighter across her chest. Hugh shut the door, and she rolled down the window as she cranked the engine. It sputtered and died.

Hugh leaned in the window. "Trouble?"

"I'm sure it'll be fine." *Shit. Come on.* She turned the key again, and this time it didn't even sputter. It made a clicking noise.

"I don't think you're going anywhere in this car tonight, Bree."

She banged her forehead on the steering wheel. "This can't be happening."

Hugh reached through the window and lifted her chin so she was looking at him. "I can fix it tomorrow. I'll give you a ride."

"You can fix it? Are you a mechanic?"

"I know a lot about cars, but I actually meant that I have a friend who can fix it in the morning."

"I have to work tomorrow." *Kill me now.* She ran through her contingency plan. She couldn't take her mother's car without ruining the day for her and Layla, but she might be able to borrow Kat's car. "I'll call Kat. Maybe I can borrow her car."

"Brianna, I can lend you a car," he said.

"What? You need your car." She dug in her purse for her phone.

"Bree, sweetie, take a deep breath."

She closed her eyes and breathed deeply.

"Feel better? Let's lock up your car, and I'll take you home. We can figure it out along the way. Let me make a call about fixing your car."

Her shoulders dropped and she nodded. "Thanks, Hugh. You didn't sign up for this mess when you asked me for coffee." She climbed from the car and watched him step away and talk on the phone. He seemed unflappable, not the least bit flustered by having to take her home.

When he was finished with his call, he returned to her side.

Brianna sighed. "Now your night is ruined and you have to take extra time to drive me home. I'm so sorry." She looked up at him and he was smiling again.

"Let's leave your key in the tailpipe." He tucked the key into the hiding place, then said, "Do I look like I mind?"

"No, and it's kind of ridiculous. You have to have better things to do than drive me all over creation." *I am such a loser. This is why I shouldn't date.*

"Are we going all over creation? An adventure. Now I'm excited." Hugh slung his arm around her shoulders and pulled his jacket tight across her chest. "Come on. Our adventure begins. So tell me, where is this place…Creation?"

They walked around the corner, and as much as Brianna tried to deny the feelings that were building inside her, she loved being pressed against Hugh's sturdy body. He made her feel feminine and safe, and his arm felt deliciously sexy around her shoulders.

The parking garage was quiet and practically empty. Every *click* and *clack* of her boot heels echoed as they crossed the garage to the elevators. When they stepped out of the elevators on the top level, Brianna scanned the parking deck. There were only about a dozen cars, and Hugh took her hand and led her toward the car in the farthest corner, stopping in the center of the lot, where not a single car was parked.

"Something wrong?" she asked.

"Nope. I just realized how beautiful the stars were and I thought, as long as we're not in a rush, why not take a minute and enjoy them?"

"You're not some psycho killer, are you?" She looked at him out of the corner of her eye, wondering about the gears that made him tick. He was nullifying every assumption she'd ever had about tall, dark, and handsome men being high-maintenance, self-centered, arrogant assholes, much like men say about beautiful women.

"Not that I'm aware of. Why? Do psychos look at stars?"

"You're just so different from any guy I've ever met. I keep waiting for the skeleton to come racing out of the closet and bite me in the ass." In the dark, she couldn't see his eyes very clearly, but his hand didn't sweat, it didn't flinch, and he made no move to turn away. Instead, he took a step closer. And then another. His body was an inch from hers as he gazed into her eyes. It took all of her effort not to put her free hand on his waist, to stand on her tiptoes and kiss him. *Kiss me. Please kiss me. No. Don't kiss me.*

"Bree."

Oh, that voice. Yes, kiss me. Yes. "Mm-hmm?"

He lowered his face closer to hers and whispered, "Look up."

They both looked up, and Brianna gasped at the beauty of the tiny illuminations that peppered the dark sky. Her hand came up to his waist without any cognitive thought.

"It's so beautiful. I wish Layla could see this." She froze. *Damn it. Nothing like smothering a guy with reminders that another guy had been there before him.*

"Let's take her out one night and show her," he said, still staring up at the stars.

She held her breath. Was he serious? Should she? She couldn't introduce him to her daughter. She barely knew him.

Hugh looked down at her. "Why are you squeezing my hand so tight?"

"Am I? Sorry." *Did you mean what you said?* Thinking about Layla brought her real life tumbling back to her. "Oh no. I forgot that I have to get Layla's birthday present. I have to get my car fixed. I need to get her present tomorrow. I don't think I'll have time during the week."

Hugh settled his index finger over her lips. "Take another deep breath."

She did—again.

"I told you that I can lend you a car. You'll be fine. If you don't want to borrow a car, I'm happy to take you after my appointment tomorrow. We can get her present while my friend fixes your car."

"Do you really have an extra car?" *Who has extra cars?*

"Yeah, and I really have a friend who will fix your car. He's picking it up as we speak, and he'll try to get whatever parts are needed and have it fixed by whatever time you need it. I told him by two since you said you had to work in the morning anyway."

She was thankful that he was willing to help her, but she really needed to use her own mechanic so she could make payments if it was too expensive.

"What's the worry I see in those beautiful eyes?" he asked.

She looked down, and he lifted her chin again, using the hand he had interlaced with hers.

"This is so embarrassing." She looked down again, but their hands were right there again, bringing her eyes back to his.

"Unless you stole that car, there's not much that can be embarrassing."

"Oh, yes, there is."

He took a step backward, but she clung to his shirt at the waist where her hand had been resting. He looked down at the tether that kept him close.

"Brianna, if you're married, I'm not that kind of guy. I like you, but I won't be with another man's wife. I can just give you a ride home and—"

"Married? I'm definitely not married."

He brought their clasped hands up and ran his knuckle softly along her jaw. "Then what is it? What's embarrassing?"

She held his gaze. He was so nice. How could she do anything but tell him the truth? *Great. Now you'll know I'm a broke loser.* "Hugh, you're so helpful and very generous, but I kind of need to use the mechanic that I know in case it's expensive. He lets me work out payments."

"I understand. Let's not worry about that just yet. This

might just turn out to be nothing at all. If it's a big dollar amount and he can't work out payments, then we'll bring it to your guy. Does that work?"

He was so considerate. Even though he was right there in front of her, looking at her with those generous, thoughtful, dark eyes, she needed to feel that he was real. She pressed her fingers to his abs, just above his belt. *Real. One-hundred-percent, rock-hard real.*

Chapter Nine

AS THEY WALKED to Hugh's car, his gut twisted. With the moonlight sparkling in Bree's eyes, he'd been a breath away from kissing her. She'd looked at him with such worry in her eyes that all he could think about was how good it would feel to kiss it away and bring the sparkle back to her eyes—the one he'd caught glimpses of earlier in the evening.

He clicked the key fob and unlocked the Roadster.

"Oh my God. Is that your car?"

"I could lie and say no, but I don't really believe in being dishonest with people I consider friends." He squeezed her hand, and she slipped her hand out of his grasp.

She stepped closer to the car and covered her mouth, then looked at Hugh and shook her head. "Who are you?" she whispered.

Hugh had never wanted to be someone different in his life. He was proud of the things he'd accomplished with his racing career, his college degree, and his family. But at that moment, with a hint of fear in Brianna's eyes, he wished he were Joe Nobody. He stepped closer to her and ran his hands up her arms to her shoulders. She felt so small beneath his jacket.

"I'm the same guy I was in the bar and the same guy you

had coffee with. I'm Hugh. Hugh Braden." He shrugged.

She drew her eyebrows together again, and the worried look deepened, stealing her smile and replacing it with a serious mask. "But who are you?"

"How can I answer that, Bree? I'm a son, a brother, a friend to some people. That's who I am. And a guy who wants to get to know you better." He knew he couldn't avoid telling her what she wanted to know, but every bit of him screamed, *Let her see the real you first!*

"What do you do for a living?"

He slid his hands across her shoulders and cupped her face with his hands. "Does that really make a difference?"

She stepped out of his grasp. "Maybe."

"I'm not a drug runner, or a thief, or anything else that you'd be ashamed of." The muscles in his neck knotted.

"Is it that difficult to tell me? Are *you* married?"

"No."

"Ever been?"

"No, Bree." He stepped forward, and she stepped backward. "Bree." He glanced away and ran his hand through his hair. "All I wanted was to get to know you without my career hanging over our heads. That's all. It's so hard to be normal when people know who I am."

"So you're someone important?" She crossed her arms.

"No. I'm not." He stepped closer. "I'll tell you who I am, but please don't judge me by it, and don't...change. You're so sweet and kind and good."

"I'm pretty sure I can remain the person I've been for the past twenty-eight years even if I know who you are."

"Are you sure? Because I really enjoy spending time with you, and once you know who I am, you might see me differently." *Like everyone else I've ever met.*

"Hugh, why would I do that? You are who you are."

Hugh didn't know what drove him to take her face in his hands, or to look her in the eyes and ask, "May I just kiss you once before you know who I am?" but when she nodded in agreement and he lowered his lips to hers, he was damn glad he'd done it. Kissing Bree was the sweetest thing he'd ever experienced. Her lips were soft and full, her tongue tentative, then a minute later, eager, but not too aggressive, and she made the sexiest little moans that he wasn't sure she realized she'd even emitted. He wrapped his palm around the base of her neck and deepened the kiss, slowly loving her delicious mouth, and then her delicate hands were on his waist and every bit of him hungered for more as she ran her fingers up his back and their bodies came together. They kissed until they had no fresh air in their lungs. Every breath of his became hers, and when they came away, Hugh was numb, breathing hard and fighting the desire to take her in another greedy kiss.

"Thank you." He kissed her forehead and moved to open the trunk of the car so he could show her his racing jacket.

"Wait." Bree grabbed him by the back of his shirt. Her fingers trembled against his skin. "You're really worried that it'll change how I see you?"

He shrugged. "I hope not, but I wanted you to know me for who I am before you knew me as what I do for a living. But…"

"And you're not going to tell me that you're something bad? Someone I should be afraid of?" She closed her eyes. "Wait. That's a stupid question. If you were, you wouldn't tell me."

He leaned his forehead against hers. Her perfume wafted up at him again and he nearly lost his voice. "Bree, you don't know me, and I barely know you. And I know you have no reason to believe or trust me, but I promise you that I will not ever lie to you, even if I worry that it'll hurt you. I think honesty is one of the most important things a person can promise someone, and I promise you honesty."

"Hugh, this is so unfair." She put her hands flat on his chest.

Her touch felt so good, so right, so different from that of the grabby, forward women he was used to being with. He placed his hand over hers just to feel the realness of it.

"I want to know who you are because I can't protect my daughter unless I know who I'm involved with. I respect your worry about things changing, and you're right, I don't know you, but I think for Layla's sake, I have to risk things changing. I have to know who I'm with to protect her."

Hugh's heart swelled in his chest. He nodded, unable to find words to express how beautiful that love for her daughter made her appear. He opened the trunk and took out his racing jacket, emblazoned with the logos of his sponsors, and his black driving gloves. Without a word, he handed them to her.

She ran her fingers over the logos, along the sleeves, and she traced the number thirty-two on the left breast. Then she took the gloves from Hugh and placed them on top of the jacket. She spread her petite hand over one enormous glove and smiled when her fingers reached just past the indentation of the second knuckle.

She looked up at him, then back down at the jacket. "This is supposed to mean something to me, and I get that, but, Hugh, my life is work and my daughter. I'm not sure what gloves and a jacket like this really mean. I know I sound stupid, but I'm not. I guess I just live in this tiny bubble of first grade, board games, and making ends meet."

Hugh didn't even try to fight the urge to reach out to her. He folded her in his arms and pressed her to his chest. "I really like that about you." When they drew apart, he put the jacket and gloves back in the trunk and withdrew the latest issue of *Racing* magazine, then placed it in her hands.

She looked down at it, and he watched her eyes narrow. She blew out a long breath as she ran her fingers over the image of his face. She squinted, her mouth set in a serious line. Then she looked up at him and touched his cheek before looking at the magazine and running her finger over the image again, as if she were comparing the contours of his jaw.

"So, this is you?" she said quietly.

"That's what I do, not who I am," he clarified.

She nodded. "It's dangerous, right?"

"You could say that."

"And this is why we haven't seen you around, right? You travel a lot, to race?" Her fingers were still running over his image.

"Yeah."

She nodded. "I'm glad I know." Worry lines stretched across her forehead. "I know about the race track, but honestly, I've never been. I don't have time to breathe, much less follow any sort of sports, but there are entire bars in town that cater to the fans. Restaurants too."

"I know. I purposely avoid them."

She nodded again, as if she understood, and Hugh wondered if she could possibly realize what it was really like to wonder if people gravitated toward him for what he represented rather than who he was.

He reached for the magazine, and she pressed it to her chest. "May I keep it?"

He felt the air around them shift, and he didn't like the way it blew her a little farther away than she'd been a moment before.

"Sure." He opened the car door and closed it after she was settled in the luxurious seat. "It's after two. Why don't we go by my place so you can pick out—pick up—a car. I'll follow you back to your place, so you're not arriving home alone this late, and then, when your car is done tomorrow, I'll bring it to you and we'll swap cars."

"I can't take one of your cars," she said. "By the looks of it, your cars are worth more than my mother's house."

Hugh reached across the seat and took her hand in his. "You're borrowing a car. I promised you'd have what you needed, and I always follow through with my promises."

She shook her head. "Hugh, I wouldn't feel comfortable in an expensive car. You saw what I drive. It's a nine-year-old Honda Civic. Not exactly a luxury car. And it barely runs. That's more my style."

He leaned across the seat, and he knew he was pushing his luck, but he wrapped his hand around the back of her neck and pulled her closer, then pressed another soft kiss to her lips. "I respect whatever decisions you make, but you're a working mom, and you don't have your daughter with you tonight at least partially because you need to work tomorrow. Take my car; fulfill your obligation; then you can forget you ever drove it." He started the car and drove toward home.

By the time he pulled into the garage, Brianna had been asleep for ten minutes. Hugh had a lot of experience with women. He could handle drunk women, horny women, tired and cranky women, but he had absolutely zero experience with beautiful women he actually wanted to get to know in more than a carnal way falling asleep in his car. *Should I wake her up? Carry her inside? Drive her to wherever she lives and carry her inside there?* Her face tilted toward the window and her hands were folded in her lap. She could have been just closing her eyes for a moment, save for the even, peaceful breathing that came only when all the cares of life were set aside—and he doubted that Brianna set aside her cares easily. She was definitely sleeping. She'd worked a long shift at Old Town Tavern, and she had said she'd had an appointment before that, which he now assumed, given her financial situation, was a second job of some sort. She had to be exhausted. He thought about his oldest brother, Treat, and wondered what he would do in the same situation. Treat was the epitome of a gentleman, and Hugh looked up to him for that and for many other reasons. He nodded in the silent car and made his decision.

Brianna snuggled against him as he carried her down the hall to the first-floor master bedroom, where he laid her on the king-sized bed, removed her boots, and covered her with a blanket. She rolled onto her stomach, and her dark hair fanned out from her head. Hugh had seen many women in his bed, but never had he stood above the bed and looked down upon any of them without a sexual thought in his head, as he was now. He felt a type of respect for Brianna that he had never realized was missing with other women he'd dated.

He switched on the fireplace in the corner of the bedroom, kicked off his shoes, and settled into the recliner by the window. When he took in her beautiful face against his pillow and thought of how fiercely she protected her daughter, he wondered who was protecting her. In that moment, he wanted nothing more than to be that person.

Chapter Ten

BRIANNA AWOKE TO her cell phone ringing. She rolled over and blinked away the fog of sleep. Something smelled delicious. She reached her arm straight up and tilted her head. *Why does the ceiling look so far away?* She wondered why her pillow felt insanely soft and why the room wasn't cold, as it usually was in the mornings. She shifted her eyes to the right, taking in a wall of windows. *Holy shit.* She bolted upright in the strange bed and then looked under the sheets. *Thank God.* She scrambled from the bed fully dressed, found her boots, and quickly put them on as the prior evening came back piece by piece and assembled into the lovely evening that she'd had with Hugh—the evening that never ended. *Crap.*

She saw her purse on a cherry nightstand, and beyond that, a large dresser with a family photo, Hugh's cologne, and a stack of books. She picked up the photo and scanned the incredibly gorgeous faces of the people who could only be his brothers, sister, and father. The likeness was profound. All tall and dark—except for the girl, who had auburn hair and lighter eyes than the men—and stunningly handsome. They weren't looking at the camera. They were looking at each other, laughing, as if the picture had been candid, not posed, and she wondered when people had time for such frivolity. A pang of jealousy speared her. Oh, how she longed for a little time to laugh like that. She'd had such a good time the evening before that she felt as if she'd had a taste of what it must be like to go out and enjoy an evening without real life pressing in on her. Brianna set the frame down. *Time for real life.*

She grabbed her phone from her purse and went into the enormous master bathroom, locking the door behind her. She stared at herself in the mirror. *What am I doing?* She washed her face, used some of Hugh's toothpaste on her finger, and brushed her teeth as best she could, then leaned against the counter, arms crossed, heart racing. *Who goes from not dating to sleeping at a guy's house?* She cringed at the thought. She didn't remember pulling up to the house. She had no idea where they even were. The last thing she remembered after the most intense, earth-shattering, knee-quaking kiss she'd ever experienced—a kiss so exquisite she couldn't imagine ever kissing anyone else. As quickly as she allowed herself that one taste of sensuous joy, it had been stolen away. She could never be close to a man whose life revolved around heavy travel and a job that could take his life in an instant. She could never do that to Layla. And, Brianna realized, she could never put herself in a position to compete with the plethora of female groupies that came with such a job. Hugh had been a fantasy. She supposed she should consider herself lucky. How many women get to have a romantic evening with a gorgeous man, completely out of the blue like she did?

She silenced her ringer and texted Kat. *You up?*

Yes. How was your date?

She texted as quickly as she could. *I fell asleep. I'm at his house! Awkward!*

Her phone vibrated again, and she read Kat's response. *Fell asleep after sex? That's okay.*

Brianna shook her head. *No! Fully clothed. Alone. My car broke down, and I fell asleep on the way to his house.*

The phone vibrated again, this time with a call from Kat. She pushed the green button and held it up to her ear.

"Oh my God. Tell me," Kat said.

Brianna whispered. "We had coffee; then my car wouldn't start. He was going to lend me a car. Oh my God, Kat. Who has extra cars just lying around? Anyway, on the way here, I fell asleep. He must have carried me inside. I woke up in his bed. Alone and fully dressed. He lives in this amazing house, and it smells like he cooked a gourmet breakfast." She took a deep breath, trying to keep from hyperventilating.

"Slow down. First things first. How was the date?"

"Kat! Did you hear me? I feel like a fool. The date was great. Better than great. But now I've got to take the walk of shame and I didn't even do anything." She looked in the mirror and ran her fingers through her hair. "Oh my God. I look awful, too, and you saw him. He's gorgeous. And sweet. And so…so…*Ugh!* What am I doing?"

"Bree, breathe, honey. Just breathe. You're not taking the walk of shame. You're not in college anymore. This is real life. Adult life. People have sex."

Hugh's voice came back to her. *Bree, sweetie, take a deep breath.* Brianna stopped pacing and said, "I didn't have sex."

"Okay. I know. People fall asleep. So what? If he's as nice as you say, then he won't care. Besides, if he did care, he would have woken you up and taken you home, right?" Kat spoke confidently and in a soothing tone.

Brianna took a deep breath. "What should I do? I can't

hang out in the bathroom all day."

Kat laughed. "Bree, you're a twenty-eight-year-old mother. You've handled worse situations than this. Enjoy the morning. Act like yourself. Pretend you're in a hotel and you're going out to the lobby. Natural, easy."

Natural. Easy. Brianna rolled her eyes. "I'm fucked. I shouldn't have gone out with him. The more time we spent together, the more I liked him."

"That's a good thing. Your mom always tells you that you need a life. Hell, I tell you that. You're getting no sympathy from me, honey."

"Thanks, Kat. That really helps, you brat." She sighed and flattened the wrinkles from her sweater. "Okay. I can do this." She sat on the edge of the Jacuzzi bathtub, contemplating telling Kat exactly who Hugh really was, but she worried that it would lead to one of two things—a lengthy discussion, which she definitely didn't have time for, or possibly, Kat might see him differently, as he'd thought Brianna would. She tucked away the thought until she could tell her in person and weigh her response. "Tell me I can do this."

"Bree, you've got this, honey. No sweat."

"Thank you. If I show up at your house in need of tissues and chocolate, you'll know why. And by the way, don't ever convince me to go out with a guy again. Jesus, Kat. I fell asleep. I really do suck. I love ya. Thanks for not calling me a slut."

"Bree?"

"Yeah?"

"I am so looking forward to the time I can call you a slut. Please go have sex with that gorgeous creature!"

"Goodbye, Kat."

She snagged her purse from the nightstand, and went in

search of the kindest man she'd met in a very long time.

The bedroom she'd slept in was bigger than her living room and kitchen combined. She followed the hardwood floor down a long hallway and into an enormous great room with a wall of French doors, a stone fireplace that crawled to the ceiling, two chocolate-colored couches that she was sure were like heaven to sit on, and a shiny glass coffee table. She'd never seen anything like Hugh's house, except in magazines and on shows like *Lifestyles of the Rich and Famous.* She quickly took her boots off again, worried about scuffing the floor.

"Good morning, Bree."

Brianna spun around and nearly lost her footing. Hugh wore a pair of jeans and a black T-shirt that looked like it had been painted on. Every curve of his magnificent muscles were evident beneath the thin material, from his rippled six-pack to his massive biceps that threatened to burst through his sleeves. In the daylight, his face took on a softer, sexier look—which she wouldn't have believed was possible.

"Morning," she said.

He approached her, and she held her breath. *Why am I so damn nervous?* "I'm so sorry that I fell asleep last night." She covered her face with her hands.

Hugh lowered her hands as he'd done the evening before. "You're so cute when you're embarrassed." He leaned down and kissed her cheek. "We all sleep. It's not like you got drunk and passed out."

That would have been more reasonable. Who falls asleep when they're alone with a man like you?

"Come on. I made breakfast." He placed his hand on the small of her back and guided her past the couches to a sparkling white kitchen with earthtone marble countertops and a breakfast room that was surrounded by windows on three sides. The view of the gardens didn't compare to the warmth that emanated from his hand on her back, causing a pull in her lower regions that until last night she'd done a great job of shutting out.

"Do you like Belgian waffles?" Hugh pulled out a tall chair by the curved edge of the gourmet island.

"I love them." Brianna was sure she was in some kind of time warp. A dream she couldn't wake up from. This type of man did not just waltz into the life of a woman like her. Brianna noticed photographs on the refrigerator. More candid shots. "Is this your family?" she asked.

"Yeah, my expanding family." He pointed to each one as he explained who they were. "This is Treat and his wife, Max. They just got married. Treat's my oldest brother. And this is Rex with his fiancée, Jade."

Holy cow. Even their girlfriends are hot. "They're a gorgeous couple."

"Yeah, they are. They live in Colorado. So do Treat and Max, right near my father's ranch. And this is my sister, Savannah, with her fiancé, Jack, and my other brother, Josh, with Riley. They all live in New York." Hugh touched a photo of an incredibly tan and sexy couple. "This is Dane with his girlfriend, Lacy. They live on their boat in Florida but travel a lot. And see the man in the back? That's my dad. This was taken on Dane's boat right after Lacy moved in."

She noticed how thoughtful Hugh's voice became as he spoke of his family.

"So you grew up in Colorado?" *Why do I find that sexy?*

"Yup, on a ranch. My father breeds thoroughbreds. Rex and Treat help him on the ranch, but Treat also owns several resorts around the world. He settled back in Colorado when he met Max because she was from a town nearby."

"Your whole family is so…attractive."

Hugh set a bowl of fruit on the island, then two plates of waffles. "I guess. To me they're just family. I don't mean just, as in only. Family is everything to me. I mean I don't notice the rest—the looks and stuff other people see."

"I saw a picture of your family in your room," she admitted.

"Yeah, that's one of my favorite memories. We were having a barbeque in my dad's backyard with a few relatives and friends for my father's birthday. That's my dad's thing, barbeques. Actually, from what Treat told me, it was something my mom started. She thought the sun filled our souls with happiness or something. Anyway, that day we all had so much fun. We all gathered around, you know, to watch him blow out the candles, and he was making a wish, and Josh asked him what he was wishing for, and all of us at the same time, even my dad, said, *Mom.*" Hugh shrugged. "Now that I think of it, we probably shouldn't have laughed. He was serious, and so were we. We know how much he misses her, but it was still funny."

"I think that's so sweet."

"What's your favorite memory?" Hugh asked.

She shrugged. "I could say the day Layla was born, but it wouldn't really be true. As wonderful of a moment that it was, it was painful and lonely and filled with mixed emotions. Probably my favorite memory was from when I was eight. It was right before my father left us. He took me somewhere, just me and him. I think it was a park, but I'm not really sure. It looked like a park, but there was a carousel, and he said I could ride it as many times as I'd like. Then we got cotton candy, and I just remember music and thinking that it was such a special day."

She looked down at the counter, remembering the next morning. "I realized later that that afternoon was his way of saying goodbye. He left the next day, and I never saw him again."

"Bree, that's awful."

"No, it's a happy memory. It's just what came afterward that wasn't happy. But at least I have that afternoon."

She watched Hugh process the heaviness of what she'd revealed, and she felt guilty for telling him, but something told her that he wanted to know the truth, not a fabrication of her happiest memory.

He put his arm around her and kissed her cheek. "You're right. At least you have that afternoon, and even if there's something not so happy afterward, he gave you that memory to cherish."

And there it was, the reason he needed to know. So she could see how he reacted. Now she felt validated in continuing to hold that afternoon in the high regard she always had without feeling like she shouldn't. Her mother saw that afternoon for what it was. A big show so his little girl would always think of him in a happy light. Brianna knew it, too, but she didn't care. She wanted to see him in that light. It was easier than seeing him as the man who left without anything bigger to block out the hurt.

"Would you like some coffee? Juice?" Hugh moved comfortably in his bare feet and he spoke easily, as if they'd been having breakfast together forever.

"Either's fine, thank you. Can I do something to help?" She stepped down from the tall chair, and Hugh smiled.

"Don't be silly. Sit. Relax. I never get to cook breakfast. It's a treat for me." He set a glass of orange juice and a mug of coffee before her. "French vanilla, hazelnut? Milk? What's your pleasure?"

Your lips on mine again. "Mmm. French vanilla would be delicious." She rarely splurged on flavored creamers. "Do you have Sweet'N Low or sugar?"

"Both." He set out a little ceramic bowl with several different types of sweeteners in it.

"I feel like I'm in a restaurant," she teased.

"You can thank my sister, Savannah, for that. She hired a woman who cleans the house and keeps my schedule. When I'm in town, she makes sure the house is fully stocked." Hugh handed her a glass bottle of maple syrup.

"Your sister did that for you? Now I do wish I had a sister." She laughed, but Hugh's economic status was so far out of her league that even hearing about his lifestyle seemed unreal.

"Savannah thinks I need taking care of. She worries about all of us. I guess as the only girl, and without our mom around, she probably feels a sort of obligation."

Brianna noticed his eyes soften when he spoke of his family. *I have to stop noticing things about you.*

"What time do you have to be at work today?" he asked.

"Ten." She took a bite of a waffle. "Hugh, these are amazing. Thank you."

"I have an appointment at ten, so you can either borrow a car or I can drop you off. Didn't you say you wanted to buy Layla a birthday present today?" He finished his waffles and dished fruit onto his plate.

You remembered. "Yeah. I need to do that, but I'm sure I can take a bus to the mall." She couldn't eat more than a few bites.

"Nonsense. How late are you working? I didn't even know bars opened at ten in the morning." He pushed his plate to the side while he finished his coffee.

"I'm not working at the bar this morning. I'm helping my friend Claude in his studio. I should be out by one or so." She stood to clear the dishes, and Hugh stood as well. He took the dish from her hands and began washing it while Brianna cleared the glasses.

He rotated away from the sink, and she knocked into his arm. "I'm sorry," she said, feeling heat crawl up her chest.

"I'm not."

His dark eyes stole her breath, and when he brushed her hair from her cheek, she shivered.

"Bree," he whispered.

She was rooted to the floor by his sensuous gaze. Her pulse sped up. When he ran his hands up her arms and then took a long, slow stroke back down, Brianna threw caution to the wind. She lifted up on her tiptoes, but the distance to his lips was still too great. Hugh slipped his hands beneath her arms and lifted her onto the counter, then pushed himself between her knees and took her face in his hands. *Oh, how I love the feel of your hands on my face. Leave them there forever. Please.*

"Bree," he said between heavy breaths. "May I kiss you?"

She reached behind his neck and pulled his mouth to hers. His lips were warm and tender. Every caress of his tongue sent a pulse of heat between her legs. And when he slipped his hand beneath her hair and cupped the back of her head, then deepened the kiss, all the scary thoughts about his job fell away. His hand found her waist, and in one swift and gentle move, he pulled her to the edge of the counter, his chest pressed against hers, the bulge beneath his zipper against her center. He tasted so sweet, like syrup and something more—a taste that was all his own. A taste she'd never forget. When they drew apart, they were both breathing heavily.

Come back. Please come back and kiss me again. She slid her hands to his chest, feeling the hammering of his heart against her palms.

He leaned his forehead against hers. A touch she'd already come to relish.

"Bree," he whispered. "I'm sorry." He looked down at his formidable erection.

She could barely think past her own thundering heart.

He pressed a soft kiss to her lips. "I love kissing you, but I gotta stop or I'm not going to be able to."

Then don't. Her brain told her he was right, but her body craved his touch. She desperately wanted to feel the muscles that teased her from behind his soft cotton shirt and—*Oh God!*—it had been so long since she'd been with a man. Her private parts were aching to remember the sensation of having a man's hard length buried inside her.

He wrapped her in his arms and pressed his chest to hers again; then he gathered her hair in one hand and kissed her cheek. "How about I drive you to Claude's?" He kissed her neck. "Then we can shop for Layla's gift together."

His hot breath sent a shiver down her back. She didn't want to be away from him for a second. "Yes," she whispered, and looked at him with what she hoped was a seductive expression and not some failed attempt that made her look stupid. He still held her hair in his hand, and Brianna's visceral need took over. She pressed her lips to his and buried her hands in his thick hair, pulling him into a rougher, hungrier kiss and savoring every hard swipe of his tongue. The sting of his fist clutching her hair heightened her desire, and when he reached one hand beneath her bottom and the other around her waist and lifted her up with his powerful arms, Brianna instinctively wrapped her legs around his body. His mouth left hers and found her chin, as he licked and nipped his way down her neck. She arched back, wanting to feel his mouth on every part of her. He licked a sensual line across her collarbone, and Brianna thought she was going to lose her mind. He carried her to the couch and lay down on top of her, tasting her shoulder, her breastbone, and stopping just shy of her bra.

His hand slipped beneath her sweater, and he rubbed across her rib cage with a slow, deep caress. She arched her back, urging him to touch her breast. His hand grazed the underside of her bra, and he pulled his lips from hers.

"Bree, I could make out with you forever."

She felt like she was dying of thirst and he was a river of fresh water. She couldn't get her fill. Brianna kissed him again—harder, deeper, hungrier—then took his lower lip in her teeth and drew back slowly, before releasing it and dragging her tongue across the ache she knew she'd left. His eyes narrowed, and impossibly, became even darker. They were both breathing so hard she thought their breath would fill the room.

He pressed another kiss to her lips and shook his head. "You're not that girl, Bree. I want you more than I've wanted any woman, but…"

"Not what girl?" She couldn't think straight. *What the hell?*

He wrapped his arms beneath her shoulders and looked into her eyes. She loved being in his arms, pressed beneath his body.

"You have a twelve-year-plan," he said in a serious voice. "We can't do this. We have to think about Layla."

"We?" Her voice cracked.

He nodded. "Of course. Layla owns half of your heart. Anyone in your life has to think of both you and Layla."

Why do I love that you didn't say, Your daughter? She hated that he was right. She couldn't throw away her plan and Layla's stability for a quick lay. But if he was a quick lay, would he have stopped? As she looked into his eyes, she knew he was anything but a quick lay. He looked at her like somehow during the past fifteen hours she'd become his whole life. *I've lost my mind. I'm thinking with a sex-starved brain. Shit.*

He lifted himself off of her and sat down as she righted herself beside him on the opulent sofa. He rubbed his hands over his face. "I'm sorry, Brianna. I don't know what came over me. I just…Every time I kiss you, I want to kiss you more, but you're such a loving mother. I don't want to get in the way of that."

That should have been me. What kind of a mother am I if I was ready to fall into bed with him after one night? Of all people, I know the risks. She didn't know how to respond. *Thank you? You're right? Forget my plan and take me, please?* Even though he was doing the right thing for both of them, his rejection still stung.

"It's my fault. Gosh, Hugh. I haven't even kissed a man since Layla was born, and here I was ready to…well, you know. I'm sorry. You were so kind to arrange to have my car fixed and to allow me to sleep last night—which I still feel really bad about—and then to stop me from making a big mistake." She shook her head, and when she looked up, she recognized the hurt in his eyes. "I don't mean a big mistake like sleeping with you would be a big mistake. I can only imagine…well…never mind. What I meant was that…" She sighed. "I suck at this. I'm a bartender and a mother, and you're a gorgeous, famous, race car driver. The mistake would have been yours, not mine."

He cupped her cheeks again and guided her face to his. "Is

that what you think? That I stopped us because I didn't want to get tangled up with you because you're a bartender and a mother?"

She shrugged.

"Brianna." He narrowed his eyes. "Bree, what's your last name?"

"My last name?"

He nodded. "I just realized that I don't know it."

"Heart."

Hugh smiled, and his eyes lit up. "Heart? Brianna Heart?"

She nodded.

"I love that," he said. His smile faded, and when he spoke, his serious tone had returned. "Brianna Heart, I stopped kissing you because I do want to get tangled up with you, and because of that, we need to consider your twelve-year-plan and, of course, Layla."

He moved his hand from her cheeks, and she wished he'd put them right back. "Hugh, you're a great guy, but…" *Don't say it. Just shut up and don't ruin this.*

"But?" He sat up straighter.

The life you lead isn't conducive to raising a child. But then again, you didn't say you wanted to raise my child. You just wanted to get tangled up with me. What does that mean? Sex? Just sex? If so, why consider Layla? Ugh! She'd been out of the dating scene for too long. She needed Kat to interpret for her.

"Brianna, but what?" he asked again.

She saw the worry in his eyes, but she had no idea how to tell him what she was thinking. "But my life is complicated. It's busy, and I barely get time to breathe—or sleep, as you saw last night. I don't want to bring you down."

He took her hand in his. "You light me up, Bree, not bring

me down. Can't you see that? Let's just see how things go. We'll take it day by day. I'm here through next weekend, so we have plenty of time."

"Next weekend?" She felt the pit of her stomach drop. *Plenty of time?* "Where are you going?" *What am I doing? Stop liking him!*

"Daytona. Then I have time off again."

Daytona. This can never work. Ugh! Why do I want this to work so badly?

"Hey, Bree. You okay?"

No. I suck. I really like you. "Yeah, fine." She pushed to her feet. If she was going to create distance, she had to do it now. "We should probably go. I need to go home and shower before work."

"Hey." He went to her and took her hand in his. "I'm a really good listener. Please tell me why you look sad."

She looked away. "Can you please stop being romantic…and sweet…and looking at me like that?"

He laughed. "Like what?"

I can't do this. I just got carried away. She pulled back her shoulders and feigned a smile, hoping Hugh wouldn't realize it was nothing more than false bravado as she weeded through her hormones and convinced herself that she had to stick to her original plan. *Twelve years isn't so long—is it? Oh God! It never was until I met Hugh.* "Never mind." She sighed loudly. "I've really enjoyed spending time with you. I like you. I haven't let myself even think about liking a guy in—"

"Years, I know. But if you like me, then why do you look like I killed your pet?"

She wrestled with the truth. *Because I'm too confused to think straight. You travel all the time and have all those groupies all over you. You'll get bored of my life. You'll hate having a child around all the time, and most of all, I can't bring you into our lives and have Layla worry that you'll leave—and I don't want that worry either.* "Because you're leaving at the end of next week." She hated how deflated she sounded, but it was exactly how she felt, as if she were given wings and began to fly and then suddenly the wings were whisked away and she was left floating aimlessly down to a painful reality.

"I'll be back."

"I know. But the more time I spend with you, the more time I'm going to want to spend with you." *Why am I bothering to tell you? I need to stop wanting you.*

"Well, then, we'll just have to make that happen."

Hugh put his arms around her again and she wished he'd never brought up her twelve-year-plan. If he hadn't, she'd be naked beneath him instead of convincing herself that she should never see him again.

Chapter Eleven

"YOU'RE KIDDING, RIGHT?" Brianna stood in Hugh's garage looking at his Mercedes Roadster, Aston Martin, Ferrari 458 Speciale, and Icon Sheene motorcycle. "Hugh, really? I can't even think while looking at these. They can't be real. I mean, Matchbox? Sure. Real? You can pinch me and wake me up now."

"I know it's a little much. Some guys collect baseball cards. I collect cars. So, which one should we take?" He knew he was pushing her past her comfort zone, but he'd seen the way she froze when he mentioned leaving after the next weekend. She had a child to think about, and he was hell-bent on getting to know Brianna better, child or not. Something clicked in him last night, a protective urge, a stirring of something more than sexual desire, and he had to explore the meaning of it. In order to do that, she had to know more than just what he was inclined to tell her. If he had a prayer of her accepting him into her life enough to date her and see if what he felt was real or not, then she had to see all of him—and then she could decide if he was the type of guy she wanted to be with, regardless of what he owned or what he did for a living.

She sighed. "Fine. It's probably the only time I'll ever ride in one of these anyway. The red one."

"The red one? You're so cute." He took her hand and opened the passenger door of the Ferrari 458 Speciale. "If you'd have picked any of the other cars, I would have offered for you to drive, but the 458 is more like a race car than a luxury vehicle, and I'd worry about your safety."

"Oh my God, trust me. You don't want me driving one of your cars."

Her insecurities were cute, but not at all necessary. She was obviously a bright woman who made sound decisions. He trusted Brianna, and if he was really going to show her who he was, he had to show her that, too. "You know what? How about I take you out in the Ferrari another time, and you drive the Aston Martin today?"

She backed up, waving her hands in front of her. "No. No way. No, no, no. I'm like a big gray cloud when it comes to cars."

Hugh crossed his arms and laughed. "Then I guess we're not going anywhere and you'll be late to work, because I'm not driving."

"Hugh. No." She shook her head.

"Sorry. No can do."

"Hugh," she said in a harsher tone. "How can you even ask me to drive one? They're more expensive than anything I'll ever own."

"They're cars, Bree. They're less valuable than Layla, and you trust yourself with her." He watched her lips press together, and he knew he'd struck a chord. "They're just cars."

She shook her head again with the most adorable, emphatic frown he'd ever seen. Hugh went to her and wrapped his arms around her.

"I'm not worried. You shouldn't be either." He needed her to see that cars were just possessions. They weren't what made him who he was. She needed to separate him from everything else in her mind so he could prove to her he was worth going out with again.

"Hugh," she whispered. "What if I wreck it?"

"I have insurance, so as long as you don't hurt yourself..." He shrugged.

She buried her face in his chest. "I can't believe you're making me do this."

"I can't believe you're fighting me on it." He held up the keys, and she snagged them from him.

"Fine. Whatever. Do you do this to all your girlfriends?"

"I don't have girlfriends, so the answer is no." He smiled as he opened the driver's side door for her and then climbed into the passenger side. He clicked the remote, and the garage doors lifted.

"A guy like you has girlfriends." She gripped the steering wheel so tight her knuckles were white.

"Okay, wait." He pried her fingers from the steering wheel and gently settled her back against the seat. "First of all, no, I don't. I have dated women, but I haven't had a real girlfriend, someone who I cared about and went out with more than three or four times, since I was in college. Just so you know, I've spent the last few months separating myself from that dating world of fan girls and models. Second...I'm really sorry, but you're so tense. I gotta do this." He leaned across the seat and kissed her until he felt the tension ease from her body. She met each stroke of his tongue with a passionate, hungry stroke of her own, and then he kissed her longer, simply because she was too sweet to forgo.

When he drew back, her eyes were closed. "Better?" he asked.

She blinked several times. "Yeah." She nodded. "Good. Fine. Great." She put her delicate fingers back on the steering wheel and wrapped them gently around the leather, as if she had no energy left to put forth. She shifted the car into gear, and her lips curved into a smile as she drove onto the main road.

"This isn't at all like driving. It's like flying or something."

"She's a beauty," Hugh agreed as they made their way through town.

"Still, you shouldn't have let me drive it." Bree hadn't taken her eyes off the road once, and she was an excellent driver.

"It's just a car."

Brianna parked in front of her apartment complex. She handed him the keys and tucked a strand of hair behind her ear. Hugh noticed that her hand was still shaking a little.

"I was so nervous." She let out a long sigh. "The kiss helped, but oh my God. I was sure I'd wreck it."

"I had faith in you."

Hugh surveyed the old brick apartment building. Grass sprouted through fissures in the sidewalk. Stacked boxes and plastic chairs littered the patio of the first-floor apartment to their right. A bearded man with a beer gut hung over the second-floor balcony, watching them walk inside. Hugh put his arm protectively around Brianna, his biceps and neck muscles tense.

"That guy kind of creeps me out," Brianna whispered.

Hugh stood up tall and threw his shoulders back, then narrowed his eyes and cast a harsh glare at the ogling man.

Brianna's third-floor apartment was bright and sunny. The white-tiled foyer was clean and, though small, it was functional.

There was a small table against the wall with a stack of mail and Layla's school papers. Beyond the foyer was a cozy living room with glass sliders that led to a small balcony. On the wall between the kitchen and living room was a large black-and-white photograph of a sleeping baby. The light illuminated the baby's forehead and eyes and then softened as it covered her bundled body.

"That's a gorgeous picture. Is that Layla?"

"Yeah. I took that when she was three days old. I love that picture." Brianna's eyes filled with love, and the edges of her lips curved upward into a sweet smile.

"You took that? Bree, that's amazing." He looked at her and wondered what other hidden talents she had.

"Thanks. I haven't taken pictures in about a year, since my camera broke."

A fluffy red love seat and sofa created a warm, comfortable nook in the living room. It faced three rows of white bookshelves littered with books, drawings, clay pieces that were obviously made and painted by Layla and photographs of various sizes. Three colorful throw blankets were bundled together in one corner of the couch, and a half-finished game of Candyland was spread out on the cheap wooden coffee table.

"What happened to your camera?" Hugh asked.

"Oh, Layla bumped it off the table when she was playing one day. It's not a big deal. I mean, I miss taking pictures, but it was just a hobby."

"By the looks of this picture, it could be much more." When she didn't respond, he said, "This is a sweet apartment." He crossed the floor to the bookshelves.

"Oh, please. It's a dive, but it's home. We like it." She set her purse and keys on a small table by the door.

Hugh picked up a photograph of Brianna and Layla from the bookshelf. "This is a great picture. You look radiant, and Layla is adorable. She looks like a miniature you."

Brianna laughed. "Thanks. She's my girl."

He set it down and picked up another photo of Layla sitting on a woman's lap at sunset. The woman looked too much like Brianna not to be her mother, but it was the colors and the angle that caught Hugh's eye. "Your mom?"

"Yeah."

"Did you take this one, too?" He watched her tuck her hair behind her ear again.

"Yeah. It was a long time ago."

"Bree, these are magnificent. Did you study photography?" Hugh set the frame back on the bookshelf and watched as her face flushed.

"In college." She fiddled with the edge of her sweater. "Do you mind if I shower and change quickly so we're not late?"

He set the photograph down. Brianna stood in a stream of sunlight at the edge of the living room looking so damn pretty that just the idea of her one room away, naked and washing that gorgeous body of hers set Hugh's desires aflame. He shook the thought from his head and then cleared his throat to find his voice. "Uh…Go right ahead. I'll wait here." *And try not to think about you.*

Brianna's cell phone rang. She dug through her purse for it, then put it up to her ear.

"Hi, baby. Are you having fun with Grandma?" A smile spread across her lips. "Really? For breakfast? She does spoil you." She listened for a moment.

He loved how her voice softened when she spoke to Layla.

Brianna continued talking to Layla. "I'm sorry, baby. I must have been in the bathroom. I'll keep my phone with me from now on. I know. Okay, I love you. I'll see you in a little bit. Be good for Grandma and enjoy the play." She listened again. "Always." She ended the call and let out a sigh. "See? I'm not a great mother. Layla called me this morning and I forgot to call her back."

"You're a great mother. That was probably my fault because I kept kissing you. From now on we'll make sure you keep your phone by your side and that it's turned up loud, so you don't miss her again."

She tucked her hair behind her ear again—a nervous habit Hugh already found adorable.

"You okay?" he asked.

She nodded before heading down the hall to her bedroom, but Hugh had seen the worry in her eyes. He scanned the room and saw Layla everywhere, from the sparkly little sneakers lined up by the door to the coloring books on the bar between the kitchen and the living room. He listened to the bedroom door close, then began to pace. Damn, he liked her. She was smart, responsible, family oriented. She tugged at all the right places in his heart. He picked up another picture of Layla and searched the little girl's eyes. *Day by day.* That's how he'd have to take things with Brianna, although just thinking about the man on the balcony set a fire through his veins. He was way past day by day.

"WHAT AM I gonna do? He said *we*. He didn't say that I had to keep my phone on; he said *we'd have to make sure*," Brianna whispered into her cell phone to Kat. She hoped Kat would set her racing heart straight.

"I don't see what the big deal is. He likes you, Bree. Hell, if you'd let a man near you, you'd know that wasn't a horrible thing."

"I did. Remember?" Brianna sighed.

"That was years ago. I say…You have some time before Claude's expecting you. Invite him into the shower with you," Kat teased.

Brianna stripped off her clothes as she spoke. "Kat! I'm serious. I almost had sex with him. I need you to tell me to stick to my plan. Tell me he's not a great guy, or he's a player, or something. Please."

"Okay, well, you didn't have sex with him, so that tells you something, right? He's not a dick, because if he was, you'd have had sex. He's not banging down your door when he knows you're naked in the bathroom, and that tells you he's not a bad guy, right? So, I can't do it. I can't tell you not to at least go out with him a few times. I can watch Layla."

Brianna stood in front of the mirror with her eyebrows knitted together. "Oh, Kat, I'm in trouble."

"You know what they say. If you can't be good, be careful."

"Yeah, well, that's why I went on the pill after Layla was born. Just in case." She glanced over her shoulder at the bathroom door and thought of Hugh. A pulse of heat flared between her thighs. "I gotta go. Thanks for not helping," she teased.

"You'll thank me later."

Brianna stepped under the warm spray of the shower and closed her eyes. She could feel Hugh's whiskers against her cheek, his lips pressing on hers, his tongue swiping her mouth. She slid her fingers between her legs and let out a frustrated sigh at how wet she was. She bit back a moan as she stroked herself and imagined Hugh's hands touching her, his lips trailing down her body, his tongue taking her up, up, up. Knowing Hugh was only two rooms away heightened her excitement. She held on to the tile wall as the orgasm gripped her body and clenched her teeth to keep from calling out as Hugh's name fell from her lips.

Chapter Twelve

"YOUR CAR WILL be ready by two, but I don't want you to feel trapped with me, so I can take you to pick it up or I can pick you up after my appointment and we can shop for Layla's gift together." Hugh leaned casually on the console as he drove toward town.

Brianna's mind told her to shop by herself and spend less time with Hugh, but her heart—and her body—refused to listen. The words fell out of her mouth without hesitation. "Let's go together, if you really don't mind." She'd thought her little shower release would help her stop thinking about Hugh in that way, but all it did was make her want him more. She'd even taken extra time with her makeup, and after seeing him smile at her boots the night before, she'd purposely worn them again, this time with black jeans and a flowing white blouse that was just see-through enough that it showed a hint of her laciest bra. Sitting in the confined car only increased her desires toward him. His cologne filled the air, and each time he shifted gears, his triceps jumped. She had the urge to run her finger along the defined edge of the muscle, where it curved toward the back of his arm.

"Bree?"

Shit. She didn't realize he was even talking. *Get a grip!* "Sorry, yeah?"

"You said you were helping your friend today. We're coming up on Main Street. Where to?"

She'd been so lost in him that she'd totally forgotten about directions. "Up here on the right." She pointed to the end of the block.

"Wait. CD Studios?" Hugh laughed. "No way."

"No way what?"

"That's where my appointment is. I had a photo shoot with CD Thursday for my sponsors, and we're wrapping up the last of them this morning."

No freaking way. "You're taking pictures here? Today?" *How am I going to manage this?*

"Yeah. This is great. We can spend more time together. What do you do for CD?" He opened his eyes expectantly, and then his goddamn dimples appeared again.

Why do you have to be so good-looking? Brianna tucked her hair behind her ear. "I…uh…I help Claude…CD. I do the lights, help make sure the models clothes and props are set right, you know, that kind of stuff."

He pulled into a parking space. "That's great. It'll make the shoot even more fun. I really don't like getting my picture taken, but now I'll have you to smile at."

Or I'll die of embarrassment from not being able to focus. "Yeah, great."

Hugh came around and opened her door. He pressed a kiss to her lips. Brianna's hands found his waist as he deepened the kiss, and when he pulled away, she felt light-headed again.

"Hugh." She cleared her throat.

"Yeah?" He opened the trunk and grabbed his driving suit,

helmet, and gloves.

"You can't kiss me like that." *Shit shit shit.*

His smile faded. "I'm sorry. I just assumed..."

"No, it's not that. I like when you kiss me, but I can't concentrate in there if we're..." *Shit. I sound like an idiot. No woman on earth would tell you not to kiss her.*

"I'd never kiss you like that at your workplace. We're on a side street. No one can see you."

Now she felt like a fool as heat rushed up her cheeks. "I know. Never mind. I just get flustered." She started for the building, and Hugh reached for her hand.

"Brianna, am I pushing myself on you?"

His eyes were serious, laden with concern. She couldn't play a game of push-pull with herself anymore. It wasn't fair to either of them. She was used to being completely in control of hers and Layla's lives. Organizing them, maintaining their crazy and tight schedules. And now she felt it slipping away, as if a door had opened and she wasn't sure if she should slam it to contain their orderly lives or leave it ajar and allow the chaos of the rest of the world to seep in and see what happened. Hell. This was such a mess. She could no better let the chaos in than she could lie to Hugh—or to anyone else for that matter.

"Hugh, I really like you, and I know you said we could take things day by day, but in my head I'm wrestling with everything. You travel all the time; you've got a dangerous and sexy job that makes women want you. I'm a boring, busy mom with no interest in competing with anyone, and what I want more than anything is stability for my daughter." She looked down, feeling her chest tighten at the thought of turning him away—again.

He moved in close and lifted her chin so she was looking up

at him. She loved—and hated—that he didn't let her hide from the things that she found uncomfortable.

"Has it occurred to you that I might not like those women wanting me? Or that I might be scared about dating a woman with a child?"

"That's what I mean. I've got major baggage. I understand. It's better that we end things now rather than later." She suppressed the lump in her throat that urged tears to her eyes. *Damn it. I've only known you two days.*

"That's not what I mean. Bree. I'm scared, too, but let's not run from something that might be everything we both ever wanted. Taking it slow will allow us to see if it's worth pursuing. I won't entrench myself in Layla's life. I promise you that. You lead this relationship and I'll follow. I know how much you need to protect her, and I respect that."

Brianna felt her heart soften.

Hugh continued. "I won't push myself on you, either. If you really don't want to date me, then I'll go on my way. Not that I'd want to. I want you to be happy. But if any part of you wants to…" He took her hand in his and looked into her eyes.

Brianna's knees weakened.

"The ball is in your court, Bree. Let's do our photo shoot, and afterward, you tell me if you want me to take you to get your car or if you want to go shopping together. No pressure." He kissed the back of her hand and then gently released it.

She opened her mouth, but no words came out.

"Don't answer now, Bree. Take the next few hours to think about what you want. I'm not going anywhere, and even though I'm scared, I want to spend time with you. You tripped something in me. Ever since I saw you sleeping in my bed, I had the feeling that I wanted to protect you and Layla." He ran his hand through his hair and sighed. "And, yes, I realize that's crazy. Believe me. I've never felt this way before."

Chapter Thirteen

BRIANNA FLEW THROUGH her morning routine helping Claude and trying not to think about what Hugh said, even though he was standing right there before her in his goddamn racing suit that hugged every inch of his hot body and made him look even more masculine. No wonder women loved him—between competing in one of the most dangerous and manly sports and looking like *that*, it was a no-brainer.

She adjusted lights and handed Claude lenses. Now that she'd had a minute to breathe, she was watching Claude direct Hugh into another disturbingly alluring stance. How was she supposed to concentrate with *that* going on right in front of her?

"Bree Bree, can you get those wrinkles out of his chest please?" Claude was in heaven, torturing Brianna with more costume work than ever. She had no idea if he could sense what was between them or if he just wanted them to be together. Either way, the mischievous glint in his eye was unmistakable.

Hugh stood in his racing suit with his helmet under his arm, eyeing Brianna. For the fifth time that hour, she smoothed the wrinkles from his suit. At least this time it was from his chest. The first few times it was his thighs, his groin, his waist. Claude was enjoying every second of torturing her. She ran her hands over his chest and down his sides. Hugh got that hungry look in his eyes again, and Brianna felt her heartbeat speed up. Then the muscles in her neck tensed. She knew Claude caught every glimpse and every heavy breath as he stood at the other end of the room snapping pictures. She spun around and scowled as he clicked off another shot.

"What?" Claude said. "We need shots for the studio."

"Mm-hmm."

"Let's take a few more before we wrap." Claude waved his hand at Hugh and began clicking away.

She hadn't been able to think through what Hugh had said outside because every time she looked at him she heard his voice saying all the right things. Hugh glanced her way and his words came back to her again. *I'm not going anywhere. I know I want to protect you and Layla.* He hadn't even met Layla yet. How could he want to protect her?

"Okay, I think we're all set. You can get changed, Mr. Braden." Claude stared at Hugh's ass with an appreciative grin as he walked toward the dressing room.

"That's kind of rude, you know," Brianna teased.

"Is that jealousy I hear?"

She gasped. "What? No." *Yes.*

"Based on the sparks that were flying between you two, I'd say I did the right thing bringing you in today." He pushed his glasses up onto the bridge of his nose and set his camera down on the supply table.

"Claude, you didn't?"

"Oh, yes, I did. I told you I had someone here Thursday who I thought you should meet. And now you have." He winked as he changed the lens on the camera.

Brianna shook her head. "Why does everyone think I need a

man in my life? Layla and I are doing just fine by ourselves."

Claude put his hand on her shoulder. In his jeans and sweater, he looked like he was twentysomething instead of fortysomething. "Honey, that's exactly why. Just fine is not the same as happy. You're twenty-eight years old. You're beautiful, funny, sweet, not to mention a pain in the butt sometimes, but that's to be expected with any single mother." He pretended to claw at her like a cat.

She rolled her eyes. "I am happy. Layla and I are both happy."

Claude put his hands up. "Okay, okay. But I'm telling you, a little love in your life might just do wonders for both you and Layla. Life is about more than making it through each day, and I think Mr. Braden might be just the thing you need. Did you see how he looked at you?"

Unfortunately, yes. That's why I can't think straight. He picked up another camera. "Speak of the devil," he said much too loudly. He shook Hugh's hand. "I'll be in touch with your office in the next day or two. Bree, I'll be up in my studio. Can you lock up, please?"

Hugh came to her side carrying all his stuff under his arm. "How are you holding up?"

"Fine." Her stomach twisted and her pulse raced. She grabbed a large shopping bag from beneath the table. "Here. We can put your stuff in here." She folded his suit and placed it in the bag, then set his helmet and gloves on top before she went to work putting away the lenses and moving the lights to the back of the studio. Hugh walked along beside her.

"You sure? I tried not to look at you, but, Bree, it wasn't that easy." He helped her move the equipment.

She loved having him help her, not that she needed help

with the equipment, much less anything else in life. She could manage just fine. She grabbed her purse.

"Yeah, I'm fine. Ready to go?" she asked.

He held the door open for her, and as she walked past him, he touched her lower back, sending a shiver through her. He was so damn nice and so damn considerate that he made her crazy—and Jesus, even if it was a good crazy, it made her all sorts of confused.

"Have you thought about things?" he asked.

"You're kidding, right? Do you know what it's like to see you in that racing outfit? You know what they say about guys in uniforms, right? And then everything you said pummels my mind and confuses me." *God, I sound like a bitch.* "I can't believe I'm saying this, but yes, I want to go shopping with you. I can't allow you to meet Layla, and this whole thing scares the shit out of me, but…" She tucked her hair behind her ear and looked at the car, then drew her eyes back to Hugh. "But I like you. And if I'm making a mistake, at least Layla won't know about it."

Hugh reached for her, then quickly dropped his hands, glancing back at the building. "Sorry. I forgot."

Brianna wished she'd never told him not to kiss her in front of her work.

"I have a feeling this is anything but a mistake," he said with a serious tone.

That's kind of what I'm afraid of.

Chapter Fourteen

HUGH HELD THE door open as Brianna walked into the mall. He couldn't remember the last time he'd been to a shopping mall. He bought most of his family's gifts online, and the few things he purchased in person were bought from specialty stores.

"So, where are we headed?" Hugh wanted to put his arm around Brianna, but she'd been so pensive earlier that he worried about pushing himself on her.

"Penny's. Did your friend say how much I owe for the work on my car?"

He noticed the way she avoided his eyes. He'd spoken to Art, and her car had needed a new starter. A few hundred bucks' worth of work. He knew from what Brianna had said that she couldn't afford to pay for it, and a few hundred bucks was a spit in the wind for him. What would it hurt if he took care of it for her?

"Yeah, it just needed to be jumped after all. So there's no charge."

"Are you kidding me? So we could have just jumped it?" She shook her head. "I'm sorry. And here you've been stuck with me."

That's it. Hugh wasn't going to restrain himself any longer. He reached for her hand, and after a moment of rigidity, her hand relaxed against his. "I'm not stuck with you, Bree, and it's my fault. I should have thought of the battery, but I was so wrapped up in you that my brain wasn't working right."

"Well, I feel bad. Shouldn't I pay for the tow truck or something?"

"He owns the equipment, and he's a friend. I do things for him all the time. There's no charge." He looked up at the JC Penney sign. "Shall we?"

They headed inside the store and up the escalator to the children's section. "I want to get her a winter coat."

He followed her to the children's outdoor clothing section and watched her leaf through the coats, biting his tongue about his feelings on buying a little girl a coat for her birthday. She was turning six. Wouldn't she prefer a game or something more fun? He had no experience at parenting, but he respected Brianna's financial position, and he assumed that she was buying Layla something she needed instead of a frivolous gift.

"What do you think?" She held up a pretty little pink coat with fuzzy pockets and a fuzzy hood.

"I think it's adorable. When's her birthday?"

"That was easy," she said. "Next Thursday."

Hugh made a mental note of the date. "Let's look around. We can get a coffee or a soda in the mall." He wasn't into shopping, but he'd do whatever it took to keep their time together from ending.

"Sure." She looked at her watch. "How far away is my car?"

"It's at my place. They dropped it off about half an hour ago."

Her jaw dropped open. "They dropped my car off at your

house? That's a really good friend."

"It's my pit crew chief, Art. He's a nice guy." *Except when he tries to set me up on blind dates.*

"Now I feel bad. You asked your employee to do it? He probably felt obligated." She rolled her eyes as she paid for the jacket.

Hugh laughed. "It's not like that at all. I've never asked Art to fix anyone's car besides my own, and only the cars I race. He's a friend, Bree. I'd do the same for him if he needed it." Art hadn't given him an ounce of grief about fixing her car, and he knew Art had a litany of questions he'd been holding back, but that was how their relationship worked. Respect above all else, and after the mistake Art had made with the blind date, he owed Hugh a favor.

They made their way back downstairs and into the mall. Hugh noticed two teenage boys following them, and he tightened his grip on Brianna's hand. He'd counted himself lucky not to be recognized the last time they were out together. It appeared his luck had ended. When they slowed to look in the window of the Gap, one of the boys tapped him on the shoulder.

"Um, excuse me, but aren't you Hugh Braden?" The lanky teen looked at his heavyset friend, then back at Hugh with a nervous smile.

"Yeah. Want an autograph?" The quicker he got it over with, the less chance he had of others taking the opportunity to gather around. He faced the window of the store as the boys looked at each other. "Either of you have a pen?"

They shook their heads.

"I do." Brianna snagged a pen and notebook from her purse and handed it to Hugh.

"Are you here for a race?" the taller of the two boys asked.

"Just practicing and relaxing. Hey, I'll let you watch me practice if you don't draw any attention to us. Deal?" He handed them each an autograph.

"Cool. Yeah. You're awesome," the heavyset boy said.

"Call this guy. He'll hook you up." Hugh wrote down his public relations rep's name and number and handed it to them.

"Thanks, man. We really appreciate it."

Hugh watched them walk away and breathed a sigh of relief when no one else stopped for an autograph. Without his jacket on, he rarely got stopped in public.

"Wow. That was kinda cool," Brianna said.

Hugh rolled his eyes. "I guess." He pulled her close. "But I'm a little spoiled. I don't want to share my time with you." He felt a pang of guilt, thinking about Layla. "I mean, with strangers," he added.

"I know what you meant." Brianna stopped at Gap Kids to look at a dress in the window. "Does that happen a lot?"

"Thankfully no. Not unless I'm at a race or wearing my racing jacket." Her eyes were serious, and he felt her dwelling on the autograph. "Let's go in," Hugh suggested.

"No. I can't go in there. They're a little expensive for me, and I can't walk out without a whole new wardrobe for her. It's a seriously dangerous store for me." She took a step away from the window.

He grabbed her hand. "Am I allowed to just buy her a pair of sparkly shoes? I noticed that she had a few pairs lined up by the door in your apartment, and look." He pointed to row of sequined ballet flats in various colors. "You can tell her they're from you, or from a friend."

"I can't let you do that. You haven't even met her yet."

Brianna shook her head.

"It's not like I'd be buying her a car. It's a pair of shoes. We can even get her pink to go with her new coat." Hugh hadn't expected to be excited about buying any kid a present, but now that he'd spotted those little sequined shoes that were so similar to the ones Layla had at the apartment, and he saw the idea dancing in Brianna's eyes, he really wanted to buy them for her.

"She would love them." She put her hand on the window and looked at the shoes.

Hugh took her hand. "That decides it, then." He pulled her into the store and picked up a pair of the pink flats, turning them over in his hands. "What size does she wear?"

"Two."

"They make shoes in a two?" Hugh laughed. "That seems impossible."

"Everything seems impossible until you have a baby." She looked through the boxes and found the right size.

Hugh went to a display of dresses. "Does she like dresses?"

"She's a girl. Of course she likes dresses."

"I noticed in the pictures she was wearing mostly leggings and long shirts," Hugh said.

Brianna narrowed her eyes.

"What?"

"You noticed that?" she asked.

"Of course. We were going shopping for her, so I had to see what she liked. I also noticed that she'd made a few clay pots and stuff that you had on the bookshelves. Would she like arts and crafts? There must be a craft store in the mall."

"You're so thoughtful, Hugh. I can't believe you noticed all of that in the short time we were at my apartment." Brianna crossed her arms.

"I knew we were going shopping for her." He shrugged. "What size is she?"

Hugh caught a glimpse of a young family by a display of sweaters. The little girl appeared to be around the same age as Layla. She picked up a sweater and rubbed it against her cheek, turning the sweetest blue eyes up to her father, who swooped her into his arms and kissed her cheek. His wife placed her hand on his back. Hugh felt a tug in his heart and knew that sharing Brianna with Layla could never be an issue. Treat's voice sifted through his mind. *Family knows no boundaries.* He'd heard it a million times from his father and from Treat, and it had never quite hit him the same way it did now, as he glanced at Brianna and thought of her and Layla.

"Seven," Brianna said. "She likes arts and crafts, but she's really into drama and plays right now."

He looked through the dresses for the right size.

"Wait, no. I just got carried away with the idea. We said a pair of shoes, not a dress, too, Hugh. That's way too much." She reached for the dress.

Hugh lifted it out of her reach with a laugh, Brianna's reaction was so different from that of the money-grubbing women he used to date that he found himself wanting to buy things for Layla and for her.

She shook her head. "You can't buy me, you know."

Hugh put the dress back on the rack. "You don't really believe that's what I'm doing, do you?"

"Not really, but guys don't just buy stuff for women's kids unless they want something in return."

He wrapped her in his arms and pulled her close. "Brianna Heart, you have a very poor image of men in your head." He leaned back and looked down at her. "I'm going to do everything I can to change that."

Chapter Fifteen

BRIANNA WAS THINKING of the morning when they reached Hugh's house. He hadn't wanted to stop kissing her before they'd left that morning, and he hadn't tried to kiss her—really kiss her—since they'd gotten out of the car at Claude's studio, and now that their time together was coming to an end, she wished he would.

"I had a lot of fun today. Thanks for driving me to work and to the mall, and for buying Layla those cute shoes, and for getting my car fixed." She laughed and rested her head back against the seat. "You've done more for me in twenty-four hours than anyone's done for me in twenty-eight years."

"I'm sure anyone would have done the same." He leaned closer to her and she sat up straighter. "May I be so forward as to ask for your cell phone number?" He grinned, and it made her laugh.

"Oh my God, you don't have my number and I've already spent the night at your house. I'm such a tramp."

"Somehow I missed out on the tramp part. Tramps don't go to bed fully clothed, and I'm pretty sure they don't sleep through the night or tell guys not to kiss them."

"Oh God." She groaned. "I'm sorry. I knew I shouldn't

have said anything."

"Bree, I'm teasing." He pulled out his cell phone and handed it to her. "Here, put your number right in there."

She handed him hers. "Only if you will, too."

They both put their contact information into the other's phone.

"I feel lucky that you spent the day with me, and I had fun shopping for Layla. I hope one day soon I get to meet her." He brushed her hair away from her cheek.

I want you to meet her, too. Just not yet. "She's gonna love the shoes." Brianna had built such thick walls between her life with Layla and the idea of allowing any man in her life that she felt like she'd been preparing for it as she might a war. But the closer she got to Hugh, the more it became clear that when it came to the right person, the decision was relatively easy.

"We're in my garage, nowhere near your work. Is it okay if I kiss you now?"

Instead of answering him, she leaned across the console and pressed her lips to his. He reached over to the passenger seat and scooped her into his arms, pulling her onto his lap and deepening the kiss. He kissed with slow, powerful strokes of his tongue, as if he wanted to savor every second, and the deeper he thrust his tongue, the more it aroused her. She felt so safe in his arms, like he wouldn't ever let anything hurt her. When they drew apart, she ached for his return.

"I haven't made out in a car since I was nineteen." Hugh kissed her chin. "I kinda like it."

He pulled her into another kiss and slid his hand along her hip. Brianna's brain stopped functioning. She was all senses and desires. His cologne filled the car. The muscles in his thighs were strong and hard beneath her, and his large hand gripped her hip. His other hand cupped the back of her head and pulled her into a rougher kiss. She arched into him, pressing her breasts against his chest. Just as she'd experienced with him earlier, none of it was enough. She put her hands on his shoulders and kissed the stubble of his chin. Then she wrapped her mouth around his neck and sucked, not hard enough to make a mark, but enough to taste him, to feel the rough stubble against her tongue and send a bolt of lust right through her.

"Bree." Her name was a heady whisper.

She felt a rise in his jeans, and she drew back.

Touch me. Kiss me.

"You're driving me crazy. I'm really trying to behave, but you're testing my willpower."

She couldn't weigh her response or think past right or wrong. All she could manage was, "Good," and then she took him in another insatiable kiss.

He reclined the seat, pulling her on top of him and deepening the kiss. Driven by need, she pulled up his T-shirt.

"Oh my God. Really?" She ran her hands over his six-pack abs.

Hugh laughed. "I have to stay in shape to race."

She kissed his stomach, then looked at him and bit her lower lip.

"What?" Hugh reached for her.

"I just want to put my skin against yours." She lifted her shirt up just enough to expose her stomach and lay down on top of him. She moaned. "God, that feels good."

"Do you have any idea how sexy you are?" He buried his hands in her hair and kissed her again. "Jesus, you're killing me, Bree."

Her cell phone rang, and they both froze.

"Layla." Brianna sat up, and before she could reach for her purse, Hugh had snagged it and pulled her phone from the side pocket.

"You promised her. Here." He thrust her phone into her hand.

"Hi, baby," Brianna said.

Hugh righted the seat beneath them, and when she tried to crawl from his lap, he held her in place. He fixed her shirt so it hung properly and covered her belly.

"I'll be there soon, honey. How was the play?" Brianna mouthed, *Sorry*, to Hugh.

He mouthed, *It's fine*, and ran his hand down the back of her hair. She felt silly sitting on his lap and embarrassed to have been interrupted. *There's no way he'll want to see me now.* She tried to focus on Layla.

"I'm so happy for you, Layla. Okay, tell Grandma I'll be there in twenty minutes. I miss you too, baby." She purposely didn't look at Hugh, afraid to see the disappointment in his eyes. "Okay, see you soon."

She ended the call and tried again to move from his lap, but he held her still.

"How'd she like the play?"

"She loved it. Hugh, I'm so sorry." She chanced a glance at him and he was looking at her with warmth and interest, not disappointment. His lips curved up and then he tilted his head to the side.

"I love hearing you talk to her. Your whole face lights up. There's no need to be sorry."

She struggled free and moved to the passenger seat. Hugh wrinkled his forehead.

"Why are you in such a hurry to move away from me? I like

when you're close."

"I was embarrassed. There we were, making out, and I had to stop to take a phone call." She shook her head and reached for the door handle.

"Hey, Bree." He grabbed her hand. "Layla comes first. I get that. It's the way it should be. I respect you for it. My father did the same thing with us. I'm not upset, and I'm not some kind of animal driven by sex."

"Hugh," she whispered, "you're a little too good to be true. I'm waiting for something bad to bite me in the ass."

He raised his eyebrows. "If you're into that sort of thing."

She pushed him playfully away with a little laugh. "You know what I mean."

"I do, and I'm sort of waiting for the same thing, but right now, I'm not gonna fight it. I like to be with you, and you have a daughter. It's an easy equation to understand. The more difficult part is, when can I see you again?"

Brianna pressed her lips together. "That's the hard part. I have Layla every minute I'm not at work. This weekend was a fluke." Kat had offered to babysit, but with working so many hours, Brianna would feel guilty leaving Layla after not seeing her all day.

He nodded. "Okay, well, I have a few things to do throughout the week, but can I come by your work and see you?"

"Of course, but, Hugh, I know what my life is like, and I know it will seem insurmountable to you. We've had more time together since we've met than I've taken for myself in years. I run from mommying to bartending to working with Claude, and some days I have to check the calendar twice to be sure of the day. Don't feel pressure to see me just because you were nice to me for a few days."

"Brianna, do you know what it feels like to hear that time and time again?"

It wasn't the sharpness of his tone that silenced her. It was the hurt in his eyes.

"I'm sorry." His voice softened, and he met her gaze. "I'm not angry, but I keep telling you how I feel about you and you keep pushing me away. If you really want me to walk away, I can do that. But don't kiss me like that and then shut me out. It's confusing to me, Bree. I'm not good at games. I'm a cut-and-dry guy. You either want to see me or you don't. I know you don't know me that well yet, but I wouldn't spend the day with you if I didn't want to. I'm not *that* nice of a person."

Brianna looked down. "I'm sorry. I just—"

He let out a sigh. "You need to spend time working and with Layla. I'm not asking you not to do those things. I don't know how we'll get time together, but do you want to try? Do you want me to call you?"

"Yes, more than anything."

"That's a start. You must get a lunch or dinner break at work, or have time one morning after you take Layla to school? We could meet for coffee."

Brianna felt the minutes—and her perfect fantasy day with Hugh—slipping away. "Call me and I'll look at my work schedule. I really do want to see you."

Hugh climbed from the car and opened her door. He'd been holding her hand all day, and now, as she placed her hand in his, it felt natural. It felt comfortable, and the last thing she wanted to do was walk away.

He took her in his arms again, and she was glad she'd worn her boots, because the extra three inches brought her that much closer to his lips.

"I'll call you. Have fun with Layla." He kissed her softly.

"Thank you for everything." *Why does this feel like goodbye forever?*

He walked her to her car and put her bags in the trunk. They found the key in the tailpipe, just where Art said he'd leave it. She climbed in and it started right up. Brianna felt like she'd gone full circle. They'd begun getting close the night her car died, and here she was, feeling like she'd never see him again, no matter what he'd said. She knew how crazy her schedule was, and even as they said goodbye and she tried to work through the options in her mind, she couldn't find an easy way to fit him in.

Hugh leaned through the window and kissed her again. She ran her fingers through his hair, hoping to remember everything about him—*just in case.*

Her heart ached as she drove down the driveway, and the lump in her throat that she'd fought against earlier returned with a vengeance. By the time she reached her mother's house, she felt as if she'd lost her best friend.

"Mommy!" Layla jumped into her arms at the front door.

"Hi! Wow. Did you have a great day?" She kissed Layla's cheek and set her back on the floor. Brianna had grown up in the small rambler, and she loved that her mother had the same plaid furniture and the same funky kitchen table with carved paws at the bottom of each leg. She'd freshened the rooms with paint and new carpeting throughout the years, but the bigger items remained the same. The school photos leading down the hall marked the years of change for Brianna and now for Layla, too.

"The play was so good! And you should have seen the handsome prince." Layla pulled her by the hand into the kitchen, where her mother was stirring something in a big bowl.

"A handsome prince? Tell me all about him." She bent down and looked Layla in the eye, thinking of her own handsome prince. He wore his heart on his sleeve, and everything he said and did was sincere. Of that she was certain. Brianna had never believed in fairy tales, and now, just the thought of Hugh made her consider her own happily ever after.

Layla jumped up and down in her sparkly sneakers. "Oh, Mommy! He was tall and so nice to the princess. He brought her flowers, and when he kissed her, the whole stage got bright like the sun!"

"Wow. Now, that's a kiss," Brianna said, thinking of Hugh and how her whole body sizzled when they'd kissed.

"I hope I meet a prince someday. Do you think I will?" Layla wrinkled her forehead.

"If, when you're older, you want to meet a handsome prince, then I'm sure you will, but you are a fine princess all on your own."

Layla gasped. "Is that why you call me princess? Because I'll meet a handsome prince one day?"

Brianna bristled. That's not at all what she'd been thinking when she began calling her princess. "Well, no. I call you princess because you're my princess. My special girl." She kissed Layla's forehead, hating that she wasn't even six and already worried about finding a handsome prince.

"Look what Grandma's making!" Layla pulled her toward her mother.

"Hi, Mom. Thanks for taking her." She kissed her mom on the cheek and peeked into the bowl. "Brownies?"

"Uh-huh," Layla said. "We're making them because I was so good today."

"That sounds great. I'm starved." She realized that she and Hugh hadn't eaten anything all day, and she wondered if he was starving, too.

"Did you have a nice day?" her mother asked. Jean Heart was the same height as Brianna, thicker through the waist, with the same straight, dark hair. In her jeans and sweater, she looked relaxed and happy. But Brianna knew her mother's mind never rested. Brianna had learned how to be efficient and how to multitask from watching her mother manage their lives, and she hoped she was pulling it off just as well.

Brianna sighed and leaned against the counter. "Yeah, it was okay."

Layla was doing some sort of a jumping game on the tiled floor. "Can I play in the playroom?"

"Sure. I'll get you when the brownies are ready." She watched her scamper away. "Was she okay for you?"

Her mom poured the brownie mix into a pan and handed Brianna the chocolate-covered spoon. "She's always good for me." She put the brownies in the oven.

"Thanks. I needed this." She licked the rich deliciousness from the wooden spoon. *A poor substitute for sex.*

"Want some tea? I just heated up the kettle." Her mom pulled two mugs from the cabinet.

"Sure." She set the spoon in the sink and sat down at the small kitchen table. "Mom, do you think I'm a good mother?"

Her mother set a mug of tea in front of Brianna and then sat across from her. She looked at her daughter and smiled, then picked up her mug and sipped the hot tea before answering. Brianna was used to her mother's careful answers. There was a time when her mother would rattle a quick answer without thinking about it. Much like Brianna, her mother had always worked two jobs, leaving little time for anything other than laundry and cleaning. One day, when Brianna was about twelve, she'd asked her mother why her father left, and her mother had said, *Some men can't take the heat of the kitchen, so they flee the house.* That was the day Brianna told her mother—who coincidentally burned more dinners than not—that maybe she should have taken cooking classes so that she could have a father. It was also the last time her mother had given her an off-the-cuff answer. That was one of the reasons Brianna paid full attention to Layla when she spoke to her. She never wanted Layla to feel like anything else in life was more important than her or like she'd made Brianna's life more difficult. Brianna had made her own life more difficult—and more fulfilled—all in one weekend after college graduation.

"You're a remarkable mother. All it takes is one look at Layla to know how well adjusted she is, and if you think that has to do with anything but parenting, you're wrong. She's doing well because of you." Her mother tilted her head and narrowed her brown eyes. "Why?"

Brianna shrugged. "I don't know. I just want to be sure I don't screw her up somehow."

Her mother reached across the table and laid her hand on Brianna's. "You love her too much to do anything that would screw her up. Besides, kids get screwed up all on their own."

"What does that mean?" *Are you talking about me?*

"Just that you can do your very best and kids can still fall off track for a while. Look at your graduating class from high school. The valedictorian became a heroin addict three years later. You just never know what will happen, so you do your best, and when they leave your house, you pray you raised them well enough to know right from wrong."

"Do you think I screwed up myself somehow, Mom?" She slid her hand out from beneath her mother's, unsettled by the innuendo.

Her mother sighed and her lips lifted to a soft smile that reached her eyes. She brushed her hair from her face and tucked it behind her ear, just like Brianna. "I don't think you're capable of screwing yourself up. You love Layla too much. Bree, what's this about? Is something worrying you?"

Brianna weighed her answers. She could beat around the bush and maybe in an hour she'd know what her mother thought, but she was too nervous to wait an hour. "I met someone." She kept her eyes trained on her tea.

Her mother leaned across the table and whispered, "You did?"

Brianna lifted her eyes and was surprised to see her mother's face alit with interest.

"Brianna Marie, come over here." She took Brianna's hand and dragged her to the far corner of the kitchen.

"Mom!" She stumbled behind her.

"Out of earshot. Met someone? A man? And?" Her mother touched her arm.

"Why are you so excited?" Brianna had to laugh. She'd expect that reaction from Kat, but not from her mother.

"Because I've been worried about you. Twenty-eight-year-old women are supposed to date, Bree, and you know how I feel about you making Layla your whole world."

Brianna rolled her eyes. "Healthy people have diverse lives. I know, Mom, but you said yourself that I'm a good mother and that Layla's well adjusted."

"She is, and you are. But a little ego boost for you isn't a bad thing. Is he a good person?"

That question was the heart of why she adored her mother. She didn't ask if he had a good job, or if he was attractive. She cared most about the person he was inside, which is where Brianna had learned it from and probably why she was having such a confusing time deciding how to move forward—or if she should move forward—with Hugh. For six years, living a life without complications beyond taking care of her daughter and making ends meet had been easy. No man had been too kind or too interesting to ignore…and then came Hugh.

"He's a remarkably good person."

"Oh, Bree!" She wrapped her arms around Brianna. "How did you meet? When have you had time to see him? You worked today." She tilted her head, looking out of the corner of her eyes at Brianna. "You were working, weren't you?"

"Yes, of course. I worked and then we went shopping. Oh, and my car broke down last night." She leaned against the counter.

"Oh no. How much is that going to set you back?"

"It's not. He…" She paused, wondering what her mother's reaction would be to what he did for a living. If she was ever going to figure this out, she needed to be honest. "He's a Capital Series Grand Prix driver and his pit crew fixed it."

"Capital Series? A race car driver? How on earth did you meet a guy like that here? I mean, you never go to the track, and I know you don't hang out at the places in town where the Grand Prix fans hang out." Her mother crossed her arms and tapped her chin with her index finger.

"He was in the tavern one night and we talked." She watched her mother pace the small kitchen.

"At Old Town? Really? Gosh, I must be way too far removed from that world. I had no idea that those guys hung out there. You've never mentioned it."

"They don't, Mom. He avoids those places."

"Brianna, I don't know. He must travel a lot, and what do you really know about him? I mean, guys like that? They scare me a little." She stopped pacing and looked at her daughter. "I'm not judging him sight unseen, but you're my little girl. Do you have your eyes open? Does he have women everywhere? I mean, how long is he even here for?"

"I know, Mom. Believe me. My eyes are wide open. Wide open. He travels, but he said he gets time off soon."

"They only race about nine or ten months out of the year or something like that."

"How do you know?" *Nine or ten months?*

"Your father loved the races." Her mother tucked her hair behind her ear again. "Oh, honey. You're a smart girl. What does your gut tell you?"

Brianna pressed her lips together and tucked her hair behind her ear.

"Uh-oh." Her mother put her arm around Brianna and walked her back to the table. She peered into the playroom. "We'll whisper," she said as she sat beside her. "You have that look on your face that you had when you told me you were pregnant with Layla." She held Brianna's hand. "Tell me."

Brianna's stomach twisted as it had earlier that day. She tried to formulate a response, but as she opened her mouth, the truth fell out without any cushioning at all.

"I like him, Mom. I mean, I really, really like him, even though it's only been a few days. He treats me well, and he's so thoughtful." She felt her cheeks rise with a geeky, gushing smile. She crossed her arms on the table and rested her forehead on them. "What am I gonna do?" She felt her mother stroking her head, and she peered out from beneath the veil of hair that had fallen over her face.

"What do you want to do?" She asked it with such gentleness that Brianna knew her mother wasn't judging her, as she'd done for a brief time right after she told her she was pregnant.

Brianna lifted her head. "I want to see him. More." She glanced at the playroom.

"And what about Layla?" Again she asked with tenderness, not accusation or judgment.

"I told him he can't meet her. I'm afraid to let him. What if Layla adores him and then we break up?"

"I think you mean what if you adore him and then you break up, too."

Brianna dropped her eyes. "It worries me. He's a little too good to be true." She leaned forward, and her mother met her halfway across the table as she whispered, "We could have…you know…and he knew that I was worried about getting too involved because of Layla. So we didn't." She leaned back, then admitted, "He wouldn't."

Her mother's jaw dropped. "Brianna!"

"What?"

They both laughed, and Brianna covered her face with her hand.

"Oh, honey. It's okay. You're allowed to…do that."

"I know, Mom, but if I get close to him and it doesn't work out, then what?" As the words left her mouth, her heart squeezed. She realized for the first time how very badly she wanted to be with Hugh and how she'd been blocking those feelings because it's what she'd told herself she needed to do for so very long. *Please tell me it's okay. Please, please. I want to be with him more than I want almost anything else in the world.*

"Well, I don't know anything about any of the men you've dated over the past few years or how it worked out with them." She narrowed her eyes, and Brianna knew she was expecting an admission.

"None. No one since." She nodded toward the playroom.

"No. That can't be." Her mother shook her head. "I thought you were just being careful about telling me or letting Layla know. No one? Not once?"

Brianna shook her head. "I was planning on waiting until Layla was eighteen so I didn't complicate her life."

"Oh, honey. I take back every thought I ever had about me being a good mother. I'm a terrible mother if that's what you've been doing. Brianna, you can't be the best mother you are capable of if you aren't fulfilled, too, and fulfillment comes from all angles."

"So you want me to sleep around?" Brianna teased.

"No!" She leaned forward again. "But you don't have to be a nun. Enjoy life a little. Date; go dancing; hang out with Kat more than just at work. Layla's almost six; she's not a toddler. I can take her sometimes. Good Lord. Eighteen? That's twelve more years. I promise you: If you do that, you'll spin around in twelve years and wonder what the hell you accomplished."

"But our lives are so complicated. I work all the time, and I need time with Layla."

"You do, yes." Her mother tapped her finger on the table with an unfamiliar glint in her eye, and the right side of her mouth lifted in a mischievous smile. "But you also need to honor your own feelings and your needs as a woman. If you feel this guy…what's his name?"

"Hugh Braden." Saying his name made her heart race.

"Hugh Braden. If you feel he's not a gigolo of some sort and he treats you well, go on a date or two. See how it goes. I'll watch Layla, and she won't have to know until you decide she should."

"No one says gigolo anymore, Mom." Brianna laughed, but inside she was both relieved and scared shitless. She'd been counting on her mother to talk some sense into her and talk her out of following her heart. She'd felt her heart opening to Hugh already. What would it do if they became intimate?

Chapter Sixteen

HUGH ROUNDED THE bend at the bottom of the hill and ran at a quick pace beneath the colorful poplar and maple trees that lined the road in front of his house. He'd been too edgy after spending the day with Brianna to sit still in his house, and it was too late to go to the track. He finished his four-mile run with a sprint up the driveway. He stretched and headed to the back door to spend an hour in his home gym. Just walking by the garage made him think of Brianna and the way she'd leaned over the console to kiss him and then pressed her bare skin against his. She was so damn sexy that he'd been ready to take her right there, just flip her over and make love to her in the driver's seat. It was probably a good thing her phone rang. Sex in the car might have been hot, but it was not where he wanted to make love to Brianna for the first time. He'd envisioned her beneath him in his bed since they'd been intimate on the couch, and after spending the day together, his attraction to her had only become stronger, deeper, more layered.

He worked his biceps and triceps in front of the mirror. His T-shirt was drenched with sweat and stuck to his body like a second skin. He ran his hand through his hair and slicked it back away from his face. His massive quads were even more pronounced from the hard run. Hugh loved the adrenaline rush of working out, but as he pumped his arms with each heavy lift, he thought about how he'd rather be spending the hour with Brianna.

He set the weights down to answer his cell phone.

"Hey, Treat."

"Hugh. How's it going?"

It was good to hear his brother's voice. Hugh had been so young when his mother died, and Treat, as the oldest, had been eleven. Treat had taken it upon himself to ensure each of his siblings knew what their mother was like, and to Hugh, those stories became real, as if he'd been there to experience them himself.

"Great. I'm in Richmond, and you know, keeping it real." Hugh had always tried to play things casual with his brothers, and they called him on it as often as Savannah did. "How's Max?"

"She's great. Your last race of the season is next weekend, right? Max and I want to come down for it."

"Really? Man, that would be awesome. It's in Daytona. Are you sure you can make it?"

"Hugh, have I ever said I'd make a race and not made it?"

Treat always kept his promises. *Always.* "No. I'm heading down Friday night."

"I know you can't stay out late or anything Friday night, but we can get together after the race, can't we?"

Hugh's mind was already racing. He wasn't like Treat. His family was used to him taking off right after awards and races, usually to avoid the media rush, but he was already thinking about flying back to Richmond right after the race. He hated to blow off his brother if he was taking a trip just to see him, but the thought of blowing off Brianna was even more painful. "I'm not sure if I'm sticking around after the race."

"Do you have another event?"

He heard the disappointment in Treat's voice, and guilt sucked the enthusiasm from his voice. "No. No event."

"Then why not hang out?" Treat pushed.

Hugh sighed. "I met someone here in Richmond, and I'm thinking about coming back to see her." He closed his eyes, ready for the razzing his family had always given him.

"What's another date with another model compared to spending time with family?" Treat's voice had become serious.

"She's not a model, Treat, and she's not a fan either." If it had been any of his other brothers, he'd have joked his way out of a serious conversation, but Treat had never steered him wrong and he was less judgmental than the others. He called Hugh on his shit, but he offered advice instead of just judgment. Right then, Hugh could use a little advice. In his brother's silence he read disbelief.

"It's the truth, Treat. She's a single mom, and I like her. A lot." Hugh sat down on the weight bench and wiped the sweat from his forehead.

"A single mom."

Maybe Hugh had given up his hand too early. He detected something akin to judgment in Treat's voice.

"Yeah, a single mom." Hugh sat up straighter.

"Hugh, what are you thinking? Single moms have responsibilities. They can't be out until two in the morning drinking, and I doubt she'll want her daughter around a guy who dates a different woman every night."

Hugh pushed to his feet. "You don't know me that well, Treat." Anger crept into his voice. "I haven't dated like that in months."

"Months?"

"Yes, months. I know how it seems to all of you. I'm the irresponsible youngest Braden, the one who you all laugh about when I leave family gatherings early because you know it's just who I am. I get it, man. I created that image, but it's not me any longer, and it hasn't been for a long time."

"Months," Treat repeated.

"Yes, months."

"Really? Months? Well, I thought you meant, you know, a few weeks. How could I not have known that?"

"Despite what you think, you don't know everything about all of us, Treat. Even with your ability to make a phone call and learn all the dirty details of people's lives."

"Hugh, I'm looking at an *Enquirer* from two months ago with my brother on the front, on the arm of a leggy model."

He heard the smirk in Treat's voice. "You believe those bullshit magazines?"

"Not usually, but this sort of fits your rep, bro."

"Yeah, it fit the rep I had. Look carefully, Treat. Do you see where it says *2012 Parade* on the sign behind the blue car? The motherfuckers didn't Photoshop very well, did they?"

He heard paper crumbling.

"Why are you reading that shit anyway?" Hugh asked. "Don't you have better things to do with your time?"

"I'm at a doctor's office, and it was here on the table. Now it's in their trash can."

"Doctor? Is everything okay?" Hugh sat back down. His father had a heart issue a little over a year ago, and now Hugh's chest tightened at the thought.

"Yeah. Max wasn't feeling well. We're waiting to see the

doctor."

"Oh, thank God." Hugh let out a loud breath. "I don't mean that. I thought it was Dad. I hope Max feels better."

"She will. It's not Dad; don't worry. I'd have led with that if it were. So tell me about the woman you met."

He heard Max in the background. "Hugh met a woman?" He pictured her pulling out her cell phone and blasting a text to his entire family and their significant others: *Alert! Hugh met a woman he actually likes!* There were no secrets in the Braden family. Their grapevine ran strong and often.

"Bree." Hugh paced again. "She's…I don't know, Treat. She's different from anyone I've ever met. She's more real. She's responsible, sweet, careful. She's very careful." He paused, and when Treat didn't fill in the gap, he knew he was waiting for more, but he couldn't define what it was about Brianna that tweaked his heart. He just knew that she had.

"Where's the hot, sexy, awesome in bed stuff you always spout off?"

"Jesus, Treat. She's not like that. We haven't even done that stuff. I mean, she's beautiful, and she's beyond sexy in a wholesome, natural way." He paused again, thinking about Brianna's smile and the way it lit up her eyes. "She's nothing like the women I've dated. She's better in every way."

"Hugh, I'm sorry, man. I didn't realize you were serious. What about her daughter?"

"I haven't met her yet. I actually could use some advice on this, Treat, and I really don't have anyone else to turn to. I really like Bree, and yes, it surprises me, but I can't turn away from the way I feel. I haven't known her that long, but when I took her to her apartment, I didn't like the feeling I got. Some scuzzy guy was eyeing her, and I wanted to protect her. I mean, scuzzy guys look at women all the time, but I've never felt like I wanted to threaten one for looking at a woman I was with until I met Bree. And it worries me a little."

"What part of it?"

"It's fast. It's a strong feeling. We both think I shouldn't meet Layla—her daughter—until we're sure about us. It all worries me. I'm not exactly the most patient man on earth."

Treat laughed, a deep, hearty laugh that made Hugh smile. "You could say that again. Well, what's your plan right now?"

Hugh headed for the stairs. "For the first time in my life, I don't have a plan. I'm here until next Friday night; then I'm in Daytona. I want to come back Saturday night. Layla's birthday is Sunday, and even if I haven't met her by then, I want to be nearby in case Bree needs anything." He laughed. "That's weird as shit, right?"

"No, Hugh. That's growing up."

"Right. Whatever. Then we have Savannah's party the next weekend, and I already don't want to be away from Bree again for that."

"All I can tell you is that when fate steps in, you have no choice. You do whatever it takes to follow it."

He heard Treat kiss Max, and it made him long for Brianna. He'd been waiting to call her, not wanting to smother her. And now, hearing her voice was all he wanted to do. His phone beeped with another call coming through.

"Hey, Treat. I have another call. Wanna hold on a sec?"

"I can't. The nurse just called us in. I gotta run, but we'll touch base before next weekend. Love you, Hugh. And don't worry. You'll figure it out, and I'm here if you need to bounce something off of me."

"Love you too, Treat. Thanks."

He clicked over without looking at the screen. "Hello?"

"Hugh?"

Hugh froze; then a smile crept across his lips. "Bree?"

"Yeah, hi."

"Are you okay? Why are you being so quiet?" He went into the living room and eyed the couch where they'd made out. He had to turn away. Just thinking about it gave him a hard-on.

"I'm at my mom's, and I'm out on the porch. I just didn't want Layla to hear me."

"Is she okay? How did she like the play?"

"She's great, and she loved it. I'm actually calling because my mom offered to keep Layla again tonight, and I wondered if you were free. I know you're probably busy, but—"

"Bree, I'm free. I'm definitely free, and I want to see you. But I thought you couldn't make time." He headed for the bedroom, already thinking about where to take her.

"Well, let's just say that my mom convinced me that a twelve-year plan might not be the smartest thing for me to do."

"I love your mom already."

She laughed, and Hugh felt like the luckiest man on earth.

"Is there anything specific you want to do? When can I pick you up? Should I pick you up at your mom's?" Words fell fast from his lips. He pulled his shirt over his head and turned on the shower.

"I need to shower and change. I don't have anything specific I want to do. I just wanted to spend time with you," she said.

"Okay." Hugh's mind raced. He had a great idea for their first date, but it would require pulling some major strings, and it was a weekend, which meant he needed to also collect on most of the favors owed to him—and then some. "How about I pick you up at seven thirty? What time do you need to be back?"

She didn't answer.

"Bree?"

He read her answer in her silence. "Oh. Okay, then. I'll see you at seven thirty. Hey?"

"Yeah?" Her voice was tentative, and Hugh imagined her tucking her hair behind her ear, looking away with her gorgeous eyes.

"No pressure here. Just because we can doesn't mean we have to." Hugh never imagined he'd be the kind of guy who would say anything even remotely similar to that. His feelings for Brianna were peeling away layers of his old self, and he liked the man who was emerging.

BRIANNA STARED INTO her closet. "Come on. Come on. Come on," she said as she sifted through her clothes. She pulled open her dresser drawers and stared at the jeans she'd been wearing for three years. The same sweaters, the same blouses. She finally threw her hands up in the air and called Kat.

"What do girls wear on dates nowadays?" She paced the bedroom floor.

"You're going out with Patrick—Hugh?"

"Uh-huh."

Kat squealed so loud that Brianna had to pull the phone away from her ear.

Chapter Seventeen

HUGH HADN'T PLANNED a date since his high school prom, and even then his sister had helped him do most of the planning. He called in favors, groveled, and paid three times what he should have, but it would all be worth it. He hoped tonight would be a night that Brianna would never forget.

His heart thundered in his chest as he took the steps two at a time up to Brianna's apartment. *Why am I so damn nervous?* He took a deep breath and adjusted the gifts he'd brought before knocking at the door.

She opened the door, and Hugh lost his breath as he raked his eyes slowly down the navy blue minidress that hugged her breasts and hips like a second skin. Blousy sleeves cuffed at the wrist, and a simple neckline ignited the perfect combination of naughty and nice. The dress stopped midthigh, revealing her long, lean legs and ending in a pair of sexy black heels.

"Jesus, Brianna. You are stunning."

She dropped her eyes in that embarrassed, adorable way she had, and Hugh juggled the gifts to free his hand. He lifted her chin so he could look into her eyes. Some people wore their hearts on their sleeves. Brianna hid hers in her eyes, and Hugh had spotted it the first night they'd gone for coffee. "I'm right here, not down there." He kissed her softly, lingering with his lips against hers for a moment longer to make up for the time they'd been apart.

"What is all this?" She dropped her eyes to the package and flowers in his hands.

"These are for you." He handed her a bouquet of red roses.

"Thank you." She took the flowers, and Hugh followed her inside, closing the door behind him. "These are gorgeous, Hugh. You didn't have to do that."

"I never do things because I have to." He watched her put the flowers in a vase; then he handed her a large silver box covered with glitter and a big silver bow. "This is for Layla. You don't have to give it to her until you've decided about me, and if you decide we're not right for each other, then you can say it's from you. I didn't put a card in it."

"Hugh." She shook her head. "She doesn't need anything more."

"I know she doesn't." He wrapped his arms around her and kissed her forehead. "But sometimes girls need things just because, and how could I leave here in good conscience knowing she'd see the flowers and feel left out?"

She touched his cheek and he turned his face to her hand and kissed her palm. "You really are too much," she said.

"No. I'm just treating you both how you should be treated. Are you ready?"

"Yeah. Let me just get my purse." She grabbed a small black bag from the counter.

"Do you have your phone?"

"Yes." She furrowed her brow.

"Is it on? Loud?"

She smiled. "Yes, of course. Thank you for remembering."

Hugh held out his arm, and she took it as they walked down to the parking lot. Brianna's eyes lit up when she saw the Ferrari.

"You brought the red one!" She threw her arms around his neck and hugged him.

Seeing her reaction was more than he could have hoped for. "How could I drive anything else on our first real date?"

BRIANNA FELT LIKE she was in a fairy tale. Seeing Hugh in his white button-down shirt and dark slacks was enough to melt her heart, and when he handed her the roses, she thought she'd died and gone to heaven. But the gift for Layla had taken her right over the edge. Thoughtful was not a big enough word to describe Hugh's generosity and consideration of her daughter. He did all the right things, and his emphasis was on the things that mattered. The people that mattered.

She ran her hand along the smooth leather seats. As beautiful as the car was, Hugh had been right. It was just a car—a beautiful, extravagant car. It was the fact that he'd driven the red one, the one she'd wanted to take the day before, that made her swoon, and then when he called the evening their *first real date*, she knew she was a goner.

They drove through town, and Hugh took a back road that led behind the park. Brianna couldn't take her eyes off of him. She kept waiting for something bad to happen. For him to say he was married or had three illegitimate children. Something that would crush her hopes of allowing her heart to embrace him, but everything he did and said made him more appealing. She wondered what his father was like. Hugh was a testament to the man who had raised him. It dawned on her how similar that thought was to what her mother had told her about Layla, and that thought boosted her confidence about going out with Hugh. She was a good mother. She did deserve to follow her heart, even if carefully.

"Where are we going? Isn't this for maintenance vehicles?" Brianna asked as they drove through the open gate clearly marked *Maintenance Vehicles*.

"Yeah." He covered her hand with his. "But tonight it's just for us."

Anticipation prickled her arms. Brianna hadn't been on a first date in forever, and just being near Hugh was enough to make her nervous, but to think he had planned something special was almost too much to bear. She fidgeted with the edge of her dress.

He pulled up behind the lake and parked beneath the umbrella of a large colorful tree. Hugh opened the door for her and offered her his arm. Though she hadn't dated many men, she'd watched Kat and other women with their dates, and she couldn't remember any of the men acting consistently like gentlemen the way that Hugh did.

"Are you warm enough?" Hugh asked.

"Yeah, I think so."

He grabbed his leather jacket from the backseat and put it over his arm. "Just in case." Hugh dragged his eyes down her dress again, and Brianna looked down, wondering if she'd overdressed. She wasn't sure how to dress with Hugh. He seemed comfortable in jeans or slacks, and she was sure that even if he had shown up in rags he'd have still looked like a million bucks. Hell, she didn't know how to dress for a date. Period. Thank God Kat had some ideas, but now she questioned her selection.

"Is it too short?" she asked.

"Too…Bree, you look so hot that I'm having a hard time following through with our plans and not taking you right home to ravish you."

Ravish me? The thought terrified and excited her at once.

As they crested the small hill toward the lake, blue lights in the water came into view.

"Look." Brianna pointed toward the lake, and they walked over. "Oh my God. I haven't been here for forever, but I've never seen lights in the lake before. This is so beautiful." Brianna *ooh*ed and *aah*ed as the lights changed from blue to pink to lavender. "Oh my God. This is gorgeous. Is there something going on here tonight? Why aren't there more people here?"

"The park closes at sunset."

She looked at him, and understanding dawned on her. "You rented the park?"

"Not really. I just pulled in a few favors. But it is all ours tonight."

"Hugh? Really? I didn't even know you could do such a thing." *Oh my God! Definite fairy tale.*

"Let's walk this way." Hugh put his hand on the small of her back and guided her across the grass.

She'd already come to love the feel of his hand on her back. It was a possessive, caring touch, and she'd been taking care of herself for so long that just for one night she wished she could crawl right into his arms and let him care for her.

"I used to take Layla here when she was a toddler. There's a playground on the far side of the park, and she used to love the swings. She could swing for hours."

"Why'd you stop taking her?" he asked.

"Oh, life got busy. I had to work more to make ends meet. My mom always says life is what happens when you're busy making plans."

Hugh pulled her close. "Then maybe we should never make plans and just keep living our lives so we don't miss anything."

She leaned her head on his shoulder, adding another thing she loved about him to her mental list. *Sees the good in everything.*

They came to a large tree, and Hugh took her hands in his and looked into her eyes. It was so dark that she could barely make out his features. She took a step closer as her eyes adjusted.

"I know that giving up your time with Layla was a big step for you, and I hope that at the end of this night, you feel like it was worth it."

"Any time I spend with you is worth it." She stood on her tiptoes, and he closed the gap between them and settled his lips over hers, kissing her sweetly, then deepening the kiss and pulling her against him. His lips moved to her cheek, then found the space below her earlobe that sent a thrum of excitement between her legs.

A sensuous ache of want escaped her lips—softer than a moan, stronger than a sigh, and he licked the spot he'd just kissed. She closed her eyes and arched her neck back, wanting more of him and reveling in the feel of his tongue as it stroked the sensitive skin at the base of her neck.

"Bree," he whispered in her ear.

She thought she answered, but her lips didn't move. It was all she could do to keep breathing. She closed her eyes. *Kiss me more.*

"God, I want you so badly," he whispered against her ear.

"Yes," she managed. *Yes? Oh my God. I want you too.* Her brain wouldn't kick into gear. She was stuck in some foggy place filled with wanton thoughts and pulses of heat that filled the secret places she wished he'd touch.

He brought his lips back to hers and took her in a greedy kiss. She didn't think as her hands reached for the sides of his head and pulled him closer. When his hands found the curve of her ass, her head fell back, and he tasted her neck again, inciting another needy moan—an unmistakable take-me-now, sexual moan—filled the air. She clenched her eyes shut as heat rushed up her chest to her cheeks and he found her ear once again.

"I love that," he whispered.

Oh God, oh God, oh God. She had to regain control of her body. She clenched the muscles in her thighs. They felt foreign, apart from her. She took his head in her hands again and brought his lips back to hers. Maybe he could breathe oxygen into her failing brain. *God, you taste good.* Years of suppressed sexual desire came rushing forward.

"Bree," he said between kisses.

She blinked her way through the lust that fogged her ability to think. "Yeah?" she finally managed.

"I want nothing more than to make love to you, but..." He kissed her again. "But I planned something that I thought you might enjoy."

"Okay. Yes." *Oh my God. I'm like a sex maniac. What is wrong with me?*

They stared longingly into each other's eyes for what seemed like forever while they each found their breath—and Brianna's legs found their strength—before Hugh led her to a blanket spread across the grass beneath an enormous tree. As they approached, white lights flicked on, illuminating the branches above like a canopy.

Brianna gasped. "Oh my goodness. How did you do that?"

"Friends," he said with a shrug.

A man in a suit appeared beside the blanket, startling Brianna.

"I also realized that I never fed you after breakfast today, and I promise not to make that mistake again. So I thought we should eat dinner." Hugh thanked the man, and Brianna noticed a silver cart she'd missed when she'd first noticed him. He and Hugh spread what looked like a thin tabletop across the blanket; then the man set the makeshift table with silverware and wineglasses.

"Hugh," she whispered. "This is too much."

He took her hand and they sat down on the blanket. "Nothing is too much for you."

Brianna didn't know how to react. How did you thank someone for giving you the most romantic night of your life? Nothing could be a big enough thank-you. And still, with all the romance and forethought, even the moonlight picnic didn't compare to the gift he'd brought for Layla. He'd stolen her heart at that moment, and she doubted anything could ever top that.

After the gentleman served their dinner, he disappeared as quietly as he'd appeared.

"I brought wine, but I can't really drink, so I also have water. Which would you prefer?"

Wine. The whole bottle to calm my nerves. "I'll have one glass of wine, then water, please. I noticed that you don't drink. How come?" Brianna had forgotten until just then, and now she wondered if he were a recovering alcoholic.

"I do drink. But I have a race next weekend, and I don't drink when I have a race coming up. Dehydration is a big issue when we drive, so I'm just overly cautious."

She dropped her eyes. She'd forgotten about him leaving the following weekend. "Your race is in Daytona?"

"Yes, Saturday. Layla's party is Thursday, right?"

You remembered. "Yes. That's right. How long will you be gone?"

Hugh poured her wine and a glass of water for him. "I leave Friday, and I think I'm going to come back Saturday night. That way, if you need anything Sunday, I'll be just a phone call away."

Brianna felt Hugh's name etch deeply into another piece of her heart. "You don't need to do that. I've been taking care of myself for a long time." *But I love that you want to be here just in case.*

"I like knowing you're nearby."

Brianna's nerves were doing some sort of mosh pit dance. She nibbled on bread and cheese, wishing the night would never end.

He lifted his glass of water. "Here's to our first date."

She *clinked* her glass to his. "To our amazing first date."

Hugh leaned back on his palms and crossed his feet at the ankles. He looked so comfortable, and as much as Brianna hated herself for the thought that entered her mind, she allowed it to slip from her lips.

"Have you done this kind of thing before? You don't have to tell me. I'm just curious."

He sat up and scooted closer to her. "Nope. Not once. To be honest, I was so excited to plan our date that I could barely sit still before we got here. There's something else I wanted to show you." He stood and reached for her hand.

"More lights?"

"You'll see." They walked hand in hand down a path that led through a thick group of trees. Brianna untangled their hands and wrapped her arm in his, wanting to be closer. She rested her head on his arm and relished in the feel of him beside her. Knowing Layla was safe and happy with her mother whisked away the guilt she'd had about leaving Layla to be with Hugh.

"Are you taking me to do dirty things in the bushes?" she teased.

"Now, that's something I hadn't thought of." He raised his eyebrows in quick succession.

They rounded another group of thick trees and Hugh said, "Close your eyes."

"Okay." Brianna closed her eyes, feeling a little silly. "It's already dark. Do I really need to do this?"

"Yes. Do you trust me?" Hugh's rich voice warmed her.

"One hundred percent."

"Good. I'm going to trust you not to open your eyes." He held her hand and put his other hand on her back as he guided her forward.

Soft music filtered through the air. "What is that?"

"You'll see." He stopped walking, and she felt him move in front of her. He held both her hands, and her pulse kicked up again.

"Okay. Open your eyes, but look at me."

She looked up into his dark, serious eyes.

"Brianna, I'm blown away by what I feel for you and how fast it's happened."

Oh God. Me too. She could barely think past her hammering

heart and the blood rushing through her ears. He took her face in his hands and leaned his forehead on hers. *I love when you do that.* She held on to his waist to keep her rubbery legs from sending her to the ground. She knew if she opened her mouth she'd have no choice but for her lips to find his.

"I want to wipe away your unhappy memories and replace them with happier ones."

"Me too," was all she could manage.

Behind him, colorful lights flicked on, and the music that had been playing softly came to life. Brianna recognized the carnival-like tune. She clutched her fingers around his waist and peered around him. Her eyes filled with tears.

"Hugh." Trembling began in her chest and quickly took over her limbs as memories filtered in. *Her father holding her hand as she stepped onto the carousel. Flashes of him as she flew by riding the pink carousel horse.*

"I'm right here." He put his arm securely around her and pressed her body into his side as they walked toward the carousel. "I wanted you to have your memories of your father, but hopefully the next day's memories can be replaced with better ones."

Her throat swelled, and as she pressed into his chest, her tears sprang free. He didn't say a word. He held her tight and kissed the top of her head as she cried over the magnitude of what he'd done. She took a deep breath and wiped her eyes before looking up at him.

"I'm sorry. I—"

"Shh. I didn't mean to make you sad. I was hoping this would be a good thing. I'm so sorry."

She reached up and touched his cheek. "This is a great thing. They're happy tears, not sad. You're the most thoughtful man I've ever met, and I'm sorry I'm bawling like a baby."

He wiped her tears with the pad of his thumb. "You carry so much responsibility on your shoulders, Bree. I'm in awe of the courage and strength you have, and the thought of you being sad about the morning after such a wonderful day with your father kills me."

"I'm not courageous." She lowered her eyes.

He lifted her chin. "You're the bravest woman I know. You've given your life to make Layla's as good as it can be. That's brave, Bree. Brave is shouldering the responsibility and putting yourself last. Brave is carrying on every day against the odds. Brave is pushing past the morning your father left and making sure your daughter never has to experience that pain."

His words brought more tears. No one had ever called her brave before. How could he see those things in her in only a few short days? How could anyone?

She pressed her cheek to his chest and closed her eyes, listening to the rhythm of his heart and feeling the walls around hers crumble, piece after fragile piece.

Chapter Eighteen

THEY CLIMBED ONTO the carousel, and Brianna chose a pink horse, just as she'd told Hugh she had that afternoon so many moons ago. When she'd first teared up, he feared he'd ruined their night, but when she drew back from his chest and he saw the tenderness in her eyes, he knew he'd done the right thing. Now he sat behind her on the pink horse, her back pressed against his chest, her hair whipping with the wind. He wrapped his arms around her waist and pressed his cheek to hers.

They rode the carousel three times before climbing off.

"That was so fun. Layla would love this." Brianna's tears were gone, replaced by glistening sparkles from the lights of the carousel.

"I thought about bringing her, but this was for you. Maybe one day I can take you both on a date. She can get dressed up and feel like a big girl and we'll get a little extra time together. There's a light show at the Ginter Gardens that I think she'd enjoy, or we could go to Maymont. There's a petting zoo there and nice trails and things. Or we could see a play since she loves them."

"Hugh."

He felt his shoulders sink a little lower. "It's okay."

"No, that wasn't a *no*. That was a 'Hugh!'" She put her arms around his neck and said, "I've never taken her to the light show, and I think she'd really enjoy that." She stood on her tiptoes and kissed his chin. "She'll love it, and I can't keep you hidden forever."

Forever. Hugh hadn't been thinking in those terms, but now the word lingered in his mind in a way that would have made him bolt the other way a few months ago.

"Great, well, when you decide it's appropriate, we'll do it. And we don't have to do any of those things. If she'd rather go to McDonald's and throw a Frisbee or go to a movie, I'm all for it. I'd just like to take you both out so she doesn't feel left out."

Hugh couldn't pin down why he was feeling the need to push forward and meet Layla, but after talking with Treat and spending years not allowing his heart to be heard, it felt like the right thing to do. He couldn't help but think that maybe fate had stepped in after all. He'd been happier over the last two days than he'd been in years.

They came upon the cotton candy vendor that Hugh had hired, and he handed them an enormous paper cone of pink sugary deliciousness.

Hugh grabbed a hunk with his fingers and raised his eyebrows. "Open up."

She opened her mouth, and he placed the fluff of whipped sugar on her tongue. Brianna closed her lips around his fingers, sending a flare of heat to his loins and a groan he had to work hard to stifle to his lungs. The seductive look in her eyes drew his mouth to hers. Sugar covered their tongues and melted in their mouths. The combination of his growing feelings toward Brianna and the hope for a future together made the kiss even sweeter than their first. They kissed long after the cotton candy had melted. The music faded. The lights on the carousel went out, and the cotton candy vendor discreetly pushed his cart away. Brianna smelled so fresh, and she tasted of sugary wine. Beyond that, she tasted of Brianna. The captivating taste he'd experienced earlier that morning, when she'd fallen into his arms and he thought he'd dreamed up his perfect match.

"I have to take you home," Hugh said between kisses.

"Home? No."

Hugh pried his lips from hers. "No?"

She shook her head vehemently. "No. I want to be with you, Hugh. More than anything, I want to be with you tonight."

"Yes…my home." He put his hands on her gorgeous cheeks and took her in another hungry kiss.

They hurried to the car, kissing along the way, and jogging hand in hand. Once in the car, Brianna lifted serious eyes to Hugh. "Don't we have to clean up dinner or let someone know we're leaving?"

"God, I like you." Hugh kissed her again. "They know." He drove toward his house with a million thoughts of Brianna—and what he wanted to do with her—storming through his head.

At the house, Brianna was quiet. Hugh knew she was nervous by the way she bit her lower lip and the way her eyes darted from him to the floor and back again. Seeing her so nervous made him even more so. He didn't turn on the overhead lights; instead he went to the living room and used the remote to turn on the fireplace and the stereo, which played soft rock through the wall-mounted speakers.

Brianna set her purse on the table by the door and looked so damned seductive as she crossed the floor in the body-hugging dress that Hugh couldn't wait to strip it off of her and love every inch of her.

He took her in his arms. "I've been trying to figure out what it was about your eyes that make them so beautiful," he whispered.

Flush covered her cheeks. Feeling her body against his brought rise to his desires and a throbbing in his heart that was new and different from anything he'd experienced before.

"There's so much more to you than what anyone sees. Behind those beautiful eyes is a well of emotions." He pressed a soft kiss to her lips. "And thoughts." He kissed her cheek. "And fears." He kissed her lips again, feeling her body tremble against him.

She licked her lower lip, and his hand slid to the curve of her hip.

"Not fears," she whispered, but worry hung in her voice.

"It's just you and me, Bree." For the first time in his life, he wasn't trying to rush a woman into bed, and it struck him that everything about the way his mind reacted to Brianna was different than it had been with anyone else.

She put her hands flat on his stomach, spreading warmth beneath her palms. "Nerves. It's been a long time, and I want to be with you more than anything. I just don't want to disappoint you."

"You're here with me. Nothing could make me happier. We don't have to do anything, Bree. I'll wait until you're ready. There's no rush."

"No. No," she whispered. "I don't want to wait."

She took his hand and led him toward the hallway.

"Wait." He grabbed her purse. "You promised Layla you'd

keep your phone on."

She took his hand again and led him down the hallway to the bedroom. Every step kicked up Hugh's anticipation, and when she closed the bedroom door behind them and began to unbutton his shirt, he could barely breathe. He set her purse on the dresser and stilled her hands beneath his.

Music filtered in through the speakers, and moonlight streamed through the sheer curtains. He wrapped his arms around her and kissed her, moving his body to the rhythm of the music. Her hips moved in tune to the sensual beat, and their tongues stroked a lustful dance of their own. She gazed into his eyes and fiddled with his buttons again. Hugh took her in another desperate kiss before taking off his shirt. Brianna's fingers found the sprinkling of fur on his chest, and her tentative touch magnified his desires. She pressed her lips to his chest, flicking a warm, wet path with her tongue. If he let her continue, he'd never last. Tonight he wanted to love her like she'd never been loved. He took her hands in his and kissed her palms.

"Let me," he whispered. He gathered her hair in one hand, exposing the flawless skin on her neck. He dragged his tongue along the base of her neck before settling his mouth over the gentle curve at the back of her neck and sucking, stroking her with his tongue. She breathed harder. Her hands pressed against his chest and he drew back again and gently turned her around. He nibbled his way down the back of her neck and slowly unzipped her dress to just below her shoulder blades. Her body stiffened, and when he caught a glimpse of the black lacy bra, his body did, too. He slid her dress off her shoulders and kissed a line down her spine to the zipper, then ran his tongue up the center again. His hands trembled as he ran them along her bare shoulders—so small and feminine they made him ache. Hugh licked the arc of her shoulder, then widened his mouth and loved the gentle curve of her arm.

Brianna arched back, and he reached around her and cupped her breasts through her lacy bra as he suckled the sensitive, smooth skin on the back of her neck. She moaned in pleasure, and it took all his restraint not to rip her dress off and take her right then. Instead, he teased her nipples into taut peaks. She grabbed his hands and pressed them harder against her. He lowered his hands to her rib cage and drew them down to her thin waist.

"Hugh," she whispered.

He moved her chin to the side and kissed her hard. When she tried to turn toward him, he held her in place. He wanted her to experience desire like she never had before. He wanted her loins to ache like his did. He drew back once again and she whimpered.

"Let me love you like you deserve to be loved," he whispered. He lowered her zipper to the curve of her ass and slid his hands down her sides, gripping her hips. Her body trembled harder, and he clutched her tighter, then whispered, "You're safe. I'd never do anything you don't want me to."

"I know." Her voice was a thready whisper.

He kissed the dimples at the base of her spine, then ran his hands up her delicate back and back down her sides, grazing her breasts with his fingers. Brianna sucked in a breath, and her dress slipped to the ground. Hugh kissed along the edge of her thong, just below her hips. Then his hands found the front of her thighs, gripping them tightly as his tongue ran along the underside of the lacy string, over the arch of her cheeks, to the crest of the crack between. He felt her body stiffen again, and he drew himself up to his full height and came around to her front. Her cheeks were flushed, her lips slightly parted. He ran his tongue along her full lower lip, and she closed her eyes.

"You're so beautiful, Bree." He kissed the line of her jaw, down her neck, to the indentation at the center of her collar-bone, where he licked her gently. He wanted to taste every inch of her skin. "Are you okay?" he whispered.

"God, yes." Each word was a long, heated breath.

"If I go too far, just tell me to stop. I promise not to do anything you don't want to." *No matter how difficult it is for me.*

She lifted his hand to her breast and put her arm around his neck, pulling him into another rough kiss. Her mouth was hot and wet, her breasts soft, her nipples hard, and the combination of the feminine lace and her insistent, thrusting tongue spurred him forward. He lifted her to the bed and laid her on her back. Jesus, she was even more exquisite lying there in her sexy lingerie than he'd ever imagined. She slipped off her heels as he came down upon her and pulled the strap of her bra down her arm, freeing her beautiful breast. He ran his tongue over the taut peak, teasing her as his other hand groped her trapped breast. Brianna writhed beneath him, and he took her breast in his mouth, loving and sucking as his other hand slid down her belly to between her thighs. She arched against his hand as he slid his fingers beneath the damp fabric and into her silky, wet center.

Brianna moaned as he stroked her slow and deep, his thumb teasing her swollen nub. Her nails dug into his shoulders. His erection throbbed beneath his slacks, and in one swift move he lowered himself to her waist and ripped her thong down.

"Yes," she panted.

His tongue found her center, and her knees fell open. Hugh

licked her sweetness fast and hard. His hands slid beneath her ass and lifted her up, allowing him to taste more of her, to thrust his tongue deeper; then he took her clit between his teeth and teased her with the tip of his tongue. She cried out, and he lowered her back to the bed and slid his finger inside, licking and teasing until he felt her muscles tighten around him and she arched back, slamming her eyes closed and gripping the sheets in fisted hands. He plunged deeper, faster, taking her over the edge. Her hips rocked against him as she filled the room with his name. Every tight pulsation was stronger than the next. Instead of bringing her down slowly, Hugh withdrew his fingers midorgasm. She whimpered again, and he brought his tongue to her once again.

Brianna sucked in a breath. "Oh God, oh God, oh God."

Within seconds, she was in the throes of another powerful release. Hugh loved watching her come apart. He gripped her hips again and licked her harder, until she was breathless, panting.

"No more…please."

He honored her wish and slid up her body, unhooking her bra and tossing it to the floor before pushing her breasts together and taking them both in his mouth. She buried her hands in his hair and arched into him again. Hugh couldn't help but reach down and tease her again. She was so swollen. He couldn't wait to be inside her, but first he teased her to the edge again, sinking his teeth just below her breast while he rubbed one nipple between his index finger and thumb and thrust his fingers into her center. She cried out, and he captured it in his mouth.

"Come for me, baby."

She shook her head against the mattress.

He withdrew his fingers, keeping his promise to stop if she asked him to. "No?"

With her eyes closed, she reached down and thrust his hand back where it had been. He smiled and kissed her again, stroking her softly between her legs without entering her. She moaned into his mouth again, and he wanted to bury himself inside her. *Not yet. One more time.* She pushed his hand, urging him inside, but he continued teasing, feeling her swell beneath his touch.

"Come for me now, Bree. You can do it."

She shook her head. "Need…you," she panted. "In me."

"No, you don't. You can do this." He moved down her body and licked the inside of her thighs, the sensitive area beside her sex, while he teased her with his fingers; then he brought his tongue to her again in long, slow strokes, lapping against the spot that made her body visibly shudder.

"Hugh," she whispered.

He licked her again, focusing his attention on that secret spot, until she clenched her teeth and threw her head back. Her knees clasped against his head and every blessed pulse landed on his lips.

Chapter Nineteen

BRIANNA BLINKED THROUGH the fireworks that exploded behind her eyelids. Her limbs battled fire and fatigue. Hugh's face came into view, and she pulled his lips to hers. Hugh kissed her sensuously, his tongue running over every inch of her mouth, as if he were trying to memorize the map of it. She ran her hands through his thick hair, and he felt so right, so familiar, yet also new and different. She drew back and searched his eyes, finding the same lustful desires she felt churning within her, and then, in the next breath, even more emotion. A deeper longing, akin to the emotions she'd been trying to tamp down for fear of scaring him away.

"Let me touch you," she whispered.

He kissed her again, shimmying out of his pants and briefs and tossing them to the floor. He brushed her hair away from her face. "You don't have to."

"I want to." She kissed him and urged him onto his back. She'd been thinking about touching him since he'd taken off his shirt. She ran her fingers along his rippled stomach and realized that she'd never been with a real man—and Hugh was one hundred percent solid masculinity. She slid her body on top of his and kissed him as he'd kissed her, deep, hard, and commanding. And it felt damn good. She'd held back for so long, and with Hugh, she wanted to let it all go. She kissed the whiskers that peppered the chiseled line of his jaw and ran her tongue in the dip of his adorable dimples, which softened his intense features. She'd never explored a man's body, and as she slid farther down and touched his nipples, she wanted to kiss them. She glanced at Hugh, and his eyes were closed, so she lowered her mouth to his nipple and it pebbled beneath her tongue. He moaned and ran his hands along her arms, fueling her desire to taste the other one. She covered his nipple with her mouth and licked, then sucked. His chest tensed and his heartbeat sped up beneath her touch. She never imagined a man would like that a much as a woman. Brianna realized that she had a lot to learn, and the thought sent a rush of heat through her as her hands traveled down his perfectly sculpted torso to his powerful thighs. His formidable erection lifted from his belly, and she hovered above it. She'd been with only two men in her life. The first boy she thought she loved, her sophomore year in college, and then Layla's father, Todd. Sex had been fast and efficient with both. Never had anyone done the things Hugh had just done to her, and she'd never done what she was considering now as she looked at the length of him and knew she could never get it all in her mouth. She should have asked Kat for pointers.

Brianna closed her eyes and let her heart take the lead. She kissed his hip, his massive thigh, then moved her hands to his shaft and wrapped her fingers around him. He was so thick that she had to see for herself the distance between her fingertips. She ran her tongue from base to tip and felt him shudder beneath her. She smiled, wanting to please him as much as he'd pleased her. Now she wished she'd spent at least a little time learning something more about sex. She always figured things would happen naturally, but she felt lost. She licked him again and he groaned. There was no hiding her lack of finesse as she paused again. Her mind screamed, *Just do it!* But her heart told her she needed guidance, and she wanted that to come from Hugh. With his careful hands and thoughtful eyes, she felt safe to explore with him.

Hugh opened his eyes and touched her cheek. "Come here," he whispered.

She joined him, feeling her cheeks flush.

"You don't need to do that, Bree. I just want to be close to you." He kissed her softly.

"I want to. I've just never done it before." She searched his eyes for the slightest hint of laughter, but they were filled with warmth.

He came up on one elbow and pulled her against him. "Oh, baby."

Brianna took a deep breath and closed her eyes, then whispered, "Show me?"

"Bree, you really don't have to." He drew back and took her face in his hands. "I wanted to love you and make you feel good. I don't expect anything in return."

When she looked into his eyes, she saw that he was telling her the truth. He didn't expect a damn thing, but she wanted to touch him, to taste him, to be as close to him as he was to her. "I want to. I want to be close to you and make you feel good, too. I just..." She looked down.

"You sure?"

She nodded. He took her hand in his and wrapped it around his hard length. His hand was warm and big, engulfing hers entirely. He kissed her cheek and whispered, "Lick me. Get me wet."

She slid down the bed and licked the length of him again; then she wrapped her hand around him again, and he wrapped his hand over hers and gently squeezed.

"Lick the top," he whispered.

She lowered her head and licked the tip as he moved her hand in tight strokes; then she took the whole head in her mouth. He moaned, still guiding each stroke as she teased him with her tongue.

"Jesus, Bree. You don't need any help."

She took him in deeper, and he moved her hand down, cupping his balls. His other hand tangled in her hair, and he rocked his hips, moving himself in and out of her mouth. Brianna was surprised to feel the heat between her thighs increase and swell with desire. She licked the length of him again, then ventured lower, licking his balls. They tightened beneath her tongue, and Hugh sucked in a breath. She did it again, enjoying the empowering feeling and the way it made her pulse ratchet up. She wrapped her hand around the base, and his hand fell away as she buried him in her mouth. She took him as deep as she could, then sucked as she drew him out slowly, centering her attention on the tip, while her hand continued long, luxurious strokes. His other hand found her head again and urged her faster, deeper. When she felt his erection grow a fraction harder, she pulled back, exposing his wet shaft to the cool air. He groaned, a guttural, hungry sound that spurred her on. She moved between his legs and licked his balls, stroking him with her hand. She watched him clench his jaw and close his eyes.

"Bree," he whispered.

She continued licking, stroking, then took his full length in her mouth again.

"Bree." Her name was an urgent warning.

She pulled back, worried she'd hurt him.

"Jesus, Bree. You're gonna make me come."

Isn't that the point?

"I want to make love to you," he said quickly. He reached over to his nightstand and grabbed a condom from the drawer, ripped it open with his teeth, and slid the thin latex on. She lay beside him, and his eyes softened again. "Okay?"

"Yes, yes. Stop asking." She wiggled beneath him, and he looked down at her.

"I just want you to be sure. I don't want to—"

She leaned up and kissed him. "Take me, Hugh. Please, take me, love me, fuck me."

He entered her slowly, filling every bit of her. The pressure was so intense, she gasped. Her hips rose to meet each slow thrust, which took her closer to the edge again. Brianna had never had an orgasm with a man, much less multiple orgasms. He lowered his mouth to hers, and she wanted to kiss him forever. His tongue moved in the same slow cadence as his sex, and she wanted more, harder, faster. She reached for his hips and urged him faster. He deepened the kiss, burying his hands in her hair again.

"Bree," he said in one long breath between kisses. "Ah, Jesus. I'm not gonna last."

Brianna could barely concentrate. She heard the words, but her body was already in a frenzy of need and want, her muscles clenched around him. She felt every blessed inch as he penetrated her deeper, harder, the tension of his hands in her hair bringing a wild mix of pain and pleasure. When he settled his teeth over her neck and his tongue lapped at her before he took her neck in an intoxicating mix of nips, sucks, and licks, she spiraled over the edge. Her hips bucked and rocked. She clawed at his shoulders and called out his name with no ability to quiet her voice. Hugh's release was seconds behind. He buried his face in her hair and groaned and grunted through each powerful thrust. His sexual energy aroused her even more, and she felt her body climbing up, up, up. She wrapped her legs around him, and in one swift move he pushed a pillow beneath her hips, lifting her to the perfect angle for him to take her up and over the peak of another mind-numbing climax.

Chapter Twenty

BRIANNA LAY ON her back with her arm over her eyes. She never imagined that making love could feel so good, and she wondered if that's what it was like for everyone. Had she just been too young to know any better before? Is that why Kat always pushed her to get close to someone? Jesus, her whole body was on fire, humming with a gratified afterglow. If she'd known sex could be this amazing, she'd never have waited so long. Now that she'd experienced making love with Hugh, there was no turning back—and there was definitely no carrying out a twelve-year plan. *What on earth was I thinking?*

Hugh came out of the bathroom naked and ridiculously handsome, with a playful smile on his lips and a contented look in his eyes. He climbed onto the bed beside her and laid his hand across her belly.

"You okay?"

"You've asked me that a hundred times. I'm more than okay." She touched his cheek. She loved how he worried about her, but she didn't want him to think of her as fragile. "Hugh, I'd let you know if I wasn't all right. Okay?"

He nodded.

"You're so thoughtful, but you don't need to ask to touch

me. I love when you touch me, and you should just know I'm okay unless I say otherwise, or I look like I'm having trouble."

"Okay, fair enough. I just don't want you to feel pressured. I really like you, Bree, and I feel like I want to protect you from everything. I don't think I've felt this way about anyone. Ever." He drew circles on her belly with his finger. "It kind of scares the crap out of me, so I'm probably being even more careful."

Relief swept through her. "Oh, thank God."

"Thank God it scares me?" He wrinkled his brow.

"Kind of, yeah, because I feel the same way. I feel so comfortable with you, and I never knew...*that*...could be so amazing."

He laughed. "It's not. I think it's only amazing when you have feelings for the person; otherwise it's just kind of a lot of energy for a few minutes of pleasure. The reason everything feels so good between us is because of the emotions we have for each other."

"Are you a secret sex-ed teacher?" She ran her finger down the line of his jaw.

He kissed her forehead. "Hardly. I just know that there's a lot of emptiness that goes along with meaningless sex." He looked away, and this time, she drew his eyes back to her.

"My turn to ask. Are you okay?"

He nodded, but his eyes were solemn. "There's just all this stuff going through my head. When I look at you, I want to be sure you're happy. When we were close, my thoughts weren't about me or even about being inside you. I was thinking about what I wanted to do for you. How I hoped you felt. And afterward, I couldn't help but think about Layla." He lay back down beside Brianna and held her hand. "I want you to be sure of me before she knows about us, even if that takes a long time.

I already feel so much toward you that the thought of not being with you is painful. I can't imagine what it would be like to get close to Layla and then be out of her life for whatever reason. For me or for her. It would be confusing for her, hurtful for me."

"Okay," she whispered. "You do that a lot, you know."

"What?"

"Take Layla's feelings into consideration. That means a lot to me."

His dimples appeared when he faced her. "I told you. She owns half your heart. I'll always consider her."

Brianna felt another tug on her heart.

Chapter Twenty-One

HUGH CLIMBED FROM bed at five o'clock the next morning and took a shower. He hoped to get a run in before Brianna woke up. He'd slacked off in the last few days, and it was imperative that he was in top shape for the race. She looked so cute curled up beside him that he hated to move from beside her naked body, but if he had any hope of being at the track by eight, he had to get a move on. He couldn't remember another Sunday when he wasn't itching to get to the track. Today he wished he had another twelve hours—hell, he wished he had another month—before he had to leave again.

He came out of the bathroom with a towel wrapped around his waist and found Brianna leaning on her elbow looking at her phone. Her hair cascaded over her left breast, and when her eyes darted to him, she set her phone on the nightstand.

"Now, that's a welcome sight in the morning," she said, then licked her lips.

He sat down on the edge of the bed and kissed her. "So are you."

"Were you planning on leaving me here? I guess you can't exactly take off after sex when you're in your own bed. I'm sorry. I'll just shower really quickly and go." She started to climb out of the bed, and he pinned her to the bed with a hot stare.

"Take off after sex? After everything I said to you last night?"

She shrugged, and a mischievous smile played across her lips. He tickled her ribs, and she screamed with delight.

"Okay, okay. I was kidding." She hung on to his hands.

He kissed her again, feeling a tightening in his groin. "Yeah? Well, I'm more sensitive than I look. You'd better be careful, or you'll hurt my feelings." Hugh ran his hand through his wet hair.

"Maybe you could ugly yourself up a little. Then I'd want to leave," she teased.

He pulled the blanket back, exposing her naked body in all its glory. "Maybe you could put some clothes on and I wouldn't want to stay."

"Maybe I'll just stay naked forever then." She ran her eyes down his chest.

The hell with my run.

AN HOUR LATER, they climbed into the Roadster and headed toward Brianna's apartment. She couldn't take her eyes off of Hugh while he drove. She could hardly believe the last few days had really happened. Every few minutes, he glanced over and smiled.

"That was an amazing night and an even more wonderful morning." Brianna touched his shoulder. She hated the idea of not being with him for an hour, much less a day or several days. They hadn't made any plans beyond taking her home, and for an organized, scheduled woman like Brianna, it was unsettling.

Hugh pressed a kiss to the back of her hand. "Maybe now you can hold on to those happier thoughts of your dad from the afternoon before he left, and when you think of the next morning, instead of seeing the end of your life with him, you can see the beginning of ours together."

Ours. Together. How did that happen so fast? She had no idea, but the butterflies in her stomach told her not to overthink it. She fidgeted with the edge of her dress.

"I will." She thought about earlier that morning, when she'd seen Hugh coming out of the bathroom in nothing but a towel. All of the hot and heavy feelings she'd experienced the evening before had come rushing back. She was glad she'd had time to text Kat while he was in the shower. She'd asked what the morning after was supposed to be like, and Kat had answered, *As hot as the night before. Or hotter.* That was all the rationalization Brianna needed to allow her desires to take over. She'd woken up wanting him all over again, but she'd worried that she was only feeling that because it had been so long since she'd had sex. One kiss from Hugh and his tented towel had told her that he'd had the same urges. Making love with him in the morning had been as earth-shattering as it had been the night before.

"What's your plan today?" Hugh asked as they pulled into the parking lot of her apartment complex.

"I work from three to eight at the tavern, so I was gonna hang out and play a game with Layla, but I think I'll take her to the park. She'd like that."

Hugh parked the car and opened the door for Brianna. "Is your mom watching her while you work?"

"Not tonight. Her neighbor Mrs. Cranston is taking her. I've known her forever. She's like seventy years old and Layla loves her. She watches her sometimes when my mom can't."

"Do you get a dinner break?"

"Twenty minutes around seven. You don't have to walk me up to my apartment. I'm just gonna change my clothes and then pick up Layla."

"I want to. What kind of boyfr—"

Boyfriend? She pretended not to notice his use of the word, even though her skin tingled with excitement. *Boyfriend.* She loved the sound of it.

He pulled her closer. "Boyfriend." He looked at her and smiled. "Do people still say that when they're my age, or is that a high school word?"

"You're asking the wrong girl." *Yes! Use it!*

"Is it too possessive? Too limiting for a girl like you?"

She saw the tease in the lifting of his brows and decided to tease him right back. "Well, it is a bit limiting."

"Yeah, that's what I thought." He focused on the building with a serious look in his eyes.

She'd expected him to laugh. Disappointment filled her heart. Did he think she'd meant it? Hugh put his arm around her and pulled her close, his eyes trained on the bearded guy who watched them from his balcony. She hated the way he stared at her. She had become so used to it that she usually just stared at the ground or put a protective arm around Layla and hurried past. She was glad when Hugh had insisted on walking her inside.

Upstairs, Brianna fumbled for her keys, chewing on the idea that he'd nixed the use of the word *boyfriend. It's just a word. So why does it hurt so much?* She dropped the keys, and Hugh bent down and picked them up, then found the proper key and unlocked the door.

He pushed the door open. "After my girlfriend." He waved a path for her to enter.

She couldn't keep the silly smile from her lips, then kissed him as she walked past. "I like that," she admitted.

He pulled her into his arms and kissed her again. "So do I."

The apartment smelled like fresh roses. Brianna added fresh water to the vase. "I hope these last forever."

"I would say nothing lasts forever, but I'm not sure I believe that anymore."

She glanced at his profile as he went to the glass doors in the living room. He was nothing like the man she'd thought he would be. He flipped the lock on the slider, and it dropped without clicking.

"Doesn't this lock?"

"No. It never has. But we're on the third floor, so I'm not too worried." She set the vase down on the counter.

"Do you have a screwdriver?"

"Sure." She dug through a kitchen drawer and handed it to him. "It's really fine. I don't think anyone's gonna go Spider-Man on us and scale the wall."

He was already taking the lock apart.

"I'm gonna change real quick." While she changed her clothes, she called out to him, "What are you doing today?"

"I'm going to the track. I've gotta meet my pit crew and spend a few hours practicing and going over things for next weekend."

"Are you excited about it?"

"I love to drive, but I'm not excited about not being with you," he said.

Brianna pulled on a pair of jeans and a sweater. She put on makeup, spritzed perfume, and found Hugh looking over the photographs on the living room shelves. "You really didn't have to wait for me."

"I wanted to walk you back down. Besides, I'll take whatever time I can get." He held up a black-and-white photo of Layla in a red wooden frame. "You're really good at photography. Maybe we can get your camera fixed." He set the frame down on the bookshelf.

She shook her head. "It was old and not a very good one." She slid her feet into a pair of flat boots. "One day I'll get another one, and when Layla's a little older, I'll take pictures again. Right now there's no time anyway, so I'm not missing much."

He drew his brows together and spoke softly. "You're so patient, Brianna."

"Moms have to be."

"I put your screwdriver back in the drawer. The lock is missing a piece. It's like it's been taken apart and put back together without a key element. I can fix it for you while you're at work if you want." He put his arm around her as they locked the apartment and headed back downstairs.

"You don't have to do that. Even the maintenance guy couldn't fix it. They offered to replace the door, but it was really pricey." *I love that you want to fix my lock.*

"I'm a little smarter than a maintenance guy. I can have it fixed before you guys get home tonight."

"Sure." As she took her key off of her keychain, she realized that she didn't have an ounce of hesitation about giving him a key. She trusted him completely, and the ease with which that realization came shocked her.

"Wait. You'll need it to get in before work."

"I have a spare at my mom's. I'll pick it up when I get Layla."

"Okay, and I'll bring this one back to you at work."

He smiled and she knew he didn't mind, but she felt guilty after everything he'd already done for her. "Hugh, you don't have to do that. I can get it the next time I see you."

"Good, because that will be the next time you see me."

He walked her to her car, and she felt like she was in high school, waiting for the cutest boy in school to kiss her goodbye, even though Hugh wasn't a boy and they'd moved way beyond goodbye kisses. She tucked a strand of hair behind her ear and leaned back against the car.

"Can I text you later?" Hugh put his hands on her waist and a thrill ran through her.

"Of course. You can call if you'd like." As much as she appreciated his consideration of her, she wished he'd take for granted that he could call her, kiss her, or hug her anytime. Only she knew he couldn't, and she'd made that clear outside of Claude's studio. *Talk about sending conflicting messages.* But hadn't everything changed since then? Or was that only in her head?

"I don't want to complicate things for you and Layla. Your life runs like a finely tuned automobile, and I know how a tweak in the wrong direction can make for a bumpy ride." He kissed her cheek. "I had a great time last night."

"I've never had a better time, and I hate that we have to be apart." She touched his stomach with her fingertips. The memory of their lovemaking snaked its way into her head, and a shiver trailed down her back.

"It'll make our time together that much sweeter when we see each other again."

HUGH WATCHED BRIANNA drive away before heading back toward her apartment. He took the steps two at a time to the second floor. He pulled his shoulders back and stood up to his full six-foot-three inches before knocking on the door of apartment 202, the only one on the right that faced the parking lot. The last time Hugh had challenged a man about a woman was when Savannah was a sophomore in college. She'd come home for spring break and some jackass from out of town had been visiting his cousin. He made a comment to Savannah when she was riding by on her horse, and by the time Savannah arrived home, she was livid. With Treat, Dane, Rex, and Josh away at school, it was up to Hugh to set the guy straight. All it took was staring down his nose at the squirrely kid and Savannah had an apology within the hour. Now, as he stood outside the bearded man's door, Hugh had no idea what he might say to him. The man hadn't done anything more than leer at Brianna, but it was enough to give Hugh a bad feeling about him. For all Hugh knew, he was a nice guy, but he'd stake his claim and make sure that Brianna and Layla didn't run into any trouble.

The door swung open, and the scent of body odor wafted out the door. The bearded man looked like he belonged on *Duck Dynasty* with his thick, unkempt beard and beer gut that threatened to rip his dark T-shirt at the seams. The guy narrowed his beady green eyes and looked Hugh up and down. "Wadda you want?" He stood a solid eight inches shorter than Hugh with soft, doughy arms and an unwashed face.

Arms crossed, Hugh flexed his biceps. "Saw you eyeing my girlfriend."

His eyes shifted to the left, then back to Hugh. “And?”

Hugh lowered his chin, set his jaw, and pinned the man with a rottweiler’s death stare. “And there’s nothing but trouble waiting for you there.”

The man swished his jaw from side to side, his long, straggly beard moving along with it. He pushed the door closed.

Hugh reached out with his left hand and stopped the door, then closed the gap between them. He looked down at the man and gritted his teeth. “Make no mistake about what I’m saying. If she or her daughter so much as feel uncomfortable coming home at night, I won’t ask questions.” His chest expanded with each breath. He felt his nostrils flare as he tried to rein in the urge to grab the man by the throat and throw him up against the wall. “We straight?”

The man swished his jaw again.

Hugh stepped closer, hunkering over him and narrowing his eyes. “Got it?”

“Yeah, man. I got it.”

Chapter Twenty-Two

"MOMMY, LET'S SWING!" Layla ran toward the playground in her striped leggings and sweatshirt. Her pigtails bobbed with each step.

Brianna pushed her on the swing, thinking about last night. The park felt like an entirely different place. Last night it was an enchanting wonderland for just the two of them, which incited heightened emotions and well-hidden memories. Today it was anyone's park, as if the carousel and the lights had never existed.

Her phone vibrated with a text from Hugh. *How's Layla? Having fun?*

She smiled as she responded. *Great. At the park. Miss you.* Her finger hovered over the send button. She quickly deleted *Miss you,* then pushed send.

When he responded, her pulse sped up. *Wish I was there with u.*

She responded, *Wish u were 2. Miss you.*

Hugh texted back a minute later. *Gotta drive. Pit crew's waiting. Xox.*

She closed her eyes and thought, *Hugs and kisses. God, I miss your hugs and kisses.* She texted back, *Xox,* then put the phone in her pocket and returned her attention to her daughter, who was chatting about all things prince and princess.

"Grandma says we can make puppets and put on our own play with them," Layla yelled from the swing as she pumped her legs. Her white sneakers were covered with blue sequins that swirled and sparkled in the sun.

"That sounds like fun. I'd like to do that, too." Brianna had always enjoyed playing with Layla, and guilt tightened in her chest as a thought whispered through her mind. *I miss Hugh.* Dividing her attention was so unfamiliar that Brianna felt a twinge of guilt.

"I want to make a princess, a queen, and a prince."

"We can paint a castle for the background." Brianna smiled at the innocence of Layla's comment, and how the image she conjured up to meet her daughter's puppets was of her, Layla, and Hugh. Her cell phone vibrated, and she read the text from Kat.

Epic morning? She and Kat usually referred to Kat's sex life as epic or amazing. That she was about to text about her and Hugh sent a thrill of excitement through her.

Beyond. At park with Layla. Will fill u in 2nite.

The phone vibrated again with a response. *Yay! C U at 3.*

"Can we make the castle now, so we can surprise Grandma with it?" Layla asked.

"We sure can."

BACK AT THE apartment, Brianna carried Layla's overnight bag and held her hand. The bearded man was on the balcony when they arrived, and Brianna put her arm protectively over Layla's shoulder and trained her eyes on the sidewalk. She caught movement in her peripheral vision and lifted her gaze, catching sight of the man as he disappeared through the glass slider. Brianna breathed a sigh of relief.

She unlocked the door and Layla ran inside.

"Mommy! Someone brought flowers! And look, a present!" She grabbed the glittery box from the counter.

Darn it. She'd forgotten to hide the gift. "That was for you, actually. From a friend of mine."

Layla gasped. "For me? Can I open it?" She sat cross-legged on the floor and tore open the package.

Brianna's stomach twisted, easing only after she noticed that the present had sidetracked Layla from asking who had brought her flowers. She watched her lift the top of the box and set it on the floor, then leaf through a mound of tissue paper.

"Mommy, look!" Her eyes bloomed wide as she pulled out a pink dress—not the dress Hugh had shown Brianna earlier in the day, but a fancier one with white lace along the bottom edge, a white collar, and tiny polka dots that spread from the bottom and faded as they reached the waist.

"That looks like a birthday dress to me," Brianna said. Her heart beat so fast she put her hand on her chest. The box was much too big to hold only a dress. She watched Layla dig through the remaining tissue paper and pull out another box. She ripped off the wrapping paper and jumped up and down with the box in her arms.

"Mommy, Mommy, Mommy! Look!" Layla held up the box to show her.

"Drama Queen? What's that?"

"It's a game where you make your own stories! It's like a play only not in real life, and you get to make lots of stories not just one. Miranda has it!"

How did Hugh know about this game, and how come I didn't have a clue about it?

"Did you want that game?" She took the box from Layla and opened it. Then they sat at the coffee table in the living room and set up the game beside Candyland, the drawing and making of a castle forgotten.

Brianna spread the pieces of the game across the board and was surprised when Layla didn't reach for a single one.

"Layla, did you want this game?" she asked again.

Layla nodded. "Mommy, did Kat give me this?"

Brianna didn't have an answer ready. "Um, no."

"Was it really you? Did you get me this? Because if you did, you can take it back. I don't need it." Layla's eyes were so serious it brought Brianna to her side.

"Layla, why would I bring this back?"

"Because Miranda said it costs a million dollars, and we don't have a million dollars."

Brianna kissed her forehead, hating that Layla was aware of their financial situation at all, much less that she probably hadn't told her mother she wanted the game because it was expensive.

"I think Miranda was exaggerating." *But I'll Google it and find out.* "A different friend gave these things to you. He wanted you to have it. Otherwise he wouldn't have bought it for you." Part of her worried about Layla receiving an expensive gift. She didn't want to set up unrealistic expectations, and she definitely didn't want her daughter bragging to other kids and making them feel bad. As much as she hated adding a lesson to a happy moment, the mother in her wouldn't let the opportunity pass. She placed the game pieces on the board. "If I were you, I'd be careful how you tell your friends about this."

"Why?" Layla picked up the figurines and inspected their dresses and tiaras.

"Because maybe their parents can't afford this game, and you don't want your friends to feel bad because they don't have one." She watched Layla knit her eyebrows together. "How did you feel when Miranda told you she had it and that it cost a million dollars?"

Layla set the figurines down and shrugged.

"Well, you didn't ask me for the game, so I'm guessing you didn't feel happy, but maybe a little sad?" She lifted Layla's chin as Hugh had done so often to her, and the sadness in her daughter's eyes slayed her. She wanted to pull her close and tell her how sorry she was that she couldn't afford extravagant gifts and how much she loved her, but instead she used those feelings to teach Layla about kindness. "You wouldn't want your friends to feel that way, would you?"

Layla shook her head.

"I know you'll want to tell them about your new game, and that's okay, but maybe instead of saying, *Guess what I got*, the second you see them at school, you could tell them that you can't wait to share your new game with them on your birthday."

Layla's eyes lit up. "That's nicer, and they'll want to play it, too. I know they will. Miranda said we couldn't play it because she didn't want to lose any pieces, but I'm a good sharer. I don't mind."

Pride swelled in Brianna's chest. "The best sharer ever." She wondered if Layla would ever be okay sharing her with Hugh.

Chapter Twenty-Three

BY SIX THIRTY the dinner crowd had filtered from the tavern into the restaurant, leaving just a few customers in the bar. Brianna was glad for the break. She'd been watching the couple in the corner booth sucking face for most of her shift. They kissed every minute, and that only made her miss Hugh even more.

She wiped down a booth, picked up a tip from another table, and went behind the bar to catch up with Kat, still drawn to the kissing couple. She was mesmerized at how they kissed and pawed at each other. She knew Hugh was being careful with her, but she wanted more. She looked at the couple again. *I want that.*

"What's the plan with lover boy?" Kat lifted her eyebrows in quick succession. She wore her blond hair in a high ponytail and her tightest Old Town Tavern V-neck T-shirt.

"We don't have a plan."

"Oh no, and what does that do to your overscheduled little brain?"

"This is why I hate you. Do you really have to point out the obvious?"

Kat shrugged.

"Can I ask you something?"

"Go for it," Kat said, eyeing the couple who were now practically having sex in the booth.

"Can a guy respect you too much?"

"Oh God. What happened?" Kat set down the glass she'd been holding and folded her arms across her chest.

"Nothing. Hugh's just careful. He asks permission sometimes, and I know it's because I'm a mom and he respects me and all that, but I kinda want…" She looked at the couple in the corner again.

Kat smacked her chewing gum and followed her gaze. "Ah. So, tell him. Or show him. I vote for showing him."

Brianna purposefully stopped looking at the couple. "How do I do that without looking like a slut?"

"You've already slept with him. There's nothing left to look like. Just, you know." She moved in close and whispered, "Take him."

"Take him?" She narrowed her eyes. "Oh, *take* him. Right. I've already told him he didn't have to be so careful, but…"

Kat winked. "You go, girlfriend. But how are you holding up without a plan? You're not like that. Overplanning is how you manage."

"I'm trying to not be *that* person."

Kat put her cheek next to Brianna's and whispered, "I've got news for you, hon. You *are* that person." She patted Brianna's cheek. "That's why you're so great at being a mom. You think ahead in ways I never could."

Brianna sighed. "You know, while I was at the park with Layla, I thought about Hugh the whole time."

"Yeah, and?" Kat blew a bubble with her chewing gum.

"And…I've never done that before, thought about being

with a man when I'm supposed to be thinking about my daughter. I don't want to be one of those women whose mind is somewhere else when her child needs her." Brianna wiped her hands on the towel that hung from her belt. "It felt weird."

Kat shook her head. "You really have lived in a boxed-off mommy world for too long. Every parent thinks of other things or people when they're with their kids. That's normal, Bree. Just ask Mack. He'll tell you."

Mack walked behind Brianna to the far end of the bar. "Ask Mack what?"

"Mack, when you're with your daughter, what do you think about?" Kat crossed her arms and smacked her gum.

Mack had a daughter two years older than Layla, and he and his wife, Tami, had been married for ten years. "I don't know. Sports. The bar. My wife. Why?" He grabbed a large bottle of liquor and walked past them again toward the back room, stopping beside Brianna. "Something going on that I should know about?"

Brianna rolled her eyes. "No."

"She's thinking of a guy when she's with Layla," Kat said.

"Kat! Jesus, can't I have any privacy?" Brianna covered her face so Mack wouldn't see her cheeks flush again.

"What guy?" Mack asked.

"The guy from the other night," Kat explained. "Patrick Dempsey's look-alike."

"Oh my God, Kat. Really?" Brianna pushed past Mack and went into the stockroom. A second later, the door opened and Mack walked in.

"You okay?" He leaned against a metal shelf and crossed his arms.

"Yeah. Fine." She grabbed two bottles and headed for the

door.

Mack put his hand on her arm and lowered his chin. "Bree?"

She sighed. "Okay, fine." She set down the drinks. Mack was the closest thing she had to a big brother, even though he acted more like a father, and she knew she could trust him. "I went out with Hugh, the guy from the other night, and I really like him. A lot."

He crossed his arms and pressed his mouth into a tight line. "You know who he is?"

She nodded.

"I figured it out at about two in the morning after I met him. The name clicked." His eyes searched hers. "Capital Series driver."

"Yup."

"Bree, that's a fast crowd. You sure he treated you okay?" His eyes softened.

"Yeah, Mack." She leaned on the shelf beside him. "Better than okay. He's probably the nicest guy I've ever met." She smiled up at him. "Besides you, I mean."

He nodded unconvincingly.

"Mack, he's careful with me, and protective, but not overly possessive, and he's always concerned about Layla and not messing things up for us."

"Just promise me you'll be careful and be smart. I'd hate to have to kill him if he hurt you."

Brianna leaned against his side. "Thanks, Mack. Can I ask you something?"

"Anything, you know that."

"Am I weird?" She watched his eyes shine with laughter, then grow serious.

"What do you mean?"

"Kat thinks I'm weird because I'm used to giving Layla my full attention. I just don't want to be one of those women who slights her kid, you know? But I also don't want to be some kind of freak who isn't relatable. I don't want to turn around when she's eighteen and have been so blocked off that even she thinks I'm weird." She sighed. "I wish parenthood came with a handbook."

Mack put his arm around her. "Don't we all? You're weird, Bree—that's for sure—but not a bad weird. We're all a little weird. I've watched you raise Layla since she was a baby, and you're a little overly focused, but that doesn't mean it's a bad thing." He started to reorganize the bottles on the shelves. "You spend all of your time with Layla or at work. All your brain thinks about is what you know, right? So since Layla was born, you've been thinking about work and Layla. You talk with Kat, or go shopping, or whatever, spend time with your mom, I guess. But that's a really small piece of your life. Suddenly Braden shows up." He winked at her.

She couldn't help but smile.

"He comes into your life, but you're so focused on this safe world you set up for yourself and Layla that you don't really know how—or if you want to—venture outside of that world. So now you've got life over here." He waved his left arm. "And over here." He waved his right arm. "And in the center are you and Layla. You're playing a game of tug-of-war. But, Bree, that game is all in your head, because every day your daughter goes out into the world with her friends. She laughs; she plays; she does schoolwork. She's growing up and learning, but you..." He frowned and narrowed his eyes. "You don't give yourself a chance to expand your own life experiences."

"So what are you saying? I should join more of life and forget about doing the right thing by my daughter?"

"No. Definitely not." He took her hand and led her away from the shelf. "Bree, you're twenty-eight. You're still a kid yourself. You deserve to fall in love, have fun, learn, take pictures, for God's sake. You used to do that all the time."

"My camera broke."

"You know what I mean. Being a good mother and being a woman don't have to be mutually exclusive. Look at Tami. She's a mom, but she's also a woman, with me and in general. She gets her hair done, she goes out with friends, and she still comes home and loves us all up. And I think it makes her a better mother by doing those things."

Brianna sighed. "So why do I feel so guilty?" She covered her face.

"Because you've been perfect—and weird—for a very long time. And because you care. Trust your instincts, Bree. If Braden isn't the right guy for you, you'll know it in your heart. If he is..." He shrugged. "You'll know that, too. But you have to start by allowing yourself to be a woman. It's okay to think about a guy you like while you're with Layla. I'd worry you didn't like him very much if you didn't think about him. Especially this early on in a relationship."

She sighed. "Thanks, Mack. Why is it that when you explain it to me, I get it, but when Kat says it, I feel like she's just pushing me to go out and have fun?"

"Because I'm old and she's young. And with age comes a false facade of being wise."

Brianna arched a brow.

"Or some shit like that." He laughed.

The door opened, and Kat popped her head into the stockroom. "Bree, lover boy is here."

"He's here?" *Oh my God. I look like hell.* She reached up and patted her hair.

"You look beautiful," Mack said with a smile. He looked at his watch. "You're on break anyway. Go."

HUGH HAD WAITED all day to see Brianna, and as she came through the stockroom doors, he felt a flutter in his chest. It took all his willpower not to sweep her into his arms and kiss her right then and there.

"Hi." He reached for her hand and brought it to his lips.

"Hi. What are you doing here?" Her eyes darted around the bar, and he realized that Mack and Kat were both watching them.

He released her hand and nodded at Mack, then waved at Kat. "I know you only have twenty minutes, but I thought I might monopolize at least fifteen of them."

She tucked a strand of hair behind her ear. "Sure." She pulled the towel from her belt and set it on the bar. "Let me get my jacket."

He watched her walk away in her curve-hugging jeans and flat-bottomed boots. She was so damn sexy, and she didn't even know it. Even her Old Town Tavern T-shirt made her look like the most exquisite and seductive girl-next-door he'd ever seen.

They walked down the street hand in hand. Hugh had been trying to be respectful of her time, her space, and her reputation, and even though she'd given the green light to their intimacy, he still held back. Hugh was used to moving fast, and he worried that if he let his true emotions take control, he might smother her—or worse, scare her off completely. He had to test the waters.

Hugh pulled her around the side of the building and took her in a long, avaricious kiss. "God, I've missed you."

Brianna hooked her finger in his belt. "Me too," she whispered.

He took her cheeks in his hands and pressed another kiss to her lips. They were definitely in sync. Her eyelids hung heavily, and her lips remained parted. Holy hell, she was so damn hot that he had to remind himself she had only a few minutes. He drew further away to calm his desires.

"I…uh…I fixed your lock, and I saw that Layla opened her gift. I'm glad you gave it to her."

Brianna held his gaze. "She found it on the counter and she loved it. Thank you, but you really didn't have to buy her those things. She's just fin—"

Jesus, I want to kiss you. He shoved his hands in his pockets to keep from touching her. "I wanted to. I'm glad she loved it." He didn't have a plan for the fifteen minutes with her. He'd just needed to see her.

Brianna fiddled with the edge of her jacket.

"Hey, you okay? Did I overstep my bounds with the kiss? Or the gift?" His stomach lurched.

She shook her head and took a step closer to him; then she reached up and took his cheeks in her hands and stood on her tiptoes. He lowered his mouth to hers and kissed her again, soft and tender.

"I've been thinking about you all day," she whispered.

She kissed him again, and Hugh backed her up against the wall, allowing himself to kiss her like he *needed* to kiss her—like he'd *wanted* to kiss her all afternoon—passionate and deep, until neither of them had any breath left in their lungs. She ground her hips into his and he couldn't help but run his hand down the delicious curve of her hip and grab hold of her backside.

He pulled back, and she said, "Kiss me," in one long breath. She grabbed the back of his head and pressed his lips to hers again, capturing his next breath.

Jesus. She drove him crazy. He'd have to walk back to the bar with a hard-on and no hope of being able to hide it.

"Next time, please don't hesitate." She looped her index finger in the waist of his pants.

"I was trying to be respectful."

"I got it. You respect me. Hugh, I want to experience the real you, and whatever that is, I'm not afraid of it."

"You may not realize what you're asking. I'm a thrill seeker—not with other women, but once I let my emotions take over, my carnal desires won't be far behind. I might smother you." He dragged his eyes down to her heaving chest and let his eyes linger there, then brought them back up again, weighing her expression, which got hungrier with each breath. "I don't want to screw things up with you. I force myself to slow down and ask if I can touch you." He cupped her hip in his hand.

"Don't," she commanded, with serious eyes and an expression to match.

He took his hand off her hip and she grabbed it and put it back.

"Don't think of me like that," she said. "I mean, think of me with respect, but I can tell you're holding back, and I want to experience you full-on, Hugh. If I'm going to risk my organized and overly scheduled life, then I want to do it right. I'll never do anything that'll jeopardize Layla or the world she knows, but if we're alone, or in bed together…" Her cheeks flushed.

"Love you like I want to?"

She nodded.

He breathed heavily. "You might want to retract that the next time we're alone together."

She bit her lower lip again, before whispering, "Good."

Sweet Lord, Brianna had no idea how his feelings for her had multiplied over the afternoon, or how much he wanted to crawl right back under the sheets with her.

"When I get back from my race next weekend, I have a couple months off, and I've been thinking that I'd spend them here with you and Layla. You might regret your decision when you see me more often."

She narrowed her eyes. "I can't wait to find out."

Chapter Twenty-Four

BRIANNA'S HEART FELT as if it might explode. She couldn't believe she'd told Hugh what she wanted, and when she saw the dark, wild look in his eyes, a shock of apprehension ran through her—and just as quickly excitement chased it away. He held the door to the tavern open as they returned.

"Did you say you get a couple months off? Months?" she asked as he helped her take off her coat.

"I usually take off some of November, December and January. I'm an on-again off-again road warrior for most of the year." Hugh looked around the busy bar.

"A road warrior?" She grabbed her towel from behind the bar and looped it over her belt, then grabbed an order pad as she noticed two couples settling into the booths.

"The race schedule runs thirty weeks out of the year. When I race the circuit, I'm on the road a lot of that time. Listen, you need to work. I'll sit down and have a soda and watch you for a minute or two." He raised his eyebrows with a coy smile. "Then I'll take off so you're not distracted. You can call me after Layla's asleep and we can talk."

Road warrior? What was I thinking? The thought of being apart for even half of that time was too much. She felt her heart breaking and knew she couldn't mask the ache.

"Okay," she managed. She headed for the new customers before Hugh saw her face. *Thirty weeks. Oh my God. I can't do this to Layla. Or myself.* Hugh settled into a seat at a nearby table, and her heart twisted; her stomach ached. She took the customers' orders and went behind the bar to make their drinks.

"So? Did you show or tell?" Kat whispered.

Brianna's lower lip trembled. *Don't cry. Don't cry.*

"Bree? Oh my God. Bree. What happened?" Kat took the glass from Brianna's trembling hand. "Honey, what happened?"

She opened her mouth to speak, but nothing came out. Tears tumbled down her cheeks.

"Mack?" Kat called.

Mack came behind the bar and stopped cold when he saw Brianna's tear-filled eyes. "What happened?" Mack shot a look at Hugh and took a step in his direction.

Brianna grabbed his shirt. "Mack, no," she whispered. "He didn't do anything. It's not that."

"Then what is it?" Mack kept his eyes trained on Hugh.

Brianna glanced across the bar at the same time the door to the bar opened and Layla and Mrs. Cranston walked in.

"Oh God." Brianna wiped her eyes.

Layla ran up to the bar. "Mommy! Mr. Cranston had to go to the hospital and I need to stay here."

Brianna looked at Mrs. Cranston. She had a frightened look in her red-rimmed eyes. "What happened?"

"We're not sure. He had chest pain, and you know Mr. Cranston. He could have had it for weeks before saying anything. I'm sorry, Brianna. Your mom is out until midnight with that evening job, and I didn't have anyone else to take her."

"Don't be silly. Go, and thank you for bringing her here. Do you need a ride to the hospital?" Brianna came around the bar and hugged Mrs. Cranston.

"No, thank you, dear. I've got my car. I'd better go." She hurried out the door.

"Of course. I hope he's okay." Brianna put her hand on Layla's shoulder and looked at Mack. "Mack." She glanced down at Layla, then at the full tables and booths.

Mack blew out a breath. She could see that he needed her to work. Brianna took Layla's hand and walked her to the end of the bar. "You can sit here and color while I work." *Shit, shit, shit.*

"Brianna, she really needs someone to watch her. We're too busy for you to do both, and we can get into trouble with her at the bar." Mack's gaze was soft, and Brianna knew he wasn't trying to be a stickler, but he was right. She was too busy to be a mom and a bartender. Something had to give.

Hugh came to the bar, and Mack moved beside him.

Brianna shot a look at Mack. "Mack, please." She caught a glimpse of Kat, who was rushing from table to table.

Mack crossed his arms.

"Hi, Mack." Hugh smiled at Mack, then narrowed his eyes. "Why are you looking at me like that?"

"You tell me," Mack said.

Hugh's eyes darted between the two. "Bree?"

"*Ugh.* Mack, I told you it wasn't him. Hold on, Hugh." She waved a hand at Layla. "Honey, I'll be right back." She dragged Mack to the other side of the bar with Kat on her heels.

"It's not him. Okay?" Brianna said to them. "He didn't do anything. I just didn't realize how many weeks he traveled each year, and once I did..."

"Brianna, that's why you were crying? Jesus, you scared the shit out of me. I didn't want to be known as the guy who beat up Hugh Braden." He pulled Brianna out of earshot of the customers. "Bree, if you guys really stay together, you won't be apart during that time. Lots of those guys are married. Their wives and children travel with them and they bring along tutors for their kids, or they travel back and forth. Listen, if you were all broken up over being apart, then you must really like him. Give it a chance." He took her by the shoulders and turned her around. "Look."

She watched Hugh drawing with Layla at the bar. His dimples deepened and his eyes smiled…at her daughter. Brianna melted beneath Mack's grip. "Oh, Mack. I'm in so much trouble."

"Things could be worse." Mack nodded at Tracie, who was headed directly for Hugh.

Brianna groaned. "I got this."

Kat cut her off. "No. This one's on me."

Tracie pressed her body against Hugh's back and whispered in his ear, "Are you back here looking for a date?"

Hugh cringed and shifted his body like a protective shield in front of Layla.

Kat narrowed her eyes and slammed her order pad on the bar. Hugh drew his eyebrows together, and before she could utter a word, Hugh said, "Actually, my date nights are filled up for the foreseeable future. And if you'll excuse me, Layla and I would like to finish our game of tic-tac-toe."

Tracie pursed her lips, glanced over at Layla, and then shot a scalding stare at Brianna.

"That's right, Red. He is taken with a capital T," Kat said with a shake of her head.

Tracie stomped off through the restaurant doors. Hugh nodded at Kat. "Thank you, Kat."

"My pleasure." Kat leaned down and whispered, "I've been wanting to do something like that for months." She tapped the napkin in front of Layla. "Hey, beautiful. You've got the most handsome date in the place."

Brianna put her hand on Layla's shoulder. She watched her daughter look from Hugh to Kat, then back again. "He's not my date." Layla giggled. "He's my handsome prince."

Brianna didn't know it was possible for a heart to break apart and reassemble so quickly.

Hugh caught her eye and winked. "I can entertain Layla while you work." He looked at Layla and smiled. "We'll be just fine, won't we?"

Layla nodded. "Yes, Mommy. Please?"

I think he just might be my handsome prince, too.

Chapter Twenty-Five

"I DIDN'T MEAN to force myself into Layla's life. She was there, and you seemed upset, and you said not to hold back. I just let my instincts take over." Hugh stood beside Brianna while she wiped down a booth. Mack had already closed the bar, and Layla was at another booth half awake, drawing pictures.

"That's okay. I'm glad you did. It kind of makes things easier. I wasn't sure how or when to introduce you. Now I don't have to worry about it." She let out a sigh and looked at Layla. "She just sort of goes with the flow, doesn't she?"

"She's pretty remarkable. I was the scribe to her muse. She sure does love princes and princesses."

Brianna laughed. "She's in a princess stage right now."

"You're going to think this is a frivolous waste, but would it be terrible if she got some dress-up stuff for her birthday? A Disney princess dress or something like that? Little girls love that stuff."

She closed her eyes and sighed. "I'm not sure what I think about her believing in all this fairy tale stuff. It's not real life, and it sets her up to be hurt by the harsh realities of life."

Hugh's eyes narrowed and his voice grew serious. "Dreaming is all you have as a kid. It's what pulls you through the difficult times and inspires you to work harder."

"My childhood wasn't exactly filled with dreams. It was filled with worries. Hopes maybe, but not really dreams," she admitted.

"Then don't you want something more for Layla?" He wrinkled his forehead.

"Is this what I have to look forward to? She'll wrap you around her little finger and you'll spoil her rotten and then I'll have a monster on my hands? She'll expect life to be one big fairy tale."

Hugh wrapped his arms around her waist. "Look at that face." He looked at Layla sitting sleepily in the booth across the bar. She yawned and rubbed her eyes. "Does she look like she could ever be a monster?" He kissed Brianna and felt her stiffen within his arms. "Bree? I thought you told me not to hold back."

She pried herself from his arms. "I did, and I meant it. But…" She nodded at Layla. "I need to explain to her that we're seeing each other or she's gonna be mighty confused."

"Of course." *Shit.* He'd been so wrapped up in Brianna's desire for him not to hold back his emotions that he wasn't thinking straight. "Do you want me to be there when you tell her?"

Brianna looked at her daughter and sighed. "I think I'd better talk with her first." She leaned against the booth, fidgeting with the towel. "Hugh, before I talk to her, I think we need to talk. Can we talk after she goes to bed?"

"Sure. Should I be worried?"

"No. It's just that telling her is a huge step, and I want to be sure we've thought things through before we do that." She touched Hugh's arm, but her eyes remained trained on Layla.

"Do you want me to wait and walk you to your car, or would you rather I didn't?"

"Yes, please. I want you to."

Hugh breathed a sigh of relief. "I'll go wait with Layla."

BY THE TIME Brianna finished cleaning up, Layla had fallen asleep across Hugh's lap. He sat with his head back and one arm protectively around her.

"I'm sorry." Brianna slid in across the booth from him. "The night ran much later than I expected."

Hugh spoke softly. "My only plans for the night were to work out and think about you." He reached across the table and held her hand. "I got to meet Layla and I was near you. Double bonus."

"It seems like you're always rescuing me, and before I met you, I never seemed to need rescuing." Brianna had been protective of Layla for so long, and with Hugh the introduction came so easily. Naturally. She'd anticipated Layla being confused or at the least upset when she met Hugh, but he'd woven his way into their lives seamlessly. And from the look of Layla sleeping peacefully on his lap and Hugh looking perfectly content as her pillow, she realized it was because it was *him*. Everything about Hugh felt right. *Even this.*

"Sometimes it's the people who don't know they need rescuing that need it the most. But the truth is, you didn't need rescuing at all. I have no doubt that you would have figured out your car situation, and you would have figured out tonight, when Layla showed up, too. But it never hurts to have someone to help share the burden of these little snags as they arise. Come on. Let's get this little princess home." Hugh gathered Layla's stories and put them in his pocket; then he picked up Layla and covered her with his coat. She snuggled against his shoulder. With one arm around Brianna's shoulder and the other safely holding her daughter, they left the bar.

Brianna wished she had a working camera. Layla's cheek rested beside Hugh's, and the moonlight cast a romantic glow across them both. She imagined the angles she'd shoot and envisioned the finished photograph hanging on the wall above his fireplace. *I'm getting way too far ahead of myself.*

He settled Layla into her booster seat and hooked the seat belt, then covered her with his jacket. "She's out like a light." He closed the car door softly. "Did you decide if I can do something princessy for her?"

He looked so hopeful that she couldn't say no. "One princessy thing. Deal?"

"Deal. Every little girl should have one princessy dream to hold on to. Why don't I follow you home and carry her upstairs?"

The image of Hugh carrying Layla to her apartment incited thoughts of a future together, and Brianna's stomach fluttered again. "I can do it. I've been carrying her since before she was born."

"I know you can. Let me ask you another way. Is it okay if I come with you and carry her upstairs? That's kind of what boyfriends do."

"You're so…chivalrous."

"You're so…beautiful." He stepped closer to her. "Smart." He kissed her lips. "Sweet." Hugh kissed her neck. "Loving," he whispered against her ear.

Brianna's fingers grazed his stomach. "Hugh," she whispered as he lowered his mouth to hers again, pressing his body to hers. Her back met the cold metal of the car. His arms enveloped her, stealing the cold and replacing it with excruciating heat that radiated from his body right through hers. She wrapped her arms around his neck, enjoying the feel of his body, the taste of his lips, the passionate swipe of his tongue. His hands roved over her back to her hips, her ass, and back up again. Every caress pulled at her most sensitive areas. He had to feel the way her legs lost their strength as she clung to him for support. When he settled his mouth around her neck again and buried his hands in her hair, tugging her head back, she could barely contain the begging moan that welled within her. His hips gyrated against hers, and another rush of heat settled between her legs. With a final—*Oh God*—hot stroke of his tongue, he pulled back from her.

Come back. Brianna's eyes fluttered open, and when he whispered in her ear, *Should I follow you home?* It took all her focus to manage a nod.

Chapter Twenty-Six

DUCK DYNASTY WAS outside when Hugh and Brianna arrived at the apartment complex. Hugh carried Layla, and when his eyes met the bearded man's, the man went inside. *Damn right.* He reached for Brianna's hand and mounted the stairs with a little stronger peace of mind.

Layla awoke when Hugh laid her down. She looked from Hugh to Brianna, and a smile crept across her lips.

"Good night, Mommy." She reached her arms up for a hug.

Brianna kissed her forehead. "Good night, princess."

Layla reached her arms up toward Hugh. "Good night, Prince Hugh."

Hugh brought her covers up to her chest and kissed her cheek. "Good night, Princess Layla."

She curled around her Piglet doll, and within seconds, she was fast asleep again. Brianna took Hugh's hand and led him out to the living room, closing Layla's door behind them.

Hugh tried not to notice how sexy Brianna looked with her sleepy eyes and graceful movements, but damn it, how could he not? Brianna nibbled on her lower lip, and he went to her. She wanted to talk and he wanted to kiss. How could he be expected to want to do anything else so soon after she'd given him the green light to act upon his feelings? That's all it had taken for a flood of emotions and desires to surge forward. Her whole damn body had reacted to the kiss in the parking lot—and left him wanting more. A taste of Brianna just wasn't enough. With one hand on her waist, he glanced at Layla's toys on the counter and it returned his mind to what mattered most.

"You wanted to talk?" He buried his face in her neck, taking one small taste to hold him over.

"Yeah," she whispered.

He reluctantly pulled away. "Let's sit down."

The scent of her perfume called to him. She was close enough that all it would take was leaning over a handful of inches and his lips would meet hers, a few more and their bodies would be intertwined. *Jesus. What am I doing?* Just because she said it was what she wanted didn't mean he needed to go into full-on make-out mode.

He brushed her hair from her shoulder and rubbed the knot at the back of her neck. "What did you want to talk about?"

Brianna sighed. "That feels so good. Thank you."

"You worked hard tonight." Brianna had glided through her busy night at the tavern without so much as a complaint. She didn't fall apart when Layla showed up unexpectedly, and she didn't get flustered when she had five booths and two tables of rowdy couples to wait on. She was one of the most in-control women Hugh knew.

She smiled, but it didn't reach her eyes. When she tucked a strand of hair behind her ear, Hugh knew that whatever she wanted to discuss was not only important, but unsettling.

He held her hand between his. "Tell me."

She let out a loud breath. "I'm probably jumping way too far ahead here, and I feel stupid even bringing it up, but…" She glanced toward Layla's room.

Hugh drew her face back toward his. "You're worried about Layla? I shouldn't have offered to stay with her at the bar. I'm sorry, Bree."

She shook her head. "No. That's not it at all. I love that you did that."

Hugh never claimed to be an expert at understanding women, but he was pretty sure he didn't suck at it. However, at that moment, he had no clue what Brianna was trying to tell him. "You're totally confusing me."

"I know. It's because I'm confused, so how can I be clear if I'm not even sure what I'm thinking?" She withdrew her hand from his and rose to her feet. Her eyes narrowed and her lips pinched tight.

Hugh's stomach knotted. He forced himself to remain seated, giving her space to pace, as she was doing now, with her arms folded over her stomach. He wanted to take her in his arms and tell her that whatever it was, they'd work it out, but as she took her lower lip between her teeth again, he held back, allowing her to tell him whatever was eating at her when she felt ready.

A moment later, she stopped pacing. Her eyes filled with sadness and her brows pinched.

He couldn't take another minute of it. "Bree?" He reached for her, and she sank to the couch. "You're worrying me."

She blew out another breath. "I like you a lot."

*But...*He held his breath. He finally met a woman who sparked the emotions he hadn't been sure he'd ever feel, and now his heart was going to get crushed? This couldn't be happening. Hugh wasn't the dumpee. He had always been the one to walk away. This was all wrong, and damn it, he didn't want to walk away from Brianna—or Layla.

"Bree—"

"Let me get this out, please. Hugh, seeing you with Layla made me realize how much I like you, and I'm afraid it's a lot more than *like*."

Hugh closed his eyes for a breath. *Oh thank God.* When he opened them again, she was holding her lip captive again. *Shit.*

"It's just…Can we talk about our lives for a minute?"

"Of course. Whatever you want to know. My life is an open book." He'd been asked all sorts of intimate questions by previous lovers, and none of it worried him. He'd always been careful, protected himself from sexually transmitted diseases, and though he'd slept with many women, he'd promised Brianna that he'd always be honest, and he intended to honor that commitment.

"Tell me about your schedule." She tilted her head, her brows still knitted together.

My schedule? She didn't want to know about his past lovers, or if he'd told women this or that. Of course she didn't. Brianna was practical, responsible. She had a daughter to worry about.

"What do you want to know about it? We race February through October, typically two races each month. I used to do the larger circuits and race weekly, but recently I've cut back and joined the Capital Series."

"Capital Series. What does that mean?"

"It's just the name of the race series. What it really means is that I have an innate need for speed and I thrive on the thrill of racing at mind-blowing speeds."

Brianna nodded and pressed her lips together again. Hugh could practically see the gears in her brain processing and conjuring up the best way to ask whatever was on her mind.

"If you love it, why did you cut back?"

Hugh leaned forward, resting his elbows on his thighs. He rubbed one hand with the other. He hadn't shared the truth of his answer with anyone. When the press questioned him, he gave them an off-the-cuff answer. *I want to try a different circuit. Don't want to get stale. I'm looking into other endeavors.*

Brianna's trusting eyes pulled the truth right from his heart. "Please don't repeat what I tell you, because I haven't been forthright with the press, and managing public relations can be a nightmare."

"I promise. But before you tell me, is it some awful reason that will make me want to turn away? Something scandalous that if I knew about it, I'd want to protect Layla from it?"

There they were again. Her mama instincts taking over. *God, I love that.* He shook his head, wanting to smile and assure her with a happier face, but the truth was not easy to spell out, and he felt as solemn as he knew he looked.

"It's nothing like that." He stretched one arm over the back of the couch, more for something to hang on to than for comfort. "You know I grew up without my mom."

"Yes," she whispered, and at the same time, she placed her hand on his thigh.

Hugh's chest tightened. "I've always been the live-fast, no-tethers guy in the family. I breezed in and out of family gatherings like the wind, even though my family is the most important thing in the world to me. But I think it's because I know they'll always be there. To be honest, I did the same with women."

Brianna dropped her gaze.

"Please look at me, Bree. I will always be honest with you, and this isn't easy for me. I need to know that you see me when

I say it, and that you don't see an image of me that my admission conjures up."

She met his gaze.

"I've stopped doing that crap, so before I continue, just know that that's who I was, not who I am." He ran his hand through his hair and took a deep breath. "I've never brought a woman home to meet my family, and when discussions grew deeper—with family or women—I've always made light of them. Then my father had some heart problems, and something in me clicked." He paused, thinking of how his father's illness had hit him like a knife to the chest. "Life moves fast, and my life moved even faster than most people's. Without anything to ground me, I had no limits."

Brianna pulled her hand from his leg. "Drugs?"

"No. Bree, I've never been a guy who wanted to ravage his body with drugs, so you don't have to worry about that. Nothing illegal. Just…life. Ride hard, play hard. That's who I was." He leaned forward again, rubbing his hands together. "My dad still lives every day for my mom. He talks to her, and I swear, sometimes I can feel her around, you know?" He drew his eyes to hers. "She had this horse. Hope. My dad still has Hope, and he treats her like Mom is part of her." He knew how crazy it all sounded, but even as a lump swelled in his throat, he continued. "So there I am, looking at the man who is everything to me. The man who filled the hole my mother's absence left, and I'm thinking, *What happens when you're gone?*" Hugh's eyes welled with tears, and he pressed his finger and thumb to them. "I haven't learned enough from him yet. God, I sound like a fool."

"No, you don't." Brianna scooted closer. She tucked her legs beneath her on the couch. Her knees brushed his thigh.

He nodded, unable to look at her until he got it all out. "After that weekend, I took a long look at my life. My crazy, whirlwind, no-ties life, and I realized that besides my family, my life was pretty damn lonely. I realized that I had learned what I needed from my dad after all. I just hadn't listened to what he'd taught me." He blew out another breath, relieved to get some of the feelings that he'd kept trapped for so long off his chest. She watched him intently, and her trusting eyes gave him the strength he needed to continue.

"Brianna, I thrive on thrills, but it's not who I am. I spent a few months trying to figure out who I was. I always thought I was so different from my brothers and my sister. They always seem to do the right thing. Even my love for them never kept me tied to the family gatherings for very long. I always had to be moving forward, looking for the next thrill. I'm not proud of all of that, but I am proud of the changes I've made."

"Cutting back on your racing?" she asked.

"That and other changes. I'm reaching out more to my family, spending more time with them. I spent time with Dane on his boat recently. Just stuff like that, and I'm taking more downtime now. I think one reason I never took time off before was that I had built this rep that everyone expected of me, so I felt like I had to live up to it." Hugh felt the tension in his neck ease. "I like who I am, Bree. It took a little getting used to, not going out all the time, slowing down, but I'm a good man. I'm a nice guy, and I'm learning about things I've never even considered before. And mostly…" He took her hand in his. "I realized that I want what my father had."

"Hugh, you don't have to tell me all of this." In Brianna's eyes he saw the same unconditional love that his father had for him. He knew she didn't need to know everything he was telling her, but he wanted to tell her.

"You asked about my schedule, and I know I'm giving you a diatribe about my life, but I think you need to understand why I made the changes. The main reason I cut back on racing was that while it filled my need for thrills, it left other parts of me empty. I can't build a relationship or have a family if I'm racing every week. I need to nourish all the parts of me, not just the thrill-seeking part. I want to love the way my father loved and the way my brothers and sister love their partners. I want to be a good boyfriend and a great husband, not just a fun guy. I want to have children and raise them to be good men and women." He searched her eyes for a hint of what she was thinking. She swallowed and licked her lips. What did he expect? He just laid a future out before her when she'd asked for a little background.

Brianna looked down at their hands; then she put her hand on his cheek and said, "You are a good man. I always thought Mack was the best man I knew, but you're right there with him."

He tried to swallow past the lump that was now firmly lodged in his throat. In lieu of words, he kissed her hand again. He loved her hands. He loved when she touched his cheek, or held his hand, or touched his body. *I love her. All of her.* He suppressed the urge to tell her. She had a heavy enough load as it was.

"Can I ask you something else?"

"Anything," he answered.

"How does it all work? If you race twice a month, where do you live? How would you maintain a relationship with so much travel?"

Hugh reached around her and pulled her closer. She stretched her legs out behind her on the couch and leaned across his lap. Gazing into Brianna's eyes, Hugh didn't need to dig too deep to find the answer. Truth found his lips again.

"Until I met you, I didn't have to worry about that." He leaned his forehead against hers. "All I know is that I don't want to leave your side, and now that I've met Layla, I don't want to leave hers, either."

Chapter Twenty-Seven

BRIANNA COULD COUNT on one hand the number of times she knew she was making the absolute right decision in her life. The first was when she went away to college. The second was when she decided to study photography. She'd always felt as though she was looking at life through a filter, trying to rid what she saw of the blurry edges and bring it all into focus. The third time was when she found out she was pregnant and knew she was going to keep the baby. There had been a click in her brain that afternoon, probably much like the click Hugh spoke of a few minutes earlier. Each of those decisions had been the right ones, and they'd led her to a happy, productive life that had served her well, even if it was a bit closed in. Now she looked into the dark eyes of the man she was falling head over heels in love with. The man who was kind, generous to a fault, and the most honest man she could ever ask for. Brianna knew this fourth and most important decision in her life came with major consequences. She had Layla to think about after all. The words balanced on the edge of her tongue, and she closed her mouth to keep them in. What if she was wrong? What if he meant every beautiful word he said, but meaning them wasn't enough? What if…No. She wouldn't go down that road tonight. She'd asked him what it all meant, and he'd told her. She owed him the same honesty.

She placed her hand on the spot on his stomach that she'd come to believe was hers and hers alone. The spot just above the rivet of the right pocket of his jeans. The spot where her fingertips melded perfectly to his abs. The spot that always rewarded her with a widening and then, almost instantly, a darkening and narrowing of his eyes as he leaned forward and—*Oh God, yes*—lowered his mouth to hers. Every kiss was like a renewal, a crazy tossing up and mixing together of the lust and love that bloomed within her, spilling over with each press of his lips. And, Jesus, he tasted good. She wrapped her arms around him and he moved with her, pressing his chest to hers and dragging his hand—*How I love those big, glorious hands*—down her side the way he did, making her feel feminine and aroused in ways she never dreamed possible.

He slid his hand beneath her T-shirt, caressing her bare skin and sending a shock of greediness right through her. He read her need with pinpoint accuracy, cupping her breast and moving his mouth to her neck as he whispered her name.

"Bree..."

His voice slayed her as it had since the first night she'd met him. He came in like the wind, soft and alluring. He brushed softly against the walls she'd erected, and they fell away when she wasn't looking, leaving her with only a few thin layers of protection around her heart. Hugh lifted those layers right off of her with every consideration, every loving kiss, every longing look, exposing her vulnerable heart—and now, as he lifted her shirt and settled his mouth over her breast, she never wanted to find a windless spot again.

With one arm beneath her and one arm around her waist,

Hugh shifted his body above Brianna's. He felt so damn good—every hard inch of him. She tangled her hands in his hair and brought his mouth to hers again, disappearing into the heat that arched her hips to his and pulled hungry moans from deep within her lungs.

"Jesus, Bree." He moved down her body, kissing her stomach and shifting his hips to the side. His mouth found hers again as he slipped his hand down the front of her pants, his fingertips brushing her center. He groaned against her lips. "You're so wet."

Hearing him talk dirty spurred her to him again, and she met his mouth with a clash of tongue and teeth as he pushed his hand deeper. His fingers entered her, and she pulled back from his mouth with a whimper of need. She tugged at his shirt and pulled his bare stomach to hers, pressing her hips against his. He took her in another rough kiss, and the combination of want and need meshed together with the sensations of his loving touch and sensuous tongue and she spiraled up and over the edge. Her head fell back, and he captured her cries of pleasure in his mouth as a thousand pinpricks lit her limbs on fire and stole her concentration. As she eased down from the blissful crest, their kiss became tender.

"Wow," she whispered, brushing her hair from her face.

Hugh glanced down the hall. "As much as I want to take you into your bedroom and make sweet love to you, you haven't told your little princess about us yet. I have a feeling that if she woke up and found a strange man in her mother's bed, it might ruin her for life."

Brianna traced the outline of Hugh's biceps with her finger. "Don't you mean her handsome prince?"

Hugh smiled down at her. "Well, there is that." He scooped

her into his arms. "So, mama bear, how does this work?"

"What do you mean?"

"Was there anything else you wanted to know about me before you talk to Layla?" The seriousness returned to his voice.

"I feel like you've bared your soul to me, and everything you've told me just draws me even closer to you. I'm just trying to figure things out, and I know we've only been seeing each other for a few days…"

"It feels like a lifetime."

You have no idea. "For me too. I just worry that if we continue to get close and then you're gone for weeks at a time, that'll be really hard on Layla." *And me too.* "I'm not trying to push our relationship forward. I just…as a mother, I have to think ahead. What I do affects Layla."

"Bree."

She felt completely off balance. She wanted to crawl into his lap and stay there, safe and sound, but what if safe and sound really meant only a few weeks each year of safe and sound?

"Bree," he said again.

"Yeah?"

Sitting beside him like this, his hands on her arms, his dark eyes telling her he'd never hurt her, made her worries fall away, but one glance down the hall to her daughter's bedroom tripped her up again.

"There are plenty of guys who bring their families with them when they travel. They bring tutors for the kids. Some have a home base and they travel back and forth. If that's where we're headed, we'll figure it out together and do what's best for Layla."

What's best for Layla. His constant commitment to Layla's well-being and the way his thoughts repeated Mack's about how things might work out brought the word *fate* to the forefront of her mind.

He tucked a wayward lock of hair behind her ear, and she closed her eyes and just breathed for a minute. "Okay. Thank you."

"Stop thanking me." He put his arms around her again. "What are your plans for the week?"

She cringed. "Back to real life. I work from ten to ten Monday and ten to five on Wednesday. And I'm working with Claude Tuesday and Thursday morning from eight to one, and then I'm at the tavern from two until ten Tuesday and two to five Thursday because I have Layla's birthday party late Thursday afternoon. Normally I'd be there until nine or ten. Then I'm back at the tavern again Friday from nine to five."

Hugh arched a brow. "You're working almost fifty hours Monday through Friday?"

"That sounds about right. They didn't have any hours for me Saturday. So unless Claude comes through with something, I'll have that day off, too, which right now would be a blessing." She leaned against the couch, watching worry lines travel across his forehead.

"When do you have time with Layla during the week?"

She lowered her eyes. "I never have enough time with her, but we fit it in. We have breakfast together, and I'll spend time with her in the evenings, just not much time." Familiar guilt knotted in her stomach. "What are your plans for the week?"

"I've got a few things to take care of before I leave Friday morning. I was hoping to see you at some point, but you have so little time with Layla that I don't want to interfere."

"I don't go into work until ten on Monday and Wednesday. We could see each other before work if it fits with your schedule."

"I'll make it work Monday, but Wednesday I have a meeting with a sponsor. Are you talking to Layla about us tomorrow?"

"I think so, but I can't do it before school in case it upsets her. She'll be exhausted Monday night, but that's probably the best time. I'll let you know how it goes."

"If things go well, and if you feel it's appropriate, can I take you and Layla out on a double date Wednesday evening?"

"She'd really like that, but don't feel pressure to do it." The idea of it sent a thrill through her.

He inched closer. "I'll tell you what. You talk with her and let me know what you think. In the meantime, where do you want to meet tomorrow morning? Do you want to have breakfast together? Do you have any errands you need to run during that time? I can tag along. I don't care what we do as long as I'm with you."

She'd be damned if she'd waste the little time they had together running errands. "Nope. I'm good."

"Okay, then why don't you come over after you take Layla to school and I'll make you breakfast?"

"Sounds perfect." She mentally ticked off each of her sexy undergarments.

Pink. Definitely pink.

Or maybe...none at all.

Chapter Twenty-Eight

THE NEXT MORNING, Layla sat on her knees on the kitchen chair, stabbed a piece of her pancake with her fork, and shoved it in her mouth. "I had fun last night. Can I go to your work again tonight?"

"I'm sorry, sweetie, but children really aren't supposed to be at Mommy's work. Mack made an exception last night, but he can get in trouble if we do that too often. Besides, Grandma rented *Tangled* to watch with you tonight." She took a bite of her pancakes and watched Layla crinkle her nose. "Is something wrong with your pancakes?"

Layla shook her head and stuck her lower lip out in an adorable pout. "I wanted to see Prince Hugh again."

Brianna's body tingled with the anticipation of seeing him. *I don't blame you.* "Did you have fun with him, or was it just fun because you were at my work?"

"I had fun with him. He's nice and he's just like the prince in the play I saw with Grandma. He played with me and made up stories and some girl asked him on a date and he said no so he could play with me." She flashed her tiny Chiclets teeth—and the gap where one was missing—as she put another piece of pancake in her mouth.

Since they were on the topic of Hugh and Layla appeared to hold him in a positive light, Brianna decided not to wait to discuss their relationship with her. "I wanted to talk to you about him." She set down her fork and folded her hands under her chin, weighing Layla's reaction. Of which she had none. Zero. Not even a modicum of interest that would dissuade her from the pancakes as she speared another piece with her fork. "Hugh is a friend of mine. A special friend."

"I know."

Brianna lowered her hands to her lap. "You know?"

Layla shook her head. "Uh-huh."

"How do you know he's my special friend?" *I'm going to kill my mother.*

She shrugged.

Brianna's pulse sped up. She lifted her eyebrows. "What do you think a special friend is?"

Layla took a drink of her juice, then speared another piece of pancake. "Someone who you like a lot. Like Kat. Kat's a special friend."

Brianna smiled. "You're right. Kat is a very special friend."

"And Mack. Mack's a special friend." She shoved the pancake in her mouth.

"Yes, Mack is too. But Hugh is a little different kind of special friend," Brianna explained. How the hell was she supposed to do this? She had no idea how to differentiate between one kind of special friend and another.

"Marissa's mom has a special friend, and she said they kiss. Do you kiss Hugh?"

Brianna blew out a breath. *I guess that's how I differentiate.* "Would it bother you if I did?"

Layla puckered her lips and wiggled her mouth from side to

side. "Do you really like him? Because Grandma said girls should only kiss boys who they really, really like. And she said you have to kiss a lot of frogs to find a prince."

"Grandma is right." *And she has a big mouth.* "You should only kiss boys that you really, really like, and yes, I really, really like Hugh."

Layla sat back on her heels and put her fork down. "I like him too."

"That's good, Layla, because he likes you as well. He'd like to take us out Wednesday night. Would that be okay?"

She bobbed her head up and down with a toothy grin. "Where will we go?"

Brianna's heart soared. "I'm not sure yet. Someplace special."

Layla furrowed her brow. "Anywhere?"

"I think so. Where did you have in mind?" Brianna began clearing the table.

"I don't know. You decide." She jumped off her chair and ran to the table in the living room. "Do we have time to play Drama Queen?"

And just like that the conversation was over. She'd stewed all night over telling Layla about Hugh, and thirty seconds after hearing it, her child brain had already switched gears. *If only it were that easy for adults.* "Not before school, but you should know that Hugh is the one that bought that for you." She checked her watch. In thirty minutes she'd be at Hugh's house. In thirty-one minutes she'd be in his arms.

Layla bounced up and down. "Hugh bought this for me? How did he know I wanted it?"

Brianna smiled at her daughter's enthusiasm. "I don't know, but we'd better get your shoes on or we'll be late." She had decided to swing back by the apartment after dropping off Layla at school to change before going to see Hugh. Her stomach flipped and dipped.

In the foyer, Layla slid her blue-stockinged feet into her blue sneakers. "I know how he knew, Mommy. He's magical. All princes are magical."

He has magic hands, but I'm not sure he's magical. "I think he's just a really good guesser."

Chapter Twenty-Nine

HUGH PORED OVER the race schedule for the following year. He ran his hand through his hair, trying to figure out the best way to navigate a relationship with Brianna and still maintain his rigorous schedule. He'd been staring at the damned thing for more than an hour, but no matter how much he tried, he couldn't focus. It was a good thing he'd lessened his schedule. If he was having this much trouble with an abbreviated race schedule, there was no way he'd have been able to manipulate his way around the heavier competitions and fit in a relationship. *Damn it.* The thought of Brianna working fifty hours in five days killed him. She needed more time with Layla, and certainly Layla needed more time with her mother. He pushed away from the table and paced.

The twisting in his gut told him it wasn't just Layla he was worried about. How would he and Brianna find any time to be together? Racing took his entire focus. For three days of each race week he'd eat, breathe, and sleep racing. There would be press conferences before or after every race, sponsor shoots, dinners, award ceremonies. There was no way his girlfriend could work fifty hours each week and still attend events with him. Hell, if she were his—really his—she wouldn't have to work a day in her life. She could get back into photography, have more time with Layla and with him. Hugh knew himself too well. He was an obsessive, competitive bastard, and the feelings he had toward Brianna weren't that different from the ones he had toward racing. Since they'd met, he'd eaten, breathed, and slept with thoughts of her every second. He needed more time with her. *Fuck.*

He walked to the glass doors in the living room and pulled them open, inhaling a deep, cleansing breath of the crisp morning air. It did nothing for him. He took another one, thinking about how women had always been like a new set of tires. He'd ride 'em hard and toss them away, never to think about them again. Brianna stuck in his mind like tar. Hot and present, impossible to shake off. And he loved her, damn it. He wanted more time with her, not less.

He wasn't leaving town for another four days, and even then he'd be gone for only a night or two and it was already destroying him. He worried about Brianna working too many hours and he worried about Layla not spending enough time with her mother. He worried about the bearded man he'd had a talk with, even though he seemed to have listened. Jesus, he worried about how he'd sleep the night before the race with all this shit running through his head. As it was, he was up half the night wishing she were beside him. How the hell did that happen so fast?

When his doorbell rang, he hadn't even prepared breakfast, as he'd planned. He closed the glass doors and crossed the floor in his jeans and bare feet, then took a deep breath, trying to calm down. He reached for the doorknob, and only then did he realize his hands were fisted, the muscles in his arms and neck strung so tight he could play a tune off of them. *Shit.* The doorbell sounded again.

Brianna stood before him wearing a short coat that belted around the waist and stopped midthigh. Her legs were bare and shivering. Hugh's eyes were on a downward scale, and the shivering should have stopped him, but the stiletto heels that she stood upon had him getting hard despite his earlier frustration. Holy hell, was she a dream come true. He had no idea what she had on under that little coat of hers, but there was no way in hell she was wearing that to work. Not today. Not ever, if he had anything to say about it. He forced his eyes back up her crazy, sexy outfit and lingered just above the belt, where his eyes caught on a swatch of skin. He followed the path of silky skin up between her breasts, clear to her succulent lips. Even through his hard-on fog it registered that she wasn't wearing a bra, and more likely wasn't wearing anything beneath that coat. *Jesus.* He pulled her inside and closed the door.

He backed her up against the wall. Adrenaline had already taken over his body before he opened the door. Now it mixed with testosterone, and he feared he might burst. God only knew how he'd made it through the night without relieving his sexual tension, but he'd made it through. He'd planned a lovely breakfast and a loving intimate interlude—until he'd received the revised race schedule when he'd checked his email, and he'd gotten lost in trying to reconfigure his life. Now Brianna's scent assaulted him, and just knowing what she probably wasn't wearing beneath that coat drove his mouth to hers.

"Well, hello to yo—"

He cut her short. All of the wanting of the last twenty-four hours and the emotions that made his chest ache and his groin yearn for Brianna exploded in a frenzy of erotic thoughts and carnal needs. He tangled his hands in her hair and tugged her head back, just enough to angle her mouth up so he could kiss her deeper, plundering every breath from her lungs. She made that sound that took him over the edge, a desperate, hungry moan that began somewhere deep inside her and vibrated through her chest. Hugh tugged at the belt on her jacket as she groped his body, fumbling with the button on his jeans and whimpering when she couldn't set him free. God, how he loved that sexy whimper.

With a grunt and a groan, he ripped the button off his jeans with one hand and managed to untie the belt of her coat with the other. Her lapels fell away, exposing a perfect path of skin down the center of her beautiful naked body. For a breath he was stunned. Frozen. He couldn't think. The provocative look in her eye coalesced with the lust coursing through his body, and in that second he knew he'd never be able to be apart from her. She narrowed her eyes, and her lips parted for him as she reached between his legs and cupped his balls through his jeans.

"Jesus, Bree." He wasn't sure he actually said the words. Did they make it from his brain to his lips? All he knew was that in the next second his hands were on her ass, squeezing, taking hold and pulling her against him. The feel of her cold skin against the heat that boiled within him made him want more of her. His mouth found her breast, teasing her nipple, then grazing it with his teeth. She buried her hands in his hair and held on with a death grip. One hand found her deliciously wet center—and he couldn't stand to tease her. He had to be inside her. He plunged his fingers in, and she lifted up on her toes with a gasp, lifting her four-inch heels right off the ground and sending his desires into overdrive.

Brianna reached for his pants, tugging one side of his fly. His jeans fell open, revealing the tip of his erection trapped beneath the waistband of his briefs. She looked down and licked her lips. The innuendo stopped him cold. She ran her fingers down his stomach in a way he'd come to crave, gentle and seductive. She hooked her thumbs in his briefs and tugged them down. They caught on his massive thighs, and she bit her lower lip again, looking up at him through her thick lashes as she bent down to greet his thick length with her mouth. Hugh groaned as she licked every inch, then took him in deep. *Holy shit.* Had she practiced overnight? He wanted to crawl out of his skin.

She stood, guiding his back to the wall where she'd just been and playfully held him there.

"Bree."

"Shh. My turn."

She brought her mouth to his and pinned him against the wall with her hands, rocking against him. He grabbed her hips, and she pushed his hands away, drawing back from his mouth and snagging his lower lip in her teeth before releasing it and slicking her tongue over the sore spot.

"Who are you?" He swallowed to settle the eagerness in his voice.

"I thought about you all night, and I know how much you respect me. The only way I'm going to get through to you—really make you understand how *not careful* you have to be—is to show you that you can treat me like a woman." She licked her lips again. "Seven years is a really long time." She shimmied down his body and looked up at him again before whispering, "Don't come."

He closed his eyes and groaned as her hands and tongue worked their magic. He gripped her shoulders, forcing himself not to help her rhythm. God knew if he did that, he'd never last. Her mouth was so hot and—*Oh Jesus*—his eyes sprang open. *What the?* A sensation he'd never felt before sent a thrill right through him. She glanced up. She was using the underside of her tongue to tease him.

She flashed a mischievous grin and arched a brow. "*Cosmo* and *Redbook*. They have great online tips."

"Holy fuck." He clenched his eyes shut as she turned her attention to his balls. "Bree," he said in one long breath. "Brianna." She quickened her pace, using both her hand and mouth. He grabbed her head and pulled himself free.

"Don't. Come."

"You're killing me." He threw his head back against the wall.

She pried his hands from her head and began working him with a fast rhythm, five fast strokes, four, three, two; then she worked her way up with slower, longer strokes, rousing any remaining sanity that he might have had left.

"Bree. Bree."

"Don't," she commanded. She didn't miss a beat. She brought him right up to the edge, then backed off, giving him just enough relief to regain control before taking him up to the edge again.

Every nerve burned. In one swift and sudden move, he lifted her off the ground and into his arms, wrapping her legs around his waist. She grabbed his face with her hands and took him in another intoxicating kiss. Control was not something Hugh was used to giving up. He could barely think, but he held on to one string of thought.

"Condom."

"On the pill." She kissed him again.

"Bree?" He pulled back and looked into her loving, trusting eyes. "I'm gonna make a bride out of you one day, and not an accidentally pregnant one. The next time you get pregnant, it'll be your decision." He kissed her as he carried her—still straddling him—into the bedroom, where he grabbed a condom from the bedside drawer. Together they rolled it on. No way was he putting her down for one measly second. Having her in his arms, holding on to him like he was her everything, shot a burst of love right through him.

"What did you just say?" she asked tentatively.

"It's madness, I know. I don't want a night here or there, a date when we can fit it in. I'm not pushing, and I don't think I'm crazy. I just know I never want to be without you, and I want to take care of you and Layla with every piece of my heart and soul."

Her lips curled up and her eyes filled with more love—if that were even possible. She took his face in her hands. Her lips parted, as if to speak, before a tear dropped from her cheek and she lowered her forehead to his. As she slid down his body and took him in her mouth, the anxiety from the morning evanesced, leaving his heart whole and his mind free to embrace the woman that he loved.

Chapter Thirty

THE BEGINNING OF the week went by in a blur of work, romantic phone calls and texts, and nervous excitement. Brianna was finishing up her shift Wednesday evening at the tavern when Kat sidled up to her.

"So, any more bride talk?" She leaned back against the bar and lifted her eyebrows. Today she wore a coral-colored lipstick, which gave her a fun, youthful appearance.

"I haven't seen Hugh since Monday." She had hoped to see him before work that morning, but he'd had to meet with a sponsor. Each time they'd spoken since Monday, they'd talked about Layla and caught up on what each of them had done that day. They swooned about how much they missed each other and both professed how they couldn't wait to see each other again. Brianna should have been over the moon, but she realized that morning that Hugh hadn't brought up what he'd said while they were making love—*I'm gonna make a bride out of you one day*—and the worry had expanded like a sponge in water throughout the day, lodging itself in her chest. The clock couldn't reach five fast enough.

"Does this mean you're going to move away from me? What will I do all alone here with no one to talk to?" Kat smacked her gum and dropped her gaze.

Brianna tucked her hair behind her ear and let out a frustrated sigh. "I don't think that's what it means, Kat. I really don't know what it means." She threw her towel down on the bar.

"Whoa. What's up with that?" Kat picked up the towel and folded it, then tucked it back into Brianna's belt.

"*Ugh.* I don't know." She bent down and whispered, "He hasn't brought it up again. At all. Should I worry? I mean, what does that mean? Does he regret it?"

"Shit, no. The man's crazy about you. He rented a freaking carousel, Bree." She poked Brianna in the side of her head. "Think. Use your head for a minute. He told you he's gonna make a bride of you. The guy who rented out an entire park, who fixed your car, who bought your daughter a hundred-dollar game. Do you really think he says things he doesn't mean? Or...do you think he can't bring it up again unless he's really ready to propose? In case you haven't noticed, this guy doesn't do things halfway."

"Maybe." Brianna looked up at the ceiling. "But he could regret it," she said quietly.

"You're insane. What does your mom think?"

Brianna bit her lower lip.

"Brianna! You didn't tell your mother?" Kat crossed her arms. "You are worried."

"I just want to know he's sure. I don't want to get all"—she waved her hands up over her head and used a high-pitched voice—"*I'm getting married!* only to find out that he said it in the heat of passion and didn't really mean it." The damn lump she'd been fighting all morning lodged itself in her throat and pressed tears to her eyes.

Kat put her arm around her shoulder. "Bree? Has he done something to make you think he doesn't adore you?"

Brianna shook her head. "No. He's great. Better than great, and it's scary as shit. What if I'm in some dream world and I screw up Layla? She talks about him nonstop after spending only one evening with him. What if once he spends more time with me he finds out how complicated my life really is and he decides that it's not for him? What if he decides—"

Kat pulled her close. "Honey, he's not your dad, and he's not Layla's father, either. Take a deep breath. You've got yourself stuck in a tunnel of doubt."

Brianna nodded as she pulled away. "Jesus, Kat. I never cry. I'm like a bundle of nerves and girlie emotions. What has happened to me?"

"You fell in love, Bree. That's what it does to you. It turns you inside out and fucks with your mind…and your body." She sighed dreamily. "I can't wait until it happens to me."

Brianna laughed. "You're a glutton for punishment."

Kat smacked Brianna's butt. "Maybe, but only sometimes." She winked.

That little tap veered Brianna's mind to the sex-tip articles she'd been reading, which made her think about making love to Hugh. Her nipples perked up as she wiped the last of her tears from her eyes. *It turns you inside out and fucks with your mind. I'm totally fucked. No. I'm totally in love with Hugh Braden.*

Chapter Thirty-One

LAYLA AND HER grandmother were sitting on the floor playing with Barbies when Brianna walked into her mother's house.

"Mommy! Is it time for our date?" Layla rose to her feet and jumped up and down.

Brianna kissed her on the cheek and ran her hand over Layla's silky hair. "Almost, princess. Why don't you put the toys away and get your shoes on?" She watched Layla gather her dolls and pulled out her phone to read a text.

Hi, beautiful. I'll be there at seven thirty. Can't wait to see you both. Xox, H.

She texted back. *Us too. Xox.*

Her mother rose to her feet. "Can we talk in the kitchen?"

"Sure." Brianna stuffed her phone into her pocket and breathed deeply to calm her erratic pulse. By the serious tone of her mother's voice, she assumed Layla had said or done something that concerned her, which did nothing to help her calm down. "What's up, Mom?"

"I received a phone call today from Maureen Hooper." Maureen Hooper had worked for the city of Richmond for the past twenty-five years, and she was the biggest gossip on this side of town.

"Yeah. And?" Relieved that Layla hadn't picked up some bad words at school or said something off base, she was completely thrown by her mother's serious eyes and pinched lips.

"Bree, why didn't you tell me about what Hugh did for you?"

Brianna's breath caught in her throat. What she saw wasn't seriousness at all; it was hurt. *How the hell did I miss that?* She was too damn wrapped up in herself.

"I'm sorry, Mom. I thought it might upset you because of Dad."

Her mother put her hand over her mouth and shook her head. The sadness in her eyes was now unmistakable. She pulled Brianna into a hug, startling her.

"Mom, what's wrong?"

"Oh, honey. I'm sorry." She crossed her arms. "When Maureen told me about the carousel and the park, I put two and two together and realized how much you must have hurt from your father's leaving. I mean, that's the last time you were on a carousel, so it wasn't hard to figure out why he chose that. Let's face it. That night made a huge impact on you."

"So did the next morning, Mom, when he left. Remember?"

Her mother dropped her eyes. "Yes. Of course, and I'm sorry for anything I've done to make it even harder."

"Mom, you didn't make it harder." *At least not on purpose.* She clenched her eyes against the tears that threatened. Was her entire night going to be spent in tears?

Her mother nodded. "Yes, I did. I was so angry at him. I know what I did, and I was aware of it at the time, but I couldn't stop myself from saying all those things about him. I never should have said a negative thing. I should have just said the marriage ended and it was both of our faults."

"You never said much, Mom. You just said he couldn't stand the heat or something." She remembered every word her mother had said and how it had struck her like a brick to the chest, but there was no need to make her mother relive that too. She knew her mother had been overwhelmed, and the pain in her mother's eyes was apology enough.

"Yes, but sometimes it's not what you say. It's how you say it." Her mother hugged her again.

It's not what you say. It's how you say it. Shit. She'd spent the afternoon in a tizzy of worry over nothing. Every word Hugh said over the phone, every text he sent, was laden with love. She had been too worried to see them for what they were. He didn't need to hammer home the idea that he wanted to marry her with those very words. He'd already done it in a hundred different ways. Everything was happening crazy fast, and even if he wanted to slow things down, that wouldn't mean that he felt any differently about her.

"I know, Mom."

"Okay, well, you didn't tell me how romantic he was." Jean brushed Brianna's hair from her face.

"I know. I still can hardly believe it."

"Well, I fed Layla, and I hope tonight is wonderful for all of you."

Brianna wondered where they were going that evening. Hugh had texted earlier and said to dress up and to feed Layla a little something before he picked them up.

"It sounds like this is serious. How do you feel about him?" Her mother searched her eyes, and as her mother's hand flew to her mouth, Brianna knew she'd seen the answer written all over her face. "Brianna, you love him," she said from behind her hand.

Heat spread up her neck and cheeks. She held her mother's gaze and nodded.

"Oh, Bree!" She wrapped her arms around Brianna and whispered, "Do I ever get to meet him?"

"Maybe Thursday. At Layla's party, if that's okay?"

Layla walked into the kitchen. "What's happening at my party?"

Brianna and her mother exchanged a smile. Brianna crouched down to speak to Layla. "Would you mind if Prince Hugh came to your birthday party?"

"I would like that." She spun in a circle with her arms out to the sides. "Are you gonna kiss him?"

Jean covered her mouth and said quietly, "I forgot to tell you that she's been very focused on you kissing your *special friend*."

"I'll try not to, Layla." *But I'm not making any promises.*

Chapter Thirty-Two

FRESHLY SHOWERED AND dressed in a tuxedo, Hugh stood in the expansive walkout basement of his house. His legs were planted hip distance apart, his arms crossed, muscles flexed. The room was perfectly appointed with rich furniture and a seventy-two-inch television, complete with surround sound and two smaller televisions on either side of the larger one so he could watch multiple shows at once. It was a media setup that most guys would love. Hugh never watched television. He read sports updates on his phone and couldn't stand to sit and stare at a television. Before Brianna books had held his attention. Now even his reading time was minimal—and that was just fine with him.

The carpet still looked model-home new, and the walls were a pristine color that hovered between latte and cream. A fully stocked mahogany bar graced the corner of the room, and beyond that, the entrance to the gym stood ajar. The nine-foot ceilings and wall of French doors overlooking the perfectly manicured lawn and gardens gave the room an airy, open feel, and still, it felt flat. Lifeless. Stale.

He imagined a large coffee table, five feet wide and close to the floor. Something Layla could kneel beside and play her games or color, or whatever put a sweet smile on her lips. He had been roaming the house for the last hour mentally redecorating. Fitting Brianna and Layla into his life. He walked upstairs and into the office that he never used. It was far too big for an office and would be better suited as two rooms, a library and a darkroom for Brianna's photography, which he hoped she'd one day have time to enjoy. She was too damn good at it to let her talents go to waste.

Hugh pulled out his cell phone and called his father as he crossed the living room.

"Hey, Dad."

"Hugh. How's my boy?" Hal Braden's deep voice never failed to bring a smile to Hugh's lips and fill his mind with warm memories.

"Good, Dad. I miss you. How are you doing?" Hugh had been thinking about his father, remembering the way his father used to chide him for riding the horses hard and fast. *If I were that horse, I'd buck your ass right off.*

"I'm good. The ranch is going along well. Construction is done on Treat and Max's house. It's gorgeous, of course. Leave it to Treat to create a spectacular living space, and Max has put some real nice finishing touches on it. Rex and Jade's place is equally as beautiful. You'll see them when you come out next weekend for Savannah's engagement party. You are coming, aren't you?"

His brothers had both bought property in Weston, and now, as Hugh thought about his family, he wondered why he owned seven houses and not a single one in Weston. He thought about logistics, mulling over the distance to the airport, race locations, and, of course, Brianna and Layla. Would they want to move away? Their friends were in Richmond, and

Brianna's mother lived there, too. He pushed the thoughts away for now and returned his attention to his father.

"Yeah. I'm coming. Is it okay if I bring someone? Two people, actually?" He settled into the couch.

"You can bring anyone you want; you know that. It's always been your choice. Why would this be any different?"

He knew damn well that his father had already put two and two together. But just as his father would never tell him what to do with his life, he would walk with the same cautiousness around matters of Hugh's heart. "I don't know. I guess because it's Savannah's engagement party. Maybe I should call her and ask if she'd mind." He ran his hand through his hair.

"Probably a good idea, though I can't imagine she'd give a hoot."

He heard a smile in his father's voice.

"Your last race is this weekend. This is about the time of year when you get itchy for the next adventure. How're you holding up?"

His father knew him too well. In previous years, it had taken Hugh a solid month to settle back down and not feel the need to drive fast or party all night. Hell, that part of him never really settled down until recently, and it was exactly why he had phoned his father.

"I'm holding up just fine with regard to racing, Dad, but I kinda have something else on my mind." He checked his watch. He had to walk out the door in five minutes if he was going to pick up Brianna and Layla on time. "I met someone, Dad. Someone I really like." *Love, damn it. Someone I love.*

"I might have heard something about a woman."

Hugh closed his eyes. *Of course you have.* The phone call with Treat came back to him.

"And if I heard right, a child, too." Hal's voice carried no judgment. He had always been careful not to tell his children what to do, but he never failed to point out his thoughts in subtle ways. Ways that usually ended up revealing more about the person's hidden feelings without them even knowing it.

Now it was Hugh's turn.

"Brianna. She has a daughter, Layla."

His father inhaled deeply and then blew it out slowly. "Well, children are blessings. How do you feel about Brianna?"

He had so many memories of driving his father crazy by wrestling in the living room with his brothers or sledding over the fields his father had told him to stay off of—but where the other kids sledded was too slow for thrill-seeking Hugh. He could hardly believe his father coined children as blessings, even if his father's love was limitless. *Rascals*, maybe. *Pests that he loved*, definitely. But just blessings with no mischief wrapped around it? Five boys and one feisty girl couldn't have been easy on him as a single father. Although now that Hugh thought about it, he couldn't retrieve one memory where his father made him feel as though he were a burden.

"I love her, Dad." There. He'd said it. He hadn't even told Brianna yet, at least not in so many words. Hugh had never told a woman he loved her before. He'd always been too independent and self-centered to put a woman's needs ahead of his own. Until Brianna.

His father made a *hmph* noise. "And Layla?"

"That's kind of why I wanted to talk to you. I don't understand what's going on with me. I've only spent a little time with Layla, but I swear, Dad, I have loved her since I fell for Brianna. It's like because she's Brianna's daughter, she's automatically in that love zone. Is that totally wacked or what?" He paced again, waiting for his father to tell him that he had no business with a woman and a child because he had no idea what love was, or he was too self-centered. And maybe he'd be right. Hugh had no idea if what he was feeling was crazy or not. He didn't wait for his father's answer. "Every time I think of not being with them, it's like someone reaches into my chest and tears out a piece of my heart. It's pretty messed up, right?"

"Well, son. You've always known when things were right in your life. I remember when you were home on a college break and I asked you what business you wanted to go into. You had no idea. You looked at me like I look at Max when she talks about that damn interweb."

"Internet."

"Whatever," his father said. "So I asked you what brought you happiness no matter when you did it."

"And I told you that I loved racing more than anything even though it was supposed to just be a hobby that I did on weekends and in my spare time. Then you told me to do it. I remember."

"I raised you and your brothers and sister to love with your whole hearts. God only knows why it took each of you so long to realize that, or to allow yourselves to love. That's probably my fault, too. But you, Hugh, you love completely. So all you have to do is ask yourself if Brianna is the woman who makes you happy no matter what. And then you need to think hard about that little girl, because there will be times when she's a teenager and she sneaks out of the house or brings home some crappy guy who only wants to get in her pants, and you gotta know in your heart that even when she lies or when she goes against your words, you'll love her through it. No matter what."

Hugh pictured his father looking over the horses in the

fields and replaying memories of the trying times from Savannah's teenage years. And smiling.

His father continued. "You asked me if it was wacked that Layla fell into the love zone before you spent much time with her, and, son, love has no zones. Love is whatever it is, and trying to fit it into a box all neat and tidy will never do anything but drive a man crazy. Love isn't neat and tidy. Love's messy and, in some ways, indefinable. I don't think what you're feeling is wacked at all. You're an all-or-nothing guy. Always have been. If you've made up your mind with Brianna, and Layla is part of her life and part of her heart, then of course you've embraced her. That's love, Hugh."

An unexpected feeling of peace washed through Hugh, followed by a rush of adrenaline.

"Thanks, Dad. This is all so new to me that I wondered if I was losing my mind." Hugh looked at his watch. "Hey, Dad. I gotta run. I'm taking Brianna and Layla on a date and I'm late, but your advice means the world to me. Thank you."

"I look forward to meeting your ladies, son. And do me a favor, will ya?"

"Anything, Dad."

"Let Treat in on your feelings. That man worries about you as if he were your father, and Lord knows you've still got me for that."

Hugh laughed. "Sure. I'll call him tonight. I love you, Dad."

"I love you, too, son, and I'm damn proud of you. You had me worried for a while there. I wondered if I had somehow turned you off toward love. That would have broken my heart."

"No, Dad. You're the one who made me realize how important love is and how much I should treasure it."

Chapter Thirty-Three

"I'LL GET IT!" Layla pulled the door open. "It's Prince Hugh!" She jumped up and down in her new pink dress. Her brown hair tumbled past her shoulders.

Brianna smoothed her black knee-length dress over her hips, and when she looked up, her breath caught in her throat. Hugh stood before them wearing a black tuxedo, looking as if he'd just walked out of *Esquire* magazine. She'd been nervous before he showed up; now she breathed a little harder, her legs became wobbly, and her heart beat a little faster. Definitely more nervous than on their first date and maybe even more nervous than the morning she'd seduced him before work. Would the butterflies in her stomach ever get used to him? Brianna wasn't sure if she hoped they did or didn't.

"I've missed you." Hugh kissed her cheek. "You look gorgeous." Before she could respond, he bent down and said to Layla, "And I've never seen a more beautiful almost-six-year old than you."

Layla's eyes widened, and her smile spread even farther across her pink cheeks. She put her hands behind her back and twisted from side to side, swinging the skirt of the pink dress Hugh had given her. Brianna's hand settled on Layla's shoulder, more for her own stability than for Layla's benefit.

"I brought you something." Hugh brought one hand out from behind his back and presented Layla with a wrist corsage.

"What a beautiful corsage," Brianna said.

"Mommy, put it on me!" Layla jumped up and down.

"May I do the honors?" Hugh asked.

"Yes!"

Hugh put the wrist corsage on Layla's wiry arm. Then he reached inside his jacket and pulled out a small, flat box. "And this is for you." He handed it to Brianna. His dimples appeared when his smile reached his eyes, stealing nearly all of the remaining strength from Brianna's legs.

"Hugh, you didn't have to do this." Her voice was just above a whisper, and as he came into the apartment with Layla holding his hand, she realized her hands were trembling. She lifted the top of the box and sucked in a breath.

"Show me, Mommy! Show me!" Layla stood on her tiptoes.

Hugh lifted her into his arms so she could see. Her eyes danced with delight. "Oh, Mommy. That's beautiful!"

Brianna lifted the necklace from the box and ran her fingers around the diamonds that framed the round pendant, which was about a quarter of an inch thick with tiny charms between the glass front and the gold-plated back.

"It's a locket," Hugh said.

"Lemme see!" Layla pleaded.

Brianna read a tag that hung from the gold chain beside the locket. "Loved."

"Because you are," Hugh said softly.

She inhaled deeply and read the inscription on the gold plate inside the glass locket. *Strength. Truth. Courage.* She looked up at Hugh.

"You're the strongest and bravest woman I know. You're my truth, Bree, and you're Layla's truth, too." He drew his dark eyebrows together, and she touched his cleanly shaven cheek.

Thank you, she mouthed. Her voice was trapped by her swollen heart.

Layla wiggled in Hugh's arms. "What are those things floating in it?"

Brianna drew her eyes back to the little charms inside the locket.

"The heart that says family is for you and your mommy and your grandma." He leaned forward and kissed Brianna's cheek.

Brianna inhaled his scent, lost in the feel of his freshly shaven cheek and the thoughtfulness of his gift.

He whispered for only her to hear, "And I hope one day, for us."

Don't cry. Don't cry. Brianna tried to force her trembling lips into a smile, but she knew she failed miserably. Her chin was shaking too much.

Hugh looked down at Layla and continued. "The tiny camera—can you see that, Layla?" He held her closer to the locket.

"Mm-hmm."

"That's for your mom's passion for photography. And do you see the little heart that has the pink baby feet?"

"Is that for me?" Layla asked.

"Yes. And it has your birth date on the back," Hugh answered. He held Brianna's gaze while he spoke. "Since it's a locket, we can add to it anytime."

"What's the other thing?" Layla pointed to a little gold car with number thirty-two inscribed in it.

"That's for Hugh," Brianna said. Tears streamed down Brianna's cheeks, but she couldn't reach up and wipe them away.

"Mommy, why are you sad?" Layla asked.

She was frozen in place, staring at the man who'd waltzed into her life unannounced and broken down her walls, then stolen her heart while she was busy worrying. With Layla cushioned against him, holding on to his muscular arm like a security blanket, the heart she thought had room only for her daughter expanded and opened—accepting Hugh completely. *It's not what you say. It's how you say it.* He couldn't have made his love for her any more clear.

"I'm not sad, baby girl. These are tears of happiness."

Hugh put the necklace on Brianna and pulled her close. He kissed her forehead, and then he did the same to Layla. "Are my two leading ladies ready for a big night?"

Brianna wondered how she'd make it through the night on rubber legs and without a voice.

"Yes!" Layla squealed. She threw her arms around Hugh's neck and kissed his cheek.

Luckily, with Layla around, she wouldn't need her voice, and as Hugh guided her out the apartment door, she knew he'd provide all the strength she'd need.

Chapter Thirty-Four

THE CENTERSTAGE THEATER marquis was lit up like old-time Hollywood with white letters on a black background and illuminated in hundreds of small yellow bulbs. The theater was built on a corner, and the sign wrapped elegantly around the curve of the building.

"Oh my goodness, Layla. Look at that." Brianna read the marquis aloud. "*Special Showing. Sassy and the Bird, by Layla Heart.*" Brianna glanced at Hugh, who was giving nothing away as he trained his eyes on Layla.

Layla jumped up and down. "That's my story!" She took her mother's hand, then situated herself between Brianna and Hugh before reaching for Hugh's hand too. "How did my story get up there?" She looked from her mother to Hugh.

Hugh shrugged. "We'll have to go inside and see."

"Her story?" Brianna asked.

He winked, and her heart threatened to burst right through her chest.

They walked beneath the marquis and across the red carpet that covered the floor of the elegant theater. The seats were empty. Every seat.

"Hugh?"

Layla ran ahead of them down the aisle. Hugh put his arm around Brianna and whispered, "I wanted her to have a night she'd never forget…minus a hurtful morning after." He kissed the corner of her mouth, and it took all of Brianna's willpower not to deepen the kiss. "Is it okay? I know it's extravagant, but look at how happy she is."

Layla stood at the railing above the orchestra pit wiggling back and forth.

"It's okay, but she'll learn to expect these things, and that worries me," she said honestly.

"We can make sure she doesn't." He ran his knuckles down her cheek. "I know how much the afternoon with your father meant to you, and I wanted her to have something equally as special."

"Okay, but please, no more for a while, okay?"

Hugh shifted his eyes to the ceiling.

"Feigning innocence doesn't work with me." She looked at Layla heading back up the aisle toward them.

"I might have a little something else planned. Well, maybe a few little things."

She poked his side. "I work really hard to make sure she has what she needs, and now she's going to think she *needs* so much more." *Ugh! I sound so ungrateful.* Layla stopped short of them and ran into a row of seats.

"You're right. I should have run it by you first. I'm sorry, Bree. I've never done this before, and I guess I got a little overzealous."

Oh my God. I'm a bitchy girlfriend. What am I doing? He was doing something for Layla that she might never have the opportunity to do again. Maybe being romantic and thoughtful was simply who Hugh was, even if he was over-the-top. She touched her necklace and held on to his hand.

"It's okay. I'm sorry," she relented.

Layla stood in the center of the aisle again, beckoning them with one hand while smelling the corsage on the other.

"I promise, from now on I'll run everything by you." They took two steps and he stopped again. "I'd better amend that." His voice deepened with a serious tone. "I promise that I'll try to run everything by you, but honestly, I know myself, and there will be times that I forget, or I'm excited, or I want to surprise you both." He wrinkled his forehead and curled his lips into a sweet, tentative smile.

How could she deny those dimples and such a kind heart? "You kill me with honesty," she teased. "Okay. Deal."

LAYLA SAT BETWEEN Hugh and Brianna. She bounced her feet as Tami, Mack's wife, entered the stage wearing jeans and a white long-sleeved shirt. Her hair was pulled back in a high ponytail, and in her arms she carried a large fake tree. She set the tree beside a chair and stood at the front of the stage. *Tami?*

Layla gasped. "It's Tami! Tami's here!" Layla jumped up to her feet and held on to the seat in front of her.

Brianna whispered to Hugh, "You brought Tami here? What story?"

"Layla wrote a story at the tavern. Remember?" Hugh winked.

Brianna knitted her brows. "What?"

Hugh took her hand in his, then put his finger to his lips and nodded toward the stage. "Watch. You'll see."

"This is the story of Sassy and the Bird, written by Layla

Heart," Tami began. "Once upon a time, there was a yellow cat named Sassy. She had a bell on her collar that she got from her owner, and she loved the bell."

Kat crawled onto the stage on all fours. She wore a yellow long-sleeved shirt, yellow sweatpants, and a headband with two cat ears poking up from the top of her head. Tami shook a bell and the *tinkle, tinkle* sound followed Kat across the stage.

Oh my God.

"Kat! Mom, it's Kat!" Layla laughed.

Brianna's throat tightened. She squeezed Hugh's hand, and he moved into Layla's seat and put his arm around Brianna.

Tami continued. "Every morning Sassy followed her owner outside."

Jean walked across the stage wearing a pretty blue dress. She picked up a purse from a table and pretended to open the door to leave. Kat crawled behind her, scooting out the door alongside her.

"It's Grandma!" Layla climbed into Hugh's lap, and Brianna felt all the pieces of her world coming together.

"Sassy climbed a big tree where she could watch two baby birds play in their nest."

Kat climbed on top of the chair next to the tree and perched like a cat on all fours.

Mack and his daughter, Karen, entered the stage with big painted wings strapped to their arms. They sat in a big wicker basket that looked a lot like an enormous nest.

Layla laughed. "Look, Mom. Mack and Karen are birds!"

Brianna couldn't believe that Hugh had orchestrated the entire production without her knowing—and all for Layla.

Tami continued. "One day when Sassy was in the tree, one of the baby birds fell out.

Oh my God. Hugh pulled Brianna closer and kissed the side of her head.

Karen climbed over the side of the basket and yelled, "Ouch!" She held one wing up in the air.

"Sassy climbed down the tree as fast as he could." Tami rang the bell as Kat climbed off the chair.

Layla yelled, "I wrote that!"

Hugh put his arm around her and whispered, "You sure did."

Kat walked across the stage in silence and stopped by Karen. She touched her neck and curved her mouth into a frown.

Tami began again. "Sassy lost the bell she loved in the tree, but she saved the bird."

Karen climbed on Kat's back and, Brianna, Hugh, and Layla all laughed as Kat transported her into the pretend door to the house alongside Jean.

Jean picked up Karen and set her in a gigantic cage that seemed to appear from nowhere, but Brianna realized Mack had also disappeared. She'd been so busy watching Karen and Kat that he must have slipped out the other side of the stage.

"For lots of days," Tami continued, "the bird was in the cage getting better. Sassy was sad that she couldn't be with the bird inside the cage, so she watched from beside the cage."

Kat wiped her eyes and frowned, staring longingly at Karen through the bars of the cage.

"One day, the lock on the cage broke, and the owner had to leave it open when she went to work."

Jean opened the cage and walked out of the pretend door again.

"Look at Grandma." Layla laughed.

Brianna looked at Hugh. He squeezed her hand and nodded

toward the stage.

Tami continued. "Sassy climbed into the cage and snuggled with the bird until its wing felt better."

Kat climbed into the cage on all fours and rubbed her body against Karen's side.

Jean came back onto the stage.

"When the bird's wing was better, the owner took the bird outside and set it free," Tami said in a solemn voice.

Jean held Karen's hand and guided her out the door. Then Karen pretended to flap around the stage, and she climbed onto the chair beside the tree. Karen used her nose to poke at the tree.

"The bird had a surprise for Sassy," Tami said.

Layla jumped off of Hugh's lap. "Can I go to the front?" she asked.

Brianna agreed and watched Layla run down the aisle to the railing again, where she waved at their friends on the stage.

She forced her brain to work and hoped her voice would follow. "I can't believe…" She blinked her damp eyes and swallowed to gain control of her shaky voice. "You did all of this."

He touched her chin. "I'd do anything for you and Layla. She was so excited about this story, and I wanted to support her interest in the arts."

Brianna touched the locket he'd given her and wondered how she'd gotten so lucky to have been working the night he came into the tavern for the first time.

Tami smoothed her shirt, then continued. "That afternoon, the bird flew into the house when the owner came home."

Karen flapped her arms and ran into the door beside Jean.

Layla laughed hard and loud.

Karen dropped something by Kat, and Tami rang the bell as she said, "The bird gave Sassy back her bell, and the owner left the window open every day after that so Sassy and the bird could be best friends forever."

"And they lived happily ever after," Tami and Layla said in unison.

Tami curtsied and clapped as Kat, Karen, Jean, and Mack stood up and bowed. Layla clapped, and Brianna's jaw hung open, awestruck at the story her daughter had written and the man who had helped it come to life.

Hugh stood and clapped. "Bravo!"

Brianna looked up at him with damp eyes. Even blurry, he was the most handsome man she'd ever seen, but she was looking—again—beyond his facial features and broad shoulders. She saw right through to his generous, loving heart.

Hugh took her hand and led her down the aisle, where she scooped up Layla.

"That was the most beautiful story," Brianna said.

As they mounted the stairs to the stage, Layla said, "I wrote it. Me and Hugh did."

Halfway across the stage, Layla wriggled from Brianna's arms and wrapped her arms around Hugh's legs.

"That was the best play ever!" Layla gushed.

Before Brianna could pull herself together enough to thank him, and her mother, and Kat—*Oh God, everyone did this for me? For Layla?*—Hugh leaned in close and whispered, "What do you think of your little playwright now?"

Layla has such a kind heart. She looked at her daughter, grinning from ear to ear and jumping up and down like she was the star of the show. Which, of course, she was.

She snuggled against him. "I'm beginning to believe in fairy tales."

Chapter Thirty-Five

THE CATERED DINNER arrived as scheduled and was swiftly set up in the reception area. Just beyond the table, Tami stood with Layla and Karen, all three of them giggling with their heads huddled together. Hugh watched Brianna, Kat, and her mother talking off to the side. Her mother shrugged, then looked at Hugh and winked, and he knew Brianna was chastising Jean for not revealing that Hugh had secretly gone to her work and introduced himself. He didn't like to keep secrets, but the dreamy look on Brianna's face that had remained since they'd stepped from the car was worth it.

"That was really something, Hugh." Mack appeared by his side with a drink in hand. Without his tavern T-shirt, he looked older. Dress pants and button-down shirts tended to do that to men. He offered a drink to Hugh.

"No, thanks. Racing this weekend." He held up his glass of water.

"You know, you set the bar really high for normal guys like me."

"Do I?" Hugh looked at Mack and saw the tease in his eye, but Mack was right, and that realization brought him back to Brianna's earlier comment about spoiling Layla. He made a mental note to watch the lavishness of his gifts. Brianna had worked hard to provide for her daughter, and Hugh didn't want to create an alternative lifestyle for her. They'd have to find a middle ground. As he watched Brianna touch her locket and then glance at him and smile, he knew that together they could do anything.

"Hell, it's okay." Mack glanced at Brianna. "I've never seen her so happy. She's a good egg, Hugh. She works hard, she's a wonderful mother, and she really cares about people."

"I feel like there's a threat coming, Mack."

"No threat." Mack pulled his shoulders back. "Just a word of advice."

Hugh raised his eyebrows.

"She doesn't love easily. I've watched guys try to catch her eye, ask her out. Hell, one guy even brought her flowers every day for a week. And still she held back. She let all those walls down for you, and I would hate to see her name in a rag magazine with the byline *Jilted Spouse*."

Hugh's chest tightened. He narrowed his eyes and met Mack's gaze. "I'm not that guy, Mack."

"Yeah. You don't seem like it, but tabloid tales don't exactly show a monogamous lifestyle."

Tabloids. Fucking tabloids. "How many women did you date before marrying Tami?"

Mack let out a quiet laugh. "Shit. I don't know. Twenty? Thirty?"

Which Hugh translated as ten or fifteen. "Did you love any of them?"

"Hell no. I don't think I knew what love was until I met Tami."

"Yeah, the right woman pulls it out of you. There's no

doubt. Now, let's say a photographer followed you around and your picture ended up in the paper with each of those women before you met Tami. How would she have reacted?"

Mack shifted his gaze to Tami. "She wouldn't have given me the time of day. Tami's not one for competition."

"Fair enough. But should the rest of the world judge who you are based on those pictures?"

A deep V formed between Mack's eyebrows. "What are you getting at?"

"That reality isn't necessarily depicted in rag magazines, Mack. My dating years were captured on film. Yours weren't." Hugh shrugged and took a drink of water. He took a step away and Mack grabbed his arm. He stared at Mack's hand until Mack released him.

"I just don't want her to end up hurt."

Hugh patted him on the back. "I love her, Mack. The last thing I want to do is hurt her. Or Layla." He noticed Brianna crossing the floor toward them. "We're on the same team, Mack, and if she ends up a jilted spouse, then you can come kick my ass." Hugh asked quietly, "What makes you think I'm gonna propose?"

Mack's cheeks lifted to a smile that immediately reached his eyes. "Guys get a look before they lock down their woman. I'm sure they had it all the way back in the caveman days before they dragged their women off to their cave. You've got that look, Hugh."

Brianna's hand on his shoulder softened all of the hard edges that remained from the threat that wasn't a threat. He knew from the wave of pleasure that passed through his body from the simple brush of her hand against his cheek as Brianna came around to his side that Mack was right.

"So, Mr. Secret Keeper. You enlisted all of my friends for this without me even knowing? How did you do it?"

"I'll leave you two alone," Mack said before leaving to join Tami and Karen.

"A gentleman never tells his secrets." Hugh pulled her close and pressed his hips to hers. "Do you think Layla enjoyed her surprise?"

Brianna looked down and her cheeks flushed. "Yes, but I'm ready for mine now." She rocked her hips against him.

He groaned. "That's unfair. We won't be alone tonight."

She blinked her lashes seductively.

"Excuse me, lovebirds." Brianna's mother, Jean, joined them.

Brianna took a step back. Her cheeks flushed red.

"Jean, thank you so much for playing along."

"Are you kidding me? This is about the most romantic thing I've ever heard of. Well, the carousel was pretty romantic, too, but look at Layla." She nodded toward the girls. "She'll never forget this night."

"That was the plan," Hugh said. He reached for Brianna's hand. "But I'll make sure I don't do too much spoiling. I know it's important to keep her well grounded."

"Oh, phooey," Jean said, waving her hand. "A little spoiling is a good thing."

"He doesn't know what the word *little* means, Mom."

Her comment conjured all sorts of dirty thoughts involving *big* things. Jesus, it was like she'd flipped a horny switch in him tonight. What the hell was going on?

He gulped down the rest of his water. "I do know what it means, and I am going to work on it. I didn't give her the tiara I had backstage."

Brianna blinked several times. "You bought her a tiara?"

"I say give it to her. What can it hurt?" Jean shrugged. "She's had a big night. What's a little more?"

Brianna crossed her arms and cast a harsh glare at her mother. "I have no idea who you are anymore."

"Bree, I did my best with you with what I had. Layla has a chance to enjoy some of the things I couldn't have dreamed of giving you. Why not allow her those pleasures?" Jean winked at Hugh.

Brianna rolled her eyes. "Great. The two of you ganging up on me. Just great."

Hugh reached for her hand. "No one's ganging up on you. Besides, I'm not giving it to her. She's had enough."

Brianna narrowed her eyes. "Really?"

"Yeah. You were right. I do need to be careful. And Jean's right, too. Layla should be able to enjoy some of the nicer things in life, but not too many. She'll look beautiful in the tiara on her birthday."

Brianna's lips curled up. "Thank you for understanding."

"I'll always try," he said. Hugh turned his attention to Jean. "And I think your mom is right, too. We can find a happy medium that we all agree on. Jean, I can't tell you how much it means to me that you were able to come and support Layla tonight."

Jean looked at Brianna and her eyes softened. "I wanted to support all of you."

"Thanks, Mom."

Jean folded Brianna into her arms. "I love you, baby girl." She drew back. "Hugh, you're leaving Friday? When do you return?"

"I'll be back after the press conference Saturday night." A

pang of loneliness touched his heart at the thought of leaving Brianna behind. Before he could weigh his thoughts, he suggested, “Why don’t the three of you come with me?”

“I have to work Friday,” Brianna said. “So does Mom.”

“We could fly you out right after,” Hugh offered. “It’ll be a fast trip, but you’ve never seen me race, and I like the idea of you being there.”

Brianna lowered her eyes. “I don’t know. After working all day, trying to rush through the airport, and you have to be there more than an hour early to fly because of security. Layla would be exhausted.”

“What about if you didn’t have to wait for the plane or show up early?” he offered.

Jean raised her eyebrows at Brianna, and Brianna shrugged.

“Bree, I can fly you down on a private plane,” Hugh explained.

“See. No idea of what little means,” Brianna said to her mother.

“It might be an adventure,” Jean said excitedly. “And Layla can sleep on the plane.”

Hugh saw a shadow in Brianna’s eyes that he couldn’t read. “Excuse me, Jean. Do you mind if I speak to Brianna alone for a moment?”

“No. Go right ahead.”

He led Brianna a few feet away. “What is it? Is it just the extravagance? Because, Bree, I have enough money to—”

She shook her head. “It’s not that.”

He brushed her hair away from her face. “Then what is it?”

She let out a breath and closed her eyes for a beat too long. Hugh’s chest tightened again.

“Bree?”

She placed her hands on his forearms. "This is going to sound stupid, but I went online and I saw all those pictures of you and women—lots of beautiful, rich-looking, sexy, too-hot-to-deny women—and I read about accidents that happen at the track, and it all kind of scares me." Her grip tightened.

"What are you saying?" He could barely breathe.

"If I don't go to the race, I can pretend it's not dangerous, and if I don't see the women all over you, it will be like it doesn't really happen." Her eyes filled with worry.

"Brianna." He took her cheeks in his hands. "Baby, I need you there. I want you there. I can't change the danger. We both know it is what it is. But the women? When I'm at the tavern, I see men looking at you and it kills me, but I know that you'd never hurt me. Can't you see the same in me? Don't you trust me?"

She held on to his arms. "I do trust you."

"Then nothing else in the world should matter." He brought his lips to hers and felt tension in the stiffness of her body. He deepened the kiss, and her lips parted; her body relaxed into him. When they drew apart, he took her hand in his and brought it to his lips. "I love you, Bree, and I love Layla. I'm not going to do anything that could hurt you. I promise you that."

She dropped her gaze and nodded.

He lifted her chin and their eyes caught. "Brianna, if you don't trust me, then we have no future." *Trust me. Please tell me you trust me.* Hugh hadn't given a thought to how he looked to the world when he'd been flaunting a different sexy woman on his arm every week. Why would he? It was all fun and games, and he had no attachments. Now he saw it all much differently. "I can't change my past, Bree. But I am the man you see in front of you. The man who wants to have a family and wants nothing more than to settle down and love you and Layla." Why wasn't she telling him how much she loved him? *Shit, shit, shit.*

She looked at Layla for a long time without saying a word. Every second that passed twisted his gut a little tighter.

"My mom trusted my dad," she whispered. "He left, and look how messed up it made me."

He moved in front of her eyes. "You're not messed up, Bree. Haven't I shown you how much you mean to me?"

She nodded.

"I don't understand any of this." Hugh took a step backward. "I get why you worry, and I know you're protecting Layla, but I haven't given you any reason to believe I'd hurt you. Not one."

She looked him in the eye. "No, you haven't."

"Then what the hell is going on?" His muscles corded. He felt them strain against his neck, felt the room go quiet, and knew all eyes were on them.

"No one plans to walk away," Brianna said softly. "What if we do go with you and you suddenly realize that this time in Richmond has been fun, but it isn't what you really want? What if you realize that you miss the faster lifestyle?"

His gut reaction—born of hurt and anger and not at all how he really felt—was, *What if I do? Then fuck me. It's my loss.* He clenched his jaw long enough to ensure his voice would not take flight without consulting his brain.

"What if you go into work tomorrow and meet a normal guy who won't spoil Layla and has never been photographed with another woman? What if you come with me and decide you can't take it? What if you're intimidated by the fan girls or hate the travel?" It could happen, he realized, and his stomach knotted tighter.

Their eyes locked. Brianna reached up and touched her locket. She tucked her hair behind her ear, and Hugh felt his heart cracking. He registered voices behind him but couldn't comprehend the words. His mind was in a vacuum, focused solely on Brianna's response.

"Maybe…maybe it's safer…for us…you and me…if Layla and I don't go." Brianna's voice was barely a whisper.

Hugh ran his hand through his hair and noticed the rest of their guests gathering their coats. He had no experience with this—with relationships. All he knew was that the idea of going to the race without her sucked and it pissed him off that she'd give up being with him because of her insecurities.

The muscles in his jaw twitched as the anger was pushed aside and disappointment filled his heart. "Let's get Layla home and we can think this through."

BRIANNA'S STOMACH LURCHED as she watched Hugh walk onto the stage and disappear behind the curtain. *He's getting Layla's tiara.* Even when she was turning their lives upside down, he was still thinking of Layla.

As soon as Hugh was out of sight, Kat joined her. "Hey, you guys okay?"

Brianna shook her head, blinking away tears that burned her eyes. "What have I done?" she whispered.

Kat dragged her into the ladies' room. Brianna spun around, her face hot, her heart racing.

"What the fuck is wrong with me?" she cried. "Oh my God,

Kat. I'm such a fuckup." She caught a glimpse of her red face in the mirror and turned away.

"What happened? It was a perfect night, and then all of a sudden everyone's looking at you guys and you both look like you've had your hearts ripped out." Kat grabbed her by the shoulders and spun her around. "Look at me, Bree. Spit it out, and if he said something that hurt you, I'll kill him."

Tears streamed down her cheeks. "Do you really think he'd hurt me? Look around you, Kat. Where are we?"

The bathroom door burst open, and her mother walked in. "What's going on?"

Brianna turned her back to her mother and crossed her arms over her chest.

"Brianna?" She touched her shoulder, and Brianna shrugged her off. "Kat?"

Brianna imagined Kat holding her palms up toward the ceiling.

"Brianna Marie Heart, turn around," her mother said in a motherly voice that commanded attention.

She rotated slowly, her eyes trained on the floor.

"Bree, talk to me. Please. What the hell happened?" She opened her arms, and Brianna collapsed into them, sobbing into her mother's shoulder.

"It's me. I can't do this. This is why I had a twelve-year plan, because relationships are too complicated."

"My ass," Kat said under her breath.

Brianna pushed away from her mother, grabbed a tissue from the counter and wiped her eyes. "What's that supposed to mean?"

"You're the most organized and efficient woman I know. For years you've juggled two jobs and a daughter." Kat stepped closer with a challenge in her hooded eyes. "There's nothing too complicated for you."

"Great friend you are," Brianna snapped.

"I am a great friend and you know it. Whatever you did, you did because you're afraid or something." Kat leaned against the sink and looked at her nails.

"You don't care." *Why am I being such a bitch?*

Kat rolled her eyes.

"Oh, that's real nice," Brianna spat.

Her mother shook her head. "Okay, girls, hold on." She stood between them. "Bree, what happened out there? He just invited you to see his race. How did that lead to *this*?"

Because I'm afraid. Because maybe I won't fit into his lifestyle. Because maybe a child is too much for him and he just doesn't know it. "How the fuck should I know?"

"Because whatever happened, you just said you did it." Kat glared at Brianna. "I love you. You know I do, but I'm not going to sit here and mollycoddle your ass when you're freaking *Pretty Woman* and Richard Gere is right outside that door waiting to sweep you off your feet."

Fresh tears filled Brianna's eyes.

"Sorry, Bree. No pity here." Kat held her gaze. "Either give it up and tell us what he did that led you to do whatever you did, or I'm walking out that door and I'll see you at work tomorrow. Did he hurt you? Demand you do something you don't want to? Is he a control freak? Does he have inappropriate thoughts about Layla?"

"Kat!" Jean snapped.

Brianna leaned against the cold tile wall. Hugh's sad eyes were seared into her memory. She slid down the wall, wishing she could disappear. She closed her eyes against the fluorescent lights that echoed off the yellow walls—and against her mother and Kat's disbelieving eyes.

"There are too many what-ifs," she finally said.

Her mother crouched beside her. "What-ifs?"

Kat paced. "What-ifs. What if he leaves me?" she said in a mocking voice. "What if he doesn't like me in a year? What if my daughter's too much for him?"

"They're real concerns, Kat," Brianna snapped.

Kat sat on the floor beside her and gently took her hand. "Yes, they are," she said in a soothing voice. "They are one hundred fucking percent valid concerns." Kat pressed her lips into a line and brushed Brianna's hair from where it had stuck to the tears on her cheek. "There are no guarantees, Bree. None. You could decide tomorrow that you don't want to be a mom anymore."

Brianna gasped. "I'd never do that."

"See what you felt right then?" Kat poked Brianna above her heart. "That pain that speared you when I said it?" She paused. "That's what you did to him."

"This is my fault." Her mother let out a loud sigh. "You worry because your dad left and because Layla's father left. You've never trusted men, and I never did anything to teach you otherwise." Her mother held her other hand.

"That's not true." It was one hundred percent true about most men, but she wasn't going to admit to *that* weakness. "I do trust Hugh." *I really, truly do. With my life and with Layla's.*

"Then what is this all about?" her mother asked.

"It's me, Mom."

Her mother shook her head. "I don't understand. Are you worried that you'll change your mind about him?"

"She's weird, but she's not crazy," Kat said.

"No. I love him. I know I do, but how do I make myself not worry? I have all this shit in my head." Brianna fidgeted with the hem of her dress. "I think about what *could* go wrong..."

Kat pushed to her feet. "Okay, so go back to your twelve-year plan, but I don't see how twelve years will change anything. Some guy will fall in love with you twelve years from now, and you'll worry that he'll leave you in a year or six. You'll just be older with saggy boobs and bigger hips. Layla will be off to college, and...Oh, you know what? Maybe we should just fill your house with cats now instead of later."

Brianna rose to her feet. "You're being a jerk."

"No. I'm a realist, which is what you have always been, but somehow you morphed into a wishy-washy wimp, which I totally don't get." Kat crossed her arms, and Brianna did the same.

"Oh my God. It's like you're both twelve years old." Jean looked between the two of them. "Brianna, you need to talk to Hugh. If you really think the *what-ifs* are too big, then follow your heart and walk away. If you think you can overcome them, then stop hemming and hawing and give this relationship a fair shot—or don't, but you gotta let him know one way or another. He's not a college kid, Bree. He's a man, and a man who seems to be head over heels in love with you and Layla."

"Tell me how." The severity of her own voice surprised her. "All I need is to know how to turn off the worries. You've seen him. He's drop-dead gorgeous. If I go to the race and see women all over him, I'll want to rip their heads off or run away, and which do *you* think I'll do?"

"Run away," her mother and Kat said in unison.

"Exactly."

"I could come with you and I could rip them off of him.

You know I'll do it." Kat smiled and fisted her hands.

"Then the real question is, what would make that feeling go away?" her mother said softly. "Because unless you're dating a dog of a man, you're gonna deal with that anyway."

"Why are you always the voice of reason, Mom? Can't you just say, *I'm totally with you here, Bree. I get it. It's fucked up, but I see why you're afraid to face it.* That would make me feel better."

"I did say that, honey. You just didn't hear me."

There was a knock at the bathroom door.

They all froze.

"Bree?"

Hugh. "Yeah?"

"Layla's really tired. Are you almost ready to go?"

Her heart squeezed so tight she thought she might cry again. "Yeah. One sec, please." Brianna blew out a breath. "I'm going to go home and think about it, and I'll decide tomorrow."

"Tomorrow?" Kat raised her eyebrows again.

"Yeah. I can't think right now."

Her mother ran her hands up Brianna's arms. "Honey, he isn't asking you to marry him. He's asking you to go watch him race."

I'm gonna make you a bride one day. Brianna nodded. "I know. But everything I do, every step I take, impacts Layla, too. It's like having a super coupon for dating. I have the power to screw up two lives instead of one. What if I go to the race and realize I can't watch him be pawed at?"

"You're so weird," Kat said. "He's racing, not pole dancing."

"I gotta tell you, honey. I don't get it either. When are you worried about him being pawed at? I was so caught up in your hysteria that I didn't even think about it." Her mother looked at her expectantly.

"Ugh! I don't know. I went online and there are all these pictures of him with gorgeous women. He's near race cars and tracks in some and in others he's signing autographs." She watched the two of them exchange an eye roll. "What?"

"Signing autographs?" Kat shook her head. "So you're worried about what exactly? You're not worried about him cheating on you? You're literally worried about him being pawed at?"

"I guess. Yeah. Why are you guys staring at me?"

"Because, Bree, if you trust him, why do you care if women paw at him when he signs autographs? And pictures on the Internet? He's a big-time racer. Of course he's going to be photographed with women. Was he cheating on a wife or a girlfriend? Did you read anything about him doing dastardly things?" Kat asked.

"Well, no." She sighed.

"Bree, you're pawed at all the time at the tavern. Should he not trust you?" Kat asked.

"See. It is me. I told you." *Shit. I'm an idiot.* "I'm overthinking again."

"You're protecting yourself and Layla," her mother said. "I understand. Go home, think about it, and the right answer will come to you."

She found Hugh carrying a heavy-lidded Layla on his shoulder.

"Hi, Mom," Layla said with a yawn.

She put her hand on Layla's back and kissed her cheek. "Sorry I took so long, princess. I'm sorry, Hugh."

"That's okay." His voice no longer carried the upbeat bravado that it had before Brianna had reached into his chest and pulled his heart out. She cringed at the thought of how she'd hurt him.

The tension in his voice tugged at her heart.

"Let's wait for your mom and Kat to get their jackets. I don't want them to walk out alone."

His compassion tugged her heart in a different direction.

Jean and Kat's faces were solemn.

"That was a really sweet thing to do," Jean said to Hugh.

"I think Layla enjoyed it. Thanks again for helping. And, Kat, you were awesome. Thanks."

Hugh pushed the glass door open and held it for the women to pass through. The second he walked out the door, flashbulbs blasted his eyes. Women called his name. He held a hand up. "What the—"

"Oh my goodness," Jean said. She grabbed hold of Brianna's and Kat's arm.

Hugh pushed through the crowd, one hand shielding Layla, the other protecting Brianna, Kat, and Jean. "Stay with me," he said to them.

"Hugh! Can I get your autograph?" a heavyset woman yelled.

"How long are you in town?" a man with a television camera hollered.

Hugh didn't answer. He continued moving toward the car and pulled Brianna closer, situating himself in front of her mother and Kat.

A beautiful blond woman with enormous breasts and a tighter-than-tight short dress pushed in front of Hugh and Brianna and shoved a pen at Hugh.

"Hugh, you can sign my cleavage?" She somehow managed to sound seductive even with the chaos.

"I don't think so," Kat yelled and yanked her away from

them. "Told you," she said to Brianna with a smile.

Hugh unlocked the car and settled Layla into her booster seat. He opened the passenger door while watching Kat and Jean hurry to their cars. The cameramen and fans stuck by Hugh, making an arc around him, shoving papers and taking pictures.

Brianna started to climb in.

"Wait." He put his arm around her and whispered, "Please do this with me."

Her mind wasn't functioning. She wanted to run. Running seemed like a great idea. Only it didn't. Running away from Hugh seemed like a really stupid idea. Her head nodded, though she didn't tell it to, and then he faced the cameras with Brianna pressed against his side. She clung to him with one hand on his abs—in her favorite spot, and damn he felt so good—and the other hand clinging to the back his slacks. The bright flashbulbs left her seeing spots.

Hugh held up one hand, and Brianna's eyes adjusted, allowing her to see the group more clearly. There were a handful of women and men, all with hopeful eyes and their arms stretched out toward Hugh. Two men with cameras were either filming or taking pictures; she couldn't tell which, as the lights were now trained on them. A black van with television station call letters emblazoned across the side was parked at the curb.

Brianna sucked in a breath. *Filming?* She stood up straighter, feeling totally out of sync with her body, and she looked over Hugh's shoulder, relieved to see that Hugh had placed himself in front of Layla's window.

"I'll answer three questions, and I'll sign autographs if you don't approach the car."

"How long are you in town?" a short man yelled.

"Two more days," he answered.

"Why did you rent out the theater?" the buxom blonde asked.

Hugh tightened his grip on Brianna, and she watched his dimples appear as he gazed lovingly into her eyes. "To do something special for my girlfriend and her daughter."

The women in the crowd *aww*ed.

My girlfriend. He'd claimed her. In front of the television camera and strangers, and he'd done it while looking at her in a way that no one could misinterpret—not even Brianna.

"Will you marry me?" a woman yelled from the back of the crowd.

"That's number three, and I'm already spoken for," Hugh answered.

The crowd moved forward, and Hugh held up a hand. He opened the door for Brianna. "Thank you," he whispered, and pressed a kiss to her lips. She climbed into the car and watched him work—and control—the crowd like he'd been doing it his whole life.

Pride swelled in her chest, and the twisting ache that had pierced her gut began to ease. He'd taken care of Layla and he'd watched out for her, Jean, and Kat, and he'd done it all on instinct, it seemed.

He claimed me.

In front of the world, he claimed me.

Brianna had no idea if the filming would end up on television or even if it was actual footage or just still pictures, but that was immaterial. What mattered was how Hugh had instantly sprung into action to shield them and what was reconfirmed during the chaos.

He loves me.

Other women don't matter.
He matters.
We matter.

Chapter Thirty-Six

THEY DROVE TO Brianna's apartment in silence. Hugh's stomach had been tied in a knot since their earlier conversation. The crowd outside the theater had pulled the noose a little tighter. He was proud to have Brianna by his side and was surprised when she'd agreed to stay with him instead of hiding in the car. It gave him hope that the look he'd seen in her eye in the theater had been something other than what he feared—that she had thought up some crazy reason to end their relationship. He'd racked his brain the whole time she was in the bathroom with her mother and Kat, and he hadn't been able to come up with one single thing that rationalized the thought of her breaking up with him.

He parked the car and caught a glimpse of Layla, fast asleep in her booster seat. Brianna looked beautiful with the splash of light from the moon that cut through the window. He reached over and cupped her cheek. Her skin was warm and smooth. She was frustrating, moody, so damn sexy, and sensuous beyond his wildest fantasies, and until just a little while ago, she was all his. He let his hand slide from her cheek with the thought.

"Let's get Layla to bed," he whispered.

Upstairs, he laid Layla in her bed and waited in the living

room while Brianna changed her into her pajamas and tucked her in. He noticed the copy of *Racing* magazine that she'd asked for on her counter, and he thought of the first night they'd met and how tough Brianna had acted. She walked into the living room, her black dress swishing against her legs, her bare feet padding softly across the floor. The hardened layers that held her together had been stripped away, revealing the warm, sensitive, and brave woman he'd fallen in love with. She reached for his hand, and without a word, he gave himself over to her, allowing her to pull him down beside her on the couch. Her head rested against his shoulder and her sweet scent enveloped them. He closed his eyes for a moment and just breathed her in, remembering the feel of her naked body beneath him, the way she closed her eyes when he kissed her, and the sexy little sounds she made when she came. His lips curved up when he thought of her telling him to stop asking if he could kiss her and how cute she looked when she said she was a tramp for spending the night at his house before he even had her telephone number.

He couldn't imagine a life without her.

He didn't want to imagine it.

Her lips on his cheek pulled his eyes open.

"Yes," she said.

"Yes?"

"I wanna go to your race. Me and Layla, and I think Mom will go too."

Her brown eyes searched his, and he knew he should respond, but his words were trapped against his heart, afraid to come forth lest she changed her mind again.

She furrowed her brow. "Is that still okay?"

"Yeah," he whispered. "But I need to understand what happened back there."

She looked down. "I'm sorry. I had a little freak-out moment."

"Bree, don't you trust me?" He felt like his heart was in her hands—literally. One wrong move and it'd shatter.

"I do. I really do. I wasn't sure if I trusted me."

"I'm sorry, but huh?"

She stared at the floor.

"I need to see your eyes, Bree. Tell me what's going on. You broke me back there, and I'm not an easily broken man." He felt raw. Exposed. Vulnerable. *What the fuck happened to me?* One look at beautiful Brianna and he had his answer. *I fell in love.*

"I was afraid of how I'd react. I might come across as brave, Hugh, but I'm pretty insecure. I'm not a beautiful, buxom blonde. I'm not the life of the party or the sexiest girl around."

"You're right. You're more beautiful than any blonde could ever be, and you're the sexiest *woman* around. I'm not looking for a party girl, Bree. Didn't I make that clear the first night I met you?"

She nodded.

"Bree, I'm not a halfway guy."

"I know, and I'm not a halfway girl."

She moved closer to him, and he pulled her onto his lap. He needed to feel her close, to know he wasn't losing her.

"I guess my father's leaving did have a profound effect on me. I worry about it. I worry that no matter how much someone loves me, how much you love me, you might find someone better along the way and Layla and I would get really hurt. But it's not just you. I think I'd be that way with any man, which is probably why I wasn't so upset about Layla's father not wanting to be involved from the beginning. It was easier to be alone than to worry about being abandoned."

He felt his heart come back together. If Hugh had learned one thing about himself over the past few days, it was that he was capable of love. He knew he was loyal and honest and, without hesitation, he loved Brianna. He'd never abandon her. Before he could reassure her, she continued.

"I was afraid I'd run if I saw women all over you, because running away would be so much easier than being left behind. But then I saw you with those women tonight, and you didn't give them a second glance. Your entire focus was on our safety. Our feelings."

"Of course," he whispered.

"Maybe to normal people it would be a *duh* moment. An *of course* moment. To me, it was an awakening."

She touched his cheek. "You love me," she said. It wasn't a question. It was a confirmation.

He closed his eyes for a beat, relishing in the feel of her. "I do. Very much." Relief eased his shoulders down a little lower.

"And you love Layla."

"Very much."

She nodded and pressed her hands against his chest. "Does that happen a lot?"

Her hands stirred a different type of warmth in him. "What?"

"Autographs, cameras."

"Yes. Sometimes. Someone from the theater must have leaked that I was there. I'm sorry you had to experience that." He laid his hand on her bare knee.

"I'm not. It helped me realize how silly I was being. I worried so much about Layla getting hurt—about me getting hurt—that I was ready to hide for eighteen years. I can't hide from what we have, Hugh. Tonight I realized that I don't want to. And the next time I fall into a *what-if* stage—and trust me, I will—will you please remind me that I'm being an idiot?"

He felt his cheeks lift with a smile. "No." He laughed under his breath. "I know better than to do that. If you're anything like you were tonight, it wouldn't have mattered if I had carried you behind the curtains and made sweet love to you." Damn, now he had that image in his head. "You were in a place all your own. Untouchable." Mack's words came rushing back to him. *She doesn't love easily.* "Teach me how. I'll do anything for you."

She leaned forward and pressed her lips to his.

"That wouldn't have worked. You were too upset. You would have smacked me. Help me help you, Bree. I'm being sincere. How can I break through next time without upsetting you further?"

She unbuttoned his shirt and slid her hand across his chest. Holy hell. Now he had a hard-on again. She was seriously fucking with his equilibrium.

"Next time I do that…" She leaned in close and took his neck in her mouth, sucking lightly. "We need a code word."

He was still stuck on her tongue on his neck. "Code…"

"Mm-hmm," she said. "If I get the what-ifs, you say—"

"Sidecar."

She wrinkled her nose. "Sidecar?"

"Yes. It will remind you of the night we first met." He pulled her mouth back down to his neck.

"Sidecar," she whispered before taking his neck in her mouth again.

His broken heart reassembled and slammed against his chest. Her tongue stroked his neck. She came away from his neck with her lips parted, curling into a coy smile as he lowered his mouth to them, filling her with all the love he had. Their mouths fit together perfectly; their tongues moved in tandem; their bodies melded together. He slid his hand beneath her dress, stroking her through her damp panties. She looked at him hungrily, and he knew they were once again in sync. He slid his fingers beneath the thin fabric and groaned as he entered her. Brianna pressed her hips into him. He slid her dress open and took her breast in his mouth, inciting the sexy little moans that sent his desires into overdrive. Christ, she was hot. He felt her thighs tighten, and he moved his fingers quicker. His tongue teased the taut peak of her nipple, and she grabbed his shoulder in her fist, digging her nails into him. He loved the pain and pleasure all at once. She called out his name, and he brought his lips to hers to muffle her cries as the orgasm tore through her and she kissed him like she needed him to survive. He brought her down easy, replacing his fast strokes with lusciously slow teases. She sighed a sweet, gratified breath, and he leaned his forehead against her chest.

He listened to her heartbeat calm, felt her body find that boneless, after-release sedation.

"Bree?"

"Mm?"

"Don't scare me again, please." He looked up at her, and all the feelings he had for her collided together—the love, respect, lust, worry—and he needed all of her. Right then, right there. *Bad idea.* He glanced down the hall.

"I promise. Sidecar. Just remember sidecar." She slid off his lap and reached for his zipper.

"No, not here." He lifted his chin in the direction of Layla's door.

She stood and took his hand. He followed her down the

hall, past Layla's door, and into her bedroom, which felt insanely naughty.

"You sure? What if she wakes up?"

"I locked the door. We'll just have to be very quiet." She fumbled with his button, and he settled his hand over hers.

"Bree. I can wait."

"I can't."

THERE WASN'T TIME to think or even to breathe. Brianna had made one giant mistake that evening, and she'd never be so foolish again. The fear of losing Hugh intensified her desire to erase what she'd done. As their mouths mashed together and they fumbled with each other's clothes, she let her mind go where she had been tethering it from meandering before. To the place that scared her the most. *The future.* He laid her down on the bed, and she closed her eyes, waiting for the fear to settle in as it had earlier. She felt his hands on the insides of her thighs, pushing her legs open, and she heard his whisper from earlier. *Please do this with me?* She summoned the fear, imagining herself at the race, watching women reach for Hugh.

His hands traveled up her sides, rough and sure.

She tried harder to bring the fear forward. Trying to imagine him closer, using the buxom blonde from earlier in the night as a visual, testing her own fear. She closed her eyes and tried again to imagine Hugh moving toward the blonde. She needed to see if the fear was lingering somewhere deep within her brain.

Hugh wrapped his lips around her hip and stroked her skin with his tongue. She rocked against his teeth, wishing he'd go lower.

The blonde pushed herself in front of him, and no matter how much Brianna tried to conjure an image of him moving toward the blonde with a wanton look in his eyes, his eyes remained trained on Brianna. The fear would not come out to play.

"Yes," she called out in excitement. Her hand flew to her mouth, and Hugh looked up.

"Did I miss a home run?" he teased.

"Sorry," she whispered. She bit her lip but could not suppress the smile that stretched her lips.

Then his body was on top of hers, and he was kissing her, hard and deep, and she could feel his hard length against her, and—*Oh God*—she wanted him so badly. She pulled at his hips, and he rolled to the side and snagged a condom from his wallet.

"Hurry," she whispered.

He made a dramatic display of opening it painfully slowly and then rolling it on at the same treacherously unhurried pace. She groaned, and he slid back up her body, the tip of him resting against her center.

"What was the cheer for?"

"Come on," she urged, hoping he'd drop it.

He pulled back, and she grabbed hold of him, pulling him up once again. "Okay, okay." She sighed. "I was trying to envision you with a fan girl."

He pushed himself up on one hand. "While I was…"

"Mm-hmm."

"Why?"

"Because I wanted to make sure the fear was really gone."

"You tried to bring a fan girl into the bedroom with us to make sure it didn't scare you?" he teased.

"No!"

"Shhh." He pressed a kiss to her lips. "I don't swing that way, sweetheart. I'm a one-woman man. So if you need more than just me to satisfy you, you need to tell me now."

She shoved him playfully. "Shut up."

"I'm being serious." He grinned and brought his hips between hers again.

"So am I. I can't summon the fear. I'm sure it's still there, lingering and waiting to attack at the worst time, but I'm going to tattoo *sidecar* on our wrists. Then we'll be safe forever."

He took her hands in his and stretched them above her head, holding them with one hand.

"Forever. I like that," he whispered, then lowered his mouth to hers.

Within seconds, she was lost in the kiss. The best kiss of her life. He held her arms captive, rendering her defenseless and unable to pull his hips to hers. She arched in to him, and he teased her, sinking just the thick tip of himself into her, then drawing it out. She gasped with each withdrawal, her wrists straining against his strength. When he drew back, she was breathless, but not too breathless to plead for more of him.

"Make love to me," she panted.

He sank the tip in again and then—*Oh yes!*—a little more.

"Yes. More."

He withdrew again, and a cry escaped her lips. He tried to catch it in his mouth and was too slow. "Shh," he reminded her.

How the hell was she supposed to be quiet when he was bringing every nerve in her body to a tantalizing, brain-numbing ache of need?

"Please," she begged.

He sank his teeth into her neck and drove her up to the edge with three hard sucks and another taunting tease down below. She closed her eyes and groaned, struggling to free her arms and loving the restraint.

"Open your eyes," he said. "See me. Feel me."

The promise of feeling him drew her eyes open. She was so close to coming apart that when he said, "I love you, Bree," it almost took her over the edge. She closed her eyes to savor the moment.

"Open your eyes. See me, Bree. Be with me."

His voice was rich and smooth, and oh so sexy. She opened her eyes, and he drove into her, every magnificent inch of him, filling her completely, touching all the right spots as he thrust again and again, withdrawing almost completely and then returning with fervor, each time taking her higher. His eyes darkened and narrowed, but he held her gaze, and the strain of her arms against the thrust of his hips and the love in his eyes collided in a flash of lights as she reached her peak, and this time he caught her passionate cries in his mouth. A minute later, oxygen from his lungs filled hers as he found his release, and she held their silence by swallowing his gratified groans.

Chapter Thirty-Seven

IT WAS ALMOST three when Hugh arrived home. He showered and checked his email, then wandered around the house that didn't really feel like a home. Brianna's apartment felt like a home. No, that wasn't right either. Wherever Brianna was felt like home. Yes, that was it.

He picked up his cell and punched in Treat's speed-dial number.

"You'd better be dying," Treat groaned.

"Nice welcome for your baby brother," Hugh teased.

"Hold on," Treat grumbled. Hugh listened to him walk across the floor. A door opened, then closed. Treat sighed, and Hugh pictured him in his boxer briefs, his enormous body stumbling in the dark house Hugh had yet to see.

"You all right?" Treat was more awake now, with a sharp, irritated edge.

"Sorry for calling so late. I need a favor."

Treat sighed again.

Hugh ran his hand through his hair. "Treat. I don't know who else to ask, man."

"Of course. Whatever you need."

And just like that his eldest brother, the person who had

always watched out for him, taught him, riled him up like no other, and above all else, loved him, was ready to help. That was the kind of man who Hugh was striving to be.

"When you proposed to Max, remember how she rushed to our house and you showed up and she backed into your car?" He spoke fast, anxious to get his point across.

"Like it was yesterday." Treat yawned.

"Were you guys having trouble? Why was it all so…urgent?" Hugh stood before the glass doors in the living room, one arm crossed over his abs, his other elbow leaning on his wrist.

"Hugh, this is what's so urgent?"

"Treat, please."

"Yeah, okay. We were having some trouble, yes, but not trouble because we didn't want to be together. It was more like trouble because we did want to be together, but it was scary as shit."

He heard Treat breathing as if he were pacing.

"Hugh, what's going on?"

"I just needed to make sure I wasn't crazy. Are you still coming to the race?"

"Planning on it, but still waiting to hear about your plans for that night."

"Shit, I forgot. I'm sorry, man. Listen, I need a favor. It's a big one."

"Of course it is."

Not for the first time, Hugh thanked the heavens above for his family.

Chapter Thirty-Eight

BRIANNA PULLED UP in front of the school Thursday morning, and when she turned to say goodbye to Layla, a knock on her car window startled her. Marissa's mother, Cheryl, wearing thick eyeliner, red skintight jeans that accentuated her enormous ass and hips, and a thick black belt, stared into the car. She looked like Peg Bundy from *Married with Children*, complete with the eighties hair and spike heels. Brianna sighed and feigned a smile as she rolled down the window.

Cheap perfume assaulted her.

"Hey there, sugar." Cheryl peered into the backseat. "Hi, Layla. How's the birthday girl?"

"Good," she said, unbuckling her booster seat strap.

"You know Marissa will be there today, right? We left you a message."

"Yes, we're looking forward to it." Brianna glanced at Layla. "You okay, honey? You should get going."

Layla pushed her face over the front seat and kissed Brianna's cheek. "I love you."

"Love you too, princess." She watched her run out the door and into a pack of classmates, all with bright backpacks strapped to their backs like turtle shells.

"Will he be there?" Cheryl whispered.

"He who?"

Cheryl lifted her eyebrows and looked around, then pushed her head into the window and whispered, "Hugh Braden."

"How do you know about Hugh?"

"Oh please. Do you really think you can hide a man like that?" She whipped the morning newspaper from behind her back, and on the front page of the Local News section was a photograph of Hugh's smiling face, Brianna staring up at him like a star-struck groupie.

Holy shit.

She noticed two of Layla's other classmates' mothers heading for her car.

"Um, I don't know, Cheryl, but I have to get to work. Sorry to be rude." She rolled up the window and hightailed it out of the school parking lot.

She parked behind the tavern and dug through her purse for her phone. *Damn it.* She'd left it on vibrate and had three messages from Hugh. Her heart raced as she listened to them.

Hi, beautiful. Don't freak out, but we're in the newspaper. Complete with my proclamation of being off the market. Love you. I'll call you later.

She groaned.

Hey, babe. Just trying to catch you before my appointment. I'll see you tonight at Layla's party, and I'll try to call you later. Love you.

Why wasn't it Friday night? Getting out of town would be so much easier.

Hey, still trying to reach you. It just dawned on me that you might be freaking out and I wanted to say…Sidecar. Love you. Don't be scared. Nothing can ever come between us.

A call from Hugh rang through and she switched over.

"Hey there," she said, thankful that he'd reached her this time.

"Sidecar."

She let out a breath and felt her lips curl into a smile. "I'm not freaking out too badly."

"I'm on my way into my meeting, so I can't talk long, but I wanted to…no, I needed to know that you were okay."

"I'm good. I'm not going to let my insecurities or fear come between us. How do you usually handle this stuff?" Layla's lunch was sitting on the backseat. *Crap.*

"I don't pay it any mind anymore. At first it was kind of exciting; then it became a pain in the ass. But to be honest, I'm kind of glad about this picture. Now the world knows I'm with you. That's a good thing, because I'm ready to shout it from the rooftop."

She pictured his eyes lighting up and his deep dimples on his perpetually unshaven and way-too-sexy cheeks. Then it hit her like a punch to the gut. "Layla. Oh God, Hugh. They'll be all over her at school. I gotta get over there."

"Damn it. I wish I were there. I'm sorry, Bree."

She heard the distress in his voice. "It's fine. I can do this. I'm not a wimpy weak girly girl." She touched her locket. "I'm a brave, strong girlfriend."

"Yeah, you are. Love you, babe."

"Love you, too. I gotta go save my daughter, who is probably drama queening it up for the entire class about Prince Hugh."

He laughed. "I can't wait to see you."

"Oh, wait. I'm sorry. One more thing. I was mobbed at school and they were asking if you were going to be at the birthday party. That was a little freaky."

"Sidecar, sidecar, sidecar. I'll leave that up to you. I don't want to hide, and once your friends see that I'm a regular guy, they'll get used to me and the excitement will wear off. But if you worry it'll take the focus off of Layla, I'll stay home."

She sighed. "You're so good to us. I'm not missing a minute with you because of fan girls anymore. I made a promise to myself."

"Good. I gotta run, babe."

She ended the call and said, "Sidecar, sidecar, sidecar," as she threw the car into gear.

Chapter Thirty-Nine

THE FIRST THING Brianna did when she walked into the school was go to the principal's office. Principal Shue was not known for being warm and friendly. Oh, how she'd avoided that office when she was younger. But now, after seeing Cheryl's reaction to Hugh, the only thing that mattered was Layla's comfort and safety. Shue had ruled the school with an iron fist when Brianna was younger. Brianna was certain she'd enforce stringent rules when it came to her daughter's safety.

As she entered the glass doors of the main office, she remembered that Shue required appointments before ten o'clock in the morning. *I am not a weak girly girl.*

The school secretary, Ann Olephant, smiled when Brianna entered the office. "Brianna, how are you, dear?" She was a sweet gray-haired woman with a slight hunch in her back and silver glasses that hung from a chain around her neck and never seemed to find their way to the bridge of her nose.

"Fine, thank you. How have you been?" Brianna's stomach clenched when she spotted Shue on the phone in her office.

"Oh lovely, dear." She leaned across the desk and whispered, "Saw your picture in the paper."

"That's why I'm here. I don't have an appointment, but I'd

like to speak with Principal Shue, please."

"Oh yes. I think she'll make the time, given the situation. Just have a seat, and I'll let her know you're here." She pushed her stout body from her chair and hurried into Principal Shue's office.

The situation? Now Hugh and I are a "situation"?

Brianna sat in the plastic chairs by the door. Two of the lunchroom aids breezed into the office. One carried the newspaper, folded to show the photograph of Hugh and Brianna. Luckily, they were so engrossed in the damn thing they didn't notice her sitting to the left of the doors. She sank down in her chair.

"Can you believe it? I heard—"

"Brianna. It's been a very long time." All six feet of Principal Shue looked over her.

Brianna jumped to her feet. "Yes, it has. Thank you for seeing me." She followed the *clomp, clomp, clomp*, of Principal Shue's black orthopedic shoes into her office and sat across from Principal Shue, separated by a large wooden desk. She still wore her dyed-too-dark hair cropped short above her ears and layered throughout, and she still wore the same style polyester pantsuit that she'd worn when Brianna had been in school. She looked just as manly.

Brianna fidgeted with the seam on her purse, wrestling the same jittery feelings she'd had as a grade schooler.

"I hear Layla is a little celebrity today." Principal Shue leaned back in her chair and crossed her thick legs.

"Excuse me?"

"Oh, her class took a few minutes this morning to discuss what it was like to know someone famous. It was a good lesson for the children. You know, etiquette and such. The teacher did a nice job of handling it."

"Etiquette?" Brianna gripped her purse in both fists. "That is not at all appropriate for my daughter to experience in school. What our private life consists of is not up for classroom discussion."

"Oh, Brianna. You always did buck the system."

"Buck the system?" *I'll buck the fucking system all right.*

"The way you used to fight against Take Your Child to Work Day." She narrowed her eyes at Brianna, and Brianna bristled.

She'd always hated those days. They had twenty-one children in their class, and on Take Your Child to Work Day, she and the Baker twins were the only children who came to class. The Baker twins' parents also worked two jobs just to make ends meet. She'd argued the validity of Take Your Child to Work Day every year her mother was unable to take her, and every year Mrs. Shue gave her the same song and dance about the importance of children seeing what it was that their parents did for a living. Unfortunately, she never gave her the answer Brianna had needed. She never told her that her mother's boss was an ass or that at the time it had been difficult for a single mother to find employment that paid well enough to provide for them. Or what Brianna had really wanted to hear, even if it was unreasonable—that Take Your Child to Work Day had been canceled. Forever.

"I still think that day is quite silly," Brianna said. "I came in today to ask that you please monitor Layla's class and her friends now that…" *I've been photographed with my boyfriend? My lover? Oh God, what do I say?*

"Now that the cat's out of the bag?"

Brianna sighed. "Look, I don't want Layla to be the center

of attention because of Hugh's career. She's a six-year-old girl, and she's here to learn and socialize, not to become a public spectacle."

"Perhaps you should have considered that before you started dating Mr. Braden."

Ouch. Brianna stood. "Perhaps, but since this…issue has come about, can I count on you to protect my daughter or not? That's the only thing that matters at this point."

"Settle down, Brianna. Sit back down, please."

Brianna obeyed like one of Pavlov's dogs.

"Layla didn't seem to mind talking about her night at the theater, and she was commended for her creativity for writing her own play. We're certainly not trying to make a spectacle of her. There was a lot of excitement this morning, as two of the children brought the newspaper into class, and it grew from there." Principal Shue leaned across the desk.

Brianna's heart told her to take Layla and leave the school, but her mind told her to *behave* and *listen.*

"I can make certain that Mr. Braden's existence doesn't come into play in the daily classroom activities, but I'm not sure I can do much about what she'll experience on the playground. But you know how these things go. Kids will forget soon enough, and life will go back to normal."

Brianna remembered the two long years after her father left. Kids did not forget, and things did not go back to anything even close to resembling normal. And not once did any adult ask her how she felt about the name-calling or feeling left out during the special parent-child days when her mother had to work. She'd been labeled *the girl whose father left. And I'm still that girl.* There's no way in hell she'd let Layla become *the girl whose mother is dating Hugh Braden.* Brianna's phone vibrated.

"I'm sorry. Excuse me." She dug her phone out of her purse to turn it off and was astonished to see three text messages from Layla's classmates' mothers. *Now that Hugh is around, they came out of the woodwork.*

"Trouble?" Principal Shue asked.

"No." She shoved her phone back in her purse. "I guess when you date a…someone like Hugh, everyone wants a piece of him." She hated the frustration in her voice and the way her muscles all pulled tight across her neck. Was this what their life would be like? How could she protect Layla from getting an overinflated ego or from being used?

"Brianna, take a deep breath."

Brianna obeyed. *Ugh!* She hated feeling like she was back in third grade. She wondered how Layla felt. Not what Principal Shue thought was right or wrong, and not even what she thought was right or wrong. *How is Layla dealing with the attention?* She knew what she had to do.

"Principal Shue, I'd like to speak to Layla." She rose to her feet and headed for the door.

"I'll be happy to have her come down and we can speak to her."

"No, thank you. I'd like to speak with her privately." She walked out of the principal's office. "Actually, I'll go get her. I can observe through the door for a few minutes. You can tell a lot about a child's feelings by watching and even more by listening." A few determined strides later, she was rounding the corner to Layla's classroom.

She looked through the glass on the door. Layla waved her hand in the air, flapping it like a flag. Brianna smiled at her enthusiasm. *Maybe I overreacted.* She heard Principal Shue's *clop, clop, clop* echoing down the hall. She wondered if Hugh had been right and this would blow over and he'd become just "Layla's mother's boyfriend" after a while. Layla was talking to the teacher, and she looked happy enough. Brianna was about to walk away when Principal Shue appeared behind her.

"Aren't you going to speak with her?" She looked down at Brianna with the same stern look she always had.

"No. I think she's okay."

"Brianna, speak to your daughter. She'll appreciate that you did, and you'll have peace of mind."

She met the principal's surprisingly soft gaze.

"Your mother did this same thing when you were in school. After your father left, she'd come and observe about once a week. She'd feel confident after seeing you pay attention in class, or laugh at something, and then she'd go on her way. Take it to the next step, Brianna. You were never settled, and I think if your mother had pulled you from class and let you know that she cared about how you felt during school hours, it might have made you a little more at ease."

"Then why didn't you tell her to do that for me?" Brianna felt her legs weakening.

"I did. She didn't have time. She worked very hard. Two jobs, as I remember, and she'd come over on a break and have to run back to work afterward." Her gaze softened.

"She never told me." *I wish she had.*

"Many parents don't. They don't want to embarrass their children by making them think they were checking up on them. You were a pistol. You stood up to the kids who called you names." Principal Shue crossed her arms and looked as immovable as a linebacker.

"You knew?"

"Of course I knew. I tried to stop it, but you know we can't do much. We can talk to the children, suspend them for a day or two, but that's the extent of it. You held up a brave front. You gave it right back to them."

Brianna had no recollection of ever *giving it right back* to anyone. She remembered feeling alone and different. Very, very different.

Principal Shue continued, and this time she spoke in a soft tone, her eyes translating pride toward Brianna. Her normal rigid facade was now more relaxed as she gazed off to the side, as if she were watching a memory unfold before her. "A few months after your father left, you began ignoring those comments. You'd lift your little chin and act as though you were deaf to it all."

Deaf to it all? I was able to wall my emotions off then, too? Enough of that. No more. Determined not to let Layla experience the same lonely, painful childhood, she changed her mind. "I think I will talk to her. Thank you."

Twenty minutes later, after running Layla's lunch back inside, Brianna left the school with more than peace of mind. She had a contented heart as well. She hadn't yet explained to Layla what Hugh did for a living, and though her classmates made a big deal about it, Layla had raised her palm to the air and told Brianna, *All adults drive cars. Hugh's nice, so I told them that he was nice and to stop asking about his cars. Sheesh!* Unlike Brianna, Layla seemed able to handle the situation—at least for now.

HUGH ARRIVED AT Jean's house at five-thirty. "Wow, that's a big box." Brianna opened the door, and her heart swelled at the sight of Hugh. She wondered if she'd ever get used to his good looks or the sparkle that lit up his eyes when he saw her for the first time each day.

Hugh handed her a large gift wrapped in silver paper. "This one's for you."

"It's not my birthday."

"Sure it is. You gave birth to Layla six years ago. Besides, you can't get mad about this. It's a very utilitarian purchase. You need it."

They went into the living room and Brianna untied the ribbon. "Maybe I need rules about not spoiling me, too."

"I can adhere to the spoiling rule for children, but a girlfriend shall have no say on her own spoiling."

Brianna gasped as she took the camera from the box. "Hugh." She touched it as if it were made of glass.

"CD…Claude helped me pick it out."

"Oh my God. I can't accept this. These are super expensive." She put it back in the box. They'd never discussed finances, and Brianna was sure Hugh earned a lot of money given his cars and what he did for a living, but it was still too lavish of a gift for her to accept.

"Bree, if I have to accept not spoiling Layla, then you have to accept the gifts I choose for you."

"But…"

He wrapped her in his arms. "I love that you worry, but I promise you that I wouldn't ever buy anything that I couldn't afford." Hugh set the box on the coffee table and pulled Brianna down to the couch beside him. "I make more money in a year than we could ever spend."

We? She wrinkled her brow.

Layla ran into the room. "Hugh!" She jumped into his lap

and assessed the open gift. "Is that present for Mom?"

"Yup. Now she can take pictures of your party," Hugh said.

"Oh goody!" She slid off his lap and ran into the kitchen. "Grandma! Guess what Mom got!"

A knock at the door drew Brianna's attention. She should have expected that people would show up early, given the morning newspaper.

"Cheryl, hi." Brianna opened the door, very aware—by Cheryl's gaping jaw—of Hugh standing behind her.

Cheryl wore the same outfit she'd had on earlier in the day, though she had on enough perfume to gag a small army. "You must be Hugh. What a pleasure to meet you." She held out a limp wrist.

Hugh nodded and flashed his dimples. "Hello, Cheryl. Nice to meet you."

Marissa ran into the house. "See! There he is!" she yelled over her shoulder to three other little girls and their mothers. Each woman dressed as though she were attending a formal, albeit slutty, affair. Brianna had never seen these women in anything other than jeans and T-shirts. Now they flaunted cleavage, short skirts, and more makeup than Kat wore.

The children ran into the backyard with Layla, and the women swooned over Hugh, blinking their heavily mascaraed eyelashes and peppering him with questions.

"I didn't even know you lived in the area," Cheryl said.

"How did you two meet?" Lisa, a short blond-haired woman asked.

"We should get together for dinner sometime with the kids," Kelly, a short, stout brunette suggested.

Hugh put his arm around Brianna and pulled her in close. "I do have a house here, and I was lucky enough to meet Bree at her work." He kissed the side of her forehead. "Babe, I promised to help Jean with a few things. Do you mind?"

Brianna could have stayed in his arms forever, but the vultures were eye raping him. She didn't blame Hugh for wanting to escape. Of course they all watched him walk away. Brianna had to admit, he did have a hot ass. Thankfully, the parents from Layla's class never stayed at birthday parties. They always had an errand to run or another child to care for, so she held the door open for them to leave.

"The party is over at seven thirty." She watched as the women followed Hugh toward the kitchen. Brianna groaned. She picked up her new camera—relishing in the weight of it, the contoured lines, and the way it fit so perfectly in her hands—and then she went to watch *The Devouring of Hugh Braden.*

She found Hugh in the backyard with the children. He'd tied the piñata to a branch of the big oak tree. Layla was beneath the tree holding a plastic bat. Her eyes were clenched shut, and Hugh began spinning her in slow circles. Brianna brought the camera to her eye and focused on the two of them. A calm that she hadn't realized she'd missed washed over her. She took several pictures, then zoomed in on Hugh's profile, feeling her heart swell as she cataloged his features through the safety of the lens, capturing them in her heart—and on film.

"Okay, Princess Layla, swing," he coaxed.

Layla swung the bat and missed.

"Again," Hugh encouraged her.

She swung again and tapped the piñata. This time he set her in just the right position and she smacked it hard. She opened her eyes and Brianna caught the awed expression, and then she caught the embrace between the two people who owned equal parts of her heart.

Sarah, a quiet blond girl, was up next. Hugh crouched beside her. What Brianna saw through her lens was the way his eyes watched the little girl's eyes as they drifted around the backyard and how he reacted to her shyness with perfect grace, not too strong, not too soft, a sweet curl to his lips, a glint in his eye, and a moment later, Sarah's eyes followed Hugh as he settled the piñata for her turn.

When it was time for the cake, the hyenas surrounded Hugh once again. Cheryl stood behind him and put her hand on his shoulder, pretending to look around him, when, in fact, there was plenty of room for her to take a step or two to the side. Through the lens of the camera, Brianna caught Hugh's shoulders as they inched up toward his ears and the pleading look in his eyes when he turned toward her. She lowered it and watched as he twisted, disengaging from Cheryl's trap, his eyes trained on Brianna.

"You okay?" Hugh touched her cheek.

If you call wanting to claw Cheryl's eyes out okay. "Yeah."

"I'm trying to be nice to your friends, but—"

"They aren't my friends, Hugh. They're the parents of Layla's friends. Don't worry. I don't blame you for them being all over you." The women watched them as Jean handed out plates and forks.

"I can put a stop to that woman with one sentence. But I need your okay to do it."

She tilted her head, wondering what the mischievous gleam in his eyes meant.

"One sentence. That's all it takes. Something simple like, *You're really sweet, but I don't like to be touched by anyone other than Brianna.*"

Brianna laughed. "You're a goof."

"How about, *Only in your dreams*, and then I take you in a passionate kiss and press your beautiful body against mine until you can't think and I can't breathe?"

She couldn't think, and from the looks of it, he could hardly breathe. She licked her lips.

He stepped closer. "I will have to kiss you if you do that again, and I'm pretty sure that when I start I won't be able to stop."

He had a hungry look in his eyes, and when she put her hand on his stomach, she felt him shudder, which sent a pulse of heat right through her.

"Bree, Hugh, we're ready for cake," Jean said.

For a moment they just stared at each other, unable to break away from the electricity that bound them. Hugh's hand found hers, and Brianna begged her legs to remain strong.

"Hold up." Hugh held up one finger. "I have something for the birthday girl before we get started." He ran into the house and came back out with his hands behind his back.

He stood behind Layla, and Brianna focused her camera once again as Hugh settled the tiara on Layla's head.

"Happy birthday, Princess Layla."

Brianna caught on film every smile, every excited moment as Layla stood on her chair and jumped into Hugh's arms and the loving look on Hugh's face as Layla pressed her cheek against his. She lowered the camera to unveil the scene in real time. She'd never imagined that anyone could love Layla as much as she did, and there was Hugh, with a heart as big as the sun and enough love to share with both of them.

The other mothers *aww*ed, and Brianna knew that it would

never matter if women pawed at or fought for Hugh. She and Layla had already staked claim to his heart, and they hadn't even actively tried. *Maybe some things really are meant to be.*

Chapter Forty

FRIDAY AFTERNOON, THE tavern was crazy busy, which made Brianna's workday go by quickly. By the time she met her mother and Layla at the apartment, she was too nervous to be tired. Hugh's brother Treat and his wife, Max, were going to pick them up, and she had no idea what to expect. Hugh had said that she'd love them both, but that didn't stop the butterflies in her belly from multiplying.

"Are you sure you have Piglet?" she asked Layla.

"Yes." Layla and Jean were in the middle of a game of Drama Queen.

Brianna checked her bags one more time. *Clothes, shoes, makeup, birth control pills.* At exactly six o'clock, there was a knock at the door.

"Okay, princess. Let's go. Mom, are you ready?" Brianna asked.

"Of course. This will be an adventure." Jean reached for Layla's hand.

Brianna opened the door and was greeted by one of the tallest men she'd ever seen up close. He wore what looked to be a very expensive dark suit and white button-down shirt. She noted the similarities between Treat and Hugh; they had the same dark hair, though Treat's was cut a little shorter, the same olive skin, and the same warm, friendly eyes.

"Hi. Brianna?" His voice was as deep as Hugh's.

"Yes, hi." Brianna held out her hand, and when he shook it, his giant hand engulfed hers. "This is Jean, my mother, and my daughter, Layla."

"Treat Braden. It's a pleasure to meet you. I've got a car waiting to take us to the airport." He reached into his jacket and withdrew an activity book, which he handed to Layla. "I thought you might like this for the trip," he said.

"You didn't have to do that," Brianna said. "Thank you."

Treat gathered their bags, and Brianna carried Layla's backpack. A black limousine waited for them out front.

Layla squealed, "Look! Look!"

Jean mouthed, *Wow*, to Brianna.

Brianna looked down at her jeans, boots, and sweater, then back at Treat's suit and cringed. Was she going to need a whole new wardrobe?

Treat opened the door, and Layla climbed into the booster seat that was already in place.

"Hi!" Layla said.

Brianna peered into the car and smiled at Max, a pretty brunette she recognized from the photograph at Hugh's house. She was relieved to see that she, too, was wearing jeans. She breathed a little easier as she climbed into the limo.

"Hi, I'm Bree, and this is Layla." Her mother climbed in behind her. "And this is Jean, my mom."

Max smiled warmly. "Hi. I'm excited to meet you. I'm Max."

Treat climbed in next to Max and put his arm around her. "My very beautiful wife." He kissed the side of her forehead.

"Oh, stop." Max laughed. "This is going to be fun."

They were on the road a few minutes later, and Max filled the quiet with easy conversation. Brianna loved her outgoing personality, and watching Treat with her reminded her of Hugh. He was just as attentive, and when Max teased him, he teased her right back. She wondered if the entire family was as openly affectionate as they were.

"Brianna, tell me how you met Hugh," Treat asked.

"It's sort of embarrassing. We met in the tavern where I work. He had a blind date, and I guess it didn't go so well." Brianna shrugged, dropping her gaze when she felt her cheeks heat up.

"That's not embarrassing. Thank God for dates gone bad," Max said.

"Have you ever been to the races, Layla?" Treat asked.

She shook her head.

"You'll enjoy it, but it's really loud, so we'll give you really cool earplugs if you want them." Max pulled a small box out of her leather bag. "See?" She handed them to Layla.

Layla looked at the box and crinkled her nose. "Do I have to wear them?"

Max laughed. "No, but if you want to, we'll have them."

"Thank you," Brianna said.

"I heard you had some excitement the other night," Treat said.

Layla told them all about the theater, and Jean and Brianna filled them in on the aftermath.

Treat's eyes shadowed with seriousness, and he set his gaze on Brianna. "Were you okay with that?"

"Not at first. It was a total sensory overload, and a little frightening, but Hugh knew just what to do. He swept Layla into the car, and he made sure we were all okay before attending to the crowd." She remembered the way he'd revealed their relationship, and it brought a warm feeling to her chest.

"I'm glad to hear he took care of it. Hugh's a good man," Treat said.

"All the Bradens are good people." Max set her hand on Treat's leg and smiled up at him adoringly.

Brianna watched them closely, finding the dichotomy of Treat's formality and Max's casual attire interesting. When Treat looked at Max, his dark eyes darkened even more, and he bathed her in love. Brianna had seen pictures in Hugh's house of his family, and as she got to know Treat and Max, the things he'd said about cars being *just cars* and his job being what he did, not who he was, made even more sense. She knew that Treat owned resorts all over the world, and yet neither Treat nor Max was pretentious. If she closed her eyes, they could just as easily have been in a station wagon.

Her mother reached over and squeezed her hand and mouthed, *Nice people.*

Nice people. That's what mattered most.

Chapter Forty-One

HUGH PACED THE hotel lobby. He'd been waiting all afternoon to see Brianna, and when she walked through the lobby doors, his pulse accelerated. He crossed the marble floor and took her in his arms, pressing a loving kiss to her lips.

"God, I missed you," he said. He held her a beat longer, feeling much more at ease now that she and Layla were there with him. "I don't ever want to be away from you guys for that long again."

Her eyes widened, then narrowed, the way they did when she had amorous thoughts. He squeezed her hand and kissed her again, before swooping Layla into his arms and tickling her belly. "And you! I missed you, too. Did you make up any great stories on the way over?"

"Treat gave me an activity book," Layla gushed.

Hugh set her down, and Brianna took her hand. "He did? Well, Treat's a pretty good guy." Hugh kissed Jean's cheek. "Was the trip okay?"

"Yes. Perfect, thank you." Jean looked pretty in her casual long skirt and blouse. "Treat and Max were wonderful hosts."

Hugh embraced Max and kissed her cheek as he had Jean's. "You look gorgeous, Max." It struck him then how similar in style Max and Brianna were, and he wondered what that said about him and Treat. Maybe they weren't so different after all. Although, now that he thought about it, none of his siblings had chosen a life partner that was pretentious or overly showy. *Dad raised us well.* The importance of Brianna's desire not to spoil Layla became crystal clear. *After tomorrow*, he'd be sure to rein it all in. *After tomorrow.*

"Bro." Hugh opened his arms, and he and Treat embraced. Treat patted him on the back. "Thanks, man. I really appreciate you taking care of everyone."

"That's what family's for." Treat put his arm around Max and kissed the top of her head.

Hugh looked at Treat, Max, Brianna, Layla, and Jean, and he felt the impact of the word like a squeeze to his heart. *Family.*

Chapter Forty-Two

THE FLORIDA SUN beat down on the bleachers, sparkling in Layla's eyes as she watched the cars speed around the track. They'd all had dinner together last night, but both Hugh and Layla had turned in early. Hugh, to be prepared for the race, and Layla from pure exhaustion. Hugh had come to see them in their hotel room earlier that morning before he left for the track. *I'm gonna win this one for you and Layla. Mark my words.* As Brianna watched his car speed by, she knew he'd win the race. She believed in Hugh. She trusted his words, and she trusted his love for her and Layla. She looked around the crowded bleachers, excited and proud to hear people cheering for Hugh. Treat and Max shared an intimate kiss; then Max went back to watching the race, while Treat's gaze remained on Max.

"How are you holding up? Uncomfortable at all?" her mother asked.

"No, actually. I realize that all that foolishness doesn't matter. Hugh loves me. The fear of wanting to run was a momentary blip on my radar screen." She put her arm around Layla. "Actually, that's not true, Mom. It wasn't that at all. I think it was Dad's leaving coming back to haunt me, and you know what? That's his issue, not mine. And definitely not Hugh's or Layla's."

"Now, that's the Brianna I know and love." Her mother bumped her with her shoulder. "Your man is doing well in the race. He'll probably win."

He already won my heart. "He said he'd win, and when Hugh says something, he means it." Hugh had told her that he'd change the way she thought about men, and while he might not have changed the way she thought about all men, he'd proven the kind of man he was, and that was all she needed to know.

"Somehow I think you're right." Jean nodded at Layla. "I think your little princess loves the races."

"I think she loves Prince Hugh." *And I know I do.*

Treat and Max rose to their feet. "The race is almost over, and Hugh asked that we meet him down by the track."

"Sure." She held Layla's hand, and they followed Treat as he descended the noisy stands. "Is this safe?" Brianna asked as they neared the track.

"Hugh would never put you or Layla in danger." Treat's commanding presence was second to the confidence in his tone. He picked up Layla and carried her safely in his arms as Hugh crossed the finish line and the crowd roared. Layla covered her ears, and Brianna and Jean cheered.

"He's gonna be pumped!" Treat squeezed Layla. "Hugh won, Layla."

"Yay!" she cheered.

"Congratulations!" Max said to Brianna.

"It's all Hugh," Brianna said. Her heart thundered in his chest. *He won. Just like he said he would.*

Max shifted her eyes to Treat. "I love to see him with Layla," Max said.

"He looks like a natural. Do you plan on having children?" Brianna asked.

"Oh, yes. Definitely." Max's cheeks pinked with her smile.

"There's no greater joy," Jean added. She put her arm around Brianna.

"Thanks, Mom. I feel the same way about Layla." She watched the cars pull into their pits.

"Come on, ladies; it's time for the winner's circle." Treat picked up his pace.

Winner's circle? Brianna's nerves took flight. She'd thought they would remain on the sidelines.

The winner's circle was inside the track and mobbed with media crews. Hugh finished his victory lap, then spun out across the grass.

When he stepped from the car, Brianna's breath hitched. He was so handsome in his driving suit, and when he whipped off his helmet, his eyes immediately found hers. A rush of heat spread through her. Hugh blazed a path toward Brianna right through the mass of reporters, who spread like the Red Sea. Treat was behind him, carrying a sign.

"May I?" Hugh took the track announcer's microphone and closed the gap between him and Brianna. He took off his glove and handed it to Max, then took Layla's hand and guided her in front of Brianna.

Brianna put her hands on her daughter's shoulders. Hugh's smile reached his eyes, and his dimples—those glorious dimples—appeared deep and true. His chest rose and fell with each hard breath. His eyes held her captive, and his rich, smooth voice sent her stomach into some kind of anxious rumba. She felt the eyes of the fans upon them, making her heart race.

"I will get on with my thank-yous in just a moment. Please bear with me." Hugh's voice boomed through the loudspeakers.

Hugh placed his hand on Brianna's, which held Layla's shoulder. "I won that race for Brianna and Layla Heart."

Oh my God! Oh my God! Brianna couldn't breathe. She couldn't move. She squeezed Layla's shoulder, and Hugh's hand lovingly held hers as he dropped to one knee before them. *One knee!* Brianna felt her knees weaken and she shifted her gaze to her mother, who was wiping tears as quickly as they fell.

"Brianna."

She drew her eyes back to Hugh, kneeling before her. *Kneeling! Oh God! Oh God!*

His eyes dampened, and Brianna's throat swelled. "You're the bravest, most loving woman I know, and when I think of my future, I see you and Layla. When I look into your eyes, I feel your love for me."

Tears streamed down her cheeks. She had no idea how she remained standing. Hell, she had no idea if she was still breathing as the man she loved said everything she could ever dream of hearing.

"My life is full of challenges and competitions, and I know I can face anything with you by my side. You deserve a man who will love and cherish you and Layla. You deserve a man who will nourish your love and feed your spirit. Brianna, will you let me be that man? Will you marry me?"

She opened her mouth to speak, and nothing came out. Her jaw trembled. The world went silent, save for her thundering heart.

"Mommy! Say yes!" Layla whispered loudly.

The reporters laughed.

"Yes." It was a whisper. "Yes." *Damn it, where's my voice?*

Hugh rose to his feet with hope in his eyes. "Yes?"

She nodded, her legs somehow propelling her forward. "Yes!"

He dropped the microphone, swooped her off her feet, and spun her around. "God, I love you!"

He kissed her in front of the world, a long, passionate kiss that stole her ability to think—as all of his kisses did.

"I ordered your ring, but I won't have it until next week. I'm so sorry, but I didn't want to wait."

"Ring?" Her mind was still in the clouds.

"Yes, an engagement ring." He hugged her again. "You've made me the happiest man on earth."

Treat held up the sign and showed it to the crowd. *SHE SAID YES!*

"Congratulations!" Her mother's voice found her.

Brianna embraced her mother. "The sign?"

"I was a little overly confident," Hugh said with a grin.

The reporters buzzed with the news. Brianna caught bits and pieces of the announcements. Her mind reeled.

"...have it folks...Hugh Braden is off the market!"

"Braden engaged..."

"Mommy!"

Her mind snapped to attention as Hugh picked up Layla and she put her little hands on his cheeks.

"I knew you were her prince! We will marry you, Prince Hugh! We will!" Layla pressed her pink lips to his cheek, then wrapped her arms around his neck.

Treat's arms came around Brianna. "Welcome to our family," he said. "He's a good man, and now he's a lucky man, too."

"Thank you, Treat." She swiped at the never-ending flow of

tears.

"Another sister-in-law!" Max hugged Brianna. "I can't wait to get to know you better. And you'll love the rest of the girls, and of course the men, too, but you know what I mean." Max sighed. "I never imagined I'd have so many sisters."

Jean pulled Brianna into a hug before she could say another word. "This, I had no idea about."

"He didn't tell you?" Brianna asked.

"No, and I'm so happy for you, Bree." Jean nodded at Layla, still in Hugh's arms as he thanked his sponsors. "He's right, Bree. You deserve a man who will adore you and treat you well, and it's obvious that Hugh is that man."

She watched Hugh walking toward her, his broad shoulders pushed back, his chest out, and the smile that had been on his lips since he took off his helmet lit up her heart. Love coursed through her, and when he finally stood before her, her hand was drawn to his stomach. Even through his thick suit, she felt his strength.

He arched a brow. "You know what that does to me."

"I'm counting on it." She licked her lips, because she also knew what *that* did to him.

He stepped closer. "I told you that I'm not a halfway guy."

"I wouldn't have you any other way."

"What about your twelve-year plan?" He cupped his hands on her waist, and it sent a thrill right through her.

"I exchanged it for a lifetime plan." She pressed her cheek to his and whispered, "And I didn't even need a sidecar."

Chapter Forty-Three

THE WEEK FLEW by in a flurry of congratulations and too many hours of work for Brianna. Hugh waded in and out of video press conferences and interviews. By the time they arrived at Hugh's father's ranch in Weston, Colorado, Saturday morning, they were exhausted and equally as excited. It had been a week since they'd gotten engaged, and last night, Hugh wanted nothing more than to climb into bed beside Brianna, wrap his arms around her, and fall asleep, but they'd decided that they wouldn't live together until they were married, for Layla's sake. Which is how their decision to get married tonight, after the engagement party, had come about.

"This is gorgeous, Hugh." Brianna looked out over his father's ranch. "I can't even imagine what it must have been like to grow up here. It's so…fresh and free."

"We can live anywhere you want and raise our children in any state. If you want to stay in Richmond, that's fine. If you'd rather move to someplace like Weston, I'm all for it. Home for me is wherever you and Layla are."

She touched his belly, and he pulled her close.

"Other than college and your race, I've never been anywhere, but I like the idea of being around family."

"Then we can stay in Richmond. We have a beautiful house there, and Layla's friends are there." He opened the front door.

"Hugh, I meant maybe around your family. Let's see how we get along and think about it."

Hugh stopped cold. "You would move?"

"Families offer love and support. It might be nice for Layla to have more people around to love her. Let's think about it."

"Hugh!" Savannah flew out the front door and wrapped her arms around him.

"Hey, Vanny. Where's Jack?" Hugh kissed her cheek.

"He's down at the barn with Dad."

Savannah's auburn hair flowed to the middle of her back. She flashed a bright smile at Brianna and folded her in her arms. "Bree! I am so glad to finally meet you." She looked at Hugh out of the corner of her eye. "I told you you'd find her when you weren't looking."

"Hi." Brianna put her hand on Layla's back. "This is Layla. Layla, say hello to Savannah. Savannah is Hugh's sister."

"Hi, Savannah," Layla reached up to touch Savannah's hair. "Your hair is pretty."

"Thank you. Your hair is pretty, too." Savannah whispered to Bree, "She's adorable."

Layla jumped up and down. "Guess what?" Before Savannah could answer, she squealed, "We're marrying Hugh today!"

Savannah laughed. "I know! I'm so excited!"

"Savannah, are you sure you're okay with us getting married tonight?" Brianna put her hand on Layla's shoulder.

"Oh my God, really? Bree, you're gonna be my sister-in-law. Do you know how many years I spent with just brothers? Now I have five sisters in my life. I'm thrilled. We all are.

"Come on inside." Savannah took Layla's hand and walked

through the open foyer to the living room, where all of Hugh's siblings and their significant others were waiting.

Brianna hugged Treat and Max, and Max introduced her to the others. Hugh loved seeing his family embrace her and Layla. Brianna smiled at Hugh over her shoulder.

"You've gone all googly-eyed on me." Treat appeared by his side.

"Yeah. I probably have," Hugh admitted.

"Brianna's great. She and Max really hit it off."

"I know." Hugh watched Lacy hug Brianna. Lacy's golden tan set off her thick blond corkscrew curls. Layla reached up and sprang one of Lacy's curls.

Treat put his arm around Hugh. "Are you ready to be a husband?"

"More than you can ever imagine." The truth of his words nearly pulled tears from his eyes. He swallowed past the lump of love that had lodged in his throat.

"And you're adopting Layla? I'm proud of you, Hugh. I wondered if you'd ever settle down," Treat said in a serious tone.

"Says the man who was almost forty when he got married," Hugh teased.

"I was waiting for the right woman." Treat nodded toward Max. "By the way, what's up with no ring, you cheapskate?"

Hugh turned his back to the others and pulled a velvet bag from his pocket and handed it to Treat. "Cheapskate, my ass."

Treat withdrew two rings from the velvet bag and admired them. "Emerald cut, three stones, what is that? About a carat?" He smirked.

"Two, you ass. And I've got a matching wedding ring."

"And the little one?" He put the tiny ring on the tip of his pinky.

"For Layla."

"I figured since it has a diamond tiara on it. That's sweet, Prince Hugh." He elbowed Hugh and handed him back the rings.

"Bro." Dane embraced Hugh. His thick dark hair was longer than it had been the last time they'd seen each other. As a shark tagger and marine researcher, he spent about as much time on or in the water as he did on land, and his copper skin was proof that nothing had changed. "You're biting the couple bullet. I never thought I'd see the day."

"Yeah, well, the best men finish last," Hugh teased. Dane was six years older than Hugh and two years younger than Treat. He'd gotten engaged to Lacy a few weeks after Treat and Max's wedding.

"Sorry we missed your race. You guys will have to come out and see us sometime." Dane ran his hand through his hair.

"No, he should visit us more often," Rex's deep voice interrupted. He wrapped Hugh in his arms. "Missed you, Hugh."

Hugh could barely get his arms around his brawny brother. Though Rex was the same height as him, he carried an additional thirty pounds of muscle from working on the ranch. Combined with cowboy-long hair that brushed his collar and his ever-present Stetson, Rex was the epitome of a Colorado rancher.

"You too, man." Hugh felt the draw of family like he never had before. He wanted to be embraced by their warmth. He wanted to sit down and enjoy time with them and bring Brianna and Layla into their inner circle.

Jade Johnson, Rex's fiancée, joined them. She kissed Hugh's cheek. "I love Brianna and Layla. You're a lucky man." Jade's jet-black hair lay straight and thick down her back, almost to her waist. Rex slung his arm over her shoulder. Rex and Jade's relationship had ended a forty-year feud between their two families.

Hugh watched Rex place a kiss on the back of Jade's neck and thought, *Love really can conquer all.* "Thanks, Jade. I feel pretty lucky," Hugh said. "Let's go into the living room before Josh and Riley have Brianna and Layla wearing New York City wardrobes."

Josh and Riley were both clothing designers, and they lived in Manhattan near Savannah and Jack. Josh was the most reserved of the Braden men and every bit as handsome with his closely shorn black hair and perfectly sculpted physique. Josh embraced Hugh and patted him on the back.

"When are you coming back to New York?" Josh asked.

"I don't know, but I'll be a married man when I do." Patience was never one of Hugh's virtues, and his love for Brianna instilled a need to be closer to her. He glanced at Brianna and Layla. *Tonight.* Hugh couldn't wait to become Brianna's husband and Layla's father.

Riley brushed her brown hair from her shoulder. She looked pretty in her skinny jeans and sweater. Riley had grown up in Weston, and Hugh had been happy when she and Josh had gotten together. They complemented each other well. Hugh opened his arms, and Riley stepped in.

"You look gorgeous as always," Hugh said.

Hugh looked around the room and realized that he and each of his siblings had ended up with partners who seemed perfect for them.

The glass doors opened and Jack Remington, Savannah's

fiancé, and Hugh's father, Hal, came into the room. Two formidable men wearing Levi's and boots. Both had shoulders as wide as freight trains, and though Hal's hair had gone a little more gray, he was still shockingly handsome with his dark, soulful eyes and pleasant smile.

"There's my boy," Hal said. He opened his arms as he crossed the hardwood floor. Hugh fell against him and held on tight.

"I've missed you, Dad."

Hal put his hands on Hugh's shoulders and stared into his eyes. "Yup. I see it now. You see that, Jack?"

Hugh shot a glance at Jack. "What?"

"Love, son. You've got it bad." Hal crouched down and touched Layla's nose.

She put her hands behind her back and twisted from side to side. "Hi."

"Hi there." Hal's voice was so deep it seemed out of place following Layla's. He stood and opened his arms, waiting for Brianna to step in. When she didn't, he shifted his eyes to Hugh.

"You might as well step in there and hug him, Brianna, or he'll wait all night," Hugh said.

"Sorry," she said with a smile. "Hi, Mr. Braden. I'm Brianna."

"Don't be sorry. You'll be a Braden soon, and Bradens hug." Hal pulled her into a quick embrace, then put an arm around her shoulder.

"I've been waiting to meet you." He reached for Layla's hand. Together they went to the couch and sat down. "So, tell me all about Layla and yourself."

Watching his father envelop Brianna and Layla with the love he'd always bathed Hugh and his siblings in filled his heart with certainty. The next few hours couldn't pass quickly enough.

Chapter Forty-Four

HUGH'S LEG BOUNCED nervously beneath the table. Brianna's mother, Kat, and Mack's family had already arrived, and he was ready to run down the aisle and marry Brianna. Out of respect for Savannah and Jack, he made no move to rush things along. Instead, he made small talk with Jack's family, the Remingtons.

"Thanks for playing with Layla today," Hugh said to Sage Remington, one of Jack's younger brothers.

"She's a great kid." Sage's eyes were as contemplative as Brianna's and midnight blue like Jack's. A tattoo snaked out from under his shirtsleeve. At twenty-eight, he was already a world-renowned artist with work in galleries throughout the world.

"Savannah tells me that you like the outdoors as much as Jack does. Do you spend much time in the mountains?" Hugh asked.

"Not as much as I'd like, but I'm hoping to make a few changes and carve out a little more downtime."

"Downtime is overrated." Dex, Jack's youngest brother, sat on his other side next to his twin sister, Siena. All of the Remingtons had dark hair, but while Dex's eyes were midnight blue, like Jack's and Sage's, Siena, a model, had electric-blue eyes like her mother.

"I don't know. I like downtime these days." Hugh squeezed Brianna's hand.

"Dex doesn't know what downtime is. His life is all about PC game addiction," Sage teased.

"It's his business," Sienna explained to Hugh.

"He made millions in his downtime," Kurt Remington added. "But, there's no harm in loving what you do."

"Says my brother the writer, who makes up stories for a living," Dex said.

"Listen here, son," Hal began. "As long as you love what you do, then it's a fine living indeed."

After dinner, Treat stood to make a toast. "Jack, welcome to the family. We're proud to have you as a brother." He raised his glass. "To Savannah and Jack and a lifetime of love and happiness." Everyone raised their glasses, and Treat remained standing. He reached for Max's hand, and Max rose to her feet. "We have our own announcement to share." He put his arm around Max and kissed the side of her forehead. "We're going to have a baby."

There was a collective gasp.

"A baby?" Savannah squealed. She ran around the table and hugged Max, then Treat. "You're gonna have a baby! I'm gonna be Aunt Savannah. Oh, Max!" She threw her arms around Max again. "What a night. A new baby and a new sister-in-law." She winked at Brianna.

Everyone congratulated Treat and Max, and Hugh thought about how fast life was moving for all of them. He could barely believe that before nightfall he'd be married and he'd be Layla's father. Layla had asked Brianna if she could call Hugh Dad, and when Brianna told her she could, Hugh had been unable to hold back his tears.

Max threw her napkin on the table. "Okay, enough baby talk. Come on, girls. We have to help Bree and Layla get ready for their big night." Lacy, Savannah, Riley, and Jade took Brianna by the arms and headed toward the house. Jean, Kat, and Layla followed on their heels.

Savannah stopped halfway to the door and hollered, "Siena, come on! We're waiting on you. Joanie! We need another mother's opinion."

Siena and Joanie hurried toward the house.

"You've done it now," Josh said. "You'll get her back and she'll look like a whole different woman."

"A hen party," Kurt said with a laugh.

Josh leaned across the table. "Hugh, do you need help dressing?"

Hugh rose to his feet. "Shit. Not from you doofuses."

AN HOUR LATER, as the sun set behind the mountains and the wedding march played softly in the background, Hugh stood beneath a white canopy lined with white light, wearing Dane's dark suit—which fit him quite well—with a nervous ache in his gut.

Layla walked down the makeshift aisle beside Kat, looking beautiful in the princess gown Hugh'd had delivered for her from a local shop. She and Kat tossed rose petals from a basket. Hugh felt tears pressing at his eyes as he took in the love on his family's faces. His world had changed on a dime. One awful blind date. One look from Brianna's gorgeous, smart brown eyes and a first date he'd never forget.

The doors to the house opened, and Brianna walked across the lawn, her arm wrapped around Mack's. Hugh cleared his throat to loosen the lump that had lodged there. Brianna moved gracefully toward him, wearing a simple white wedding gown that cascaded over her curves and looked as if it were custom-made for her. The sweetheart neckline and short train were exactly what he'd pictured her in. Her hair hung loose and pretty, framing her face. Thanks to the owner of the local flower shop, Brianna carried a small white bouquet of roses, and as she joined Hugh under the canopy, his eyes filled with tears. He wished his mother could be there, but he felt, as his father always had, that she was with them in spirit, and as he looked at Layla sitting between her grandmother and Kat, he knew she'd have been proud of the man he'd become.

Hugh mouthed, *I love you*, to Brianna and made no effort to wipe the tear that tumbled down his cheek.

Brianna's lower lip trembled when she tried to speak.

He wiped her tear with the pad of his thumb and mouthed, "Sidecar."

Brianna smiled.

They reached for each other's hands as they turned to face Treat. Hugh couldn't think of anyone he'd rather have officiate their wedding than the brother who had been there every step of his life, supporting, teaching, and caring for him.

Treat began the ceremony. "Brianna and Hugh have found life's sweetest moments with each other. The union of marriage will become home to their honesty and affection, their courage, and their fidelity. It will also become home to the harshness of life, the sadness, and the hurt that life bestows on them. The ability to heal and rebuild is within each of you. As you create this sacred union and accept these solemn vows, remember that your partner, your lover, your spouse, will rely on, and trust in, your promise to heal, to love, and to cherish."

"Brianna and Hugh have written their own vows. Brianna."

"Hugh." Brianna's voice was soft, her eyes tender. "You came into my life when I least expected you, and you loved me and Layla unconditionally. I continue to fall more in love with you each day. I promise to be the best wife I can be, to support and love you, and never to go to bed angry."

Treat stepped forward. "Hugh."

"Brianna." Hugh heard his voice crack, and he paused to clear his throat. "I never knew how love could touch every part of a person's life until I met you and Layla. Since the first night we met, you've not only opened my heart, but you've filled it. Completely. You've shown me how to love, and you've loved me with tenderness, strength, and compassion. I promise to always put you and Layla first in my life, to honor your needs and desires, and to support your passions. I promise to be the best husband, man, and lover that I can be, and I will always walk by your side and whisper *sidecar* in your ear."

Brianna smiled despite the tears streaming down her cheeks.

"I love you, Brianna, and I am the luckiest man on earth that you have granted me the gift of being my wife."

"Dad?" Treat nodded toward his father.

Hal had changed for the occasion. In his dark suit and cowboy boots, he put an arm on Hugh's back and kissed him on the cheek. "I love you, son." He leaned in closer and whispered, "She looks just as beautiful in that dress as your mother did." He handed Hugh the rings and went back to his seat.

Mom. Tears welled in Hugh's eyes. He dropped his eyes to the gown, and his parents' wedding picture that sat on his father's dresser came back to him. Hugh felt a tingling sensation wash through him. He looked at Treat, who touched his shoulder and nodded, as if he'd known about the dress all along—and he probably had.

Treat stepped forward. "May the seamless circle of these rings represent the eternal love between Brianna and Hugh and remind them of the union they have entered into today to be faithful, loving, and kind to each other from this day forward."

Hugh held Brianna's left hand in his, each trembling hand supporting the other. He held her engagement ring and her wedding ring in his right hand.

"Please repeat after me," Treat began. "I give you this ring as a symbol of our vows and with all that I have, and all that I am, I will always honor you."

Hugh repeated the words with a shaky voice and slid the rings on Brianna's finger.

"Brianna, please repeat after me," Treat began. He stated the same vows, and Brianna repeated them while gazing lovingly into Hugh's eyes. When she slid the wedding ring on his finger, Hugh brought her trembling hand to his lips and pressed a kiss to it.

"Layla, would you please join us?" Treat held a hand out to Layla, and she came and stood beside him. "Hugh."

Hugh knelt before Layla, his heart hammering against his chest. He held her precious little hand in his and looked her in her beautiful eyes. "Layla, I promise to be the best daddy I can be. I will give you space to grow and be happy, and I will always, always love you and your mother." He slid the diamond tiara ring on her finger. Layla's mouth formed an *O*, and she jumped into Hugh's arms.

"Oh, Hugh! You really are our prince! And, Mommy, guess

what?" She didn't wait for an answer. "Grandma was wrong. You didn't have to kiss a lot of frogs before you found him!"

Everyone laughed. Treat spoke over their excitement. "I now pronounce you husband and wife. Please, Hugh, kiss your bride."

Hugh placed his hand on Brianna's cheek and kissed his beautiful wife. Then he kissed Layla's cheek.

Layla put her little hands on the sides of his head, and with a serious look in her eyes she asked, "Does this mean we're the Three Musketeers now?"

"Yes, princess, it does," Brianna answered.

Three Musketeers. Hugh didn't think his heart could hold another bit of happiness, and it opened up and swallowed that one right up.

Treat opened his arms. "Ladies and gentlemen, Mr. and Mrs. Hugh Braden."

With Layla in his arms, Hugh pulled Brianna close and whispered in her ear, "Remember when Kat asked what I was looking for in a woman?"

"Yeah. You said someone smart, honest, and family oriented."

"It could only have been you, Brianna, and it will only ever be you."

Ready for more Bradens?

Fall in love with Daisy and Luke in TAKEN BY LOVE

Chapter One

DAISY HONEY JUGGLED a cup of coffee, a cake she'd bought for her mother, a bag of two chocolate-dipped doughnuts—because a girl's gotta have something sweet in her life, and this was about all the sweetness she had time for at the moment—and her keys.

"You sure you got that, sugar?" Margie Holmes had worked at the Town Diner for as long as Daisy could remember. With her outdated feathered hairstyle and old-fashioned, pink waitress uniform, Margie was as much a landmark in Trusty, Colorado, as the backdrop of the Colorado Mountains and the miles and miles of farms and ranches. Trusty was a far cry from

Philly, where Daisy had just completed her medical residency in family practice, and it was the last place she wanted to be.

Daisy glanced at the clock. She had ten minutes to get to work. *Work.* If she could call working as a temporary doctor at the Trusty Urgent Care Clinic *work.* She'd worked damn hard to obtain her medical degree with the hopes of leaving the Podunk town behind, but the idea of relocating had been delayed when her father fell off the tractor and injured his back. She'd never turn her back on her family, even if she'd rather be starting her career elsewhere. She supposed it was good timing—if there was such a thing. Daisy had been offered permanent positions in Chicago and New York, and she had four weeks to accept or decline the offers. She hoped by then her father would either have hired someone to manage the farm or decided if he was going to sell—an idea she was having a difficult time stomaching, since the farm had been in her family for generations. Since the closest hospital or family physician was forty-five minutes away and the urgent care clinic picked up the slack in the small town, Daisy was happy to have found temporary employment in her field even if it wasn't ideal.

"Yeah, I've got it. Thanks for the cake, Margie. Mom will love it." She pushed the door open with her butt—*thank you, doughnuts*—just as someone tugged it open, causing her to stumble. As if in slow motion, the cake tipped to the side. Daisy slammed her eyes shut to avoid seeing the beautiful triple-layer chocolate-almond cake crash to the ground.

There was no telltale *clunk!* of the box hitting the floor. She opened one eye and was met with a pair of muscled pecs attached to broad shoulders and six foot something of unadulterated male beefcake oozing pure male sexuality—and he was holding her mother's cake in one large hand, safe and sound.

She swallowed hard against the sizzling heat radiating off of Luke Braden, one of only two men in Trusty who had ever stood up for her—and the man whose face she pictured on lonely nights. When she'd decided to come back to Trusty, her mind had immediately raced back to Luke. She'd wondered—maybe even hoped—she'd run into him. Residency had been all-consuming and exhausting, with working right through thirty-six-hour shifts. She hadn't had time to even think about dating, much less had time for actual dating. Her body tingled in places that hadn't been touched by a man in a very long time.

"I think it's okay." With smoldering dark eyes and a wickedly naughty grin, he eyed the cake.

His deep voice shuddered through her. *Okay, Daisy. Get ahold of yourself. He might have saved you in high school, but that was eleven years ago.* He was no longer the cute boy with long bangs that covered perpetually hungry eyes. No, Luke Braden was anything but a boy, and by the look on his face, he had no recollection of who she was, making the torch she'd carried for him all these years heavy as lead.

"Thank you." She reached for the cake, and he pulled it just out of reach as his eyes took a slow stroll down her body, which was enough to weaken her knees *and* wake her up. She'd left Trusty after high school and had purposely found work near her college and med school during summers and breaks, so her memory of the people she'd gone to school with was sketchy at best after eleven years, but his was a face she'd never forget.

"You've got your hands full. Why don't I carry it to your car?" His dark hair was cut short on the sides. The top was longer, thick and windblown in that sexy way that only happened in magazines. His square jaw was peppered with rough stubble, and Daisy had the urge to reach out and stroke it. *His stubble, that is.*

Luke looked like one of those guys who took what they wanted and left a trail of women craving more in their wake, and in high school his reputation had been just that. *Carry the cake to my car? Like that won't end up with you trying to carry me to your bed?* The idea sent another little shudder through her. It was exactly what she'd been hoping—and waiting—for.

He had been two years ahead of Daisy in school, and because she'd spent her high school years fighting a reputation she didn't deserve, she'd kept a low profile. She'd darkened her hair in medical school to combat the stereotypical harassment that went along with having blond hair, blue eyes, and a body that she took care of. Now, thanks to a six-dollar box of dye every few weeks, it was a medium shade of brown. She'd never forget the time in her sophomore year when Luke had stood up for her. She'd carried a fantasy of him thinking of her for all these years. *Was I really that invisible to you?* Apparently, she was, because by the look on his face, he didn't recognize her. It stung like salt in a wound.

Her eyes caught on a flash of silver on his arm. Duct tape? She squinted to be sure. Yes. The wide strip of silver on his bulging biceps was indeed duct tape, and there was blood dripping from beneath it.

He followed her gaze to his arm with a shrug. "Scraped it on some wire at my ranch."

She should take her cake and walk right out the door, but the medical professional in her took over—and the hurt woman in her refused to believe he could have forgotten her that easily. She took a step back into the diner. "Margie, can I borrow your first-aid kit?"

Luke's brows knitted together as he followed her inside. "If that's for me, I don't need it. Really."

Margie handed Daisy the first-aid kit from beneath the counter. "Here you go, sugar." She eyed the tall, dark man, and her green eyes warmed. "Luke, are you causing trouble again?"

He arched a thick, dark brow. "Hardly. I'm meeting Emily here, but I'm a little early."

"Good, because the last thing you need is more trouble." Margie gave him a stern look as she came around the counter, and he flashed a warm smile, the kind a person reserved for those he cared about.

Daisy felt a stab of jealousy and quickly chided herself for it. She'd been back in town for only two weeks, and she had kept as far away from gossip as she could, but she couldn't help wondering what type of trouble Luke had gotten into. Her life was crazy enough without a guy in it. Especially a guy with enticing eyes and a sexy smile who deserved the reputation she didn't. She focused on his arm and slipped into doctor mode, which she was, thankfully, very good at. In doctor mode she could separate the injured patient from the hot guy.

Luke shot a look at Daisy, then back to Margie. "Can't believe everything you hear."

I bet.

"Glad to hear that." Margie touched his arm like she might her son. "I have to help the customers, but it's good to see you, Luke."

He flashed that killer smile again, then shifted his eyes back to Daisy, who was armed and ready with antiseptic. "I don't allow strangers to undress my wounds." He held out a hand. "Luke."

"You really don't remember me." Even though she'd seen it in his eyes, it still burned. "Daisy Honey?"

His sexy smile morphed into an amused one, and that amusement reached his eyes. "Was that Daisy, honey, or Daisy Honey, as in your full name?"

She bit back the ache of reality that he didn't even remember her name and passed it off with an eye roll. She turned his arm so she could inspect his duct-tape bandage. "Daisy Honey, as in my given name."

He laughed at that, a deep, hearty, friendly laugh.

She ripped the tape off fast, exposing a nasty gash in his upper arm.

"Hey." He wrenched his arm away. "With a name like Daisy Honey, I thought you'd be sweet."

She blinked several times, and in her sweetest voice, she said, "With a name like Luke Braden, I thought you'd be more manly." *Shit. I can't believe I said that.*

"Ouch. You don't mince words, do you?" He rubbed his arm. "I was kidding. I know who you are. I get my hay from your dad. I just didn't recognize you. The last time I saw you, your hair was blond." He ran his eyes down her body again, and damn if it didn't make her hot all over. "And you sure as hell didn't look like that."

You do remember me! She ignored Luke's comment about her looks, secretly tucking it away with delight, and went to work cleaning his cut. "How'd you do this, anyway?" She felt his eyes on her as she swabbed the dried blood from his skin.

"I was walking past a fence and didn't see the wire sticking out. Tore right through my shirt." He rolled down the edge of his torn sleeve just above his cut.

"Barbed wire, like your tattoo?" *Your hot, sexy, badass tattoo that wraps around your incredibly hard muscle?*

He eyed his tattoo with a half-cocked smile. "Regular fence

wire."

"Was it rusty?" She tried to ignore the heat of his assessing gaze.

He shrugged again, which seemed to be a common answer for him.

"When was your last tetanus shot?" She finished cleaning the cut and placed a fresh bandage over it before wrapping the dirty swabs in a napkin.

He shrugged. "I'm fine."

"You won't be if you get tetanus. You should stop by the medical clinic for a shot. Any of the nurses can administer it for you." She tucked her hair behind her ear and checked the time. She was definitely late, and he was definitely checking her out. Her stomach did a little flip.

"Are you a nurse?" He rolled up his torn sleeve again.

"Doctor, actually," she said with pride. She wondered if seeing her helping *him* stirred the memory of when he stood up for her all those years ago. By the look in his eyes, she doubted it. He had that first-meeting look, the one that read, *I wonder if I have a shot*, rather than the look of, *You're that girl everyone said was a slut.*

He nodded, and his eyes turned serious. "Well, thank you, Dr. Daisy Honey. I appreciate the care and attention you've given to my flesh."

He said *my flesh* with a sensual and evocative tone that tripped her up. She opened her mouth to respond and no words came.

Margie returned to the counter. "Can I get you something, Luke?"

Thankful for the distraction, Daisy pushed the first-aid kit across the counter, then gathered her things. "Thanks, Margie."

"I'd love coffee and two eggs over easy with toast," Luke said.

Daisy felt his eyes on her as she struggled to handle the cake, bag, and coffee again.

"Coming right up, sugar." Margie disappeared into the kitchen, and Daisy headed for the door.

He touched her arm and batted his long, dark lashes. "You're just going to dress my wound and leave? I feel so cheap."

Despite herself, she had to laugh. "That was actually kind of cute."

He narrowed his eyes, and it about stole her breath. "Cute? Not at all what I was going for."

Then you hit your mark, because it wasn't cute that's making my pulse race.

He held the door open for her. "I hope to see you around, Daisy, honey."

"Tetanus isn't fun. You should get the shot." She forced her legs to carry her away from his heated gaze.

To continue reading, buy **TAKEN BY LOVE**

Have you met the Remingtons?

Fall in love with Dex and Ellie in GAME OF LOVE

Years ago, Ellie left like a thief in the night, leaving Dex a numb and broken man. Now she's back, and a chance encounter sparks intense desires in Ellie and Dex—Desires that make *her* want to run, and make him want to *feel.* This time he's *not* letting her go.

Chapter One

DEX REMINGTON WALKED into NightCaps bar beside his older brother Sage, an artist who also lived in New York City, and Regina Smith, his employee and right arm. Women turned in their direction as they came through the door, their hungry eyes raking over Dex and Sage's wide shoulders and muscular physiques. At six four, Sage had two inches on Dex, and with their striking features, dark hair and federal-blue eyes, heads spun everywhere they went. But after Dex worked thirty of the last forty-eight hours, women were the furthest thing from his mind. His four-star-general father had ingrained hard work and dedication into his head since he was old enough to walk, and no matter how much he rued his father's harsh parenting, following his lead had paid off. At twenty-six, Dex was one of the country's leading PC game designers and the founder of Thrive Entertainment, a multimillion-dollar gaming corporation. His father had taught him another valuable lesson—how to become numb—making it easy for him to disconnect from the women other men might find too alluring to ignore.

Dex was a stellar student. He'd been numb for a very long time.

"Thanks for squeezing in a quick beer with me," he said to Sage. They had about twenty minutes to catch up before his scheduled meeting with Regina and Mitch Anziano, another of his Thrive employees. They were going to discuss the game they were rolling out in three weeks, *World of Thieves II*.

"You're kidding, right? I should be saying that to you." Sage threw his arm around Dex's shoulder. They had an ongoing rivalry about who was the busiest, and with Sage's travel and gallery schedule and Dex working all night and getting up midday, it was tough to pick a winner.

"Thrive!" Mitch hollered from the bar in his usual greeting. Mitch used *Thrive!* to greet Dex in bars the way others used *Hey*. He lifted his glass, and a smile spread across his unshaven cheeks. At just over five foot eight with three-days' beard growth trailing down his neck like fur and a gut that he was all-too-proud of, he was what the world probably thought all game designers looked like. And worth his weight in gold. Mitch could outprogram anyone, and he was more loyal than a golden retriever.

Regina lifted her chin and elbowed Dex. "He's early." She slinked through the crowded bar, pulling Dex along behind her. Her Levi's hung low, cinched across her protruding hip bones by a studded black leather belt. Her red hoodie slipped off one shoulder, exposing the colorful tattoos that ran across her shoulder and down her arms.

Mitch and Regina had been Dex's first employees when he'd opened his company almost five years ago. Regina handled the administrative aspects of the company, kept the production schedule, monitored the program testing, and basically made sure nothing slipped through the cracks, while Mitch, like Dex, conceptually and technically designed games with the help of the rest of Thrive's fifty employees—developers, testers, and a host of programmers and marketing specialists.

Regina climbed onto the barstool beside Mitch and lifted his beer to her lips.

"Order ours yet?" she asked with a glint in her heavily lined dark eyes. She ran her hand through her stick-straight, jet-black hair.

Dex climbed onto the stool beside her as the bartender slid beers in front of him and Regina. "Thanks, Jon. Got a brew for my brother?"

"Whatever's on tap," Sage said. "Hey, Mitch. Good to see you."

Mitch lifted his beer with a nod of acknowledgment.

Dex took a swig of the cold ale, closed his eyes and sighed, savoring the taste.

"Easy, big boy. We need you sober if you wanna win a

GOTY." Mitch took a sip of Regina's beer. "Fair's fair."

Regina rolled her eyes and reached a willowy arm behind him, then mussed his mop of curly dark hair. "We're gonna win Game of the Year no matter what. Reviewers love us. Right, Dex?"

Thrive had already produced three games, one of which, *World of Thieves*, had made Dex a major player in the gaming world—and earned him millions of dollars. His biggest competitor, KI Industries, had changed their release date. KI would announce the new date publicly at midnight, and since their game was supposed to be just as hot of a game as they expected *World of Thieves II* to be, if they released close to the release for *World of Thieves II*, there would be a clear winner and a clear loser upon release. Dex had worked too hard to be the loser.

"That's the hope," Dex said. He took another swig of his beer and checked his watch. Eight forty-five and his body thought it was noon. He'd spent so many years working all night and sleeping late that his body clock was completely thrown off. He was ready for a big meal and the start of his workday. He stroked the stubble along his chin. "I worked on it till four this morning. I think I deserve a cold one."

Sage leaned in to him. "You're not nervous about the release, are you?"

Of his five siblings—including Dex's fraternal twin sister, Siena, Sage knew him best. He was the quintessential artist with a heart that outweighed the millions of dollars his sculptures had earned him. He'd supported Dex through the years when Dex needed to bend an ear, and when he wasn't physically nearby, Sage was never farther than a text or a phone call away.

"Nah. If it all fails, I'll come live with you." Dex had earned enough money off of the games he'd produced that he'd never have to worry about finances again, but he wasn't in the gaming business for the money. He'd been a gamer at heart since he was able to string coherent thoughts together, or at least it felt that way. "What's happening with the break you said you wanted to take? Are you going to Jack's cabin?" Their eldest brother, Jack, and his fiancée, Savannah, owned a cabin in the Colorado Mountains. Jack was an ex–Special Forces officer and a survival-training guide, and he and Savannah spent most weekends at the cabin. Living and working in the concrete jungle didn't offer the type of escape Sage's brain had always needed.

"I've got another show or two on the horizon; then I'll take time off. But I think I want to do something useful with my time off. Find a way to, I don't know, help others instead of sitting around on my ass." He sipped his beer and tugged at the neck of his Baja hippie jacket. "How 'bout you? Any plans for vaca after the release?"

"Shit. You're kidding, right? My downtime is spent playing at my work. I love it. I'd go crazy sitting in some cabin with no connectivity to the real world."

"The right woman might change your mind." Sage took a swig of his beer.

"Dex? Date?" Regina tipped her glass to her lips. "Do you even know your brother? He might hook up once in a while, but this man protects his heart like it carries all of the industry secrets."

"Can we not go there tonight?" Dex snapped. He had a way of remembering certain moments of his life with impeccable clarity, some of which left scars so deep he could practically taste them every damn day of his life. He nurtured the hurt and relished in the joy of the scars, as his artistic and peace-seeking mother had taught him. But Dex was powerless against his deepest scar, and numbing his heart was the only way he could survive the memory of the woman he loved walking away from him four years earlier without so much as a goodbye.

"Whoa, bro. Just a suggestion," Sage said. "You can't replace what you never had."

Dex shot him a look.

Regina spun on her chair and then swung her arm over Dex's shoulder. "Incoming," she whispered.

Dex looked over his shoulder and met the stare of two hot blondes. His shoulders tensed and he sighed.

"It's not gonna kill you to make a play for one of them, Dex. Work off some of that stress." Sage glanced back at the women.

"No, thanks. They're all the same." Ever since the major magazines had carried the story about Dex's success, he'd been hounded by ditzy women who thought all he wanted to talk about was PC games.

Regina leaned in closer and whispered, "Not them. Fan boys, two o'clock."

Thank God.

"Hey, aren't you Dex Rem?" one of the boys asked.

Dex wondered if they were in college or had abandoned their family's dreams for them in lieu of a life of gaming. It was the crux of his concern about his career. He was getting rich while feeding society's desire to be couch potatoes.

"Remington, yeah, that's me," he said, wearing a smile like a costume, becoming the relaxed gamer his fans craved.

"Dude, *World of Thieves* is the most incredible game ever! Listen, you ever need any beta testers, we're your guys." The kid nodded as his stringy bangs bounced into his eyes. His friend's jaw hung open, struck dumb by meeting Dex, another of Dex's pet peeves. He was just a guy who worked hard at what he loved, and he believed anyone could accomplish the same level of success if they only put forth the effort. Damn, he hated how much that belief mirrored his father's teachings.

"Yeah?" Dex lifted his chin. "What college did you graduate from?"

The two guys exchanged a look, then a laugh. The one with the long bangs said, "Dude, it don't take a college degree to test games."

Dex's biceps flexed. There it was. The misconception that irked Dex more than the laziness of the kids just a few years younger than him. As a Cornell graduate, Dex believed in the value of education and the value of being a productive member of society. He needed to figure out the release date, not talk bullshit with kids who were probably too young to even be in a bar.

"Guys, give him a break, 'kay?" Regina said.

"Sure, yeah. Great to meet you," the longer-haired kid said.

Dex watched them turn away and sucked back his beer. His eyes caught on a woman at a booth in the corner of the bar. He studied the petite, brown-haired woman who was fiddling with her napkin while her leg bounced a mile a minute beneath the table. *Jesus.* Memories from four years earlier came rushing back to him with freight-train impact, hitting his heart dead center.

"I know how you are about college, but, Dex, they're kids. You gotta give them a little line to feed off of," Regina said.

Dex tried to push past the memories. He glanced up at the woman again and his stomach twisted. He turned away, trying to focus on what Regina had said. *College. The kids. Give them a line to feed off of.* Regina was right. He should accept the hero worship with gratitude, but lately he'd been feeling like the very games that had made him successful were sucking kids into an antisocial, couch-potato lifestyle.

"Really, Dex. Imagine if you'd met your hero at that age." Sage ran his hand through his hair and shook his head.

"I'm no hero." Dex's eyes were trained on the woman across the bar. *Ellie Parker.* His mouth went dry.

"Dex?" Sage followed his gaze. "Holy shit."

There was a time when Ellie had been everything to him. She'd lived in a foster home around the corner from him when they were growing up, and she'd moved away just before graduating high school. Dex's mind catapulted back thirteen years, to his bedroom at his parents' house. "In the End" by Linkin Park was playing on the radio. Siena had a handful of girlfriends over, and she'd gotten the notion that playing Truth or Dare was a good idea. At thirteen, Dex had gone along with whatever his popular and beautiful sister had wanted him to. She was the orchestrator of their social lives. He hadn't exactly been a cool teenager, with his nose constantly in a book or his hands on electronics. That had changed when testosterone filled his veins two years later, but at thirteen, even the idea of being close to a girl made him feel as though he might pass out. He'd retreated to his bedroom, and that had been the first night Ellie had appeared at his window.

"Hey, Dex." Regina followed his gaze to Ellie's table; her eyes moved over her fidgeting fingers and her bouncing leg. "Nervous Nelly?" she teased.

Dex rose to his feet. His stomach clenched.

"Dude, we're supposed to have a meeting. There's still more to talk about," Mitch said.

Sage's voice was serious. "Bro, you sure you wanna go

there?"

With Sage's warning, Dex's pulse sped up. His mind jumped back again to the last time he'd seen her, four years earlier, when Ellie had called him out of the blue. She'd needed him. He'd thought the pieces of his life had finally fallen back into place. Ellie had come to New York, scared of he had no idea what, and she'd stayed with him for two days and nights. Dex had fallen right back into the all-consuming, adoring, frustrating vortex that was Ellie Parker. "Yeah, I know. I gotta…" *See if that's really her.*

"Dex?" Regina grabbed his arm.

He placed his hand gently over her spindly fingers and unfurled them from his wrist. He read the confusion in her narrowed eyes. Regina didn't know about Ellie Parker. *No one knows about Ellie Parker. Except Sage. Sage knows.* He glanced over his shoulder at Sage, unable to wrap his mind around the right words.

"Holy hell," Sage said. "I've gotta take off in a sec anyway. Go, man. Text me when you can."

Dex nodded.

"What am I missing here?" Regina asked, looking between Sage and Dex.

Regina was protective of Dex in the same way that Siena always had been. They both worried he'd be taken advantage of. In the three years Dex had known Regina, he could count on one hand the number of times he'd approached a woman in front of Regina rather than the other way around. It would take Dex two hands to count the number of times he'd been taken advantage of in the past few years, and Regina's eyes mirrored that reality. Regina didn't know it, but of all the women in the world, Ellie was probably the one he needed protection from the most.

He put his hand on her shoulder, feeling her sharp bones against his palm. There had been a time when Dex had wondered if Regina was a heavy drug user. Her lanky body reminded him of strung-out users, but Regina was skinny because she survived on beer, Twizzlers, and chocolate, with the occasional veggie burger thrown in for good measure.

"Yeah. I think I see an old friend. I'll catch up with you guys later." Dex lifted his gaze to Mitch. "Midnight?"

"Whatever, dude. Don't let me cock block you." Mitch laughed.

"She's an old…not a…never mind." *My onetime best friend?* As he crossed the floor, all the love he felt for her came rushing back. He stopped in the middle of the crowded floor and took a deep breath. *It's really you.* In the next breath, his body remembered the heartbreak of the last time he'd seen her. The time he'd never forget. When he'd woken up four years ago and found her gone—no note, no explanation, and no contact since. Just like she'd done once before when they were kids. The sharp, painful memory pierced his swollen heart. He should turn away, return to his friends. Ellie would only hurt him again. He was rooted to the floor, his heart tugging him forward, his mind holding him back.

A couple rose from the booth where Ellie sat, drawing his attention. He hadn't even noticed them before. God, she looked beautiful. Her face had thinned. Her cheekbones were more pronounced, but her eyes hadn't changed one bit. When they were younger, she'd fooled almost everyone with a brave face—but never Dex. Dex had seen right through to her heart. Like right now. She stared down at something in her hands with her eyebrows pinched together and her full lips set in a way that brought back memories, hovering somewhere between worried and trying to convince herself everything would be okay.

Her leg bounced nervously, and he stifled the urge to tell her that no matter what was wrong, it would all be okay. Dex ignored the warnings going off in his mind and followed his heart as he crossed the floor toward Ellie.

To continue reading, buy **GAME OF LOVE**

More Books By Melissa Foster

LOVE IN BLOOM SERIES

SNOW SISTERS

Sisters in Love
Sisters in Bloom
Sisters in White

THE BRADENS at Weston

Lovers at Heart, Reimagined
Destined for Love
Friendship on Fire
Sea of Love
Bursting with Love
Hearts at Play

THE BRADENS at Trusty

Taken by Love
Fated for Love
Romancing My Love
Flirting with Love
Dreaming of Love
Crashing into Love

THE BRADENS at Peaceful Harbor

Healed by Love
Surrender My Love
River of Love
Crushing on Love
Whisper of Love
Thrill of Love

THE BRADENS & MONTGOMERYS at Pleasant Hill – Oak Falls

Embracing Her Heart
Anything For Love
Trails of Love
Wild, Crazy Hearts
Making You Mine
Searching For Love

THE BRADEN NOVELLAS

Promise My Love
Our New Love
Daring Her Love
Story of Love
Love at Last
A Very Braden Christmas

THE REMINGTONS

Game of Love
Stroke of Love
Flames of Love
Slope of Love
Read, Write, Love
Touched by Love

SEASIDE SUMMERS

Seaside Dreams
Seaside Hearts
Seaside Sunsets
Seaside Secrets
Seaside Nights
Seaside Embrace
Seaside Lovers
Seaside Whispers
Seaside Serenade

BAYSIDE SUMMERS

Bayside Desires
Bayside Passions
Bayside Heat
Bayside Escape
Bayside Romance
Bayside Fantasies

THE RYDERS

Seized by Love
Claimed by Love
Chased by Love
Rescued by Love
Swept Into Love

THE WHISKEYS: DARK KNIGHTS AT PEACEFUL HARBOR

Tru Blue
Truly, Madly, Whiskey
Driving Whiskey Wild
Wicked Whiskey Love
Mad About Moon
Taming My Whiskey
The Gritty Truth

SUGAR LAKE

The Real Thing
Only for You
Love Like Ours
Finding My Girl

HARMONY POINTE

Call Her Mine
This is Love
She Loves Me

THE WICKEDS: DARK KNIGHTS AT BAYSIDE

A Little Bit Wicked
Wicked Aftermath

WILD BOYS AFTER DARK (Billionaires After Dark)

Logan

Heath

Jackson

Cooper

BAD BOYS AFTER DARK (Billionaires After Dark)

Mick

Dylan

Carson

Brett

HARBORSIDE NIGHTS SERIES

Includes characters from the Love in Bloom series

Catching Cassidy

Discovering Delilah

Tempting Tristan

More Books by Melissa

Chasing Amanda (mystery/suspense)

Come Back to Me (mystery/suspense)

Have No Shame (historical fiction/romance)

Love, Lies & Mystery (3-book bundle)

Megan's Way (literary fiction)

Traces of Kara (psychological thriller)

Where Petals Fall (suspense)

Acknowledgments

Fans often ask if my heroes and heroines are patterned after people I know, and the answer is that pieces of them often come from those around me: friends, family, people I meet when I'm out and about, and even people I know only online. If you see yourself in my hero or heroine, there might be a reason why.

There are a host of readers, bloggers, authors, and friends I'd like to thank, and there is never enough space to do so. I truly appreciate your efforts and inspiration. Thank you.

My editorial team works above and beyond my highest expectations. They have worked extra hours and at breakneck speed in order to meet the intense publication deadlines for my Love in Bloom series, and they deserve a standing ovation. Tremendous gratitude goes to Kristen Weber, Penina Lopez, Jenna Bagnini, Juliette Hill, and Marlene Engel. I am forever indebted to each of you and in awe of your generosity of time, your energy, and your dedication to your craft. Thank you.

From far across the pond, author and friend Chrissie Parker has educated me on all things racing. Chrissie, many facts might not have made it into the book, and I took creative liberty to create Hugh and Brianna's world, but you gave me more information than I could have hoped for. Thank you for your support and encouragement.

I often ask my social media friends for help with my work, and I'd like to thank all of you for taking part in the contests, for encouraging me to continue, and for making me laugh (and sending chocolate!). Jen Fernando came up with the name of Hugh's racing circuit, the Capital Series Grand Prix. Thank you, Jen. It suits the book perfectly!

Kathie Shoop, you are always there to kick me in the butt or pull me through the mud when I get stuck. Thank you for your friendship and your ability to help me see path beyond the trees when I'm lost.

Russell Blake, six books ago you pushed me to take the Bradens further than I had planned, and ever since, you have proved a trusted and solid friend and a source of competition. Thanks, skater boy. Write on.

Hugs and kisses of gratitude and love to my understanding and supportive family. You make my world beautiful every day, and I appreciate you.

Melissa Foster is a *New York Times* and *USA Today* bestselling and award-winning author. Her books have been recommended by *USA Today's* book blog, *Hagerstown* magazine, *The Patriot*, and several other print venues. Melissa has painted and donated several murals to the Hospital for Sick Children in Washington, DC.

Visit Melissa on her website or chat with her on social media. Melissa enjoys discussing her books with book clubs and reader groups and welcomes an invitation to your event. Melissa's books are available through most online retailers in paperback, digital, and audio formats.

Melissa also writes sweet romance under the pen name, Addison Cole.

www.MelissaFoster.com

CPSIA information can be obtained
at www.ICGtesting.com
Printed in the USA
LVHW041639070920
665245LV00001B/60